BALLANTINE BOO

MW01617235

SHAUNA SUMMERS
Editorial Director, Dell
Ballantine Bantam Dell

Dear Reader,

The book you hold in your hands has it all. It's big and juicy, smart and thought-provoking, while also delivering a roller-coaster ride of emotions. It's cathartic, exploring female rage and complicated female relationships in a way that will have you dying to discuss it with your friends, your book club, or, honestly, anyone who will listen.

Most people have forgotten or never heard of Lady X, the mysterious vigilante who exposed and vandalized terrible men throughout New York City in the summer of 1977. That's certainly the case for Margot Cooper and her sister, Julia. While going through boxes in the attic of their childhood home, they discover stacks of newspaper clippings, all about Lady X. In fact, is that their mother's face in one of those pictures? They didn't even know she ever lived in New York City.

Jump back to 1977 where Ginger Daughtry is living the dream with her two roommates, working at the hottest club in town to pay for dance classes. Then her friend is assaulted, and when the cops do nothing, they decide to take matters into their own hands. What starts as a little vandalism soon escalates to something far more dangerous.

Molly Fader has delivered an electric, micdrop of a novel that would be irresistible at any time but also feels destined for this particular moment. The groundswell of enthusiasm and devotion for this book here at Ballantine has been something else, so I hope you love it as much as we do!

All best,

Shauna

ssummers@penguinrandomhouse.com
Ballantine Books | An imprint of Random House | A division of Penguin Random House LLC
1745 Broadway | New York, NY 10019

BY MOLLY FADER

Lady X

The Sunshine Girls

The Bitter and Sweet of Cherry Season

The McAvoy Sisters Book of Secrets

Lady
X

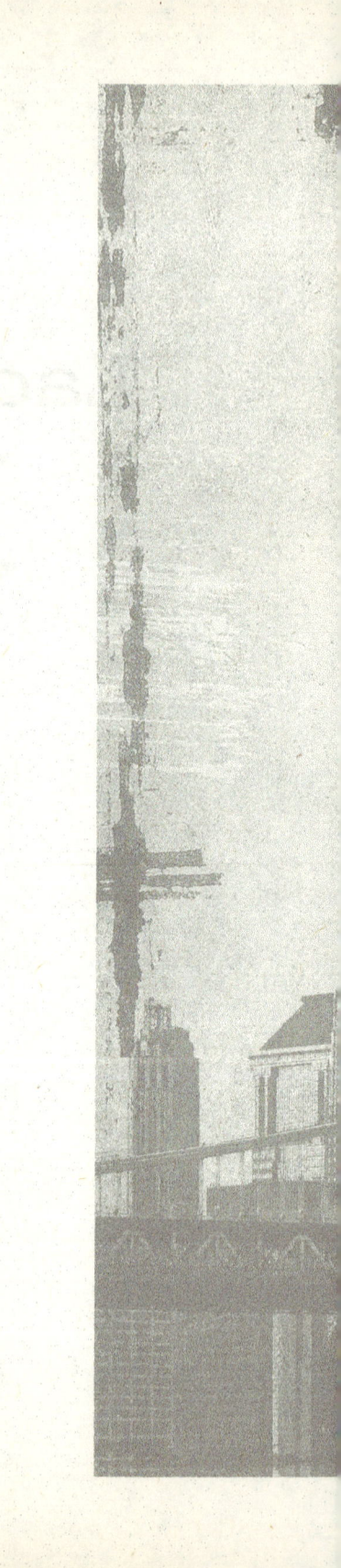

Lady X

A Novel

Molly Fader

BALLANTINE BOOKS
NEW YORK

THESE ARE UNCORRECTED PROOFS.
PLEASE DO NOT QUOTE FOR PUBLICATION UNTIL
YOU CHECK YOUR COPY AGAINST THE FINISHED BOOK.

Ballantine Books
An imprint of Random House
A division of Penguin Random House LLC
1745 Broadway, New York, NY 10019
randomhousebooks.com
penguinrandomhouse.com

Copyright © 2026 by Molly Fader

Penguin Random House values and supports copyright. Copyright fuels
creativity, encourages diverse voices, promotes free speech, and creates a
vibrant culture. Thank you for buying an authorized edition of this book and
for complying with copyright laws by not reproducing, scanning, or distributing
any part of it in any form without permission. You are supporting writers and
allowing Penguin Random House to continue to publish books for every reader.
Please note that no part of this book may be used or reproduced in any manner
for the purpose of training artificial intelligence technologies or systems.

BALLANTINE BOOKS & colophon are registered trademarks of
Penguin Random House LLC.

Hardcover ISBN 978-0-593-98366-9
Ebook ISBN 978-0-593-98367-6

Printed in the United States of America on acid-free paper

9 8 7 6 5 4 3 2 1

$PrintCode

First Edition

BOOK TEAM: Production editor: Cindy Berman • Managing editor: Pam Alders •
Production manager: Jane Sankner • Copy editor: Melissa Churchill •
Proofreaders: Barbara J. Greenberg and Kristin Jones

Book design by Caroline Cunningham

Title page image: javarman/Adobe Stock

The authorized representative in the EU for product safety and compliance
is Penguin Random House Ireland, Morrison Chambers, 32 Nassau Street,
Dublin D02 YH68, Ireland. https://eu-contact.penguin.ie.

For Lucy

Lady
X

PROLOGUE

New York City is supernaturally dark. No streetlights. Or traffic lights. The darkened buildings are looming black shadows in the indigo sky.

The Milky Way is visible over southern Manhattan, and it's not natural.

The night is loud with sirens and shouting. Something somewhere is burning.

Across the street people have gathered in the shadowy dark park with beers and a guitar because it's cooler outside and rules don't apply during a citywide blackout.

They don't seem to see the body on the sidewalk. They didn't hear it fall.

The crescent moon is reflected in the growing puddle of blood around it.

I'm sorry, she thinks.

But she's not.

Lady X is dead. She must be.

CHAPTER 1

March 2024
Montecito, California

Margot

The end, when it started, was fast. Margot had never been punched in the face, but she imagined it was a similar feeling. Painful in an extremely specific way.

Brutal.

It was a normal Wednesday morning. Jack came into the kitchen, his face creased from the pillowcase, his salt-and-pepper hair messy and not in the styled way. She always liked him best like this. So human and flawed.

"Good morning," she said, pulling cinnamon rolls out of the oven. He kissed her neck and then her cheek. "Coffee is made."

"You were up early," he said, beelining for the pot.

"The team is coming over for breakfast," she said, and belatedly realized not one of them would eat those cinnamon rolls. Oh, well. Skye could have one after school. Margot had been so excited about cooking for more than three people she might have overdone it.

"To talk about the book?" he asked, grinning over his shoulder. He was so proud of her, it made all her reservations seem ridiculous.

"The first of many—is what I've been told," was all she said.

He poured coffee into a mug and winced. "I think I hurt myself sleeping," he laughed, rolling his shoulder. "How is that possible?"

"We're not as young as we think we are," she said, and brought her mug over for a refill. He turned to her, her husband of over twenty years who just happened to be one of the most famous men in the world, and stroked the hair back from her face. She was still strawberry blonde. Painstakingly strawberry blonde.

One of the great Hollywood injustices. Men could age. Women could not.

He cupped her cheeks in his hands and smiled. "You are timeless. You always have been," he said, and kissed her lips.

Oh, she thought, her skin waking up. Her bones melting. Maybe they had time before the team came over? It had been so long, they'd both been so busy . . . She wrapped her hands around his wrists and kissed him back.

He groaned and lifted his head. "I wish," he said. "But I've got to meet my trainer in . . ." He glanced at his watch. "Shit. I gotta go. Dinner tonight? Tacos in Carpentaria?"

"Mi Fiesta?"

"Yeah, and a picnic on the beach."

"How can I say no?" It was her very favorite date night. He'd wear glasses and a hat and no one would expect *the* Jack Cooper to be eating on the beach, so they'd be left alone.

He poured his coffee out of a regular mug and into a travel mug and was gone in a whirl of high-tech workout gear. Smiling, she washed the mug he'd left in the sink.

An hour later her team arrived: Noelle, Rosa, and Paval.

"Good morning!" she cried when they'd been buzzed in the gate and finally made it into her kitchen. Rosa hugged her. Paval kissed her cheek. Noelle nodded professionally. They brought noise and chaos and shoes at the door. It made Margot so happy. Even if this meeting made her nervous.

The book.

The View from Here was the proposed title.

So pretentious, right? Ridiculous, even. This whole thing. She wanted to ask everyone in her kitchen if they thought it was ridiculous, but everyone's jobs were her and this book so they wouldn't say yes. With straight faces, they would say this book was the book people needed right now.

Her sister, Julia, would say yes. Julia would tell Margot that this coffee table book full of her thoughts on motherhood, marriage, gardening, food, and elegant hosting while rich and white was a terrible idea.

Julia would say, *They only care because your husband is Jack Cooper.*

When you are married to Jack Cooper, the world thinks that's the most interesting thing about you.

But for years she'd written popular pieces for magazines and newspapers about parenting and motherhood. It started with sneaky ways to get your toddler to eat more vegetables and the perfect menu for a little girl's tea party. That grew into stories about how hard it was to be a mom. Breastfeeding in change rooms. The foreign, weeping, sagging thing her body had turned into. What she made for dinner parties. Raising teenagers. Raising a teenager on the spectrum. Feeding teenagers. The essays morphed into guest appearances on morning shows, a popular Substack, and an elegant but affordable line of serving dishes at Target.

Her banana bread TikTok (using her mother's recipe) had over seventeen million views.

Accidentally, she'd become a brand.

As a brand, she was approached by publishers every few years. And every few years she had several reasons to say no. She didn't have any book ideas. She was already so busy.

Jack urged her to do the book, and she wanted to ask him, in all seriousness, didn't they have enough? Enough wealth, fame. Enough attention.

The social media videos and Substack were fine. Fun.

A book was officially too much.

But now her house was nearly empty and it was just Skye in high school and that was only for a few more months and Margot's days were . . . well, they were longer. Emptier. So when the book idea got pitched to her again, she'd had one clear thought:

What else are you going to do?

The "brand" barely needed her. She hated Pilates. Wasn't interested in being on nonprofit boards or doing whatever else it was that the wives of very famous men did once their kids were grown up and out of the house.

So she didn't say no to the book, and that was as good as a yes.

"This is beautiful," said Paval as he took pictures of the frittata she'd made with tomatoes from her garden, the citrus salad with pistachios, and the cinnamon buns no one was going to eat.

Paval tilted the camera so she could look at the shot. The cinnamon rolls looked amazing in the syrupy California light.

"That's not for artwork," Margot said.

"What's it for?" Paval asked.

"Eating," Margot laughed and, humoring her, Paval picked a pistachio off the salad and ate it.

Noelle Kim, Margot's assistant turned manager turned, she didn't even know what—CEO?—got everyone to the table and started the meeting.

Thank God for Noelle, Margot thought for the hundredth time that week.

When Jack's career had exploded with the first *Code Name* movie, and he was gone for months at a time, she found it uncomfortable to have other people doing the work of her life. She'd shocked her friends and the tabloids by refusing a nanny for the twins, for all of her kids, really.

But when the kids were older and there were invitations to daytime talk shows and newspaper interviews and guest editor gigs at iconic websites—she couldn't say no. And didn't want to.

It was heady and exciting to be someone other than a mom to four kids and a wife to Jack Cooper. At that time, her oldest was in college and she was ready to put on lipstick a few times a month and step out of her house. And to *talk* about being a mom to four kids and a wife to Jack Cooper. It was fun to project the image of a woman who could do it all. And do it well.

But she knew she needed help.

Despite what her mother made look so easy, Margot could not.

And, as Jack liked to joke, once you got one assistant, you got twenty. They were a Hollywood crop.

Margot didn't believe him, but once she hired Noelle, Noelle insisted Margot needed a social media manager, so they hired Rosa. Rosa insisted Margot needed a photographer and video editor, so they hired Paval.

"Let's talk about scheduling," Noelle said, scrolling up on her iPad. Her ebony hair was cut in a bob so sharp it could cut glass. The only makeup she wore was MAC Ruby Woo lipstick.

Noelle was iconic. Far more than Margot.

Margot sat, coffee in hand, at her husband's seat at the big farm table, looking out onto the sunlit Montecito garden being taken care of by its own team. Outside, the trees Jack had planted for the birth of each of their children were starting to bud tiny green leaves. A cherry for Alex. Two apples for the twins. And a plum for Skye. Jack pruned and cared for those trees as he had their children. And every late summer and early fall, he picked the fruit and she made jam that wasn't very good.

But the tradition was good. Jack was good. And she was feeling good about all of it.

Except this book? The essays and articles she wrote were very personal and revealing, but in a way that felt comfortable. The way she talked to her friends. Her sister and mom. She wasn't an actual writer like her sister Julia. Margot was just an expert on her children, channeling her mother, and being married to Jack Cooper.

This book felt . . . contrived.

"Photography starts in August, and the publisher would like Jack in some of the photos," Noelle said. "I've pushed back on the cover—"

"They want him on the cover?" Margot asked.

"God, socials would love it," Rosa said without looking up from her phone, where, it seemed, she was constantly making TikToks.

"I've pushed back," Noelle repeated.

"Jack is filming the war movie in Michigan in August," Margot said, setting her Natalie Weinberger mug on the table.

"Even if he could fly in for a day. Maybe two?" Noelle wrinkled her nose like she knew it was a big ask, but somehow unavoidable. "He is your husband. And he is Jack Cooper," Noelle said, with a sound that passed for laughter.

Yes. Jack Cooper. Who, after enjoying years of stratospheric fame, had hit a slump that he liked to joke was a grave. As her career took off, he spent ten slow years taking kids to soccer and guitar practice and doctor's appointments and out for ice cream. But now as a man with some silver in his hair and a jawline that wouldn't quit, he was having a career renaissance. He'd gone from being the actor playing the young baseball catcher who battled cancer and came back to win the World Series to playing his coach. He was playing generals instead of soldiers. Bosses instead of employees.

Funny. Jack Cooper let his hair go gray and his middle get soft and he got even more work. Even more famous. Even more handsome.

Margot refused to be bitter about it. The truth was, she'd take her husband with a paunch over all those years of extreme diets and workouts when he was playing action heroes. Paunchy Jack was a happier man.

"I'll ask," Margot said with a smile. He would do it if Margot asked. Which was why she so rarely asked. But she couldn't be Margot Cooper, domestic icon, without her very loving husband and the excellent father to her children—Jack Cooper.

When he was doing the school run and she was guest judging on Food Network competition shows, there'd been speculation that he was playing the part. Pretending to be so doting. Acting. But it wasn't a part. It was real. It was the bedrock of her life and, according to Noelle, what made her so fascinating.

Jack loved Margot. Margot loved Jack.

The way her own parents had loved each other. The way the world wished they were loved. And, outside of her kids, her marriage was Margot's greatest achievement.

Her sister rolled her eyes every time she said it out loud in her vicinity. "You're putting feminism back twenty years," she'd groan. But it was true. A good marriage—a long marriage—didn't just happen. It took physical and emotional work. Therapy sometimes. Forgiveness all the time. It was a constant balancing act between needs and wants and anger and kindness.

It only looked easy because Jack was so charming and Margot still got weak in the knees when he turned his famous blue eyes her way.

Margot checked her watch. Jack would be coming home from his training session soon. She texted him a reminder that a crowd was currently occupying the kitchen and he could go in through the back if he wanted to avoid them.

Margot put down her phone and almost immediately there was a beep. She lifted it again, expecting a response from Jack, but the screen was blank. There was another beep. Another. A chime.

Margot looked at Rosa, who gaped, open-mouthed, at her phone.

Another beep and Paval at the whiteboard went pale.

Another one. A chorus of them. Endless beeps. Social media notifications going off like land mines.

"What's going on?" Noelle asked, and Paval showed her his phone. Margot watched in what felt like slow motion as Noelle looked at the phone, read whatever was on the screen, then looked across the antique harvest table that Margot and Jack bought in Tuscany on their tenth wedding anniversary and said:

"This is bad."

"What does that mean?" Margot asked, sick with the panic that lived in a mother's body, just waiting for that phone call that someone was hurt. Scared. In trouble. "What's bad?"

Margot's phone rang and she picked it up.

"Don't answer that," Noelle said.

"It's Jack," Margot said, and the faces around her table went white.

"Oh my god," Rosa breathed. "We should leave."

Fingers shaking, Margot took her husband's call.

"Margs?" his familiar voice said. Jack had never been able to drop his northern Illinois windswept cornfield accent, no matter how many dialect coaches he worked with.

"What's going on?" Margot asked, cold in her belly.

"I'll explain when I get home. But . . . I'm sorry."

At first it was one woman. A TikToker, @yestheyarereal, who went live to tell her 1.5 million followers that she'd been having an affair with Jack Cooper. Yes. *The* Jack Cooper. She had the text messages to prove it. The pictures. There'd been hotel rooms and late-night hook-ups in her East L.A. apartment.

And she was coming forward now because she couldn't take the guilt anymore.

It had nothing to do with the blockbuster release of the movie last week.

Within five minutes another one chimed in, that she too had been fucking *the* Jack Cooper. Another one soon after who said she wasn't fucking Jack. But they'd been messaging and video calling, and he asked her to masturbate on camera for him. After then it somehow got worse, with five women saying that Jack had sent them unsolicited dick pics. And did the world want to see?

Guess what? The world wanted to see.

"Put everything to private," Rosa said. "Everything. Shut it all down."

"Won't that make Margot look guilty?" Paval asked.

"Guilty of what?" Noelle snapped.

"We need to draft a statement," Rosa said.

"No," Margot said, the word bursting out of her shell-shocked and ruined body. Was her chest in one piece? Where were her legs? "Just . . . make it all private."

"Maybe it's not him?" Rosa said, in what seemed like an attempt at comfort. "Like it's just a dick. Who knows who it's attached to?"

"It's him," Margot said. The large flat mole on his inner thigh. That's how she knew. Her husband had been firing off well-lit pictures of his hard dick scattershot across the internet. The mole on full display.

There was a text from her sister.

I'm sorry. Are you okay? Of course you're not. Call me.

And then—

That fucker. I knew something like this would happen.

Margot put her phone on silent.

Ten women. Ten incredibly young women, with fake eyelashes like caterpillars had died on their faces. With flat stomachs and giant breasts and bikini pictures as their avatars. Ten women. All of them revealing a text thread with Jack wherein they asked, "Aren't you married?" and he said things like "Do you really care?"

A few of them said, "I love your wife." To which he replied, "So do I. Show me your tits."

Margot immediately sent security for Skye at school and touched base with her other children. The twins Amelia and Ellen were in Paris, and Alex in Cape Canaveral. All of them were safe. All of them were in their homes and apartments. All of them asked if she was okay.

"Fine," she said, behind a thick glass wall. Like those scientists watching atom bomb detonations in the desert. "I'm fine. Don't worry about me."

She hung up and turned off her phone.

"You need to leave," she told her staff. "I'm sure the paparazzi are already at the gates. You should get out while you can."

Everyone left except Noelle. Noelle who'd stood, pale and trembling, unmoving for the hour of explosions.

"You need to go, honey," Margot said, taking Noelle's hand in hers. The shock of everything was a beautiful insulation. She could subvert her stress and grief and rage and concentrate on the lovely Noelle, who was blinking back tears.

"You don't deserve this," Noelle whispered.

"No," Margot said. "But I'm going to withhold judgment until I talk to Jack."

"You don't think this is real?" Noelle asked. She sounded hopeful, and the hope in Margot longed to leap on it. Combine it with her own, like proof. Two hopeful women against ten @yestheyarereal's.

"I don't know what to think," Margot answered honestly. "But I know you need to go."

Noelle left. Alone for the first time, Margot felt the first spiderweb crack in her shock. A tremble in her foundation. She braced a hand against her marble countertop.

Jack, she thought, instead of screaming. Or sobbing. *I just need Jack to come home and say this is some kind of mistake.*

They'd weathered hard things before. The usual marriage stuff and kid stuff and parent stuff. The twins Amelia and Ellen got arrested for shoplifting when they were fifteen, and the papers got ahold of it before they could manage it. Alex was neurodivergent, which took some time to diagnose and treat, and for more years than she liked to admit as a mother, Margot had insisted he was just bored.

Margot's postpartum depression after Skye had nearly swamped all of them, but Jack quit a project he'd been excited about, stayed home, and made sure Margot got to a therapist while he kept things moving at home with four kids under the age of seven.

Her parents' car accident. Dad's death. The funeral. Mom's care. That year she spent more time in Pittsburgh than she did in Los Angeles, meeting with doctors and specialists. Getting second opinions that all said the same thing as the first. Finally, finding a home that actually felt like a home for her mom. And then, when all the paperwork was signed, finally grieving.

Once a production assistant on a movie said Jack had been inappropriate with her, but no one believed her. He was Jack Cooper, after all. And people said a lot of things. None of it had ever been true.

Had it been true?

The pretty young tutor they'd had for Ellen who quit without explaining why.

Did Jack have something to do with that?

All of their normal marriage and family stuff had been strange and amplified because of who they were. But he was Jack and she was Margot and they'd made vows—not just the love and cherish ones, but Hollywood vows.

Don't do anything that will bring down what we've built. That will humiliate the other. That will bring the locusts of paparazzi to our door. Do not damage the image we have worked so hard to create.

And they'd done it.

Survived the fishbowl and the magnifying glass and they were still people. Still in love.

Skye walked in, with the usual accompaniment of slamming doors and her loafers hitting the wall. The thud of her backpack against the floor. She appeared in the doorway of the kitchen, in her blue-and-green plaid skirt uniform and her tie pulled loose. Her black hair in one long braid over her shoulder.

"Mom?" Skye whispered. As far as emotions went, Skye really only expressed various degrees of derision. Margot had learned to read those eye rolls and curled lips, but today her baby girl's dark eyeliner was streaked across her pale cheeks and the fear was obvious.

"It's okay," Margot lied, and pulled her daughter in for a hug. Skye wrapped her arms around Margot's waist, put her head on Margot's shoulder, and hugged her back. Skye was so small under her too-big blazer. Margot could feel her spine and her shoulder blades. She remembered the cinnamon rolls from earlier, but they seemed ridiculous now.

"Is it true?" Skye whispered against Margot's shoulder.

"I don't know," Margot said.

Skye leaned back, the moment over. The derision was back. "Mom, it's like . . . ten women. There were pictures."

"Did you look at them?" Margot asked, suddenly horrified and sick.

"No. But . . . everyone else saw them. Everyone at school. All my teachers."

"Okay. Okay," Margot said, squeezing her daughter close, like she might be able to squeeze her back into being ten years old. That intense, funny kid who loved the movie *Jaws*, the Go-Go's, and the *Narnia* books with such obsessiveness. She and Jack would spend whole evenings marveling at how unique she was. How fully formed outside of them. So different from their other kids.

"I know. But I'm withholding judgment until I talk to your father."

Skye stepped away. A tiny island to herself, surrounded by coral reefs of contempt.

There was the click and hum of the garage door opening and then closing. *He's back.*

Skye was poised like a deer at the edge of a highway and Jack was an eighteen-wheeler in the distance.

Run? Stay? Margot didn't have an answer for her.

She sucked in a deep breath, and it was like her ears popped and the insulation of her shock was gone. What she felt in its absence was razor-sharp and nauseating. Not rage. Not grief. Some mix of the two that made her knees buckle.

"Skye," she said, her voice a warning. A teakettle whistle. A tornado alarm.

Skye ran, her footsteps thudding down the hall and up the stairs.

She could imagine Jack climbing out of his car, still wearing the clothes he'd worn to the trainer this morning. They used to have a trainer come to the house. When did that stop? Why did it stop?

He was on the landing. Taking off his shoes. Putting his keys in the small clay dish their son Alex had made in fifth grade.

There was a trembling. A deep internal shake. The San Andreas Fault ran right down the middle of her body.

She stood in the kitchen they'd just had renovated, waiting for her life to end. Her life. Her children's lives. Everything she'd known to be true would come crashing down.

No, she thought and then again. She might have said it. Yelled it. Because Jack said, "Margot?"

She grabbed her purse. Her phone. Ran upstairs to throw things in a bag and get her daughter.

"Mom?" Skye asked.

"We need to go," Margot said, and for once Skye did not argue and that felt like proof she was doing the right thing.

They left through the back door like they were escaping a fire.

CHAPTER 2

Seven hours later
Pittsburgh, Pennsylvania

Margot

The air smelled like snow and ice salt. And hills empty of coal.
Home.

Margot touched the number six beside the door, where it sat crooked against the seven. She made it straight, let go, and it fell crooked again.

"What are you doing, Mom?" Skye whispered.

The sun had set behind the low gray-green hills, but they both wore sunglasses and hats. Disguises from home. Margot would like to believe they didn't need them in Pittsburgh. But better safe than sorry. The twins had been ambushed by paparazzi in Paris. Alex at the Kennedy Space Station (his bosses had not been pleased). It felt like the world was on fire with Jack's fall from grace. They'd been trending on Twitter or X or whatever all day. The daytime talk shows, the late shows were going to have a field day. Oprah (who she'd always considered a friend) weighed in. The internet . . . well, the internet was a place she wouldn't be visiting again.

"I feel like I should knock," Margot said.

"Mom, you're being weird." Skye pulled open the screen door and pushed the storm door open over the old front hall carpet. The smell of her childhood drifted out. Mothballs and sautéed onions, the cranberry mist candle that burned on the kitchen table after dinner for decades.

Blondie's *Eat to the Beat* was playing somewhere in the house.

Her entire self shuddered. Relief, yes. But beneath the rolled stone of homecoming was nothing but darkness.

"Aunt Julia?" Skye shouted, walking through the memories of the old house like she couldn't feel them. They both stepped into the hallway, crowded with a coat tree and a mirror, hooks for Dad's Steelers hats, and closed the door behind them. *It's so small,* she thought. But she always thought that when she stood in this foyer. She'd outgrown this house years ago, her needs and wants taking her far away. But when her life got hard, or scary, she wanted to be here. In her mother's house. With her sister.

"Did you call her?" Skye asked over her shoulder, pulling off her hat. Her hair lifted in a halo from static electricity. Margot would smile at her daughter if it wouldn't be met with a growl.

"I did not." She'd turned off her phone to silence Jack's incessant calls. Everything was one step at a time. One minute at a time. Briefly, she turned on her phone to email Noelle that everyone should stay home until it all blew over. Which it would. She was sure of it. She even added a ludicrous smiley face emoji as if to prove it.

All that mattered was getting someplace safe. And the safest place she knew was her parents' house in Pittsburgh. Now they were here, and she wasn't sure what happened next.

Julia will know.

Julia was her older sister and Julia loved to tell her what to do.

"Aunt Julia?" Skye shouted from the living room with the windows onto the street, and at the top of the stairs to the second floor came a thump.

"Skye? Is that you, honey?" Bare feet arrived on the landing. And then long, lean legs, and one of Dad's old Steelers T-shirts. Too big because Dad had been big.

And then it was her sister, dark wild hair, like Skye's. Her excellent skin she didn't take care of and didn't really have to thanks to Mom's genetics. The earrings, the nose ring. Those bold eyebrows under which her sharp dark eyes saw everything.

The trembling was back. Worse than before. Worse than ever. Margot dropped the bag she'd filled with god knows what and pressed that same hand to her stomach.

Oh, no. Don't . . . don't let that out.

"I hope . . . it's okay . . ." she said, and attempted to smile.

"You're such an idiot," Julia said, and flew down the last of the steps. She swept Skye and Margot up in her skinny arms and hugged them to her chest. Julia smelled like she had since high school, Pantene shampoo and a faint whiff of weed. The sob caught Margot by surprise. And she tried to swallow it because she had, in the last seven hours, built a home behind the atomic blast glass between her and what had happened.

For Skye's sake, she told herself.

But the truth was she wasn't sure where that one sob might lead. How that one sob might bring everything down. If she started, she was scared she'd never stop.

"Come on, Margs," Julia whispered. "You're safe here."

"Skye," Margot muttered, about to tell her that she should go in the other room. Unpack in one of the bedrooms upstairs. Play in the yard, though she was years past that. She should do anything, be anywhere, that wasn't here. Because things were about to get messy.

"She'll survive watching you cry," Julia murmured.

That nudge was all it took. The last few hours of white-knuckled control and stomach-burning fear evaporated, and she fell against her sister and sobbed her heart out. Julia patted her back and stroked her hair and didn't tell her it was going to be okay. She didn't even say that she'd always known Jack was going to cheat.

She made soft, soothing noises and let her cry it all out, the way Mom would have. And when Margot's eyes were swollen and the sobs had been reduced to deep, shuddery breaths, she said the only thing there was to say.

"Let's get drunk."

The house was a brick two-story built at the bottom of a hill, fifteen minutes outside of Pittsburgh. At the top of the hill was a country club where the families of U.S. Steel executives golfed and ate shrimp cocktails. Their houses on top of that hill had views of the Ohio River and one of the last working steel mills in the area.

Dad had worked at that steel mill and Mom had worked at that country club and their family's whole life was balanced between those two realities.

Mom had made it all look easy. Staying a size four. Working as a waitress and bartender up at that country club. On her nights off she ran what she called a living room salon, dyeing her friends' hair. Giving them perms. Doing their nails. She kept the house in shape, got dinner on the table most nights, and baked pumpkin roll for all the school bake sales.

Dad taught them how to hit a baseball in the backyard and ride a bike on the sidewalk out front.

Mom and Dad slow danced in the kitchen to Kenny Rogers, and more than once Margot and Julia had walked in on them making out. Dad's hand halfway up her shirt.

She made it all seem . . . simple.

And then four years ago, the car accident. The drunk driver who blew through a stop sign and plowed into Mom and Dad's old Volkswagen, killing Dad instantly and sending Mom into a care facility.

"Another?" Julia asked, and Margot held out her glass.

They sat in the windowless wood-paneled den with the side-by-side recliners and family pictures on the wall. The carpet was a deep burgundy and at least as old as Margot.

Julia lifted the bottle of very fine scotch they'd finished off, slipped out of her recliner onto the rug, and opened the old teak liquor cabinet in the corner.

"We're into the dregs," Julia said. "Do you want Mom's old rum? Or this?" She lifted an ancient bottle of Tia Maria.

Margot gathered all the far-flung pieces of herself. "Neither," she said, and pulled out her phone. She would have some wine delivered. Nope. Margaritas. That was what she wanted. Margaritas and some Mexican food to go with it. Skye would eat black bean burritos and guacamole all day long. And Margot was starving. Had she eaten since the citrus salad?

"What are you doing?" Julia sat curled up on the rug, looking like a teenager.

"Getting us provisions. You'll answer the door."

"I don't know if this is impressive or disturbing. Your life is falling apart and you're ordering provisions?"

While she made her order, her phone rang three times. Once from Jack. Two others were unknown numbers. One text from Noelle.

You have to make a statement.

She declined all three calls, ignored Noelle, and quickly turned off her phone. Whatever bubbled up in her chest. Behind her eyes. At the back of her throat. Tears or screams or . . . something worse. She turned it off along with her phone. There'd been enough drama; she wasn't going to add to it by screaming or vomiting or whatever it was she kept swallowing down.

"Skye is probably hungry. I'm hungry. You will be—"

"I have food! You can give up control for a few minutes. You're not even properly drunk."

"That's what the margaritas are for."

"Oh." Julia looked stymied. "Margaritas do sound good."

Julia crawled back into Dad's old recliner and the two of them sat side by side, looking at the old TV and the family portrait over it.

Mom's red hair was set in Farrah Fawcett waves and she wore a black sweater that was just a smidge tight. Cut just a little low. Dad was a giant bear of a man with a mustache, twinkly eyes, and a head of thick black hair. Margot and Julia were dressed in matching prairie dresses with maroon ribbons in their hair. Margot was smiling the smile she'd practiced in the mirror. No teeth, sparkly eyes, head tilted just so.

Julia was scowling. Arms crossed over her ten-year-old chest, with the most magnificent perm in the history of the world.

They never took another family photo again.

"Why haven't you taken that picture down?" Margot asked. Julia hated that picture.

"I did. But then the room felt so weird I had to put it back."

"Why were you so mad that day?"

"Who knows? I liked being mad. You look like a miniature Stepford wife."

She did. She couldn't even argue.

At their home in Montecito, she and Jack had a million family portraits taken by famous photographers who specialized in photojournalism. There was action shot after action shot of Jack throwing kids in the air and wrestling them on the floor. Her favorite was the one of him watching Margot as she breastfed Skye. His face was suffused with love. With adoration and wonder.

When things were hard, she looked at that photo and was, in a way, restored.

That picture wasn't a lie. She knew that. That moment, those feelings, had been real.

Or they were bullshit. Had they always been bullshit? And she was a fool who'd been polishing a lie and believing it to be true for twenty-five years?

She bit her lip against the sudden animal growl of pain in her throat.

"What did Jack say?" Julia asked. "When it all came out."

"He was sorry."

"That's it?" Julia asked, jumping to anger. Julia was good at jumping to anger. She'd made righteousness a part of her personality. As Julia's sister, Margot had made not jumping to anger part of her personality. Someone had to be reasonable. She was, currently, trying to be reasonable.

"Well, I didn't give him much of an opportunity to say more."

"What did you say?"

"Nothing." She ran her hand over the worn spot on the armrest where, for decades, her father rested his cans of Yuengling to watch the Steelers win and the Pirates lose. "I haven't talked to him."

"At all?"

Margot nodded and braced herself.

"Holy shit, Margot!" Julia cried. "You're joking." Margot shrugged and Julia reached over and grabbed her arm, pulling her attention away from her father and those sweating cans of beer. "Why?" she whispered.

Julia wouldn't understand why she ran. Julia had compromised maybe once in her life in kindergarten. She ran toward every confrontation armed with an innate sense of *right*. She'd never been conflicted or pushed around by the wants and needs of other people. Julia made decisions and never wavered. Never seemed to regret.

She never needed a goddamn minute to gather herself.

"You don't want to tell him to go fuck himself?" Julia asked with a bitter, knife-edged laugh.

Margot didn't know what she wanted to tell him. What was she supposed to say? She knew what Julia would say, but they'd never seen eye to eye on those sorts of things. She'd come here in a panic and fog to find out what her mom would say.

And she didn't want to feel shitty about that.

I just need a minute.

I just need my mom.

Julia patted Margot's hand like the older sister she was. Like the friend she was. She didn't agree, and didn't understand, but she'd keep her mouth shut about not talking to him. For the moment.

Margot met her sister's dark eyes and saw the millions of things she wanted to say about Jack. "Don't," Margot whispered. "Don't rewrite history. You did not know this was going to happen. You love Jack."

"Loved."

Margot laughed without much humor. "Fair. This has got to be some kind of midlife crisis."

"Don't do *that*. Don't excuse it."

"I'm not!"

"No, you are, you're rationalizing it. Explaining it into a little box so you can manage it."

Margot wanted to argue but couldn't. As always, her sister saw her clearly. She sighed and Julia sighed, and they reached across the small distance between the two chairs and clutched each other's hands.

"I'm so glad I'm here," Margot whispered.

"Me too," Julia said.

"Noelle wants me to make a statement."

Julia blinked at her. "What kind of statement?"

"You know, like we're working on our marriage so please grant us privacy?"

"Working on your marriage?" Julia shrieked. "I mean . . . Margot. How do you go back to him after this?"

"I don't know."

"What is a statement going to do?"

"I don't know."

"You need to divorce his ass and take him for everything. It seems pretty simple to me."

"Nothing about this is simple!" she shouted.

Margot blinked, her own anger surprising her. Julia smiled, feral and pleased. Of course Julia would love it if Margot just got mad. Just went scorched earth on everything. That wasn't something Margot had the luxury of doing. "Well, if you need someone to slash his tires or take a golf club to his Range Rover?"

"I know who to ask."

"Mom!" Skye came thumping down the stairs. "I'm starving."

"I ordered tacos."

Skye thumped back up the stairs.

"Is she okay?" Julia asked.

"I mean . . ." Tears threatened again. "How could she be? It's one thing to find out your father is a lying scumbag. But to have the whole world find out at the same time?"

"She's tough."

"I think she only acts tough." Margot squeezed Julia's hand. "Like you."

Julia squeezed her hand back.

"How is work?" Margot asked, changing the subject, but not really.

"Good. I mean . . . fine. Shit, really. I think they're going to downsize again."

Julia was a reporter for the *Post-Gazette* and had survived round after round of cuts to the reporting staff. She was currently the last man standing in what used to be a robust investigative journalism department. She had other job opportunities at bigger papers: *New York Times, Wall Street Journal, Miami Herald.*

She always said no. Pittsburgh was home. It was enough.

"I wish you'd—"

"No."

Margot swallowed the offer she'd been making for four years. Podcasts were an exciting opportunity for real journalism, and Margot would love to see her sister start one. And if it was a financial reason holding her back, Margot could take care of that.

The doorbell rang and Margot stayed in the chair while Julia handled the delivery bags, setting them in the foyer. Wine. Organic milk and fruit because Julia never bought it. Skye's favorite cereal. A sweater, because she forgot one and the house was freezing.

Dinner was delivered at the same time.

Julia shut the door and looked at the pile of bags. "Jesus. Really?"

Whenever Margot came home, she ran face-first into the reminder that what was normal in her life in Montecito was ostentatious and borderline vulgar here. And salt-of-the-earth Julia could roll her eyes all she wanted, but she'd suck down those delivery margaritas. And probably steal the sweater.

Margot stood and took some of the bags and boxes to the old kitchen. The kitchen had yellow linoleum chairs and a Formica table in the corner where Mom sat in the morning with her coffee and the paper, wearing the pink-and-red kimono she got on Canal Street when she'd visited New York. When Margot was young, she'd lay on the floor beside the chair and run her fingers through the red-and-black fringe. In her young eyes, that kimono had been the most glamorous thing in the world.

For a moment, in the doorway, Margot's hands full of luxury items her mother could never have dreamed of, Margot missed her mother more than she missed her marriage. She missed her mother like she was ten again on the first night of sleepaway camp and her chest was torn open with longing for the way Mom smelled.

"Do you think . . . we could go see her?" Margot asked. Julia leaned out of the fridge.

"Mom?"

Margot nodded.

"I can call tomorrow. I mean . . . it depends, you know."

"That would be . . . I would just . . ." She put her hands over her face. *I really want my mom.*

"Okay. All right." Julia put her arms around her again. "Sometimes when I call, they tell me she's having a good day and I go, and she remembers me and we play some music and talk shit about you . . ."

"Julia," Margot laughed.

"We'll hope for a good day," Julia said. "That's all we can do."

That's all we can ever do. Any one of us.

Margot got down plates and set the tacos on Mom's old platters. The vintage Fiestaware that was highly coveted (and maybe radioactive) and that Julia put in the dishwasher like they were from Target.

"How is it going clearing out the attic?" Margot asked, spooning the guacamole into a bright yellow bowl.

"Great."

Julia filled two glasses with ice, unscrewed the top of the ready-made margarita, and filled the glasses to the brim. She handed one to Margot and then hoisted herself onto the counter and took a noisy sip of her own. She'd pulled on ratty gray sweatpants, also too big. She was skin and bones, her sister. Mom always used to say Julia ran hot, and all that emotion burned through calories.

"You're lying."

"Am I?" Julia waggled her eyebrows.

"Julia!" Margot laughed.

"Fine. It's not going. I told you I couldn't do that without you. It's too much. What if I throw out the wrong thing?"

"You are a grown woman, Julia."

"I am. And that attic is an emotional land mine. Last time I went up there and found my old prom dress . . . I had to take to my bed."

"Take to your bed?"

"Like a character in a Victorian novel, Margot. I had the vapors."

Her sister had been living in this house for four years, since the accident, under the auspices of cleaning it up for sale. That had been Julia's plan, the thing she said at least three times a year. Selfishly, Margot liked having her sister here. It gave Margot a place to return to. A way to remind herself who she actually was, when the world of Hollywood threatened to eat her up.

But she also didn't want Julia to be overwhelmed. Or to feel like she *had* to do anything.

"I can't do it alone," Julia said. A repeat of what she'd said last Christmas. And on her birthday. "I won't."

Suddenly, fortified with a very strong margarita, some tacos, and a healthy dose of existential despair, it was obvious to Margot that the time for it to be done was now.

Work. Distraction. The tidying up of some other mess. An easy mess. A solvable problem. All of it put a collar on the low howl in her chest.

"Let's go."

"No. Come on, Margs . . ."

"It's this, cut each other's hair, or cry some more. And I don't want to cry anymore."

"I honestly think showing a little reasonable emotion here would do you some good."

"Not interested," Margot said. Emotion was a slippery slope. She needed to think. This wasn't just a marriage. It was a *life*.

And worse, it was a life in a fishbowl. Whatever she said or did would be *news*. This was already going to haunt her kids for the rest of their lives. She couldn't compound it by being reactionary.

Angry.

"Come on." She grabbed the bag of surprisingly excellent corn chips and some of the guacamole and her margarita and headed through the house. The old burgundy carpet ran through the first floor and up the stairs, where it stopped at a ragged edge one of the dogs had pulled up at the narrow hardwood hallway.

Margot knocked on her old bedroom door. The unicorn sticker she'd put on it when she was eight had no more glitter and the unicorn's face had been rubbed off.

"Tacos in the kitchen," she told her daughter. "Julia and I are going up to the attic. Come up when you're done."

The door flew open and her daughter with her big headphones and messy eyeliner blinked at her. "The attic?"

"I know," Julia agreed. "It's a bad idea."

"You'll love it up there. It's very Narnia," Margot said. She walked down the hall to the string hanging from the ceiling right in front of her parents' old room.

Margot pulled the string, and the drop ladder came sliding down along with the smell of mothballs and cedarwood and dust.

Home. Mom. Safety.

Julia caught the ladder.

"I can't believe you're making me do this," she said.

I can't believe Jack is making me do any of this. The thought was angry and bitter and not helpful in any way. She muscled it aside and smiled.

"It's gonna be fun."

CHAPTER 3

March 2024
Pittsburgh, Pennsylvania

Margot

"God, can you believe this?" Julia said. She put the old straw cowboy hat she'd worn nonstop when she was seven on her head. Dust rained down from its brim, sending Julia into a coughing fit.

"I thought I'd lost it," she finally said, her voice gruff.

The dust in places was an inch thick. And so were the cobwebs. Julia claiming she'd been up here anytime in the last year was an outright lie.

Margot wore a pink tutu skirt that tied with a ribbon around her waist and two of Mom's beauty contest sashes—Miss Lehigh Valley 1974 and Miss Pittsburgh 1975. Runner-up Miss Pennsylvania 1976. The crowns were here somewhere. Mom had made the mistake of letting Julia and Margot play with them when they were little and they had barely survived Julia's Battle Princess phase. Margot had barely survived that phase.

They were on the last few sips of their margaritas and had drunkenly embraced the attic's emotional land mines. Because there was no other way to survive it. Half measures would end up with them back in the recliners while Margot tried to ignore her phone.

"Mom hid a lot of things," Margot said, yanking the lid off the top of a plastic crate to reveal her old schoolwork and awards from high school. "Remember my trumpet?"

"Ha! Yes. She said you left it at Bonnie's at Christmas one year." Julia had not moved on from her first box of their childhood toys.

"I found it under her bed two years later."

Julia gasped, scandalized.

"I know. I might have been the best trumpeter the world has ever seen, and we will never know because Mom could not handle one more rendition of the *Hill Street Blues* theme song."

Julia cackled in her metallic-green satin prom dress, with its ruching and the gigantic ruffle at the hem and on the shoulder. Margot slipped her National Honor Society, forensic team, and Mathletics medals around her neck. They were heavier than she remembered.

"Look!" Julia cried and pulled from the bottom of her box one of Mom's crowns. It was bent and missing nearly all its rhinestones, but Julia put it on her head and lifted her hand in a beauty queen wave.

"I'd like to thank SlimFast and Virginia Slims for keeping me a size four," she said in an excellent imitation of their mother's beauty queen voice.

Margot laughed. Truly those two had been the heavy hitters in Mom's arsenal against aging. "And *20 Minute Workout*."

"Yes! Remember Bess? She was my favorite." Julia in her prom dress attempted some kind of leg lift. She toppled sideways, falling between the joists to the plywood beneath.

Skye's head popped up from the doorway in the floor. "Oh my god, what are you doing?"

Margot clapped at the sight of her. Which predictably made her teenager roll her eyes.

"It's called memory lane, honey," Julia said, sitting back up.

"Are there bats?" she asked.

"No," Margot said at the same time Julia said, "Maybe."

Skye put on a show of hating it, but she scrambled up and sat next to Margot. The floor felt like it wasn't solid, but it was. The wooden planks were splintery and there were random joists to be crawled over, but once you were sitting it was all very fine.

Julia was playing the Eurythmics on her phone and the acoustics were excellent with the pitched ceilings.

It was warm and cozy, and the world felt very far away. The paparazzi, Noelle, and Jack could not find her up here. Not ever. Maybe she wouldn't leave.

"What are we looking for?" Skye asked, her nose wrinkled, like something smelled bad when it only smelled like dust and Pittsburgh and Mom's house.

"Things we can throw out," Margot said. She pointed at the pile near the door in the floor. It was not very big, and mostly Margot's stuff. Predictably, Julia had been putting up a fight.

"What can we throw out?" Skye asked.

"Nothing!" Julia said, bending low over the boxes in front of her, like she was protecting them from Margot.

"How can you see anything?" Skye asked, peering into the shadows of the attic. There was one bare bulb with a long string illuminating the tight little circle where they sat.

"I'm not drunk enough to brave the shadows," Margot said.

"Why? What's back there?" Skye looked over her shoulder at the boxes stacked under the low eaves at the other end of the attic. The boxes were three deep and covered the window that looked out onto Irving Avenue. They'd been sitting there, just like that, for as long as Margot could remember.

"Who knows," Margot said.

"Mom and Dad's wedding stuff is over there," Julia said, pointing to the opposite corner. "Our stuff is here." She waved her hands over the mess they were currently making. "Dad's college wrestling stuff is over there. That is . . ." Julia tilted her head and the hat fell off. "I don't know."

"Maybe Nana's stuff?" Margot asked.

"What in the world would Mom keep from Nana?" Julia asked. Mom and her own mother had not been close. And Margot had very few memories of the trailer outside Allentown filled with beauty pageant memorabilia. Nana had been a narcissistic, controlling, unpleasable pageant mom before the television shows ever existed.

It made the way Mom had been so loving and warm, encouraging both Margot and Julia to be whoever they wanted as long as they were happy, even more of a miracle.

Skye scrambled sideways and crouched in front of the mystery boxes. After careful consideration she pulled out two boxes that had been hidden behind the others.

Of course she'd do the ones in the darkest corner. The ones with the most entrenched possibility and drama. Skye had always been a girl who did things in her own order. As a toddler learning to dress herself, she would put on socks first. Margot wondered if she still did and felt a margarita-inspired pang that she didn't know how her daughter dressed herself anymore.

The top box was full of old records.

"Mom?" Skye's face lit up. The twins had given her a record player for Christmas, and finding, buying, and listening to vinyl was a big part of Skye's identity these days.

"All yours, honey."

The music on Julia's phone shuffled to "Vacation" by the Go-Go's.

"I love this song," Skye said, going through Mom's disco collection.

Julia and Margot shared a quick smile.

"Hey, Skye," Julia said after a few minutes of quiet. "How are you doing? Really?"

"Fine."

Julia made a honking noise and Skye laughed. Margot's heart lifted out from the panicked spot behind her stomach where it had been hiding for the last twelve hours. She watched her daughter, the baby-fat roundness of her cheek. The black curls against her neck.

"I'm like . . ."

Margot held her breath. If anyone could pull Skye out of her teenage shell it was Julia, with her coolness and her directness and her one-step-removed-from-it-all-ness.

Skye kept her head down, looking through the box, pulling out a Chic album. Julia was doing the same, each of them pretending like everything was no big deal. Margot sat there, hands clenched. Tears hot in her eyes.

"I'm embarrassed," Skye said. "Like so many people have seen the pictures. Like the whole world has seen my dad's . . ." She shook her head. "Whatever. I'm just totally embarrassed. I can't ever go back to school. Like ever."

Those tears burned up in a sudden incendiary wave of anger.

Jack. You asshole. Look at what you've done.

If he was here—right now—she wasn't sure what she would do to him. She felt capable of anything. It was frightening and probably margarita induced.

Julia nodded. "You sound mad."

"I don't know," Skye said with a shrug.

"It's okay if you are." The words burst out of Margot's chest. "I mean, anything you're feeling is okay." Of course, the second Margot opened her mouth, the moment was over. Skye clammed back up and Julia rolled her eyes at Margot.

Way to go, Mom.

Skye put all the things she thought could be thrown away back in the box, saving the records in a stack beside her. She pulled forward the bottom box. It was big and had been closed at the top, water-damaged at the bottom. She pulled the flaps open, disrupting heaps of dust.

What diseases come from mouse poop? Margo wondered and then refused to think about it anymore.

Skye lifted something from the box and tried to tilt it into the light from the bulb in the middle of the room, but it wasn't enough and she turned on her phone's flashlight.

"Did Grandma live in New York?" Skye asked.

"No," Julia answered, digging back into the box of old toys. "She used to take us every year, though. We'd get rush seats to all the musicals."

"She loved those musicals," Margot said, stretching out her legs because her foot had fallen asleep. She took off the medals and wished for a glass of water.

"I think she wanted to be a dancer," Julia said.

"You're just saying that because of the pageants." Mom's talent for jazz dance had come out once during a mother-and-child talent show at elementary school. She'd knocked everyone dead. But she never did it again. Rarely even talked about it. "Mom wanted to be a mom," she sighed. "And a size four, forever."

"God, Margot, sometimes you have the strangest ideas about being a woman."

"What?" Margot asked. "They're not ideas. They're memories. Mom told me that. Lots of times. I'm not saying every woman wants to be a mom, needs to be a mom, or should be a mom. But Mom did. She wanted a family."

"And you don't think she wanted anything else? Ever?" This was an old argument between them and they barely got heated anymore.

"I think you're both wrong," Skye said.

"Impossible," Julia said, putting on a pair of yellow plastic star sunglasses. "We are never wrong."

"Even when we are," Margot laughed.

"This is a whole box of New York stuff," Skye said, pulling out newspapers. Faded yellow and pink flyers.

"Really?" Margot said, thinking maybe Mom saved the programs and the tickets to the musicals. They'd seen *Les Mis, Miss Saigon,* and *City of Angels* and each one had been a breathless and exciting wonder. Once Mom stole a menu from Tavern on the Green and Margot had been so scandalized she couldn't finish her meal. She'd just sat there sweating and waiting to be kicked out.

It would be very much like Mom to save that menu.

"What's the Orbit Room?" Skye asked, pulling out a piece of paper.

"You don't know what the Orbit Room is?" Julia asked, throwing the star glasses back in the box. "What are they teaching you in school?"

"The Orbit Room was a legendary disco club," Margot told Skye. "Famous people were there every night. It was the height of seventies decadence and depravity."

"Did Gran work there?" asked Skye, lifting a piece of paper. She looked up at them, her face washed in white light from the flashlight. Her eyes were dark. She looked owlish.

"No," Margot laughed. Mom worked at the Shannopin Country Club. When she retired, they named a cocktail after her (the Diz) and her picture was on a plaque behind the bar.

"What have you got there?" Julia asked, pointing at the yellowed slip of paper in Skye's hands.

"It looks like a pay stub from the Orbit Room. Made out to Ginger Daughtry." Skye bent back over the box, the light hitting the splintered wood of the ceiling. The tips of roofing nails poked out in places. "There's a bunch of them."

Margot and Julia scrambled over the floor to get to her side. "I didn't think they paid employees. Wasn't that part of why they got shut down?" Julia asked.

"Mom didn't work there," Margot said.

Margot took the handwritten stub. It was dated February 22, 1977, and it was made out to her mother.

"Mom moved in with Bonnie when she got to Pittsburgh. She didn't live in New York." Margot handed the stub to Julia. Ginger had left Allentown and ended up in Pittsburgh, where she met Bonnie at the Miss Pittsburgh contest; they'd been friends ever since. That was the story they heard every time Mom or Bonnie had a rum and Diet Coke too many.

"Yeah. That apartment in Beltzhoover," Julia said, holding the pay stub up to the light.

"It wouldn't have been New York," Margot answered definitively. "We would know if Mom moved to New York."

"I don't know, Margs," Julia said with a lifted eyebrow. "People keep secrets."

The words pierced her someplace deep and she flinched. Was everyone lying? Who could she believe?

"Hey," Julia said, immediately contrite. "I didn't—"

"I know," Margot said, absolving her sister because she just didn't want to get into it. She was rationing her strength and it was in low supply.

Skye pulled out a handful of buttons and handed them to Margot.

Purdy for New York
Safe Streets Now
Lady X for Mayor

"Lady X," Margot said. "I haven't heard that name since my women's studies elective at UCLA." It was funny to think of Mom, playing bunko and making cabbage rolls every Sunday night, at the same time as Lady X, mysterious feminist icon and violent vigilante, was trying to change the world.

"Who is Lady X?" Skye asked, pulling out yellowed newspaper clippings that were so dry they rustled like leaves in her hands.

"She was a political activist, in the seventies. A graffiti artist. Super controversial," Julia said. "Think Banksy but angrier. More violent. She was a real moment, you know."

Skye leafed through the old newsprint. "These papers say she was a criminal."

"That's not totally wrong," Margot said.

"Margot!" Julia chastised.

"What? She was!"

Skye read the headlines. "'Wounded Mets Pitcher Puts Bounty on Lady X.' 'City Held Hostage by Lady X.' 'Lady X and Son of Sam Connected?'" Skye looked up. "Who is Son of Sam?" she asked, and Julia acted like she might pass out.

"An infamous serial killer in New York City in the seventies," Margot explained. "He thought his neighbor's dog was telling him to shoot people. Mostly women."

"These are all New York City newspapers," Julia said, reaching into the box to pull out more frail newsprint. "How would Mom even get these unless she was in New York?"

Margot suddenly wanted to get out of the attic. Enough emotional land mines for one day. She was hungover and itchy. "I've got ice cream in the freezer, let's go get some."

But her sister and her daughter both ignored her.

"'John Doe a victim of Lady X. How many men has Lady X killed?'" Skye read.

"Lady X didn't murder anyone," Margot said, remembering her class. "She was killed the night of the 1977 blackout."

"No, she wasn't," Julia said. "She killed a guy the night of the blackout."

"That's not what we learned in women's studies."

"Well, it's what we learned in J-school." Julia said it as if J-school trumped women's studies every day of the week. When she was young and feeling slighted, Margot used to wonder if her mother liked Julia better because she was so sure. So confident. Margot and her mother were so alike that maybe, to her mother, she was boring. While Julia with all her fireworks was always interesting.

Skye gasped and her body went strangely still. "I think I know why Grandma cared," she whispered.

The half-delighted, half-terrified look on Skye's face promised up-heaval. Cosmic shifts. It promised something that would need to be wrestled with and Margot was wrestling with enough.

Margot put her hand up and was about to say stop. Wait.

Please don't.

But Julia, who had been an agent of chaos since birth, clapped her hands like whatever was about to come was only good times. Julia was not a person who worried about fallout. She lived for explosions.

"Let me . . ." Julia said, and took the paper. Immediately, her face folded into the exact same expression as Skye's. Horror and delight and worse . . . curiosity. A curious Julia was a dog with a bone. An ob-sessive. It was what made her a good journalist. And a pain in Margot's ass.

But Julia didn't get curious very often. Not anymore.

And that sent a spike of panic into Margot's already beleaguered body.

"What?" Margot cried. "What is it?" She didn't reach for the paper. She needed it to be translated, explained with context. Muffled. Dealt with before it came her way.

But Julia and Skye shared a look and then Julia turned the paper and held it up so Margot could see it.

There on the front page of the *Post* was a black-and-white picture of one of the Lady X crime scenes. She'd seen pictures like this in her class. But somehow in this attic, her life decimated by Jack's callous depravity and selfishness, she saw it with different eyes.

You heard the words *vandalism* and *graffiti artist* and thought of some spray paint and lewd cartoons. Something small. But this was violent and big. And pointed. An accusation. An angry, rage-filled indictment. It was a brownstone with sagging geraniums in a pot next to the black cast-iron door. And written all over the front of the building from the first to the third floor in black spray paint were the words *rapist* and *pervert* repeated over and over again, in large letters and small. Print and cursive.

It was breathtaking. Terrifying.

It was a full-throated scream of rage and pain.

Tears built up in her eyes. *Whoever did this was so mad.*

"That's a lot," Margot said, tamping down her response to all that rage. Her internal, answering howl.

"You're not even . . . you're not looking." Julia crawled over and pointed at the bottom of the picture. Where there was a woman turning away from the camera, half her face a blur, but the other half in stark relief.

Even with the blur, even in black-and-white and the separation of forty years, there was no mistaking who that woman was.

"Mom," Margot gasped. "That's . . . this . . ."

"Is Mom," Julia said.

"Have you seen this picture before?" Margot asked her J-school graduate sister. But Julia shook her head. "Me neither," Margot said.

She struggled to find some logical answer. Surely there was a logical answer. "It's some kind of accident. A mistake? She was walking by and a photographer got her in the shot?"

"I don't think so, Margot," Julia said, and handed over one last newspaper.

It was a blown-up version of Mom's face from the other picture. She looked . . . furious.

The headline screamed:

"Is This Lady X?"

IS THIS LADY X?
Daily Mail, July 13, 1977

For almost three months the violent vigilante Lady X has terrorized New York City. But, thanks to a lucky shot by a *Daily Mail* photographer, police have a new lead in the case that has held the men of the city hostage.

"The woman in the picture has been known to police since the beginning," says a source within the NYPD. "It's only a matter of time before we're able to put Lady X behind bars where she belongs."

Some citizens worry the recent cuts to the city's police force will mean Lady X won't get the punishment she deserves.

"She's a psychopath who needs to be stopped before more people are hurt. Or worse," says Jeffery Cho, who runs a newsstand across the street from the Orbit Room, the nightclub Lady X shut down in her reign of destruction. "Police are so busy chasing this Son of Sam madman, Lady X can do what she wants. The men in this city gotta organize and go after her," Cho said. "Nobody is safe."

As the city is besieged by the twin terrors of Son of Sam and Lady X, Mayor Beame's office released a statement: "There are police officers and courts for women to turn to. There's no need for them to take matters into their own hands like this. My office does not condone lawlessness or vigilante behavior. Lady X isn't a hero. She is public enemy #2. I encourage her to turn herself in before anyone else gets hurt."

CHAPTER 4

April 1977
New York City

Ginger

The Orbit Room on a Saturday night was the pulsating center of the sex- and smoke-filled universe. Even in the coatroom where Ginger was banished—cocooned by the fur and leather coats of the rich and famous and, oddly, a baby carriage—the music was so loud Ginger could feel it in her heartbeat. In her eyes. Between her legs.

It was irresistible. All-consuming.

Coat check girls weren't supposed to dance. Or drink. Or smoke. Or flirt with guests. She was supposed to stand at the coatroom door and smile. Take coats, give numbered plastic tags, while the best party in the entire world was reserved for the bar just down the hall.

It was torture. Being so close to the epic party every night and still somehow so far away.

All she wanted was to be a part of something extraordinary.

Alone, she let go of the rules and every posture correction her mom hissed in her ear and just let the groove happen.

"Ginger!" Todd yelled, and she spun around to find him lifting the gate to the coat check room. He'd been promoted from bar back to bartender and wore the skin-tight silver space suit the bartenders had to wear, like he was an extra on *The Man Who Fell to Earth*. The women were dressed like sexy space girls, with silver dresses, go-go boots, and tiny hats with red antennas.

The silver eyelashes were his own touch. As were the streaks of silver paint across his dark skin, like he'd been scratched by a space-age tiger.

"Are those roller skates still in lost and found?" he asked, his eyes bright with cocaine and another one of his fun ideas.

Ginger nodded and went back into the corner behind the coats and clothes that had all been left behind and found the two pairs of roller skates.

"What's going on?" she asked, handing them to Todd.

"Liza Minnelli and Mikhail Baryshnikov want them." He tugged on the skates but she didn't let go.

"They're gonna dance?"

Todd shrugged like he didn't know but his eyes said yes.

"I wanna see," she said.

"You know the rules."

The coat check girl could not leave her post, could not, for any reason, go into the club. If she had to go to the bathroom, she needed someone to cover for her.

"I won't go inside," she said, giving him one pair and clutching the other to her chest. "I'll just stand at the door. I promise!"

The coat check opened into the red velvet hallway, lit by chandeliers and lined with old church pews where the too drunk to stand had a place to sit. Or, in the case of two women in a dark spot between the chandeliers, make out and do cocaine off each other's bare shoulders.

Ginger couldn't imagine telling anyone from back home, especially her mother, that she worked here. She'd clutch her chest and die. Just die.

"Stand here and I'll see if I can do a little crowd control," he said. Todd was the closest thing she had to a friend in the city, but he was everyone's friend, so she wasn't special. He just made her feel that way.

He disappeared into the sweaty inner sanctum of the Orbit Room. The strobe lights froze everyone on the dance floor in place for seconds at a time and then set them free. Heads were thrown back, faces tilted to the ceiling. It smelled like burnt maple syrup from the fog machines and sex and reefer, and it just killed Ginger to have to stand in the doorway and never go in. She glanced behind her at the coat check and then stepped right up to the doorway, her silver boots on the edge of the hallway's red carpet right before it turned into the glitter-speckled black cement of the bar.

Over the dance floor spun a giant disco ball moon with a mechanical spaceship that "crashed" into it over and over again in a galactic dry hump.

The strobe lights stopped and the music paused. Todd shouted for people to make room. Get out of the way. There were grumbles and a woman yelled for the music to be put back on, and then ... an audible gasp. The sound of twenty-one hundred people at once realizing they were about to witness something incredible.

"Misha!" Liza shouted, her one-of-a-kind voice echoing in the silence. "It's been a while since I've done this."

"I have never done this," Mikhail shouted, and the funky bassline of Marvin Gaye's "Got to Give It Up" pulsed through the club.

Ginger stood on her tiptoes trying to see over the heads of people who'd crowded back to give the celebrities space on the dance floor.

"Sorry, sorry." Todd's silver space suit parted the crowd. "We just need a little space at the doorway. Fire laws and shit."

He came face-to-face with Ginger, winked, and backed out of the way so she had a minute of an unobstructed view of the best ballet dancer in the world and a New York City icon, holding hands and spinning through the Orbit Room. It was like a scene in a movie. The fog had settled toward the ground and the famous roller skaters carved through it, sending it curling up into the air. Liza's red dress and scarf billowed around her. Mikhail, strong and confident and so sexy it almost hurt, spun her and lifted her and danced around her like he was born on roller skates. He put his hands around her waist and Liza bent backward, arms over her head, eyes closed.

Full surrender.

Only here, Ginger thought and felt like the luckiest woman on Earth. Right now, at the edge of the dance floor, she was a million miles away from Allentown. From her mom. From the person she'd been. She was anyone. Could be anyone. Life had never felt more ... real.

People were screaming in joy and wonder and thrill. In disbelief at their own luck to be alive here. Now.

Ginger screamed with them.

The crowd closed back in around Liza and Mikhail and Ginger's moment was over.

"Excuse me!" someone shouted behind her. "Coat check girl?"

A man who looked familiar but whom she couldn't place stood at her coat check door with two young women. All of them covered in confetti and glitter. The chandelier lights reflecting in their shiny hair and blotto eyes. One of the women drank champagne right out of the bottle. The guy's white shirt was unbuttoned to his pants and the girl with the champagne bottle had lost her shirt altogether.

"Sorry," Ginger said, rushing back to her post.

"I lost my tag," the guy said with a shrug.

"That's okay." Everyone lost their tags. "What were your coats?"

"Fur, baby," he said, like that made him special.

Luckily, Ginger remembered him coming in and pulled out the white fur coat (not real) that he'd had on a few hours ago. Beneath it was the red car coat and a suede jacket with fringe the girls had been wearing.

"Thanks, doll," the man said with a slick grin that suddenly reminded her where she'd seen him. He was a news guy on Channel 4. He put a bill in her hand, and she waited until they were out of sight before she looked at it.

Twenty bucks. Not bad. She tucked it in the bodice of her silver space suit uniform.

Jasmine, one of the waitresses, came in a few minutes later. "I just got cut," she said, blowing her dark bangs off her forehead. "But I need to get off my feet for a second." Which was code all the bartenders and waitresses used to come and have a smoke in the coatroom. Jasmine collapsed in the big red-and-gold throne they used for private parties.

"Cut?" Ginger looked at the clock that was right above the emergency phone on the wall. It was past one. Honestly, the time here moved so fast. Ginger could have sworn her shift just started. "Hey, can you close for me?"

"Coat check?" Jasmine, a Dominican knockout from Queens, wrinkled her nose and lit a Parliament cigarette. If Ginger was being honest, Jasmine intimidated the shit out of her. She was New York City born and raised and she wasn't impressed or moved by anything.

"You'll get lots of tips," Ginger said. "It's been a good night."

"Why not? Beats going home with Carl. He's had too much to drink." Her boyfriend Carl often had too much to drink. Jasmine crossed her mile-long legs. "Why are you leaving before you get all your tips?" Jasmine asked.

"I'm interviewing for a new roommate tomorrow and she wanted to meet at nine."

"In the morning?" Jasmine gasped. "Honey, nothing gets me up at nine A.M."

"I don't mind," Ginger said. She ducked to the side of the open door so no one in the hallway could see her and took off the holster that carried two plastic squirt guns that looked like kids' ray guns. "I'm excited. I have a really good feeling about this girl."

Ginger took out the bobby pins that held the silver saucer with the bright red antenna onto her head and scratched at her scalp.

"A good feeling." Jasmine tilted her head back and blew an elaborate smoke ring. "Say no more."

"Listen, you interview as many losers as I have you start to get a sense." There'd been the woman who wanted to pay with pennies, the other girl whose boyfriend did all the talking—she knew where that was going to go. And, the worst, a girl who ate her own hair. Honestly, she did it right in front of Ginger. Just chewed it until it broke off and then swallowed it. Ginger would never recover.

Years of beauty pageants with quick changes and no dressing rooms inured Ginger to getting naked in front of other women and she shimmied out of the short silver halter dress uniform.

"God, Ginge, if Carl ever got a look at your tits he'd drop me like a hot potato."

Ginger pulled on her sweatshirt and jeans. Her tits were one of her better features, but Carl wouldn't be laying his eyes on them anytime soon. The guy gave her the creeps. She pulled on her old winter coat and tugged on her hat.

"Thanks for doing this for me," Ginger said.

"No problem. But, you're gonna take a cab, right?"

"No. I'll walk to the subway."

Jasmine looked at her like she was nuts. "Haven't you been reading about this .44 Caliber Killer? He just shot another woman like five days ago."

"Of course I heard of him. It's all anyone is talking about," she said. Was she nervous? Sure. But she didn't have money to waste on a cab. And Shane wasn't letting any of the bouncers walk with the girls heading to the subway.

"All those girls he shot?" Jasmine continued. "They're young." She held up one finger topped with a long red fingernail. "They're pretty."

"They've got brown hair," Ginger said, lifting her red hair to show Jasmine.

"Hate to break it to you, honey, but in the dark, that hair looks brown."

"But he hasn't shot anyone in Manhattan."

"There's first time for everything. Here . . ." Jasmine, who'd been working at the Orbit Room since it opened and started in the coat check, pulled a switchblade out of her boot. "You might need it."

"Are you kidding me?" Ginger asked. "You keep a knife in your boot?"

"It ain't always a roller-skating party in this place," she said. "Go on. Take it."

Ginger held up her hands, like Jasmine was pointing it at her. She wouldn't even know what to do with a knife; she'd probably cut off her own fingers. And what good would it be against a gun? "No thanks, I'm not a violent person."

"Suit yourself," Jasmine said, and tucked the knife back in her boot.

CHAPTER 5

April 1977
New York City

Ginger

Ginger forgot to set her alarm. So, when she woke up late with just a few minutes before the potential roommate arrived, she had only herself to blame.

Ginger threw the dirty dishes in the sink (that she should have washed last night) back in the cupboards.

Only one thing in this whole wide world mattered to Ginger Daughtry.

Making it in New York City. Broadway or bust, baby. At this point she'd take off Broadway. Off off Broadway. Hell, she'd take a showcase at Fazil's, her dance studio.

For any of that to happen she needed to stay in New York City, and for *that* to happen she needed a roommate, like, yesterday.

She grabbed her dirty leg warmers and leotards from the living room floor and shoved them under her bed.

This was the dream she'd been dreaming since she was a little girl in a leaky double-wide outside of Allentown.

There'd been setbacks, sure. Bonnie getting knocked up with John's baby and going back to Pittsburgh to chain-smoke at her kitchen table was obviously not ideal.

But New York City was full of women just like Ginger. Nice women who'd left behind something shitty to try for something amazing. Women who were chasing a dream and wanted to live a little.

She just needed to find one who could pay half the rent.

But coming to New York City *with* a roommate was dramatically different from being in New York City and *finding* a roommate.

She'd tried Todd at work, but he lived with his sugar daddy up on the East Side. She'd even worked up the courage to ask Jasmine before she'd found out Jasmine lived with her boyfriend.

Ginger put a notice on the bulletin board at Fazil's, but that had brought in the girl who ate her own hair and another one who wouldn't know how to have fun if it bit her on the butt.

Things weren't dire . . . yet. Bonnie had felt so bad about leaving that she'd paid her share of the rent for two months. And Ginger had been so mad about her best friend leaving she took the money and spent most of it on private dance lessons at Fazil's.

Ginger opened the cupboard under the sink and the smell of the trash was eye-watering. She took the whole shebang into the living room. Lifting the window onto the fire escape took every bit of her strength, but she got that sucker open and the full surround sound of New York City filled the apartment. Cars honked on Sixth Avenue; next door a woman shouted out her window that her man better not come home smelling like beer again. White delivery trucks rattled down West Washington Place. Kids screamed in the park. A group of teenagers whistled at every woman walking by. A car sat at the corner of MacDougal and Fourth playing Tito Puente at top volume.

The sound of the city was like stepping into a hot bath. It was almost too much, but after you gave it a second it was just enough.

Where she grew up, the only sounds were the shift whistles and the screaming of starlings.

Ginger put the garbage on the old wrought-iron steps of the fire escape where she sometimes sat to have a cigarette, contemplating the state of things.

The window shut so easily it felt like she must be opening it wrong. Even the windows were hard here.

The buzzer rang.

Well, shit.

Ginger grabbed the Jean Naté from her room and spritzed it through the apartment, hoping to cover up the smell of garbage.

She had a good feeling about this appointment. Rachel Horowitz was employed. Didn't have a boyfriend. She was the right age. And on the phone she sounded funny and smart and totally normal.

She gave all the right vibes.

Ginger lived in a fifth-floor walk-up in the Village over a pet shop called Animal Menagerie. It was cheap, and most of her neighbors were okay. With one astounding exception.

The third-floor apartment was already open when she came racing down the steps. Mrs. Reznick, in her beige housecoat and with her foul cigar and her illegal cat sitting at her feet, gave Ginger the evil eye as she flew past.

"You know, we can all hear that buzzer," the old lady said around her big brown stogie.

"You know, we can all smell that cigar," Ginger shot back. At the security door she looked out the peephole, a step she never forgot after opening the door to a man peddling fake Jehovah's Witness pamphlets, who'd tried to muscle his way inside. But there was a woman on the other side. A totally normal-looking woman. Ginger took a deep breath, rearranged her boobs in the leotard so the girls looked their best, and flung open the door.

Only to find two women standing there, as the cold, damp wind blew trash across MacDougal Street.

One had a wide smile and dark hair set in waves away from her face. She wore a thick jacket, a long burgundy corduroy skirt, and a pair of very nice brown boots with a good heel.

She could use some lipstick. And a little work on those eyebrows.

But everything about her said respectable. Friendly. *I'll pay my half of the electric and I won't watch you while you sleep.*

The other had bottle-blond hair cut in a short shag and black eyeliner an inch thick around her blue eyes. She wore red leather pants, beat-up Keds, and a bright yellow satin jacket that wouldn't keep out the wind even though it was zipped up to her chin. Blondie licked her fingers and pinched the end of her cigarette before putting it back in her pack.

She gave Ginger a floor-to-ceiling perusal and then smiled, revealing a gap between her two front teeth.

"*Bonjour,*" she said with a husky voice. She looked cagey and feral. Like something was after her, but she was after something too.

Ginger got the all-over shivers.

"Rachel?" Ginger asked, and the brunette Farrah Fawcett with the unibrow raised her hand.

"Hi. Rachel Horowitz. I have an appointment with you for nine o'clock," she said, reaching out her hand like a banker.

"I'm Faye Bouchard," said the other woman with an accent Ginger could not place. Faye didn't reach out her hand but tucked her thumbs in the tiny pockets of her leather pants. Ginger did not miss the chipped manicure. The fingernails bitten right down to the quick.

"Faye!" she cried. "I thought our appointment was noon."

From her back pocket Faye pulled the folded-up want ad section from the *Village Voice,* revealing Ginger's ad circled in red pen:

Female roommate wanted. Okay with strange hours and noise. A people person. Sunny pvt room. Fifth-floor walk-up. Safe.

"Nine A.M." was scrawled beside it.

There were four similar circles around different ads with different times . . . all of them crossed out.

"I've double-booked you," Ginger groaned. She'd been trying to be more organized, but it just never seemed to happen. She was always running late and forgetting appointments. Showing up at the wrong place at the wrong time.

But this little mistake could work out just fine. If she played her cards right, she might be able to get to that tap class at Fazil's at noon.

"It's all right," Rachel said, giving Faye a sorority girl smile. Ginger knew a bunch of girls like Rachel from the pageant circuit. People pleasers. Wouldn't say shit with a mouth full of it.

Faye shrugged, copacetic.

French? Ginger thought, trying not to be swayed by her indifferent shabby glamour. But Ginger was a straight-up sucker for glamour, shabby or otherwise.

Behind them MacDougal where it turned briefly into Washington Square West before turning back into MacDougal was full of taxis and delivery trucks heading south. The hot dog truck on the corner made the air smell like meat. It was a better smell than the stale cigar and cigarette stench of the stairwell.

"Come in. Get yourselves out of the damp." Ginger finally remembered her manners. "Since you're both here, we can kill two birds with one stone, I suppose." She climbed halfway up the first flight of steps, which was the only way they could all get into the tiny foyer. "Lock the door behind you," she said, and Faye slid the deadbolt home.

The walls of the stairwell were sticky and dark with years of smoke, and Ginger made a point of not touching them. Faye and Rachel did the same, which said they weren't dummies. Point for each of them.

"Mostly everyone in the building is cool," she said. "Except Mrs. Reznick."

"I can hear you." Mrs. Reznick's thick New York accent wafted down from the third floor, followed by the hard slam of a door.

Ginger turned and winked at the girls behind her.

"Georgio on the first floor is a little handsy, but mostly harmless." She pointed at his door as they passed it.

Faye made a sound in her throat. Part scoff. Part world-weary acceptance. It could mean anything, but in this situation obviously meant *Of course, and aren't they all.*

"This neighborhood is safe?" Rachel asked as they kept climbing steps.

How safe was any neighborhood? Especially with this .44 Caliber Killer on the loose.

"Try not to be alone at night, but if you can't help it stay away from the park. If you are really freaked out, Hongs at the corner is cool. He'll let you hang out until whatever asshole is following you moves on. Miguel, who works in the kitchen, will walk you home if it's not too busy. And the egg rolls are good."

Fourth floor was a single mom with a teenage son who kept getting in trouble. "He has pretty good weed if you're ever looking," Ginger said over her shoulder.

Ginger opened the beat-up green door to her apartment with a flourish. As if she were on *The Price Is Right* revealing the living room with warm wood floors and lots of windows. She had a couch and two beanbag chairs. A spider plant in the corner. There were actual paintings on the wall. Real ones. Not posters.

Ginger and Bonnie had bought them at a second-hand shop on Essex before Bonnie went and got knocked up when she went home for Christmas.

"Wow," Rachel said, pushing her glasses up with the back of her hand. "What a beautiful apartment."

"I know. It was a real find," Ginger said, proud of the home she'd made. "You just have to be willing to live over a pet store with live crickets that have a way of ending up in your bed."

"Is that . . ." Rachel looked at Faye and then back at Ginger. "That's not a joke?"

Ginger laughed but didn't answer the question.

"Does the fireplace work?" Rachel asked. She was walking through the room, taking it all in. Faye stood at the door, her eyes out the window at the view of the water cistern on the roof of the building next door.

She acted like she didn't care, and Ginger *loved* it.

Give her something to win over and she'd put her back into it.

"Nope," Ginger said. She pointed to the pretty arched doorway that led to the kitchen. "Kitchen is over here. I'm not much of a cook, sadly."

"Me neither," Rachel said, looking into the kitchen. "I burn toast."

"I cook," Faye said. Her smile a tiny slice of delicious secrets. *Oh, that smile said, you won't believe what I can cook.*

"Uh oh," Rachel laughed. "I'm losing already." Rachel was friendly and had a good sense of humor. Two great traits for a roommate. But her smile held zero secrets. Her smile said, *I've been a good girl my whole life.*

"Here's the room." Ginger opened a door behind the couch and flipped on the light, revealing a naked single mattress, a night table with lamp, and a bookshelf. "Bonnie left some of her stuff."

The floor creaked with every step and the view was of a plastic bag in the Hanging Elm in the park across the street. There was a pigeon on the windowsill. That pigeon was always on the windowsill. Bonnie fed the stupid thing.

"Rent is fifty dollars?" Rachel asked.

"Yep." Ginger had padded the number. There was no way she was getting caught out like her mom. Doing home perms in a leaky trailer outside Allentown because she didn't have the sense God gave a turtle. Ginger always had an escape plan.

Faye tapped the glass with her knuckle and the pigeon tapped back. She smiled.

Ginger wanted to ask her what she was thinking.

"My room is on the other side of the kitchen." Ginger led them through the galley-style kitchen to a short hallway. "Bathroom," she said, and opened one of the three doors to reveal a white-tiled room with a clawfoot tub and a shower attachment. There was a sink and a mirror and an old metal mail cart stuffed with hairspray and makeup.

"There's a closet here." Ginger opened another door to a small windowless room. There were racks on the walls but nothing hanging from them. She pulled the long string attached to a bare bulb on the ceiling and the light was so bright they all flinched away.

"That's a giant closet," Rachel said.

"I know. Bonnie and I didn't have enough clothes to fill it. She was going to get a bike and store it there, but she never got around to it."

Stupid mouth-breathing John.

Faye stepped into the room and spread her arms out. Her fingers barely touched the sides. The bottom of her jacket lifted, pulling her shirt up too. Revealing what Ginger could only call a humdinger of a bruise on her hip.

Rachel pulled in a quick breath.

Faye lowered her arms and pulled the string. The room went black.

Maybe I imagined it? Or it was a trick of the light?

Even as Ginger thought that, she knew it wasn't true.

That bruise was real. And it was bad.

"And here's my room," Ginger said, opening the third door to reveal her bed covered in scarves. Her lamp draped in scarves. Scarves over the window.

It was all very French prostitute. A look she was proud of.

"It's a fantastic apartment," Rachel said. Faye nodded, her eyes taking in every part of the room. Ginger felt like Faye could see the dirty clothes under the bed and every lie she'd ever told.

"I don't have any food, but I do have some tea, if you're interested," Ginger said, playing the part of the hostess. A role she'd learned from Miss Pennsylvania 1976, who'd invited her court to her house in Fox Chapel and served them homemade lemonade and sandwiches with the crusts cut off. She certainly didn't learn it from her own mother. Mom couldn't have been a gracious hostess if someone taught her step-by-step.

"I'm fine," Rachel said.

"Yes, please," Faye said.

Lord. I was just being polite. I hope I have tea.

Ginger filled the kettle and set it on the only burner that worked on the tiny mustard-yellow stove.

"Where are you working?" she asked, and sat down on the floor between the coffee table and the dead fireplace.

"I have a job as an assistant for Vanessa Purdy," Rachel said, sitting on the couch.

Rachel unzipped her coat, revealing one of those thick Scandinavian sweaters. With the wooden toggles at the throat. Those suckers were expensive.

Faye kept her coat zipped.

"You're kidding," Ginger said, impressed and intimidated. According to her boss Shane, women like Vanessa Purdy were what was wrong with this country. Ginger didn't agree, but the woman sure did get in a heap of trouble.

"Who is Vanessa Purdy?" Faye asked. Yeah. That accent was definitely French.

"She's a feminist writer and activist. She was on the cover of *Time* magazine two months ago?" Rachel said.

"Never heard of her." Faye shrugged with complete and total dismissal. Rachel looked insulted.

Ginger practiced the shrug in her mind. When Shane said, "Ginger, I need you to pick up another shift on Wednesday," she would give him that shrug.

"How long have you been in New York?" Rachel asked, crossing her legs like she was conducting an interview.

"Just a few months. I moved here with my best friend to be a dancer, but she had to move back to Pittsburgh," Ginger said.

"That's where you're from?"

Ginger nodded, just removing that trailer and the woman who lived there from her life like they didn't exist. What a gift, she thought, being able to re-create herself without the ugly parts. She was a new woman in New York City. She was anyone she wanted to be.

"Where do you work?" Faye asked.

"I'm taking classes like crazy right now. But I work at a nightclub as a coat check girl."

"What nightclub?" Faye asked in her blunt way.

"The Orbit Room."

"Shut up!" Rachel cried, smacking her hands on the coffee table.

"I've only been there a few months."

"How'd you get that job?" Rachel asked.

"I met someone at dance class who worked there and I . . . just . . . I interviewed," Ginger said. She flinched from the memory of that interview.

"You're so lucky," Rachel said.

"Don't I know it," Ginger said, because working at the Orbit Room *was* lucky. Last night had been lucky. Every excellent Saturday night when she counted her tips, she felt lucky.

So, she put that interview away someplace in her brain and concentrated on the luck.

"I've heard of the Orbit Room," Faye said, like her knowledge gave it a seal of approval.

"Tell me everything," Rachel said. "Does Mick Jagger actually show up every night?"

"Not every night," Ginger said. "But famous people are there every night."

"Who is the most famous person you've met?" Faye asked.

"Elton John."

Faye's eyes went wide and even she couldn't pretend she wasn't impressed. "What's he like?"

"Very short."

"You met Elton John and that's all you have to say?" Rachel asked.

"Well, we didn't actually meet. I took his coat though."

"What did he have in his pockets?" Faye asked.

"Faye!" Rachel cried. Such a good girl, honestly.

"Kleenex," she said. "And an inhaler."

Faye hooted and looked at Rachel like she'd won a bet.

"I didn't know he had asthma," Rachel said.

"You'll have to come see the club for yourself," Ginger said, like there wasn't a line a hundred people long every night, but she was made bold by their attention.

Rachel laughed, delighted, and Faye smiled, revealing that gap between her teeth.

The kettle whistled and Ginger got to her feet to make the tea and the girls followed her into the kitchen, which pleased her, endlessly.

Ginger pulled down mugs and opened up a box of orange pekoe, relieved to see a few bags left. Faye leaned in the doorway and Rachel propped herself up against the counter.

"Where are you from?" Ginger asked Faye, tossing tea bags in mugs. "Your accent is so different."

"Here and there," she said with a shrug. "Quebec for a while. London. Paris. Austria, originally."

"Austria?" Ginger had never met anyone from Austria. She wasn't sure she could point the country out on a map. It was suddenly the most exotic place she'd ever heard of.

"But you speak French? Not German?" Rachel asked.

Faye blinked as if astonished by the question.

"I speak both," Faye said, which Rachel seemed to accept.

Ginger pulled the milk out of the fridge and subtly sniffed it. It was fine. Thank God. "What brings you to New York City?"

"I just arrived here. I am actually . . ." She licked her dry, cracked lips. That woman needed some Vaseline. Quick. "Looking for my sister."

The hum of the old fridge was loud in the suddenly quiet room.

"What happened to her?" Rachel asked.

"She . . . ran away," Faye said.

"And you think she's here?" Ginger asked.

Faye nodded. "I know she is."

"Do you have a picture?" Rachel asked, and from the pocket of her jacket Faye pulled a worn and faded picture. A girl with dark hair, a hand shielding her eyes from the sun. Behind her were cows? Sheep? It was hard to say. But she looked young and pretty and a cold chill went through Ginger's body.

This city could be hard on young and pretty women.

From her other pocket Faye pulled a postcard. It said *New York City* across the front in big yellow letters over a picture of the Statue of Liberty. On the other side it said:

I'm safe. Come find me. xoxo

"Your sister wrote that?" Rachel asked, and Faye nodded.

"You'll find her," Ginger said, pressing her hand to Faye's arm. Ginger was a toucher and Faye went still at the contact. Ginger figured she'd done the wrong thing and was about to pull her hand back when Faye clapped her hand over Ginger's, holding the contact. Her palm was cold and clammy at the same time. Like a dog's nose when they're happy.

"We can make flyers," Rachel said. "Post them at the Port Authority and Grand Central Station. You can put ads in the personals section of all the papers. We can help."

Ginger nodded, though she wouldn't have volunteered any of that.

Faye blinked her big blue eyes at them as if she didn't know what to do with all this. Ginger stroked her shoulder again; she understood. She'd been used to taking care of herself on her own for a long time. It could be hard to accept help. To trust it.

"*Merci*," Faye said, her voice thick. She couldn't make eye contact anymore, like it was all too much. She looked down at the floor and fumbled in her pocket. "Can I smoke?"

"Sure," Ginger said. She wouldn't say no to Faye about *anything*.

Faye pulled the cigarettes from her back pocket. She offered them up. Ginger said no, but Rachel took one.

"These are Canadian?" Rachel said, looking at the pack.

"*Oui*. I took the train from Montreal."

"The train from Montreal," Rachel repeated like it was the most glamorous thing she'd ever heard of. She leaned in to have her cigarette lit by Faye.

"Your family must be wigging out," Rachel asked.

Faye shook her head, her eyes shuttered. "No," she said. "She left and so to them, she is dead."

Ginger handed out the mugs loaded with milk and sugar. Faye walked into the living room and, behind her, Rachel put her hand on Ginger's arm.

Give her the room, Rachel mouthed.

It was so kind. Kindness had been scarce in Ginger's life and it had never been a trait she looked for in friends. Biting humor that leaned mean and the same shoe size were what she had with Bonnie.

She found herself unexpectedly moved. Softened. Unsure of what to do.

They sat back down in the living room. Returning to the spots they'd just vacated. Spots that felt familiar, somehow. Like their names were written on the floorboards beneath their feet.

Faye took long sips of the tea and sighed like it was just what she needed.

"Do you have a job?" Rachel asked her.

"No," Faye said, as if resigned to her fate. "But I have money."

"I can get you a job," Ginger said, setting aside her tea. She really didn't like tea. It was an old box of Bonnie's.

"You can?" Faye asked. Her blue eyes were wide and not so distant anymore.

If there was one thing Ginger loved more than dancing, it was coming to the rescue. Scoring beer in high school. Getting that pervert janitor in trouble for groping her and her friends in the fifth grade. And this wasn't even a hard rescue. Helping Susan Humphries get that abortion when they were sixteen? That had been hard. This was a total cakewalk.

"With your look and accent?" Ginger shook her head, like it was a done deal. "You'll be catnip at the Orbit Room."

"If you . . ." Faye looked warily at Rachel and then back at Ginger, like she wasn't in the habit of saying thank-you. Of being grateful. It was an emotion she clearly distrusted. "If you are serious, I would appreciate your help."

"My boss will love you." Too much, maybe. But that was a different problem.

"From where are you?" Faye asked Rachel, who took a second to put the words in the right order.

"Jersey. Just over the river." She nodded her head in the direction of the Hudson.

"What are you doing looking for an apartment? You could stay home and commute," Ginger said, wishing she'd taken that cigarette. The tea made her hungry.

"Staying home was not an option," Rachel said, all that good-girl friendliness closed up tight. That was interesting. Ginger liked a secret.

"Did you get kicked out?" Faye asked.

"Oh my lord, Faye!" Ginger breathed, scandalized and delighted by her nerve.

Rachel took her tea bag out, but there wasn't any place to put it. "Yeah, actually," she said with a laugh. "I did."

Ginger slid the ashtray across the table for Rachel, who smiled gratefully and put the tea bag in it.

"Are they mad at you," Faye said to Rachel, "for working with that woman?"

"My mother is," Rachel said, shaking her hair out of her face. Her bangs were drooping. "Dad I don't think cares."

"She's scared you'll go lesbian?" Ginger asked.

"The horror," Faye said with the long-suffering sigh of a woman who wished she was attracted to women instead of the men who just disappointed her in the end.

Ginger thought of that bruise on Faye's hip.

"Trust me," Rachel said, conspiratorially. "I gave it my best try at Vassar."

Well, well, well, look at Rachel getting more interesting.

"What about you, Ginger?" Rachel asked. Ginger should have seen this coming. If they were all talking about their families, it was only natural that Ginger would do the same. It was just never easy.

"My mom," she started and then stopped. "Is complicated."

"You don't have to talk about it," Rachel said. Ginger looked at Faye, who'd been so honest to two strangers, and found herself cracked open by Faye's trust and Rachel's kindness.

"She told me if I left not to come back unless I had made something of myself."

"That's why you want to be a dancer?" Rachel asked.

"No," Ginger said, emphatically. "I want to be a dancer because that's all I've ever wanted. My mother would not be happy no matter what I do. Leave. Stay. It doesn't matter, she'll be disappointed either way."

"Oh," Rachel sighed. "Why are mothers so hard?"

Faye's laugh sounded like a dog barking. She clapped her hand over her mouth and Rachel and Ginger laughed at her without any malice. Like friends do.

"Get married. Have kids." Faye twirled her finger in the air. "That is what my mother wants for me and she does not care what I want."

"My mom's terrified I'm going to get raped and killed and cut up in a suitcase and left in a park," Rachel said. "She gave me my father's switchblade."

"This .44 Caliber Killer thing is not helping," Ginger said.

"They are scared," Faye said, quietly. "That we will do this hard thing and take this risk and that in the end we won't fail and we will accomplish what they could not."

"What's that?"

She exhaled a plume of smoke. "Freedom. Happiness. On our terms."

Goosebumps rippled up and down Ginger's arms.

"Well said." Rachel tapped the edge of her mug to Faye's.

Rachel sighed like she was setting down a heavy bag at long last and Faye lit another cigarette and blew smoke rings toward the spider plant. They both stretched out their legs and their knees touched and they didn't jump away like strangers. For a second it seemed as if they had all done this before. Like they did it all the time.

It was decided.

Ginger couldn't send one of them back into the drizzly day to look at another apartment. Rachel had gotten kicked out of her mom's house and Faye had that bruise. A sister to find.

Someone had to look after these two.

"I have an idea," Ginger said.

"The closet?" Rachel asked.

"You read my mind!" Ginger said.

"Hardly, it's a giant closet. A single bed can fit in there no problem. Maybe even a little dresser." Ginger and Rachel turned to look at Faye, who was watching them with all that hope and allure. "You can pay rent once you get a job, but until then, maybe do some cooking?"

Faye set down her tea mug with trembling hands before she clutched them in her lap. Tears filled her big eyes. Faye blinked and nodded. Blinked and nodded. Like those tears refused to stay where they were put.

"Hey!" Rachel said, throwing her arms around Faye, who could not hide her flinch. "It's all right."

Ginger leaned over the coffee table to clutch those trembling hands. "Don't cry. This is going to be extraordinary."

CHAPTER 6

April 1977
New York City

Ginger

Faye moved in with a duffel bag she'd had in a storage locker at Penn Station. She bought a crappy mattress and she and Ginger carried it over their heads for three blocks down Sixth, dodging overfull trash cans and men with bright ideas about what they could do with that mattress.

Faye put the mattress on the floor of that closet, shut the door, and they didn't see her for days. There were signs she came out, water glasses left in the sink. An ashtray full of Canadian cigarette butts. Newspapers folded open to the personals section.

Faye and Rachel whispered their fears for her in the kitchen as they waited for the coffee to percolate.

Her sister. That bruise.

Rachel's brother Simon and a friend helped her move in. Simon seemed nice enough, tall and thin with dark curly hair and excellent teeth. The friend was a real loser, though. He wore a velour tracksuit over a grease-stained undershirt. He called Ginger "miss" but his eyes never got past her chest.

"If you need anything," Simon said to Rachel, lingering at the door. Ginger tried to seem very busy in the kitchen, but she was shamelessly eavesdropping.

"I won't," Rachel said, hard as moonshine.

There was such a long moment of silence, Ginger couldn't resist and ducked her head out, thinking he'd shut the door and was gone, but they just stood there, staring at each other. Rachel looked about as sad as an angry woman could look.

"You're just being stubborn," he said.

"You don't know anything about it."

"I know you're breaking Mom's heart."

"Well, she broke mine."

"Rach—"

"Good-bye, Simon."

Days after shutting the closet door, Faye came out of her room while Ginger was home, looking so thin in the sunlight Ginger could nearly see right through her. She left the apartment without a word and came back with a pack of cigarettes, a newspaper, a jug of Chianti, a raw chicken, and a bag of potatoes.

"He is calling himself Son of Sam," she said, throwing the newspaper onto the coffee table.

"Who?" Ginger asked. She was painting Rachel's toes a bubblegum pink. Rachel leaned over to grab the paper and Ginger accidentally swiped pink polish all over her foot.

"The .44 Caliber Killer left a letter to the cops at his last crime scene. He's calling himself Son of Sam," Rachel said.

"Who is Sam?" Ginger asked, and Rachel laughed. "What's so funny?"

"You," Rachel said.

Faye came back into the living room, a cigarette hanging out of her mouth. "When will you be home?" she asked.

"My class is done at three," Ginger said. "But I have to leave for work at six."

"I'm home all day," Rachel said.

"Dinner at five," Faye said, turning back for the kitchen.

"Faye," Rachel said. She looked at Ginger and then back at Faye, rigid in the doorway. "Your sister?"

"No luck," Faye said over her shoulder and began rinsing the chicken in the sink.

At five, they gathered, Ginger and Rachel watching Faye carefully, gauging her mood. It was obvious Faye did not want to dwell on not finding her sister or Son of Sam, and Ginger was good at distraction.

So was the Chianti.

Rachel, half-blotto, was flushed and had unbuttoned her shirt a few buttons. She had fabulous tits under all those high collars.

"You're very beautiful, you," Faye said to her.

"Beautiful is a stretch," Rachel said with the humor she'd probably been taught to deflect compliments.

"You're also smart, and we are told we must choose." Faye stretched out her legs, bracing her ankles on Rachel's knee, and took a deep drag of her smoke with her eyes closed.

Rachel flinched in reaction to Faye's words, as if they'd slid like a switchblade between her ribs. Ginger half expected Rachel to stand up, she looked so uncomfortable. But then she leaned back on the couch, stretched her own legs onto the coffee table.

"Thank you, Faye. You're a good cook, did you know that?" The chicken and mashed potatoes had been the best thing Ginger had eaten maybe ever.

"I do," Faye said, as if it were boring.

"Who taught you?"

"Everyone. My mother. Her mother. Another mother at the church who taught me bread."

"What religion are you?" Rachel asked.

Faye shook her head. "No religion."

Ginger and Rachel looked at each other—*She did say church, right?*

In the background Linda Ronstadt crooned "you're no good" over and over.

"You ready for that job at the Orbit Room?" Ginger asked Faye, pulling them out of the awkward silence. As the weather turned to spring, things got busier at the club and girls were being hired and fired left and right. Faye rolled her head to look her way. Her roots were starting to show; they'd have to fix that soon. Faye wore jeans and a man's flannel shirt that was too big and made her seem very small.

It was surprising how young she looked. Ginger wanted to ask her real age, but something told her she wouldn't get a straight answer.

"Yes," Faye said. "I am ready for that job."

Rachel asked about Faye's sister and Ginger wanted to clap a hand over her mouth. God, that girl could ruin a mood. But Faye talked about going to the hospitals and shelters in Manhattan and showing people the picture of her sister.

"What about the police?" Ginger asked. Wasn't that where you were supposed to go when you needed help? The cops in Allentown had been good guys. Officer Shemansky in particular. He brought her mom home from the bar when she got disorderly instead of taking her to the station. He and his wife took Ginger out for breakfast when she graduated from high school.

"The world is a big place, honey. Get out of your mom's trailer and go and see some of it," he told her, and his wife handed her a card with twenty bucks in it.

"No cops," Faye said.

"But—"

"No cops," Faye repeated, stone-cold serious.

The needle hit the end of the first side of the record and they all jumped at the sudden thump. Ginger rushed to flip it.

"How is your job, Rachel?" Faye asked into the silence.

"Good!" Rachel said.

"What do you do for her?" Faye asked. "This Vanessa Purdy?"

"Whatever she needs. We're trying to raise money to rent a legitimate office space; until then I find free places where we can meet."

"And this is . . . fun?" Faye asked.

"It's not fun," Rachel laughed. "But it's important. It's good work. I'm hoping to get promoted so I can write her speeches and op-eds."

"Who does it now?"

"A man."

There was a moment of silence before they all cracked up.

Rachel tipped back her head and laughed. Faye laughed with her hand over her mouth like it was a secret she had to keep.

The Orbit Room without the celebrities and lights, the music and the cocaine, seemed smaller. An empty black box that smelled of industrial cleaners, cigarette smoke, and vaguely of copper from a hundred years of killing pigs in the basement. Shane didn't turn on the air conditioning until six P.M. and so in the afternoon it was getting sticky as temperatures outside were climbing.

But even without the lights and the music, it held a kind of magic. Expectation and possibility lingered in the dark corners, waiting for Grace Jones to walk in the door.

When the lights weren't on and Shane wasn't around, the staff acted like the teenagers they'd been just a few years ago. Chasing one another with underwear they found shoved in the cushions of the banquettes.

Ginger and Jasmine were cutting garnishes behind the bar. Her nail beds stung from all the lemons and limes, but Ginger was trying to make her way out of the coatroom to the bar, where the tips were better and she could be a part of the action. Last week they threw a private party for Bianca Jagger and Halston tipped Jasmine a bag of coke and a thousand dollars.

Todd, wearing the skates that had been on Mikhail Baryshnikov's feet the other night, did long, slow turns around the dance floor, backward and forward, every movement liquid.

"Are there professional roller skaters?" Jasmine asked, watching him. "Because you are that good."

"I am, aren't I?" Todd said. "I was the Dancing Queen of the Triple R Roller Rink in Rockford, Illinois."

Todd stuck one leg out in front of him and crouched down on the other one. All the staff in the bar cheered and wiped the sweat off their foreheads.

"What the hell is all this?" Shane yelled, standing in the doorway. "Roller skates?"

Todd stopped on a dime and everyone else got very busy.

Shane was unpleasant at the best of times and she didn't like talking to him if she didn't have to, but she'd been a big shot and promised Faye she'd get her a job.

"Shane!" Ginger cried as he walked past the dark bar.

"Yeah," Shane said, without even slowing down. He wore a silk shirt unbuttoned to his waist and a leather vest. His hair was long and shaggy and Jasmine said he looked like Andy Gibb. But that was what a woman said to make herself feel better about something she regretted.

Shane was the kind of guy lots of women regretted.

"Shane, wait." Ginger jogged out from behind the bar and caught him in the middle of the dark dance floor under the disco ball moon and the motionless spaceship.

"Hey doll, why aren't you in uniform?" he asked, his eyes walking all over her bell-bottoms and leather vest with fringe that hung down to her knees.

It was an hour before the place opened and the uniform was about as comfortable as a burlap bag. "I'm about to change," Ginger said with a smile. Always smiling the way Shane liked. The pageants had trained her well for this job. Smile, chin up, back straight—no matter what. "But I wanted to talk to you about my roommate. She's looking for a job."

"Yeah? She hot?"

"Yeah."

"Hot like you or hot like Jasmine?"

Ginger took a deep breath. She knew exactly what he meant, the pig. "She's white . . . Petite. Short blond hair. Big blue eyes. She's got a real Debbie Harry vibe."

He pulled a face. "That could be cool. What's her story?"

"This is what you'll love," Ginger said. "She's French. Or Austrian, I'm not sure. But she has an accent."

"No shit," he said, and Ginger knew she had him. Better, Faye had a job. "Yeah. Have her come in for an interview."

Whatever reaction she had to that word—*interview*—she buried it someplace deep where it didn't matter. Ginger had survived. Jasmine too. Every girl here, probably. Or maybe not. None of the other girls talked about it, so maybe it was just her that got interviewed that way.

Faye would be fine.

"You got a problem?" Shane asked, like he knew what she was thinking.

"Not at all," she said.

And smiled.

Lady X exploded into existence in the spring and summer of 1977 during the NYPD's disastrous staffing shortages. Lady X would have been a much bigger story if it weren't for Son of Sam capturing the world's attention with his killing spree that same summer. Starting with vandalism and ending with violence—she accused five different men of rape. Tabloid journalists and angry men accused her of violent crimes across the city—including murder—and publicly demanded the police find and stop her.

One of her victims, a professional baseball player, even offered a reward to anyone who found Lady X dead or alive. Many believe the unidentified body of a woman found near Washington Square Park after the July NYC blackout was in fact Lady X, which was why she was never heard from again.

—JENNY MIDDAUGH, *If One Burns We All Burn: Early Feminist Warriors Who Led the Way,* Margot's women's studies textbook

There are two possible outcomes for Lady X. She was killed the night of the blackout and that's why we never heard from her again. Or she finally killed a man and had to go into hiding. I know which one I'm hoping for.

—SHAWNA OSGOODE, teacher, Julia's Ethics in Tabloid Spaces class

CHAPTER 7

March 2024
Pittsburgh, Pennsylvania

Margot

Margot couldn't move. Could barely breathe. Tears leaked out of her eyes and ran unchecked into the hair at her temples. She stared up at the blocks of moonlight expanding across the ceiling in her parents' bedroom and wished she could hold on to the anger instead of the sorrow. Wished she was thinking *Fuck him* instead of *I miss him.* But she was flattened by missing him. Aching with it. With what felt like the last of her strength, she pulled the blanket up over her head.

Hiding from everyone, she gave in to the worst of her misery.

Why did he do this to me? To us?

Was it her body? Her attention on the kids instead of him?

She knew what her sister would say, but her sister wasn't under these covers. Her sister wasn't crushed by self-pity and grief.

Why wasn't I enough?

It was embarrassing to even be thinking this way. But she didn't know how to stop it. Cheating on her was about him, she got that. Intellectually. But right now it was impossible to distance herself from the betrayal.

It was impossible not to be very, very sad.

She'd thought, stupidly, that they were still *them*, despite the fame and the money. That at their core they were the kids who lived in that shitty one-bedroom off La Brea, having dinner parties with their other broke artist friends. He'd make a table out of cinder blocks and plywood and she'd make soup because it was cheap. They'd talk about books and music and about getting a dog.

They'd go to bars and have sex in the bathrooms, laughing and running out the door when they got caught.

She slept every night wrapped in his arms, dreaming of him because she could never get enough.

That was *them*. She'd been sure of it. Getting rich and famous, how could that change *them*?

When the moonlight turned to dawn she would get out of this bed and she would focus on her daughter. And hopefully seeing her mother. She would make sure all her kids had what they needed to process this outrageous turn of events. She would be *okay*. Not great. Not fine. But okay.

She would do that. Tomorrow.

More alone than she'd ever been in her life, she closed her burning, swollen eyes and wept.

Margot was a world-class hoverer.

While her own mother had been hands-off in the way of moms in the eighties, Margot had made an art form out of lingering outside her children's bedroom doors trying to anticipate their moods, feelings, and future plans for heartbreak and/or trouble.

But it was failing her now.

"What are you doing?" Julia asked, and Margot jumped away from the closed door of her childhood bedroom. Where her daughter was ... well, she didn't know what her daughter was doing in there. That was the whole problem.

"What are *you* doing?" Margot shot back.

Julia wore a Metallica T-shirt, her hair in a pile on her head. She had streaks of black marker by her ears like she'd been tucking a Sharpie there without the cap. She looked like a madwoman.

She also looked like she knew exactly what Margot had been doing last night, the self-pity she'd been wallowing in. The puffy eyes, despite all her efforts this morning to hide them, were a dead giveaway.

Julia would not approve of her crying all night over Jack, but Margot gave her a level stare that absolutely dared her to say something, anything, about it this morning.

"I was going to talk to Skye," Julia finally said, gesturing toward the sparkle-less unicorn sticker.

"About what?"

"What do you think?" Julia said, and Margot groaned. "Look, I know you're freaking out about everything. But there's nothing you can do, is there? Right now?"

Margot shook her head.

"So, this Lady X stuff is exciting and fun, and that our mom was clearly involved makes it an absolute scoop," Julia said. Margot was reminded that her sister was a world-class investigative journalist who'd broken stories of corruption in state government and had won awards for her coverage of the #MeToo movement. "And I imagine it would be a great distraction to a teenager whose father has been flashing his dick all over the place."

"I can hear you!" Skye shouted.

Margot grabbed her sister's arm before she could open the door. Her sister wasn't wrong.

"Just . . . go easy," Margot whispered, scared of one of Julia's obsessions on top of everything else they were going through.

"Easy is my middle name," Julia whispered back, and opened the door.

Margot's childhood bedroom was a single bed, a bedside table, a dresser, and a small vanity and chair all made of white wicker. When she got it from the Sears catalog as a ten-year-old it had seemed the height of glamorous décor.

Seeing her daughter in that single bed, messy braid over her shoulder, scowl in place, surrounded by such cringy retro furniture delighted her.

"Morning, honey," Margot said in a voice that sounded saccharine to her own ears.

"Why are you lurking outside my door?" Skye made a terrible attempt at hiding her phone under her covers.

"No phones in your bedroom," Margot cried, her cheerful mom act crumbling. "You know the rules."

"It's not like there's school or anything," she said.

"But I don't want you spending all night looking at what people are saying about us."

That wasn't healthy. At all.

"No time for phones!" Julia said, stepping across the room and collapsing cross-legged against the headboard beside Skye.

"Come on in," Skye said with a laugh, pulling her phone out from under Julia's bare knee and tossing it on the bedside table beside her retainer.

Margot glanced at her daughter's phone, still lit up with a recent message. From someone named Max.

It was a joke. Why can't you take a joke?

That's what she thought it said; the screen went dark before she could read it again. All of her worry sensors went haywire. *Can't you take a joke* was some gaslighting bullshit. The kind of thing a guy said to a girl when he'd crossed a line.

"Skye?" she said. "Who is Max?"

"No one," Skye snapped, flipping her phone over.

"This Lady X stuff . . . ?" Julia set her iPad, yellow notebook, and black Sharpie on the bed so she could make that head exploding gesture by her ears.

"I know, right?" Skye said. "I spent the night reading the articles we found in the attic." She pulled a stack of newspapers from the floor.

Well, Margot thought, *that's better than staring at her phone all night. I think.*

"What did you find out?" Julia asked. She was going full investigative reporter and if Margot wasn't hanging on to her life with bare-knuckled intensity, she'd be happy to see her sister so excited and sharing that with Skye. Now it only added to her overall sense of dread.

"That the New York City tabloid press was like deeply misogynistic. Like they barely stopped themselves from calling her a bitch."

Julia laughed like she wasn't shocked to hear it. "What else?"

"There were like . . . five men she targeted. A bookstore owner, a dentist. A cop! Can you believe that? She totally destroyed a cop car. She went after the Orbit Room where Gran worked. And she broke the hand of a pro baseball player." She picked up the newspaper article. "He offered a bounty for anyone who could catch Lady X dead or alive. And the press printed that! Can you believe it?"

"Honey," Margot asked, still fixated on her daughter's phone with the red hearts all over the case, "what is the joke this Max guy is talking about?"

"Mom, it was nothing," Skye said without looking at her.

"Who is he?" Margot asked, not letting go of it.

"Just a kid from school." Skye finally looked at her with wide, aggravated eyes. "Honestly. Stop."

"Well, the stuff I found online was very different in tone," Julia jumped in, as if Margot hadn't said anything. She pulled something up on her iPad. "This is from the *Untold Podcast.*"

"Wow," Skye said. The *Untold Podcast* was a big deal.

Jack had been a guest on it last year. Margot had gone to the taping and wept when he talked about the untold secrets to a long career in Hollywood.

"The secret to any success in my life springs from having the right partner. A wise counselor. A no-bullshit sounding board. A driving force. Margot is all of those and more, and she is the secret to my success." He said that. Actually said that. She felt light-headed with a sudden rage. That two-faced motherfucker.

"It was one of the first episodes that came out during the 2018 #MeToo movement," Julia said, then began reading. "'*New York City in 1977 was at a crossroads. The national government refused to bail the city out of its financial trouble. Police and firefighters were fighting with city hall. Punk was fighting with disco. Hip-hop was born. The Bronx was burning. Crime was up, but rents were down. There was a sense of lawlessness in the streets. A civilization just hanging on. Which for those who lived there at the time was as exciting as it was terrifying.*

"'For every woman who had been harassed, assaulted, raped, and silenced, Lady X was a goddamn hero. And for every man who targeted women, Lady X was a real problem.' "

Julia looked up and grinned at Skye, who grinned right back. The two of them giddy with the smell of a story.

This morning Margot had had a long talk with the twins. Amelia went back to class today at Université Paris, claiming she wasn't scared of the paparazzi. But everyone knew that was a lie. As a child she'd been traumatized by a pap who got in a terrible accident chasing them down the Los Angeles freeway.

"You don't have to do that," Margot had told her daughter. "The world won't end if you miss a week of classes." Amelia was studying fashion and apparently doing very well. Her teachers liked her, but her teachers always liked Amelia.

Ellen was happy to take a week off, which of course might lead to a month off. But that was a problem for another day.

Alex was emailing her old Gmail account no one knew about. This morning he told her that his boss was allowing him to sleep at the office, which apparently counted as a solution at NASA. Anyway, he was happy. Ellen was okay. Amelia was going to work herself into a panic attack, and Skye . . . she wasn't sure.

"Does it say anything about her killing someone?" Skye asked, looking over Julia's shoulder.

"No," Julia said, tapping her screen. "But if Mom—"

"She wasn't Lady X," Margot interrupted. It was a ludicrous thought. Their happy-go-lucky mom who made caramel corn for sleepovers and did everyone's hair for high school dances wasn't a *criminal.* "Lady X was killed," Margot said, again remembering that textbook.

"That's just one theory," Julia said. "Another possibility was that she murdered someone the night of the blackout, then left the country. Or she was a prominent person who, once the police started getting involved, had to stop. Or maybe she was actually the Mob out of New Jersey. Or she wasn't just one person but a bunch and—"

"What are you saying?" asked Skye.

"Is anyone hungry?" Margot interrupted, handing the paper back. "I was going to make some muffins."

"I'm saying no one knows who Lady X was," Julia said, ignoring Margot altogether. "No one. There are a bunch of theories and no proof."

"But the picture of Gran?" Skye said.

"I don't know," Julia said with stark honesty and a well of curiosity.

"I really want to find out who Lady X was," Skye whispered.

"Me too," Julia said.

"Should we ask Gran?"

"No!" Margot cried. "No. We don't ask Gran about this." Her mother had a fragile hold on time and place as it was, and Margot wasn't going to upset her with this nonsense, no matter how exciting and distracting it was to Julia and Skye.

"I agree," Julia said. "We don't ask Mom. But I found someone else who can help." She tapped the screen of her iPad a few times. "There was one voice of reason in 1977. A woman who was also writing about Lady X. Op-eds mostly. But with a very different angle. Listen to this . . ." Julia lifted the iPad. "'Lady X is trying to tell us something. Why aren't we listening? Why isn't anyone asking these men what they did to deserve this?'"

"Who wrote the articles?" Skye asked.

"Vanessa Purdy."

"The senator?" Margot asked. "You think she was Lady X?" This was getting ridiculous.

"Her name comes up a lot in the articles," Skye said, gesturing to the stack of newsprint beside her bed. The old yellow quilt sliding on top of them.

Julia put the marker, uncapped, back in her hair, leaving a streak of marker by her ear. Skye took it and put the cap back on before slipping it back behind her aunt's ear.

"Before she became a senator, Vanessa was a women's rights community organizer in New York City and was known to be a bit of a shit disturber. She was arrested a dozen times, once for breaking into and staging a protest inside the city prosecutor's house because he was not hard enough on convicted rapists. And she held a rally for Lady X that got violently busted up by police."

"Okay," Skye said, "let's talk to her."

"Way ahead of you." Julia turned the page on her notebook. "I wrote her last night and she answered this morning."

"She got back to you?" Margot asked. So fast? That seemed suspect.

"I might have dropped some credentials," Julia said with a shrug. "Here, listen to her voicemail."

She tapped the speaker icon on her phone.

"I don't have any answers about Lady X. I didn't know who she was then, and I still don't," said a woman with a Brooklyn accent it sounded like she'd tried hard to polish the edges of. "But everyone on my staff was passionate about Lady X. We were rooting for her until she got violent. I am all for protest and sending messages to city hall and men who break the law, but I cannot condone what she did to that baseball player's hand. And once there were rumors of murder? Well, you can understand that I had to distance myself from her."

Skye leaned forward and hit pause on the voicemail. "That sounds guilty AF," she said.

"It sounds political," Julia said, and tapped play again.

"I did have an assistant in the summer of that year who was writing a lot of my op-eds, and she was . . . obsessive about Lady X. In what I would call an unhealthy way. Her name was Rachel Horowitz."

Skye reached forward and hit the screen. "Rachel Horowitz wrote op-eds under Vanessa Purdy's name?"

"Ghost writers," Julia said. "It's pretty common." Julia hit the button again.

"I had to let her go soon after. She'd become . . . problematic."

Skye hit the pause button. "What does that mean? Problematic?"

"No idea," Julia said, and hit the button again.

"I don't have any contact information for her. I know Rachel has donated to my campaigns over the years, but otherwise we haven't been in touch. I hope that helps and, more importantly, I hope that answers all your questions."

"Vanessa sounds kinda shady," Skye said.

Julia laughed. "You have good instincts, kid."

On the bedside table Skye's phone rattled with an incoming call. Skye glanced at it but didn't pick it up. Which was something Margot had never seen her daughter do. Ignore her phone? Impossible.

"Are you going to answer that?" Margot asked when it rang again.

"No."

"Why not?"

"Because I know who it is and I don't want to talk to him."

Him.

Margot, on edge and alienated in her own bedroom, grabbed the phone from the table.

"Mom—"

Of course it was Jack. He was "Daddy-o" in Skye's phone and the picture was from one of the hikes the two of them went on to Calabasas Peak. Once or twice a month Jack put on his bucket hat and the big cataract sunglasses he wore when he didn't want to be recognized, and pulled Skye out of her room. Jack said it always took a mile of silence before Skye would open up, and then she wouldn't stop talking. Margot used to beg him to tell her what they talked about but he refused to betray her trust.

"How often has he called?" Margot asked, staring down at that goofy picture.

"A bunch."

That could be ten times. It could be three.

"You haven't talked to him?"

She shrugged.

"Why not?" Margot asked, too harsh. She knew it as the words came out of her mouth. But these sudden spikes of rage, like an erratic heartbeat, were coming out of nowhere. She took a deep breath, then another one. But she still wanted to answer the call and scream into the phone.

"What is he going to say, Mom?" Skye said, sounding like a little girl when she probably meant to sound older. Meaner. Harder. "He's sorry? He didn't mean to? It's all bullshit."

Margot didn't know what to say to make any of that right. Jack was still the goofy loving father in the picture. But he was also the man who showed his dick to girls only a little bit older than his daughters. How did you reconcile two such different versions of the same man? How did you do that when you were just a kid?

God. I'm exhausted.

"Hey." Julia showed Skye something on her screen. "I did some digging and found this email on a very old Vanessa Purdy newsletter, thanking her donors. I mean, I don't know if it's her. There are probably a million Rachel Horowitzes. And frankly, I doubt it's still active. But it's worth a shot."

Margot sat down on the bed next to Julia and tilted the screen so she could read an email Julia had drafted to rhorowitz1@hotmail.com.

Dear Ms. Horowitz, I'm writing today because my mother is Ginger Evans (maiden name Daughtry) and my sister, niece, and I have found in her attic a bunch of things that lead us to believe that she might have lived in New York City during the summer of 1977 and your paths might have crossed regarding Vanessa Purdy and Lady X. Our mother is not in a situation to answer our questions, and I was wondering if I could talk to you about this time in our mother's life. My sister and I weren't even aware she'd lived in New York City. Did you know her?

"Why haven't you sent it?" Skye asked.

"Why do you think?" Julia asked, side-eying Margot so hard she was going to have bruises. She knew her sister was just teasing her, trying to keep things light. But there was nothing light in Margot's life. Everything felt like life or death. Grief or rage.

"Because it's a terrible idea?" Margot cried, tossing the iPad back down on the bed and standing up. "Not to mention probably a dead end?"

"Lady X was an actual phenomenon," Julia said. "There were protests and marches in New York City devoted to her. There are dozens of podcasts and articles about her, and Mom was there."

"She was not *there*. Mom was standing somewhere and the photographer got her in the corner of a picture."

"Margot, she had pay stubs from the Orbit Room."

"So . . . what? Now you're lumping her into this X Lady drama?"

"It's Lady X," Skye corrected with a metric ton of brattiness.

"Don't we have enough going on?" Margot asked, trying not to sound hysterical. "We have to turn Mom into some . . . violent vigilante? Can't my mom just be my mom when I need her most?"

Julia looked heartbroken. "Margs, I've tried to tell you, she's not—"

"I know. I know. Her memory is gone. But my memories aren't." She tugged down the bottom hem of her plush green Suzie Kondi leisurewear, trying to keep herself together. "And I need them, Julia. I *need* one thing to stay the same right now. I can't be wrong about my husband *and* my mother. You want to get to the bottom of Lady X, fine. Great. Do it. Start a podcast. But not right now. I know you think this is a fun distraction, but it's not for me. It's upsetting. Please."

Julia's dark eyes met hers and the room was swarmed with a million memories. They had never been the kind of sisters who fought. It wasn't in Margot's nature to demand or argue and she'd been happy to let Julia—always so passionate—have her way.

Even when Julia was in eighth grade and started hanging out with the foreign exchange student who got sent back to Sweden for stealing. Julia had tried to alienate everyone that year, but Margot could not be held at arm's length.

"Okay," Julia said. "We can give it a rest."

Margot slumped with relief.

"Too late," Skye said. She touched the screen of the iPad and looked up with something like triumph. Something like defiance. "I sent the email."

There were 3,400 reported rapes in NYC in 1976. Reported. And we know statistically more than half of rapes go unreported. In a city with a diminished police force, that number would be higher. Tragically, much higher. So before we decide to vilify Lady X, maybe we should investigate the men she's accusing of rape. What have these men done? Who have they hurt? Because we're being told, over and over again, that they have hurt someone.

And if we don't listen now ... things will only get worse.

—VANESSA PURDY, *Village Voice* op-ed, May 28, 1977

CHAPTER 8

April 1977
New York City

Ginger

Ginger ran from the bar, down the red velvet hallway lit by glittering chandeliers Shane said were from France but totally came from Yonkers, to the coatroom to call Faye.

"Now?" Faye said when Ginger told her she had an interview with Shane.

"Some time tonight." She waved at Todd as he came into the coatroom to return the skates.

Faye agreed and hung up without a goodbye, and Ginger set the phone back in its cradle.

"I'm sorry Shane rained on your parade," Ginger said.

"It's all right," Todd said. "I was all out of tricks anyway."

Todd put the skates in the corner with the lost-and-found stuff. Which still included a baby carriage and now a duffel bag full of spray-paint cans.

"My roommate is coming to interview for a job," Ginger said. She caught herself chewing on a nail.

"With Shane?" Todd pretended to gag. *Do you know?* she wanted to ask. *Did he do it to you? To everyone?*

"*C'est la vie,*" Ginger said instead, trying one of Faye's little shrugs. It felt awful.

It was well past eleven when Faye finally came in through the side door looking like a sexy cat in a white faux fur coat and bright red hot pants. Rachel was right behind her in a T-shirt and a pair of flares with a camel-colored leather coat over the top. She was tugging at that coat like it wasn't hers.

"Hey!" Ginger said, leaning over the half door that separated the coatroom from the main hallway. She hugged Rachel and then Faye. Both were awkward huggers, but Ginger was wearing them down.

"Look at this place!" Rachel cried, turning in a slow circle with her mouth open, her eyes wide. "It's smaller than I thought."

"Everyone says that," Ginger said. "Wait until you get inside." She pointed at the strobe lights and disco ball moon just on the other side of the dark doorway. The DJ slid into an Earth, Wind & Fire song and the crowd inside went mad. Confetti fell from the ceiling, showering everyone in silver and gold.

Even Faye watched that doorway like it was something special.

"Did you have any trouble getting in?" Ginger asked. Dante, who worked the side door, could be a pest.

Faye spat something in French.

"The doorman almost didn't let us in," Rachel explained. "But Faye . . . How do you get people to just . . . do what you want?"

"I act like I don't care," Faye said, stating the obvious. She looked at Rachel over her shoulder. "You are too . . . how do you say . . ." She lifted her hands and panted like an animal. "You are a puppy and some people love to kick puppies."

"I'm not a puppy," Rachel muttered. But Faye had nailed it. It was obvious Rachel had been raised to be polite above all things. The greatest sin in her world was making anyone uncomfortable.

But now she looked hurt and Faye looked angry and that was not the vibe of the Orbit Room.

"Well," Ginger said. "You both look amazing."

"Thank you," Rachel said, touching the edges of her freshly feathered hair. Her eyes looked huge with pale blue eyeshadow up to her eyebrows and she even wore some lipstick. She was a stone-cold fox.

"You ready?" Ginger asked Faye.

She shrugged out of her fur coat, handing it over to Ginger. Beneath it she wore a pale pink silk chemise. The world could see the shadows of her nipples through the fabric. The ridges of her rib cage.

"Outta sight." Ginger tossed Faye's coat in the corner with the baby carriage and spray paint and stepped out from behind the half door. "Rachel, watch the coats."

"What? I'm not—"

"Qualified?" Ginger pursed her lips. "Vassar didn't prepare you for coat watching?"

"Fine," Rachel said, and took Ginger's place behind the half door. She sniffed and turned up her nose at the smell of marijuana and corn chips from the poppers Todd and his friends did in the coatroom during their break.

A couple came in the front door, a blast of cool marijuana-scented spring air pushing them into the foyer under the big chandelier. Rachel shot Ginger a panicked look, but they just handed her their jackets and she handed them the round tags from the hangers before they walked through the set of double doors and vanished in the crowd.

Ginger and Faye climbed the stairs that led to Shane's office.

Faye looked down at her ragged cuticles and flaked off some black polish that had been clinging there since she'd been in the city. Ginger knocked on the door, suddenly feeling nauseous.

"Faye?" A warning bubbled up to Ginger's lips. "He might..." Ginger let it trail off and Faye only blinked. "I mean, he's not . . . but he might . . ."

The door opened and Shane stood there, skinny and smooth-cheeked like a teenage boy given the keys to an adult kingdom. Behind him his office had low white couches with a long white coffee table between them. Ginger blinked and focused on Shane. "Hey, Shane," she said. "This is my roommate—"

"Faye," she said, her hand out. "*Enchanté.*" Her accent was suddenly twenty-four-carat.

Shane leered. "Pleasure, Faye. Come on in." He stood aside and

Faye swished past him. Ginger almost stepped forward into the office like she could protect her, but Shane shut the door in her face.

The music pounded in her brain like a headache and Ginger let it sweep things clean. Push out every thought. Every misgiving.

She never did any drugs on the job but had a sudden urge for a bump. Something to take the edge off.

Ginger made it across the hallway just as Todd was brushing Rachel's hair back from her shoulder. She blushed like she was having an allergic reaction.

"I mean, those are the rumors, you know? I'm not the boss's type. Thank God. I gotta run, those piña coladas aren't going to make themselves. Good to meet you, Rachel. You've got a good aura."

And then he was gone and Rachel looked after him like a puppy in a window. Todd had that effect on straight girls.

"You survive?" Ginger asked, opening the half door so Rachel could step out and she could step in. The relative quiet and warmth of the coatroom felt like a cocoon. Like safety.

"Yeah." Rachel looked around at the beautiful scantily clad people streaming into the bar and from the bar to the bathrooms to the beat of Donna Summer.

"Where's Faye?"

"Interview," Ginger said like it was no big deal, but she gave herself away when she looked up those stairs like she'd sent her kid off to kindergarten, and kindergarten was a war zone.

"What's wrong?" Rachel asked.

"Nothing."

"Ginger—"

"He's just . . . he can be . . . *you know*."

Rachel had to know. Every woman knew.

"So, you left her alone up there?" Rachel asked. Now she was looking up those stairs like it was her kid up there.

"He's not going to fuck her," Ginger said, like that was enough. "He's just gonna . . . make her take her top off. Ask for a handy. It's not my fault everyone gets left alone up there." She was working herself up. "She needs the job. That's part of the job!"

"What did he do to you?" Rachel said quietly.

Ginger felt her face go red. Rigid. She thought of the asshole sponsor walking through the dressing room of the bigger pageants she'd been a part of. Eyeing every girl there like they were his property.

"Nothing new."

"Okay." Rachel took a deep breath, steeled her spine. "I'll go up there."

"What?" *And do what?* she wondered. Stop him? Like that was a thing she could just *do?* There would be all kinds of trouble if she did that. Faye wouldn't get the job. Ginger would probably be fired.

But . . . Shane would have been told no. He would have been called on his bullshit.

A strange zip ran down her spine like she'd shocked herself.

"I have no skin in this game," Rachel said. "No job to lose. I'll just go up there and make a scene."

"You?"

"Not a puppy!" she said. Then, to Ginger's surprise and shame, she started across the hallway, dodging a man dressed like Marie Antoinette and a woman in a cake costume. Before she got to the bottom of the staircase, the door at the top opened and Faye walked out with a small stack of silver fabric in her hands. A uniform.

Ginger's soul collapsed in relief.

"That was fast," Ginger said when Faye got down to the coat check. Too fast for any of Shane's bullshit?

"I need a job and he had a job for me." Faye shrugged.

"Did he . . . ?" Rachel asked.

"Did he what?" Faye asked.

"Get handsy," Ginger clarified.

Faye shrugged and Rachel and Ginger looked at each other, unsure of what that shrug, like so many of Faye's shrugs, meant. He did and she said no and he gave her the job anyway?

"Faye . . ." Rachel said. "You can tell us. No job is—"

"I am cleaning off tables and checking the bathrooms," Faye said, shutting Rachel down. "Covering coatroom when Ginger goes on break."

Something happened up there, but Faye would not be talking about it. The subject was officially closed.

Ginger wanted to apologize. She wanted to go back and never offer the job. Really, what she wanted was to have stayed with Faye up there. Protected her instead of walking away like Shane expected.

Faye smiled quickly, revealing that gap. In the language of Faye, that smile was honest. If the shrugs were code, the smiles were real. "Thank you. Both of you. I don't like to think where I would have ended up if I didn't meet you."

"Something tells me you would have been fine," Ginger said. She was embarrassed and sick that she'd sent Faye up there without a warning of what Shane might try.

"You want to change in the coatroom?"

"This is a joke?" Faye asked, as if the idea were terrible.

"It's better than the bathrooms," Ginger said.

"You won't look?" Faye said.

Ginger made a little cross over her heart and joined Rachel at the door.

"You're a better person than I am," Ginger said to Rachel, wrapping her fingers around Rachel's. "You wouldn't have let her go in there alone."

"Someone let you go in there alone," Rachel said, and squeezed her hand. "If we want anything to change we have to talk about what men do to us in offices like that and then we have to stop leading one another into that bullshit like we don't have a choice."

Ginger nodded, grateful for the grace she wasn't sure she deserved. "Faye and I can't drink until after our shift, but if you go to the bar and find Todd, tell him I sent you and he'll make you a Tom Collins on the house."

"I could do with a Tom Collins," Rachel said. She looked over her shoulder at the dark room behind her. There were flashes of sweaty, half-naked bodies in the strobe lights. The fog machines were kicking into gear. The rocket was crashing into the disco ball moon in an endlessly suggestive way. Rachel seemed very interested.

"Go," Ginger said, pushing her into action. "Have fun for us."

Rachel headed for that hot, dark room and Ginger felt, for a moment, taller. Bigger. Like something had happened and even if she wasn't sure what it was, her body recognized that she was different too.

"Rachel?" Ginger said, and she turned just as Faye was emerging from the back of the coats, dressed in the ridiculous space uniform, looking evasive and sharp. And sexy. Very sexy.

"Yeah?" Rachel said.

"You . . ." Ginger gestured lamely toward the stairs. "You're right." It was an apology and a promise to do better, and Rachel beamed.

Something sizzled among the three of them. From Faye to Ginger and onto Rachel. It was more than candles in Chianti bottles and their spots in the living room and more powerful than laughing until Rachel cried and Faye smiled, revealing that gap tooth.

She'd never had it. Not with her mom. Not with Bonnie. It was so new she didn't have words for it and so she left it there. Recognized but unnamed.

Rachel was a loving drunk.

"You guys are the best," she said, her weight balanced between Ginger and Faye as they practically carried her out of the West Fourth Street subway station at two A.M. The stairway smelled like urine, and trash gathered in the corners of the steps. A woman pushing a cart full of broken radios walked by on her way to who knows where. "Really. I couldn't ask for better roommates."

"You're not so bad yourself," Ginger said, catching Rachel as she tripped over the curb and barely managed to miss an oily mystery puddle. Glitter rained down from Rachel's hair, sticking to her neck and chest.

"You're so beautiful," Rachel said to Ginger. "Do they call you Ginger because of your hair?"

"Yes," she said.

"That's amazing."

It wasn't, but Ginger smiled.

"If you dyed your hair black you'd look just like Betty Boop," she said.

"Oh my god, you're drunk."

"Who is this Boop?" Faye asked.

Rachel stopped and did the Betty Boop dance and song, listing off balance and knocking a VOIDOIDS AT CBGB's flyer off a lamp post.

"*Oui!*" Faye said. "I know this."

"Faye!" Rachel said, swiveling her head on what looked like a neck with no muscles. "You are the most mysterious person I've ever met."

"Because you have not met very many people, you," Faye said with an indulgent smile.

"Why did you have that horrible bruise on your hip when you got here?" Rachel asked.

This time it was Ginger who tripped. They didn't talk about that bruise. Or how it happened. Like they'd all agreed that discussing Marvin Gaye's eyes and the guy who roller skated naked through the park every dawn was more important.

But it wasn't. Of course it wasn't.

"Who hurt you?" Rachel asked, standing in the middle of the street.

The street was empty except for the racoons picking through the gutter.

Faye shrugged.

"Don't do that," Rachel said, stepping forward and grabbing Faye's arms. "You don't have to do that anymore. You're safe. We're ..." She looked at Ginger and back at Faye. "We're safe. Aren't we?"

"No one is safe," Faye said.

"*We're* safe," Rachel repeated. She clutched Faye's hands and then Ginger's. "The world isn't safe, but the three of us are. You can talk to us."

Faye stiffened, but her eyes were round and nearly pleading. "What about you?" Faye shot back. "Why were you kicked out of your house? What aren't you telling us?"

Rachel reeled in the street. "Nothing," she lied so badly Ginger laughed.

"What?" Rachel asked. "Maybe you want to tell us what happened when you interviewed with Shane for your job at the Orbit Room?"

"I don't," Ginger said with a sharp laugh. "I'm sure I don't."

"I saw that bruise," Rachel said, not letting it go. "We did. Ginger saw it too, didn't you, Ginger."

"I saw it, but if she doesn't want to talk about it ..." Ginger said. Her eyes met Faye's in the shadows of the street. *You don't have to tell us,* Ginger wanted to say. *You can pick and choose what you share, who you are. I am reinventing myself. You can too. We can be safe for that too.*

"It was old at that point," Faye said with a smile so sharp in the moonlight it looked like a snarl. "You should have seen it when it was fresh."

"Faye," Rachel pressed. "Who hurt you?"

Faye opened her mouth and Ginger held herself still, scared that Faye, the most mysterious, interesting woman she'd ever met, would trust her with her secrets and end up being ordinary, just like Ginger.

"Get the fuck off the road!" a man yelled out his car window as he blew past them so fast they jumped onto the curb in front of their building.

All at once they remembered they were three young, pretty women in a city haunted by Son of Sam.

"Come on," Faye said, slinging Rachel's arm over her shoulder. Ginger helped and they ran to their apartment door.

Ginger dug for her key and Rachel staggered back against the wall of buzzers beneath the anti-nuclear rally flyer from last month.

"Everyone okay here?" a male voice asked, and everyone jumped.

Braced to fight if she had to, Ginger turned to see Officer Boyle, a beat cop who patrolled this side of the village, west of the park. He was handsome in that baby-faced way of younger brothers. He was polite and friendly and she'd been glad to see him a time or two in the past.

"Hey," Ginger said, shooting him a quick smile over her shoulder. "Someone just had a little too much celebration."

Ginger grabbed her keys out of her bag just as the door was yanked open to reveal Mrs. Reznick standing there in curlers and a flowered housecoat, generating enough displeasure to light up the Lower West Side.

"Whoa!" Faye could not keep Rachel on her feet and Officer Boyle stepped in and grabbed Rachel by the shoulders, saving her from falling on the cement.

He stood her up and Faye put her arm around Rachel's waist, holding her tight. It looked for a second like they were playing tug-of-war. Rachel was the rope.

"Hey," Officer Boyle said, ducking his head to look at Faye. "Do I know you?"

Faye shook her head, keeping her chin tucked away from him.

"She's new in town," Rachel said. "French. Austrian, really."

"You really look familiar," Boyle said, and stepped closer to Faye.

"*Je sais pas*," Faye said, her accent thicker than it had been before.

"Get inside," Mrs. Reznick said. "Now."

Ginger didn't like Mrs. Reznick one bit, but when she talked like that Ginger was a kindergartener called to the carpet by Mrs. Knight.

"You sure you don't need any help?" Officer Boyle said, standing on the sidewalk in his heavy blue uniform, his cheeks puffy from youth, but the door was shutting in his face courtesy of Mrs. Reznick.

The four of them were crammed in the suddenly silent foyer.

"Thank you, Mrs. Reznick," Rachel said with her expansive, *I love the world* drunkenness.

"*Oui*," Faye said. "*Merci*."

Ginger said nothing, wrestling Rachel up the steps so they weren't all corralled together inside the door. There was no way to avoid rubbing her shoulder against the gross wall. Her good jacket was going to be ruined.

"Girls—"

"We're sorry," Ginger said, trying to defuse the lecture and evil eye that were undoubtedly coming their way. "Pushing the buzzer was an accident."

"Stay away from that man," Mrs. Reznick said. Her hands were clenched into fists, her face set in lines that had nothing to do with the buzzer being pushed.

"Officer Boyle?" Ginger asked.

"Yes." Mrs. Reznick made the sign of the cross and spit on the landing and Ginger's stomach heaved. Gross.

"Is she a witch?" Rachel asked in an overloud whisper that echoed in the stairwell.

"Get her out of here before she throws up on these steps," Mrs. Reznick said, and waved her hands like they were stray cats she wanted no part of.

Ginger caught Faye's eyes and they burst out laughing, hustling their drunk roommate up four flights of stairs so they could collapse in the safety and wonder of their apartment.

All of their secrets, for the moment, were forgotten.

The pageants taught Ginger a lot. Before Pittsburgh she competed against all the same girls. Pretty girls looking for a way out of their steel or coal town and hoping their looks were enough to get the job done. When she moved to the big city things changed, but not that much. Prettier girls, better talent, but underneath their swimsuits and sequined formalwear they were mostly the same. Vain, mercenary, scared shitless.

They'd stab a friend in the back for the chance to be second runner-up.

They had not prepared her for Faye and Rachel. For the kind of friendship they brought with them.

"Oh my god," Rachel groaned in the morning, bracing herself against the doorway. She was wearing her T-shirt from last night and looked positively gray. "I think I shook my tits in Cher's face."

Faye came in wearing cut-off sweatpants and a thin tank top that looked like a little girl's undershirt. She stopped in the doorway and held out her hand. Rachel gave her a coffee. They drank in silence.

"It was the man my parents wanted me to marry," Faye said. Ginger and Rachel blinked at her. "The man who gave me the bruise?"

Rachel put her mug down on the table that held the phone. Ginger stood, frozen in the kitchen.

"Your fiancé hit you?" Rachel asked. "What happened?" Like there was a sequence of events that would make it understandable. A place in the story a woman could point to and say, *Well, if she hadn't done that, it would have ended differently.*

Faye shrugged. "He hit me and I made sure he couldn't hurt me again."

"You left," Rachel said, and after a moment Faye nodded.

They stared at each other, last night's makeup in streaks on their cheeks. The sunlight hit Faye's face and made her look older. Unfamiliar. And the shabby, indifferent glamour wasn't even glamour anymore. It was something almost scary. Bare bones and raw.

"Let's go to Bigelow," Ginger said, longing for something fun. Simple. And wanting her roommates to have that too. She would rescue them from this darkness, the secrets they all carried. "My treat."

Mom had kept the wives and girlfriends of the steel workers in Allentown date-night ready for years. And Ginger had learned from the master.

Ginger spent a paycheck at the drugstore and Rachel bought donuts. At home, Ginger set Rachel's hair in bright pink ⁹⁄₁₆ perm rods and applied a bottle of Clairol's Born Blonde on Faye's.

While their hair set, they turned up Marvin Gaye on the stereo and sat on the fire escape smoking cigarettes.

"Would you please stop feeding those things," Ginger told Faye as she set Rachel's donut crumbs out for the pigeons, watching them from the railing. "I'm starting to feel like Tippi Hedren."

"Did you know birds are descended from dinosaurs?" Rachel asked, lighting a joint with the butt of her cigarette.

"Impossible," Faye said. "The dinosaurs all died. Kaput."

"What killed them?" Ginger asked, wiping a drip of Clairol Russet Beauty off the back of her neck.

"A meteor," Rachel said. "Or something like that."

"What is something like a meteor?" Ginger asked. Rachel handed her the joint and she took a hit and passed it to Faye. "An asteroid?"

"Aren't they the same thing, just . . . in different places?" Rachel asked.

"One of us really should have paid attention in school," Ginger laughed.

Faye smiled, revealing that tooth gap, and it felt like a victory.

"Those little things have dinosaur eyes." Rachel pointed to the birds that Faye was coaxing closer and closer. "They have seen everything. The end of one world, the beginning of another."

"You're stoned," Ginger said with a laugh.

"No," Faye said. "Even when you think everything is destroyed. Something survives. Something always survives."

"Exactly," Rachel said. She leaned back against Ginger's legs and Ginger leaned against Faye and the three of them tilted their faces up to the sunlight.

CHAPTER 9

May 1977
New York City

Ginger

The hallway outside the studios of Fazil's Dance School was crowded and ripe. Sweaty dancers sat on the wooden floor with their backs against the scuffed-up wall, changing out of one pair of shoes and into another and whispering shit about the choreographers.

It smelled like cigarettes, feet, and body odor.

Ginger loved it.

The only other dance studio she knew was her old grade school gym. Her canvas split-sole slippers would come away black from the fine layer of dust that settled on the wood floor.

"Can I bum a smoke?" Ginger asked Patty, a girl in her jazz class who was so good that by rights Ginger should be pissed at her, but Patty was so down-to-earth she couldn't work up the steam. Sometimes after a late class they went down to Dave's Luncheonette and shared a pickle plate and a chopped-egg sandwich.

She'd asked Patty about being a roommate, but she lived with her sister in Harlem.

"Sure." Patty handed her a Parliament and then lit it.

Ginger took a mouthful of smoke into her lungs and held it there, hoping her body would mistake it for food. But her stomach growled anyway. Patty heard it and smiled. Every dancer at the studio was on the same cigarette-and-coffee diet. They were shaky and constantly sick to their stomachs. But they were thin.

"Because of this Son of Sam asshole all the girls in my neighborhood are wearing blond wigs, can you believe that?" Patty asked.

"I can," Ginger said. "People will do anything to feel safe. You got a wig?"

"No. I'm just not going out after dark. That asshole wants to shoot me he's going to have to do it in broad daylight."

Now that Faye was working at the Orbit Room, they shared a cab instead of walking to the subway at night after their shift was over. And it was a relief that it was staying lighter longer, but the fear in the streets was getting oppressive. Son of Sam was all anyone talked about.

"They post the showcase?" Ginger asked Patty as they sat side by side smoking.

"Dean's or Brady's?" Patty asked.

"Brady."

Patty shot her a look and patted the round edges of her Afro. "What?" Ginger asked, laughing.

"Honey, you ain't gonna be on that list."

"Why?"

"Because you ain't fucking him. Unless you are and I just don't know about it."

"Are you on the list?"

"Please. My mama raised me better than that." Patty nodded toward the bulletin board at the end of the long hallway. "Don't believe me? Go look."

"It's up?" Ginger got to her feet, shoving her character shoes into her bag. "Thanks for the smoke."

Ginger ran to the end of the hallway, her bag bouncing against her hip. She found the cast list among the fliers for auditions, a shoe swap, and rides out past the bus lines.

Ginger's name was not on the list. Neither was Patty's. And Patty was the best dancer here. If she auditioned and didn't get it?

"Shit," Ginger muttered.

"Ginger." She turned to see Brady standing there in all his pretension. The man smoked a pipe, for crying out loud. Brady was not her favorite choreographer, but he got more casting directors to his spotlights than anyone else.

"You were real close, doll," he said with a sympathetic expression. "For a dancer as green as you are, you show some promise."

"What can I work on?" Ginger asked. "I know my feet aren't as good as Danica's but—"

"I'd love to talk about what you can do to be a part of the next spotlight." He stepped forward until she could smell the pastrami from the deli downstairs on his breath.

"Great." She hitched her bag up on her shoulder and stepped away. Her back hit the bulletin board.

"Why don't you come to my place Saturday night . . ."

"What?"

"Yeah, come on by. We'll have a drink and I can tell you all the things I think you can do to get in the next spotlight."

"Is fucking you on that list?" Ginger asked, her voice cracking in the long hallway. Over his shoulder she could see Patty, her arms crossed, in the middle of the hallway. Just keeping an eye. The opposite of what Ginger had done for Faye at the Orbit Room.

"You said it, doll, not me," Brady murmured, stepping closer. "What do you say, you've got the talent."

"Then put me in the spotlight."

He leered down Ginger's leotard and she stepped sideways to get past him.

"Come on, Jennifer—"

"It's Ginger, asshole," she muttered.

His face got hard. "You're the one who wants in the spotlight," he said, like his hands were tied. "I'm just trying to help."

Ginger stomped away, down the hallway. Maybe it was time for a new studio. Maybe it was time to just give up. Brady was right, she was green. Ginger was probably making a fool of herself, just like Mom said she would.

"I stopped auditioning for him weeks ago," Patty said. "The only girls he casts are the ones who suck his dick, and I don't play that game."

"The whole thing is that game," Ginger said.

"Hey," Patty said. "You're good. Don't let him get you down."

"You're just saying that."

"I don't just say anything," Patty said, her eyebrows arched, and Ginger laughed.

It was another day without any rain and it felt like the city had skipped right over spring and landed in summer, but Ginger wasn't walking through Times Square in her leotard. She pulled on a denim coat and a pair of sweatpants. "You heading to the subway?"

"Yeah."

Ginger was dreading it. But walking back to the village wasn't in the cards and she didn't have enough for a cab. The subway was filthy and full of graffiti and toughs who mugged people with deadly little knives. "I'll walk with you."

Stepping out of Fazil's and into the porn district was always a culture shock. Night was falling and the working girls stepped out of the shadows just as the marquee lights flickered on. They wore short shorts and sky-high heels, some covered bruises and needle marks with pancake makeup.

In front of them a girl leaned into the open window of a Chrysler that slowed to a stop at the lights.

"Looking for a date, handsome?" the girl asked, smacking gum. She caught Ginger staring and winked at her.

Sweaty guys streamed in and out of the porn theaters, looking for a liquor store and a pack of cigarettes.

"God," Patty said. "It's warm already and it's only May."

"I heard this summer is gonna be bad," Ginger said. Rachel told her that the other day. A heat wave summer.

"Hey mama!" some guy yelled, stepping in Patty's way. He looked like a tourist from Toledo. "How much for you—"

"Fuck off," Ginger said. She was raw from that whole nonsense with Brady and Shane at the club and maybe the last twenty years of men looking at her like she was just a pair of tits.

"I wasn't talking to you," the guy said, getting red under his collar.

"Not interested," Patty said with a polite smile, because that's how you had to be. The lamp posts were papered with flyers of missing girls the police couldn't be bothered to look for. So, women had to smile and mitigate their own disasters.

Toledo wandered off and they stopped for a light at Forty-second Street. The posters on the light posts flapped in the fetid breeze blowing up Broadway. One was a washed-out photo of a brunette with long hair. The wind curled the corner of the flyer up and Ginger reached out and straightened it.

The brunette with long hair was wearing a thick sweater and standing next to a goat.

And smiling. Revealing a gap in her front teeth.

If the woman had short blond hair and a satin jacket, it would be . . .

I mean. A dead ringer.

"Ginger?" Patty asked, halfway across the street. Someone honked and she gave them the bird. Ginger tore down the flyer and shoved it in her pocket. At the station Patty raced past the graffiti and the broken Wheel of Love game for the 2 Train to Harlem and Ginger held her breath and took the stairs down the tunnels to the southbound 1 Train. The air smelled like urine and electricity but tasted like copper. There was no winning.

There was a rat on the edge of the platform, picking its way across filthy candy wrappers and a man snoring on the only bench. The train barreled down the tunnel, blowing a hot wind in everyone's face. It slowed to a stop, every bit of it covered in graffiti, even the windows.

She found a dry seat between two women and pulled the flyer out of her pocket.

GINETTE BEAUCHAMP. MISSING SINCE DECEMBER 23. LAST SEEN TORONTO ON A BUS TO NY. SUSPECTED OF MURDER.

Murder?

On second look, she decided it wasn't Faye. Her face was rounder and her eyes were different. Wider, maybe? The longer Ginger looked at the picture the less it looked like her roommate.

That long hair made her look like the Mennonite girls in Allen

Township near where Ginger grew up. They sold jam on the side of the road and kept their heads down while riding in buggies.

Faye took the train from Montreal and she was here looking for her sister.

Ginger crumpled up the flyer and tossed it on the ground with the rest of the garbage.

Ginger climbed to the fourth floor to find Faye sitting on the steps with Mrs. Reznick, the two of them thick as thieves.

"What are you doing?" Ginger asked Faye.

"Drinking," Faye said, and toasted Mrs. Reznick with a teacup. Faye's hair looked fantastic, white-blond without any brassiness. "She makes beer." Laughing, Faye handed Ginger the teacup. "It's terrible."

Ginger took a sip and nearly spat it out. "That's not beer." She'd had her share of moonshine and it wasn't even that.

"It's free. You can't complain." Mrs. Reznick downed the last of hers and took the teacup from Faye's hand and drank that too. She went into her apartment and shut the door.

"She doesn't like you," Faye said, getting to her feet. She wore a pair of Jordache shorts that had been jeans just the other day and a white T-shirt with rainbow stripes on the shoulders that Rachel had bought last week.

"It's mutual," Ginger said as they climbed the last of the stairs to the apartment, which Faye had left unlocked.

"She says Officer Boyle makes the girls in the park sleep with him so they don't get arrested."

Ginger paused. "Really?"

Faye shrugged. "How was class?" she asked.

"Good," Ginger lied. She didn't want to talk about Brady. About being good but never good enough. It was one thing to be talented in a place like Allentown, or even Pittsburgh. But New York was full of women far more talented than her and just as beautiful.

"When can we see you dance?" Faye asked.

"You want to?" Ginger asked, soaking up that little bit of interest like it was water.

"Of course," Faye said. "I am sure you are *magnifique.*"

"You're just saying that."

"I never say things I don't mean. Not anymore."

"How did it go today?" Ginger asked. Rachel had gone with Faye to put up flyers with pictures of Faye's sister Renee at the Port Authority and Grand Central Station. Ginger thought of that flyer she'd seen in Times Square. That woman who looked like Faye, but not quite. Could it be Renee? No. There was a different name on the flyer. Ginette? Beauchamp? It couldn't be Faye's sister. It was just one of the hundreds of girls who go missing in New York City.

"Fine," Faye said as they walked into the empty apartment. "I need to get more copies made."

Rachel's loafers weren't by the door where they usually were.

"Where is Rachel?"

"She had that thing at the bookstore."

"Shit. That's right. I said I'd go." Rachel had organized a meeting for Vanessa Purdy. Advertised it in the papers. Found a bookstore on Fourth that would host it for free. She'd even gotten Faye to bake cookies for it. Little tarts with syrupy middles. Rachel had been so excited. Levitating for days. Sure this would get her promoted into Vanessa Purdy's inner circle.

God. I am the worst friend.

"I went," Faye said, kicking off her flip-flops.

"Yeah? How was it?"

Faye shrugged. "She did a good job. Made me believe it might work."

"What might work?"

"Women's rights."

"You didn't think it would work before?"

"I've never seen a woman get anything but what she fought for or stole. Where I'm from men give women babies and black eyes. And that's it," Faye said just as the front door banged open and then slammed shut. Rachel's door banged too. Faye lifted her eyebrows and they both stepped into the living room.

"Rach?" Ginger asked. "You okay?"

No answer. The hair rose up on the back of Ginger's neck, an ancient warning system, triggered by a particular kind of silence. A survival instinct passed down through women without a word ever spoken.

Faye knocked on Rachel's door and pushed it open without waiting for Rachel to answer. "What are you doing?" she asked in her blunt way.

"Packing," Rachel said. She threw her clothes into the big suitcase her brother had carried up the stairs a month ago. She wore her burgundy corduroy skirt that was too hot for the spring weather, but she'd wanted to look professional and Ginger had told her that was the most professional look she had.

"Where are you going?" Faye asked.

"Home."

"You got kicked out," Ginger reminded her.

"I got..." Rachel stopped, her shoulders curved forward as if braced for some horrible blow. Ginger couldn't take it anymore; she stepped into the room and put her arms around her. Rachel was trying so hard not to cry, Ginger could feel the tension, like every muscle was working its hardest just to stay upright. Breathing. Alive.

"What happened?" Ginger whispered. Later she would think about how she knew. Ginger knew the second Rachel banged through the front door, blown by an ill wind and full of rage. This was a new Rachel standing here. A different one.

Violently, she shrugged Ginger's hands off her shoulders.

"Don't touch me. I'm not... just... don't."

"Rachel," Faye said, her voice firm like a doctor asking where the pain was.

Rachel's face went blank. Alarmingly blank. The way Mom's did whenever Ginger asked about her father. She was burying herself deep inside her body, like coal in the hills where Ginger grew up.

Faye got up in her face. "What. Happened?"

Ginger wanted to tell Faye to stop, to leave Rachel alone, she'd clearly been through something. But she remembered Rachel's words.

If we want anything to change, we have to talk about what happens ...

Fresh tears soaked the frilly neck of Rachel's high-collared pink shirt.

"I was helping clean up," she whispered. "Stacking the chairs and taking the tables down to the basement." The word *basement* sent a cold chill through the apartment. "The bookstore owner. Mr. LeRoy? He followed me and he kissed me," Rachel said in a rush. "And I was so surprised. So shocked . . . I laughed."

Oh. No.

"Then what?" Faye asked.

"He said, 'Oh, sorry, I got the signals wrong.'" Rachel's voice was jagged. Broken. "I wasn't giving any signals. I was just excited, you know? The night had gone so well. I swear I wasn't giving him any signals."

"Of course you weren't," Ginger said. She was just happy. And for some assholes that was enough.

"He left and came down with more chairs and asked me to stack them in the corner of the storage room, and as soon as I turned around I heard the door lock."

Faye whispered something vicious in French.

"He told me nothing was free." That had been the deal. A free place for Vanessa to have her meeting. Rachel had been a hero to Vanessa and the rest of the staff. "I didn't . . . I mean I was so . . . shocked. I was . . . *shocked*. And he moved so fast and I was blocked in by the chairs and I kept thinking there was no way he was really going to do this. He just hosted a feminist meeting. He has a *baby*. And then . . . it was happening. Really happening and I was scared and it hurt and all I could think was that if I fought him . . . if I *fought* . . ."

"It would get worse," Faye said.

Ginger sucked in a breath. The shock of *worse*. The fear of *worse*. It was why Patty smiled at Toledo on the street. Why Rachel didn't fight. It was what those lamp post fliers warned them about.

"He raped you," Ginger said. The words sharp and clear, shattering the icy silence in the room.

"I didn't. I don't . . ." Rachel shook her head. Shrugged. Shook her head again. Like someone had given her instructions and she couldn't remember them. She held out her hands, then dropped them.

He raped her.

The pigeon tapped on the window. A short, sharp yes.

The three of them stood there, staring at one another. The shadows in the corners seething.

"Are you hurt?" Ginger finally said. More than the obvious. There could be bleeding. Internal damage.

"It's not . . . I didn't fight," Rachel whispered. She held out her hands again, lifted her sleeves to reveal her thin wrists. "I mean, I don't have bruises. I didn't do anything. I'm so nice I didn't even fight the man raping me." She said it again. And then again. Like she'd just realized there could have been a different option. A different outcome. And it was somehow her fault.

"The police," Ginger said. That's what you did when there was a crime. You went to the police. All you had to do was look at Rachel—shattered and shaken—to see a crime scene.

"What are the police going to do?" Rachel asked. "There's hardly any left in this city anyway." Tons of firefighters and police had been laid off because the city's budget was so bad. But they couldn't do *nothing*.

"Come on. Officer Boyle," Ginger said. Having stumbled upon this idea she couldn't let it go. The alternative was . . . what? Rachel packing up and leaving? That asshole getting away with it? Neither was right. "He's probably at the park right now. Let's go talk to him. The guy that hurt you can't get away with it."

"He's a fucking bookstore owner," Rachel said. Outside the window another pigeon arrived, starting a squabble with the other ones. "He looks like a sheepdog. He has a new baby. Who is going to believe me?"

"Officer Boyle knows us. Faye, tell her." Ginger looked at Faye for support, but Faye stood up against the dark windows, like a ghost. Glowing in the half-dark. She was . . . incandescent with something hot and internal. Everything about her seemed one breath from exploding.

She would be no help. Could, in fact, be her own problem.

Fine. The momentum would come from Ginger. She'd done worse things. Come to more difficult rescues.

Ginger grabbed Rachel's freezing-cold hands and pressed them between hers.

One of Rachel's pristine rose-colored nails was chipped and torn at a ragged edge. The nail bed was bloody. Proof of some violent thing. Of some unordinary moment. A struggle.

She did fight.

Ginger would hold up this shaking, cold hand as proof to Officer Boyle and he would believe them.

"I don't even know what's happening," Rachel whispered. The confident, intelligent woman reduced to a shaking, confused child. It was wrong. Wrong in every way.

Outside the air smelled like grease and garbage, and they turned left down the street toward the park. The day's heat had been pushed out by cold spring air that felt damp and dirty. Like sweat drying in places no one wanted it.

"I don't feel good about going to the park at night," Rachel said.

"What is there to be scared of?" Faye's laughter the bark of a wild dog in the woods. "The worst has already happened."

Officer Boyle was by the fountain chatting up two working girls. He had his foot on the cement ledge by one of the women's hips.

"Officer Boyle," Ginger said. When he turned to face them, the two girls beat feet in the other direction.

"Hello, ladies," he said, lifting his hat up higher on his wide forehead. "What are you three doing here at night? There's a serial killer on the loose. It's not exactly safe for girls like you."

A hysterical sound erupted from Rachel's throat and Ginger knew what she was thinking. "Girls like you"? What did that mean? And what was safe? It wasn't any safer for the women walking away as fast as they could.

And if a bookstore wasn't safe, no place was.

"We need to report a crime," Ginger said. "A bad one."

"Yeah?" The smile faded from his face. He looked serious and she felt dizzy with relief. Sure, there were bad cops, but there were good ones too. And they had found one. "What happened?"

"Rachel was attacked."

"They took your purse? Broke into your place? I've been telling Mrs. Reznick to do something about that fire escape."

"I was raped," Rachel said quietly. The streetlight turned everything blue and white, and she looked like a statue. Grim-faced and stoic. She should have a stone sword and be on that arch behind her. Valor or dignity in human form.

"No shit." He stepped sideways into the light cast by a streetlight. "Come here, sweetheart."

Rachel stepped into the pool of light and Ginger followed.

"Can I?" he asked, reaching for Rachel's chin. Permission? It was like he understood. Ginger glanced at Faye where she stood in the shadows. Nothing about her seemed relieved. Or comforted. She was sharpened by the light. Poised on the edge of something wild.

Rachel lifted her face. He took her chin between his thumb and finger and tilted her head back and forth in the light. "You don't look hurt," he said.

"I didn't . . . he didn't hit me," Rachel said quietly. She pulled her chin free.

"On the face?"

"At all."

He reached for her hands and pushed back the sleeves of her sweater. No permission that time, and Rachel flinched.

Faye's lips parted in a silent snarl.

"I ain't gonna hurt you," he said with a hard edge Ginger didn't like. "He didn't tie you up? Hold you down? You got bruises anywhere else?"

"No. I . . . I didn't fight him."

"Didn't fight him?" he asked. "Did you want to have sex with him?"

"No!"

"You make that clear? Because sometimes you girls, you tease a guy and he thinks it's a done deal and you change your mind last minute and that ain't fair, is it?"

Ginger immediately regretted pulling Rachel out of the apartment into this oily night, to reveal her wounds to this monster of a man.

"Look, you have a fight with your boyfriend"—Officer Boyle held up his hands—"that's between the two of yous."

"He's not my boyfriend. He . . . has a wife. A kid."

"Jesus, you're trying to bust up a family and you come to me to get him in trouble?" He shook his head, lip curled. Just so disgusted with the group of them. "Like we cops don't have enough to do. We got an actual serial killer on the loose—why the hell are you wasting our time with this shit? You know something, I should have you arrested for this. Disturbing the peace. Soliciting . . ."

Faye said something sharp and furious in French and Boyle stiffened.

"What was that, kraut?" he asked, turning on her where she stood in the shadows.

"She's Austrian," Ginger said. Like it mattered.

"I don't care if she's the fucking queen of England. Speak English."

That didn't even make sense.

Faye walked out of the shadow and into the light, making explicit and bold eye contact. Dangerous eye contact. Antagonizing. And when she got right in front of him, she laughed in Officer Boyle's face. She smeared her disdain all over him, like mud. Like shit.

She put her arm around Rachel and walked her out of the light and into the shadows, heading for the street.

Leaving Ginger behind in the air that had changed the way only men could change it. Sulfur and venom. The threat of violence.

He was embarrassed. Put out. Faye made him feel foolish, and there was only one way to deal with that.

Ginger turned and ran, following her roommates, her hands at their backs, pushing them so they'd run.

"No," Faye said, pushing against Ginger's hand. "Don't give him the satisfaction."

She forced them to walk away like tonight didn't have teeth. Fists. Sharp edges that tore at their clothes. Grabbed at their hair. Faye walked through all of it like she couldn't feel how threatening the world was around them.

Like the worst had already happened.

I don't know who this Lady X lady is, but she mad. She real mad.

—New York City citizen

Who is Lady X?

—*New York Post*, June 10, 1977

CHAPTER 10

March 2024
Pittsburgh, Pennsylvania

Margot

Julia called The Oaks and got the okay for a short visit with Mom after lunch. Margot changed her clothes, wrapped up muffins she'd made for the staff, and met her sister in the cranberry-carpeted living room.

"Is Skye coming?" Julia asked.

"I didn't ask."

Margot didn't know how to say that, if it was possible, she wouldn't have Julia there either. If it was possible, she'd go alone and put her head in her mother's lap like she used to and cry until she was empty.

"You're mad she sent that email."

Of course she was mad.

"I don't care that she sent the email," Margot snapped. "I don't care about this Lady X crap. I am up to my ears with a real crisis."

"I know, but it's not crap to your daughter," Julia said. The subtext here was *It's not crap to me.* God, wasn't this just like her sister. Margot's house was on fire and Julia was watering her garden.

That wasn't fair. It might be true, but it wasn't totally fair.

"Don't ask me to care right now, Julia. Mom was Mom. I'm not entertaining the idea that she kept secrets from us. Because I can't. I am full up on secrets right now."

Julia lifted her hands. "Of course. I'm sorry." Margot didn't think Julia meant that apology, not even for a second, but the effort was nice. They got into Julia's old soft-top Jeep Wrangler, a vehicle she kept alive for reasons absolutely beyond Margot.

The bitter air whistled through the zippers and even with the heat blasting there was no way to stay warm. The radio, to be heard over the wind and the engine, had to be played at eardrum-splitting decibels and even then was fairly incoherent. The whole thing was just loud chaos.

"Why don't you get a new car?" Margot shouted over all the noise. Her sister made good money at the paper and she lived rent-free.

Julia reared back in outrage. "The Jeep is perfectly fine. She's been checked out by the finest mechanic in Allegheny County."

"John?"

"Of course John."

John was Dad's old football buddy from high school and married to Mom's best friend Bonnie. He'd owned a repair shop on Neville Island and took care of everyone's car until he sold the shop. It was nice he was still looking after Julia.

"So . . . Mom," Julia said.

"Yeah."

"Her memory is really deteriorating. Even on good days . . ."

"I know."

"You don't. Margot, you haven't been here in six months. I'm trying to tell you, she thinks she's staying in a hotel. And that Dad is going to walk through that door any minute."

Margot wanted to protest, say something in her defense, but what could she say? Six months was way too long.

Margot paid for Mom's very good and extremely specialized care. But Julia was *here*. She visited more often, had a closer relationship with the staff and caregivers. And that was all that mattered.

Julia parked in the small parking lot in front of an old Victorian house set in the hills of Sewickley. There was a gorgeous wraparound porch and bright white gingerbread tucked like handkerchiefs in the peaks of the roofline. You could see glimpses of more modern buildings set behind the house, the medical and rehab facilities. But the house with its rocking chairs and pine trees just looked like a really nice house.

The people inside probably didn't know or care. But the people who visited were extremely relieved.

"You coming?" Julia shouted and Margot jumped out, nervous despite all her best efforts. She tried, she really did, to make this not about her. She reminded herself that she had to meet Mom where she was and not bring all her wants and needs into the room.

The air smelled like pine and the sound of the highway at the bottom of the hill was a steady, nearly comforting hum.

Julia pressed the buzzer and leaned toward the speaker.

"Julia and Margot to see Ginger Evans."

A heavy lock disengaged followed by a buzzer, and Julia opened the oak security door disguised to look like a part of the house. They were greeted by a lovely and calm receptionist in business casual who hit a different buzzer that opened another door and they were met by another lovely and calm woman, this time an aide, who would walk them to Mom's apartment.

Speaking the whole time in a calm and reasonable voice. Everything calm. Everything reasonable.

Margot used to love that about the place, was so drawn to it. Had joked (badly, she knew it was a bad joke) with Jack that he could move her here when the time came.

Now, all this calm and quiet and reasonableness gave her a foreign impulse to trail her hand across one of the shelves and knock everything to the ground.

She wanted to *ruin* it.

The thought was startling. Scary, almost. She adjusted her rings, the bracelet the twins got her for Christmas, trying to set herself right.

They walked through the lovely common room that led to a gorgeous solarium. The door to the music room was open and one of the residents, a man who had been a percussionist in the symphony, sat at a piano. Not playing. Just looking at the instrument like he couldn't remember how to turn it on.

In the back of the house there was a short hallway with four rooms branching off.

Four private apartments.

Mom's was on the far right.

"We've told her you're coming," said the aide with a smile. "She's very excited to see you."

She stepped away and Julia knocked on the door before turning the knob.

"Mom?"

"Darlings!" she cried, her voice only a little muffled. "Come in. Come in!"

They followed the sound of her voice to the sitting room with a love seat and Mom in her specialized recliner. They'd made the room as familiar as possible. Blankets and pillows from the house. Pictures. Even the ridiculous Betty Boop doll their mother had kept in a place of pride on the windowsill above the kitchen sink.

Margot braced herself but seeing her mom was still a shock.

She's so small.

Like she'd lost an inch and ten pounds.

Was that normal? Should she be worried? Who did they need to talk to?

Mom's hair was thin and the kind of beige that happened to natural redheads. The left side of her face was not as frozen as it had been after the accident and the strokes. The physical therapy here was pretty amazing. But her left arm had not regained much movement.

Still, she wore lipstick and had bright red nails and while the rest of the world might have given up on bras after COVID—not Ginger. She filled out her black sweatshirt like the beauty queen she'd been.

"Margot, honey!" Her blue eyes filled with tears and Margot crouched to hug her mom in her chair.

"Hi, Mom," she said, her voice rough with emotion. Gratitude and sadness and an ache so deep it felt like it was carving her out. Mom smelled the same. Shalimar and baby powder.

"Where are my grandkids?" Ginger asked, looking past Margot's shoulder.

"They didn't come this time."

"Well," she said, her bright blue eyes narrowing. "I don't have all that many times left, sweetie."

"Don't say that, Mom," Julia said, stepping in for her own hug. "You know it always makes Margot cry."

"Hardly," Mom said. "Margot is tough as nails. You"—she squeezed Julia—"are the one with the waterworks."

"Blasphemy." Julia bent and kissed Ginger's cheek. "How are you?"

"Just fine." She leaned forward and dropped her voice. "Did you bring any of that reefer you brought last time?"

"Julia!" Margot gasped. "You did not."

"I did. I talked to her doctors and they said it was fine. But no, Mom, I didn't. Instead I brought the fun police."

"Yes," Mom said, patting Margot's hands and then lifting them to her face to kiss them. "She always was a little serious, wasn't she? She could use some reefer."

"Yes!" Julia laughed. "Yes, she could."

"Could you imagine," Mom asked, swaying in her chair. "We could get high and dance to Marvin Gaye just like we used to?"

Margot and Julia looked at each other. They'd danced with their mother plenty. Kitchen dance parties to Billy Joel and Whitney Houston. But never high.

"So, Mom," Julia said, pulling Margot down with her onto the love seat. "Give us the good gossip."

"Oh!" Mom's face lit up. She loved gossip. Always had. When Julia and Margot came home from school, they'd sit around the kitchen table and have graham crackers with homemade buttercream frosting and fill her in on all the goings on at Avonworth High School. And Mom ate it up like it was a soap opera.

Ginger craned her neck forward, lowered her voice.

"Eddie, next door?" she whispered.

"Yeah?" Julia asked.

"Chlamydia."

"Again?"

"He's a dog. I swear."

"As long as you're not letting him sniff around you."

"Can you imagine? Your father would have something to say about that."

Margot opened her mouth to correct her mom, but Julia put her hand on her knee and squeezed.

"Speaking of fathers, how is Jack?" Mom was Jack Cooper's number one fan. She fell for that man's charm hook, line, and sinker. Margot was grateful that her mother had no way of knowing what had happened.

"Fine."

"When is his next movie coming out?"

"Summer." Though, that was probably getting pulled if it hadn't already.

"We just loved his last one," Mom said. "Did we tell you that? Dad and I went to see it in the theaters and, oh my lord, we were on the edge of our seats. *No Man's Land* was his best one yet."

No Man's Land came out eleven years ago.

"Mom," Margot said, her voice catching. She cleared her throat and tried again. "It's good to see you. I've missed you."

"Oh, I've missed you too. I don't know why you had to go all the way to UCLA when Carnegie Mellon is right here."

"I like the sunshine," she said, her old argument. When what she'd really wanted was to stretch her wings as far as they could go. God, she hardly recognized that girl who made such big and bold decisions, who knew what she wanted and went after it.

What happened to her?

"You are just like your father. That man never passes up a chance to get a sunburn."

"Mom," Julia said. "Remember all those trips we took to New York City?" Margot turned and glared at her sister. Hadn't they agreed not to do this very thing?

"Goodness. Yes," Mom said. "Didn't we have fun? Remember when I stole that menu from Tavern on the Green and Margot nearly had a heart attack." Ginger stroked Margot's face. "So serious. So ethical. My little thinker. I used to worry about you, thinking yourself into a standstill."

It was too much. Her mother seeing her so clearly from her mechanized chair in her memory care facility, miles from Margot's life. Her hard edges, her barriers and walls, crumbled with the sweetness of it. The bitter pain of it.

Margot was a kid. And she just needed her mom.

There was no holding back the sob.

Julia put her hand on Margot's knee, her fingers digging deep like they were at church and old lady Moss behind them farted.

"Did you ever live in New York?" Julia asked, and Margot was not having that.

"Did Dad ever cheat?" Margot asked right over her sister.

"You have got to be kidding me!" Julia said under her breath.

"Your father?" Mom asked, her right hand pressed to her chest. "Cheat? On me? What kind of question is that?"

"A terrible one," Julia said.

"I'm just curious. You were married for so long . . . and I don't know, sometimes people cheat."

"John did. That fool almost destroyed the best thing that ever happened to him. I swore to your father that I'd never tell Bonnie, but you can believe I let John know what I thought of his bullshit." Margot could feel Julia staring at the side of her face, but they would dissect that bit of information later. "But no, honey. Your father would never. He knew where his bread was buttered." She looked at her old watch. "Where is he? We've got reservations downstairs at ten. Honestly, this is the best hotel."

"What would you have done if he had cheated?" Margot asked, and Julia nudged her with her elbow.

"Oh, well, I guess . . ." Mom tilted her head to the side. "I never thought of that. It depends, I suppose."

"On what?" Julia asked, like the idea was ridiculous.

"Is he in love? Does it mean anything to him? Were you two little?" Mom shrugged. "Was it once? Was it a relationship?"

"So, you're saying you might forgive him?" Margot asked.

"No," Julia snapped. "She wouldn't have. Because you don't forgive people who cheat."

"*You* don't," Margot snapped back.

"Margot," Mom asked, "did something happen?"

She could tell her, unload all of this and maybe her mother could handle it. She seemed so good right now, so much like herself. Maybe everything would be all right. She needed just one thing to be all right.

"Mom," Margot whispered, the tears back in her eyes, her throat suddenly thick. "I don't know what to do."

"Oh, honey," Mom whispered, stroking her hands. "Tell me what's got you in such a state. Your father worries about you, you know? Out there in Hollywood with people who don't really know you."

Julia kicked her foot and Margot moved it out of the way. Didn't she deserve this? Couldn't she have this? One thing? What more did she have to give up?

"Jack's done—"

"Hey, Mom," Julia said, talking right over Margot. "What can you tell me about this picture?"

From the back of her tight black jeans Julia pulled the folded-up front page of the *New York Post*. She unfolded it, revealing the picture of the graffitied dentist's office and her mother's face captured in the corner.

The soft energy in the room sizzled and snapped. The mother Margot knew vanished, right in front of her. It was like she folded herself up and put herself away and in her place was someone who looked like Mom but was too sharp. Too cold.

A furious stranger.

Margot glared at Julia.

"What is this?" Mom took the picture in her good hand. "Oh," she said, her right eyebrow lowering in sharp disapproval. "Where did you get this?"

"Skye found it in a box in the attic," Julia said in her journalist voice.

"The attic?" Mom said. "What are you doing up there?"

"Just cleaning things up. We found this box of all these New York things."

"New York?" She dropped the photo and it fluttered to the floor.

"Yeah. Mom, you never told us you lived in New York City. And you worked at the Orbit Room. And Lady X. Mom . . . she was such a badass." Julia stood to grab the picture from the floor.

"Lady X," Mom said, turning to look out the window. The blue sky and bare limbs of the maple trees. Her hand trembling as she picked at the sleeve of her shirt. "I don't know . . ."

Margot pulled Julia back down to the couch and pinched her like they were girls.

"Ouch," Julia whispered. "You want to ask more questions about Dad?"

"Why are you asking me this?" Mom asked.

"Because you kept all this stuff—"

Mom pressed a hand to her head. "It was months ago." She looked up at them with narrowed eyes. "It wasn't me."

"I didn't think it was," Julia said quickly.

"I had nothing to do with it." Ginger began to fidget in her seat, lifting herself as best she could with only half a working body.

"Of course not, Mom. We're not saying you did."

"I was just there. It's not my fault someone was taking a picture." She tried to get out of her chair without using the motor that would lift the seat so she could get to her feet easier.

"We know that," Julia said. "I'm sorry, Mom. Please don't get upset."

"I'm not upset. You're the one asking me. And I've told you over and over."

Ginger fell hard back into the chair. Margot grabbed her but she pushed her hands away.

"I'm a citizen, and I haven't done anything wrong. You keep showing up at my house and asking me the same stupid question," their mother yelled, her voice tremulous and heartbreaking. "This is harassment!"

"Does she think we're cops?" Julia whispered.

"Mom. We don't think you did anything," Margot said, putting her hand on her mother's back. "Do you want some tea?"

"Get your hands off me!" she cried.

"Shit," Julia said, and reached forward to push the distress button hanging off the arm of Mom's chair.

"Why haven't you asked those men about their crimes?" She tried again to get to her feet.

"Mom, please calm down."

"I've had enough of this bullshit," Ginger said, shoving her hands away. "Knocking at my door at all hours because some woman has got you looking like a fool in the papers. I am not Lady X. I don't know who Lady X is. But I hope you never catch her."

Mom finally got to her feet and stayed up, but she didn't have her walker. She had only rage and half a mobile body. She tried to take a step and would have crumpled to the floor if Margot hadn't caught her.

There was a quiet knock on the door and one of the reasonable, smiling aides walked in.

"Mrs. Evans?" he said.

"Where's Peter?" Mom asked, her words slurring, her pitch climbing. She was scared. They'd scared her. Margot wanted to erase everything. They never should have come. How could she have been so selfish? "He's supposed to be waiting for me. Peter?" she cried.

"Mrs. Evans. Let me help you get back into your chair."

The aide reached for Ginger and she tried to smack him. "I said keep your hands off me."

She was shaking with a terrible mix of chemicals from a brain that couldn't be trusted.

"Peter!"

The room was suddenly full of people. No one was smiling anymore and a nurse quickly injected Mom with a mild sedative. Margot made a low keening sound and had to look away as the nurses murmured and hushed and shuffled Mom, calmer now, to her bedroom.

Margot and Julia stood there staring at each other.

"This was a mistake," Margot said.

"Mom knows more than she's saying," Julia said.

Margot gasped. "That's what you have to say? We upset her so much she had to be drugged, Julia."

"I'm not the one asking about her dead husband."

"Fuck you," Margot snapped.

Margot grabbed her purse and shoved past her sister. She thanked the staff as she went, apologized for disturbing the peace of The Oaks. Hoped she didn't upset any of the other residents.

The man at the piano, as she walked by, looked up at her but still did not play.

"That's the chlamydia guy," Julia whispered just over her shoulder.

"Jesus. Have some respect," Margot snapped.

She hit the door and stepped out into the brilliant sunlight and icy wind. Margot put on her sunglasses.

The Jeep didn't lock, so she climbed into the passenger seat, put her Birkin in her lap, and waited for her sister. It had been years since she'd felt this kind of shame. The shame of putting your needs in front of someone else's and making things worse. She would remember her mother's fear until she died.

"That was awful," Margot said into the silence of the car after Julia slammed the door.

"It wasn't great," Julia admitted. "We are the worst."

"We really are."

"I'm sorry."

She looked over at her sister in surprise.

"What?" Julia asked. "It's so shocking?"

"It is, actually."

"It's hard," Julia said. "Because she's there but she's not. Or she's there and she's gone. And she's still so young and it's all just really unfair." Julia took a deep breath that shuddered, and Margot set her anger aside and gripped her sister's hand. "But there's no way Mom would have forgiven Dad if he cheated."

"Oh my god, just drive, would you?"

"Let's go get a pepperoni roll," Julia said.

"Yes," Margot sighed. "Let's."

Twenty minutes later, loaded up with fresh, warm pepperoni rolls from Mancini's, they pulled up in front of the house. They weren't even halfway up the walk before the front door was flung open and Skye stood there, trembling. Eyes wide.

"What's wrong?" Margot walked faster and then ran to the door. "What happened?"

"I'm sorry . . ." Skye whispered.

Instinctively, Margot looked around for paparazzi. She imagined someone knocking on the door and Skye answering and getting photo-bombed and peppered with awful questions about her father's sex life. "Come on, let's get inside."

She crowded her daughter into the foyer. Julia came in after her and shut the front door. Locked it for good measure. Watched out the window for the bad guys.

"I didn't know what to do," Skye whispered.

"About what?" Margot asked.

"Hello, Margot."

It was a painfully familiar voice. Masculine and rich, touched with his Midwestern roots he couldn't shake when he wasn't playing a character. It was a voice that used to send shivers across her skin. In certain times and circumstances, his voice made her cry. Made her wet. Made her laugh her head off.

Standing in the living room of her safe place was her husband Jack.

Women can't just go around accusing people of crimes they didn't commit. That kind of behavior ruins lives. And whoever this Lady X is, she's gonna have to answer for what she's done to people. It's not right.

—Officer Sherman Boyle

Lady X Strikes Again

—*Village Voice,* June 3, 1977

CHAPTER 11

May 1977
New York City

Ginger

The chill from the night followed them into the apartment, settling into their bones and turning to panic. Helplessness. The apartment Ginger had lived in for the better part of six months looked completely foreign to her. The spider plant. The dishes on the coffee table. Rachel's coffee cup from that morning.

All signs of a life lived before this unfathomable moment. It was like going into a museum and seeing the dinosaur exhibits.

Ginger stood in the doorway of Rachel's room and watched her pack, not sure how to help when she'd just made it so much worse.

"I'm sorry," Ginger said. Which was stupid. But she couldn't stop herself. There was nothing in her to adequately meet this moment. Ginger hadn't learned grace from her mom. She hadn't learned how to make right what she'd ruined.

"For what?" Rachel spat.

"For making you go talk to him." Ginger carefully walked into Rachel's room, like there were land mines buried under the hardwood. She leaned against the window, the glass cold at her back.

"It's not your fault," Rachel said, and wiped the tears from her chin. Her neck was wet. Her eyes were swollen. Ginger wanted to get her a damp washcloth, something cold to put over those sore-looking eyes.

"Are you really going to leave?" Ginger wanted to hug her so bad, but Rachel was shrouded in barbed wire and no trespassing signs.

"How do I stay?" Rachel cried. "How do I . . ." She gestured around the room. "How do I get up in the morning? How do I go to bed tonight? How do I walk around a city filled with men who would hurt me if given a chance? What do I do with all this . . . ?" She made fists of her hands and screamed in her throat.

Ginger thought of Shane at the Orbit Room asking for that hand job like he was asking for a cup of coffee. Like it was both Ginger's job and nothing at all. And Ginger had turned her face to the side and closed her eyes and thought about the starlings at home and how they flew together, hundreds of them making those shifting, changing, eerie formations. Her fifth-grade teacher told her the smaller things worked together to scare off the bigger things that would hurt them.

When the hand job was over, Shane had handed Ginger her uniform. In the bathroom she cleaned herself up and buried that memory down deep with the rest of the bad ones. But now Ginger wondered, what if she had said no? How far would Shane have gone to get a fucking hand job?

As far as the bookstore owner?

"He shoved me against the table I had stacked. The table I set up and stood behind and poured coffee at. The table I *organized*," Rachel said.

Faye stepped into the room and walked right up to Rachel, ignoring the land mines. She wiped Rachel's eyes with the flats of her hands. A gesture that was so tender and so practical at the same time.

"And I said stop and he said I could scream but no one would hear me. So I didn't scream. I didn't scream." Rachel shrugged. "I didn't. I don't . . . is it the screaming that makes it rape? Is it the bruises? I said stop. I said no. I asked him. Begged . . ." She stopped and reached for more clothes, throwing them in the suitcase.

"This does not get better if you go home," Faye said.

"Then how does it get better!" Rachel shouted. "How?"

"It doesn't." Faye's words were like a death knell. Ginger wanted to argue that surely it had to get better. Something had to make it better. If she buried these memories in some dark place and never thought about them? Pretended it never happened. Built something different on top of the night's rot.

Rachel closed her swollen red eyes. The tears were gone. Her breath heaving and heaving like she was running and couldn't stop.

"I have to *do* something. I can't do nothing," Rachel whispered.

When she opened her eyes, they were stone-cold. Gunmetal. She was a soldier home from war who had to live with what she'd seen.

"I know something we can do," Faye said. "And it will make you feel better."

"What?" Ginger asked, scared of the look on Faye's face.

"Something that will hurt him."

"I want to hurt him," Rachel said, as bloodthirsty as Faye.

"Hold on a second," Ginger said, trying to pull on the reins. "Is it bad?"

"Is what happened to Rachel bad?" Faye snapped, and Ginger felt a thick, sticky wave of shame. "Is what Shane did to you in that office bad?"

Ginger stiffened. She hadn't told her. She hadn't told anyone. It was the vile secret she kept swallowed. But of course Faye knew. Faye knew every vile secret.

"Of course it's bad. But I don't want her to end up in jail on top of . . . everything else."

"Everything else?" Faye said, her eyes narrowed, her voice just one shade from a sneer. "You can't even say it."

Ginger didn't want to say it. Didn't want to watch Rachel flinch every time she heard the word. Ginger wanted to make this better, not keep hurting her.

"Rachel." Faye turned to her, ignoring Ginger. "Do you want to get revenge on the man who raped you?"

Rachel nodded.

"Won't he know it was her?" Ginger said.

"He would have to confess what he did," Faye said. "And he'll never do that, will he?"

"I don't care. I want him to know it was me," Rachel said.

Faye nodded like the deal was struck, and never in Ginger's life had a night moved so fast. Not even the night she left home, her mother screaming from the door of the trailer. Every second that passed was some new thing. Every second that passed, Rachel reinvented herself into a new person. And Faye burned brighter. And Ginger was trailing behind.

"In or out?" Faye asked, like she'd been waiting for this moment.

"What are we doing?" Ginger demanded.

"I don't care," Rachel said. "I'm in."

At three A.M. they were alone on the city streets. They kept to the shadows near the buildings on Fourth. Stepping over garbage and foul puddles, startling rats and avoiding the lights. The bookstore when they got there was surrounded by other dark windows. A poster shop and a hardware store with ladders on display.

Ginger could hear the diesel engines of the meat delivery trucks rumbling down Bleecker, but otherwise the night was quiet. The three of them stood in front of the window, under the awning that hadn't been rolled up for the night.

He was too busy raping Rachel to bother.

Anger swamped Ginger's fear. Her trembling hands, cold with nervous sweat, curled into fists.

They wore black sweaters and hats despite the heat. In a night that felt horrifically dramatic they were dressing the part.

She'd brought up Son of Sam, that maybe they should be scared going out alone so late, but Faye and Rachel didn't care. They were the scariest things in the city tonight.

Faye dropped from her shoulders a dark blue duffel bag with red straps that Ginger recognized from the coatroom at the club.

"What are you doing with that?" Ginger asked, as if stealing from the lost and found even registered in the crime count for the night.

"It's been there for weeks. No one is coming back for it."

"When did you take it?" she asked, like it mattered.

Faye ignored her and unzipped the bag, revealing a crowbar and cans of spray paint. Rachel reached in and took the crowbar, smacking it against her hand and smiling at the heft of it. The night was spinning toward chaos and Ginger didn't know how to stop it.

Didn't know if she should.

Or wanted to.

Rachel reached up with the crowbar and tapped the canvas. And then, like she was opening a beer, she tipped the crowbar, caught an edge, used all of her strength, and ripped it right down the middle.

Rachel laughed, a manic sound at odds with her tear-swollen face.

"Shhhh," Ginger said, rushing to stop her even though she was only doing what they were there to do.

"*Jésus,*" Faye sneered. "Why did you come?"

"To stop you two from being arrested!"

There was the *click, click, click* of a spray-paint can being shaken, then Faye sprayed the word *RAPIST* in huge letters across the front glass. The word filled the whole window. Top to bottom.

It was like a scream. A pointed finger. An accusation not even Boyle could dismiss.

This was happening. It was now.

"No one is going to save us. No one is going to care," Faye said. "We have to do it ourselves."

Ginger remembered all at once every shitty thing she'd buried deep. The bones on which she'd tried to reinvent herself. The pervert on the express train who pretended to fall asleep and put his hand on her thigh. The men her mom dated who leered at Ginger. The janitor who groped Brenda. Mr. David who always stood too close in math class. A million shitty dates who thought buying her a hamburger gave them a free pass to her body. Shane and his hand jobs. Brady at the dance studio.

Come to my place on Saturday. Show me what you've got.

Ginger held out her hand. Faye's smile was feral. The gap in her teeth held monsters in the shadows. She smacked a can of spray paint in Ginger's hand and another one in Rachel's.

This is what I've got.

Ginger stepped forward and wrote the word *liar* across the top of the door. *Liar. Rapist.* The tiny white nozzle was nothing under the pressure of her finger. The smell of ozone and paint made her high. She started drawing dicks on the awning. A doodle Mick Palmer taught her in fifth grade when he thought he was being so naughty.

Mick Palmer once tried to pay her five dollars to lift her skirt for him and his friend, whose name Ginger couldn't remember. She almost did it too. Five dollars was a lot.

"What are you doing?" Rachel asked.

"Drawing his tiny dick."

Rachel hooted and clapped a hand over her mouth.

"Hurry," Faye said. "Before someone calls the cops."

Faye's comment sobered them, and they got serious about the job. Rachel and Faye wrote *rapist* over and over again in big letters and small, across the door, the window, the sidewalk in front of the building. What was left of the awning. And Ginger kept on with the dicks. A hundred of them.

"You need to sign it," Faye said.

"She can't put her name on that!" Ginger protested, pointing at the door.

"Not *her* name. *A* name," Faye said, as if the distinction was clear.

"A nom de plume," Rachel said, like she loved the idea. The writer in her coming out to join the fun. She shook the can and in an empty space in the middle of the door, right above the mail slot and below the window where it was framed prominently, she wrote:

Lady X.

"I love it," Ginger said.

They stepped back to examine the work. It was violent. Furious. It demanded to be seen. Dealt with. He couldn't hide this or pretend it didn't happen.

"*Parfait,*" Faye said, like the front of that store matched the dark inside of her body.

Rachel, who'd been a trembling, untouchable monolith all night, threw her arms around Faye. And Faye wrapped her arms around Rachel. Ginger piled in too. Holding them tight. Breathing them in. Someone was laughing. Someone was crying. Might have been all of them.

"I'm not going to cry anymore," Rachel said, wiping her face, like she could just get rid of her tear ducts all together. "It's over. All over."

Faye hummed and looked up at the moon, luminous and distant, half-hidden behind some silver-lined clouds. "I think it's just starting," she said.

Blocks away a police cruiser siren screamed in the night.

Faye grabbed the bag and they sprinted down the street, through the shadows.

Rachel made a noise. A bark. Part laughter, part exalted shout, part scream of rage. Ginger felt the same thing roll through her, sharp and bright. Something between grief and joy. But all wild. Soon they were all laughing, howling, sprinting through New York City.

For once, for now, they were the fiercest, most dangerous creatures in the night.

And Faye was right, they were just beginning.

If it had just been vandalism, the city, which was full of broken windows and graffiti, wouldn't have cared. Even the word *rapist*, written over and over again in a mostly white neighborhood, would have eventually been drowned out by the Son of Sam. But 1977 was a tipping point. And women were really fucking tired. Tired of being victims. Of being voiceless. Of managing the consequences of the crimes committed against them. Lady X was the match that lit the powder keg. And thanks to community organizer Vanessa Purdy, she just kept burning.

—Elaine Moore, *Women Behaving Badly* podcast

CHAPTER 12

March 2024
Pittsburgh, Pennsylvania

Margot

J ack Cooper had the bluest eyes she'd ever seen. That's what Margot thought in the deli section of that Ralph's grocery store a million years ago and that's what she thought standing in her mother's house after the man had taken a hammer to their lives.

Really. They were just so blue.

"Get the fuck out," Julia snarled over Margot's shoulder. Through the thin curtains, Margot scanned the road for odd cars. The glint of long-range lenses.

"Julia, please," Jack said, lifting his hands as if to show he had no weapons. "I just want to talk to my wife."

"Mom," Skye said, standing there with all her armor and eyeliner. "I'm sorry I let him in. I didn't know what to do."

"Honey, it's okay." To her surprise, Skye let Margot wrap her arms around her. She pulled Skye against her chest and thought it probably wasn't healthy to be grateful for Jack's intrusion just because it let her hug her daughter.

You can be grateful for the trauma that lets you heal.

That was some bullshit one of the Instagram girls had posted on their page. Why in the world Margot remembered *that* was a real brain mystery. But there it was, and here he was, and if Margot didn't snap into action, Julia was going to draw blood.

And what would be wrong with that? she wondered. If she let Julia at him. If she joined in? Suddenly she wanted to *bite* him. Sink her teeth into his billion-dollar body until he screamed.

Jesus. Margot. Get it together.

"Julia," Margot said, squeezing her daughter one last time. "Just give us a minute, would you."

"What?" Julia cried. Of course she didn't see why Margot would give Jack a minute of her time, but that was the difference between her and Julia. One of a million.

"It's okay. I swear." Margot patted Julia's shoulder and tried to hang as much assurance on her face as she could manage. A lie, but hopefully a good one.

Clearly, Julia didn't believe it, but she allowed it. "Fine. But you get five minutes and that's it."

"Julia, honestly, we don't need your refereeing," Jack said, but Julia growled at him as she walked past. "Come on, Skye," she said, looping an arm around her niece's shoulders. "Let's eat some ice cream and eavesdrop."

"Please don't," Margot said.

Julia offered no assurances. "She's totally eavesdropping," Jack muttered when the living room was empty.

"What do you want, Jack?" Margot asked. Exhausted by loving him and hating him and hating herself for caring at all. Margot wished she could be more like Julia, but she was stuck being herself. She remembered when they found out she was pregnant with Alex. They'd barely been dating five months. She was just starting her junior year at UCLA. She'd been accepted on the biophysics research team, studying REM cycles and brain activity in Parkinson's patients. It was everything she wanted to do, and a baby was going to put all of it in jeopardy.

She had taken the test in Jack's apartment and burst into tears.

Jack was thrilled about the baby. He lit up like she'd never seen him, not even when he got a recurring role on that sitcom that kept winning Emmys. Jack listened to all of her concerns and he agreed it would be hard, but he rejected that it would be impossible. Their moms could come out and help. They could go down to city hall that day and get married. A ridiculous idea that she rejected.

Because a baby was a blessing.

In fact, he insisted so hard and so well that she swallowed down the word *abortion* and never thought it again. Well, that wasn't true. When she lost the spot on the research team because the morning sickness was so profound, so unfixable, and so unbearable that she couldn't drive a car. Or even be in a car. Or stand up. She tried. She did. Harder maybe than she'd ever tried at anything before, but she missed three half days in the first six weeks of the program and she'd been asked to step aside.

That day she sat in her car and cried and thought the word *abortion*.

But then the sickness faded, and she was able to go to class, and then Alex was born, pink and screaming with a head full of dark hair. He was set at her breast, and everything shuffled around him. Sweet Alex. Her first. With his inquisitive, methodical mind. They spent hours outside looking at birds' nests and spiderwebs.

School, the focus of her whole life, was replaced by that boy. With being a mom.

When she got pregnant again so quickly, and with twins, it was just a matter of survival. She turned her back to the world and wrapped her arms around her family. She thought of the way her mother had made her feel when she was young, so seen and so important, and she just tried to do that. To be that.

The sob she'd been swallowing down, all the sobs she'd been swallowing down, they rose up in her throat. She pressed her fingers to her lips and tried to breathe through the pain.

Jack had gotten his first movie and then his second and he was gone for long stretches, but when he was around, he was deeply focused on the family. When he got big enough that they could go with him, well, those years had been the happiest. For her. Life kept happening and she just held on.

What came next might have been the happiest for Jack. Those years of mega fame. Of stratospheric money and recognition. His choice of projects. Of co-stars and directors. Challenge followed by challenge. His first Academy Award for the baseball movie. They finally got married. A splashy ceremony in the hills above Santa Barbara.

But then a sudden softening of box office numbers. The new script for the next movie in his *Code Name* franchise was put on hold, then the part in the Ron Howard film he'd been sure was his went to that handsome Australian actor. And then he was offered a rom-com that he took with the promise that he'd be playing opposite Reese Witherspoon, but Reese was replaced by an unknown and far too young actress and the chemistry had been so awful the movie didn't just tank, it became a laughingstock. He was a meme and one of his terrible lines was a viral TikTok sound and he couldn't get away from any of it.

"Honey." He stepped forward now and Margot flinched back. He noticed and blanched. "I just want to talk. You left and we . . . we didn't talk."

"What is there to talk about?" she asked. "All of it is true, isn't it? You . . ." She lost the words. Fucked those girls. Masturbated in front of them with and without their consent. Sent dick pics all over the internet. Harassed women barely older than his twins.

"I'm sorry. The last thing I ever wanted to do was hurt you."

"Bullshit!" Julia shouted from the kitchen.

"Julia!" Margot cried. "Please."

She heard the creak of the stairs as Julia and Skye went up, and Margot let out a shaky breath. "How in the world did you think this wouldn't come out?"

He shrugged, pale and haggard, and she knew. She saw him. Those places in him so inured to shame, wiped clean by all his money and all his fame. Protected by his reputation as the Nicest Guy in Hollywood. He thought he wouldn't get caught. That the world would always bend toward him.

Had he always been like this? Had she just refused to see? Or had he just been a man, granted so many freedoms and privileges that he lost touch with himself? With decency?

She thought of all the ways she'd compromised over the years, letting go of little things, because he seemed to care more. But had he? Or did he just expect her to agree? To do what he wanted?

Is that why he cheated? she wondered. *Because I was a doormat? Because I never put up a fight?*

She thought of what her sister would think of her taking responsibility for his shit behavior and forced herself to stand up straight and keep her chin in the air. He cheated, not her. This was all on him.

"I was an idiot," he said with utter and complete conviction. "And I'm sorry to just show up like this, but we have a crisis and you're not answering your phone."

"I don't want to talk about it yet, Jack. I don't know how to make that any more clear—"

"The publisher pulled the book."

Margot blinked. "What?"

"Your business, your *brand*, is in trouble, Margot. You need to make a statement."

Margot shook her head. None of this was making sense. "You're here because of the *book*? That's the crisis?"

She saw how he wanted to cloak himself in this lie, pretend that he was noble and caring. But he couldn't do it. She didn't have to call him on his bullshit. He was doing it himself.

"No," he said. He wore the blue sweater she'd bought him for Christmas. She bought him a blue sweater every Christmas because on their first Christmas she bought him a blue sweater and he loved it so much. It was one of a million jokes between them. Small traditions. Little things that made up a gigantic life. She felt another sob rise up, or maybe it was a scream, possibly vomit? Whatever it was, she swallowed it down. "Of course that's not the only crisis."

Margot cocked her head, examining him. "It's just the one you wanted to lead with? Like maybe I cared more about my 'brand' than my marriage."

He took a deep breath and looked down at the floor. His hands on his hips. "Of course not."

"Then cut the crap, Jack, and tell me what's going on."

"The studio is putting the war movie on hold."

Margot sucked in a deep breath and forgot to exhale. *Good*, she thought. *Good*.

"Margot, you can hate me. You can divorce me if we get to that place. But a statement right now, from you, from us, would go a long way to saving both our reputations."

"What kind of statement do you think I should make?" Margot was lightheaded and would have sat down in her dad's old armchair but she didn't want that power differential for the rest of this conversation. She needed all the power she could get.

"That we're committed to our family. That we are committed to each other. That we're working our way through this as authentically and as respectfully as we can as a family."

That language bothered her. It bothered her because it was so perfectly suited to her *own* brand.

Jack wouldn't use the word *authentic*. She remembered when Noelle put that word in Margot's mission statement, he'd asked Margot what it even meant. Not that he didn't know. He just didn't understand how you lived a life authentically. Didn't the decision to be authentic and then live that way make it unauthentic? Performative.

There was a buzzing in her brain, a waiting calm. And she wanted to cling to it even as the penny dropped.

Noelle had helped him.

Noelle, her trusted and valued employee—her *friend*—had talked to Jack. And had helped with that statement. Probably got him on the jet to Pittsburgh. Lord knows he hadn't made his own travel plans in twenty years.

She could have screamed. But she didn't. For that she gave herself full marks.

"Did you talk to the kids?" she asked instead.

He opened his mouth and then shut it. He wanted to argue more about this statement, she could tell. "I tried. Ellen is the only one who talked to me."

That made sense; Ellen had always been a daddy's girl. Crying out for him when she got sick. Calling him for money when Margot cut the purse strings.

"Alex emailed," he said. "He's . . . disappointed."

Yes. He would be. Her moral son who saw the world in black and white. "Amelia texted. But Skye. . . ." He blew out a breath.

"She's mad."

He nodded. Outside a bird flew past the window and lingered at the bird feeder the twins had given her mother for Christmas years ago. The bird was a blue jay. They were mean. Territorial.

"Margot," Jack snapped, pulling her attention from the window back to him. "Can we please just talk? We don't need to make any decisions, but we need to talk. You're my wife. I . . . miss you."

Again, he wasn't lying.

She missed him too.

That was the part she didn't know how to deal with. The rage felt appropriate. So did the grief. But missing him? Missing the man who made her a laughingstock in front of the world? What kind of woman was she? She could never say that out loud to Julia; she'd lose her mind.

But it was true. She missed the way he smelled. The sound of his feet on the steps. She missed his hand on her back as he got the cream out of the fridge while she poured coffee into two mugs every morning. She missed the way he told her about the show he watched after she went to bed.

She missed *them*. She missed their home and their life and the way people revered them. Did that make her shallow? Probably.

"I'm not ready to make a statement," she said, turning away.

"Margot," he said. "This is millions of dollars, hundreds of jobs."

"How in the world is a statement from me going to fix that?"

"You haven't looked at social media?"

She didn't even bother answering.

"It's a forest fire and it's taking over everything. People are making up lies and stories, and without a statement it's just burning through everything we've worked for."

"I still don't understand how a statement from me changes anything."

"People need assurances. Without that, the news cycle is endless with speculation and gossip. You say something and it will die down. Without a statement it's never-ending."

"Well, you should have thought of that before you sent pictures of your dick to a bunch of women on the internet. I appreciate you trying to make this my fault, but I'm going to have to remind you, you did this to yourself." She spat the words at him and it felt good. Righteous.

"Margot." He stepped forward again, his hand reaching out for her. She watched it coming and for some reason didn't flinch away. It was a science experiment. Would her husband's touch feel the same after what he'd done? Their bodies were the same. Their skin cells. Nerve endings. His biochemistry was familiar. Beloved. His hand wouldn't have changed. Neither would his smell.

His palm curved around her shoulder, the way it had a million times before. They'd been married a long time, and his touch had been a lot of things, but it had never made her skin crawl before. It had never made her feel hunted.

Used.

Manipulated.

Now it did.

She smacked his arm away and stepped back.

His hurt expression, which was hilarious, quickly hardened into anger. "I'm staying at the William Penn downtown."

"What?" she cried. "Jack! What are you doing?" It would only be a matter of time before the paparazzi found him. Which would lead to her and Skye.

"Trying to keep my family together!" His veneer cracked and she could see the panic in him. The pain. And she was white-hot with rage.

"This isn't about your family. It's about your career."

"You're the one who combined them. You're the one who put our kids center stage. Put *us* center stage. You're the one who had to be so good at something, you turned the only thing you were doing into a goddamn brand."

She shook her head, backing away, terrified suddenly of how badly she wanted to smack him. To rake her nails across his face. She wanted blood.

How *dare* he?

"You did this," she said. "I'm not fixing it."

The door to the kitchen opened and she expected Julia to come storming in, waving a wooden spoon at him. But it was Skye, shell-shocked and furious.

"Dad," she said. "You need to leave."

In the face of his daughter's stoic anger, he had the good grace not to argue. Margot stepped around him to stand beside Skye. The two of them stared at him until he threw his hands up. "Fine," he said. "But Skye, I'm just downtown if you want to talk."

"I don't," she said.

"Margot," Jack said, his blue eyes beseeching. Begging her to clean up after his disgusting mess.

"Go," she said. "I'll call when I have something to say."

He grabbed his coat off the old blue-patterned couch. Weak sunlight dribbled in through the windows and illuminated his face. The tiny scars behind his ears. Hidden in his brows. Despite the money spent on the discreet doctor tucked behind Rodeo Drive, he looked old. He looked chased down and worried. Margot hadn't seen him looking like that in a long time. If ever. Even when his career started to slip, he'd seemed rather sanguine about it.

It was a strange relief to see him affected by the danger he'd put their family in.

Or maybe he was just worried about his movie.

At one time she would have known without a doubt, but now she couldn't trust him or her reactions to him. And she'd never really understood how much of her life was her reaction to him.

It was rather appalling.

He turned and maybe it was the sleepless night, or the betrayal, but for a second he was a stranger to her. Just a man. A tired old man. And for that second she could actually breathe. She'd think more about that later. The relief of not knowing him. How it might allow her to skip over all the pain. But in the next second he was Jack again and the pain and anger was a prison.

"Did you tell your mom what's going on with Max?" he asked, and it took her a second to realize he was talking to Skye. She glanced down at Skye only to find her red-faced. Her eyes squeezed shut.

"Jack," Margot said, wanting him out of this damn house before he could lob any more hand grenades at them.

"You think you're the better parent. You always have," he said, softly. An evil, insidious whisper. "But she didn't tell you about Max." He opened the door and a black sedan she hadn't noticed pulled away from the curb across the street to idle in front of the house. Bruno, his driver, in the driver's seat. Jack got in the back, surrounded by dark windows and steel, and left.

She and Skye watched until the car turned left at the stop sign and vanished.

"Max?" Margot attempted, because what else could she do, really. "The boy who was on your phone? The boy from school?"

Can't you take a joke?

"What did he do, Skye?"

"Nothing."

"That's clearly not true."

"Nothing I want to talk about," she snapped.

Her daughter was a turtle; she'd just pulled herself entirely inside her body. Margot took a deep breath and told herself not to cry.

"It's already handled, Mom," Skye said. "Like . . . the whole thing is over."

"Your father had something to do with that, I guess?" she said. Which meant it was something Skye wanted to go away. Because that's how Jack handled the hard things. He used his influence or his money to make them small and then make them vanish.

The unbelievable amount of stress that was currently flattening Margot to the ground was doubled. Tripled. Her knees buckled and she had to put her hand against the wall. She could barely breathe for the weight.

Is this a heart attack? she wondered.

"Mom," Skye said. "I'll tell you if I need to. But I promise it's over and it's fine."

Margot's laugh sounded like a sob, and she tried not to be passive-aggressive. She tried to be sympathetic and patient with her daughter, who was going through her own hell. "That's all I can ask for," she said, and amazingly it didn't come out sarcastic.

"The paparazzi are going to find us, aren't they?" Skye asked.

"I don't know."

"I do," Skye said with the assured fatalism of a teenager. "They'll find us."

That night, in her parents' bed, she tried to focus on her anger. But her brain fixated on the memory of a camping trip she and Jack had taken to Joshua Tree. There'd been a rattlesnake sunning itself in the middle of the road and Jack had thrown orange peels at it, to try to get it to move. She'd been sure it was dead and to prove it she walked up to the snake. When it rattled at her, she'd screamed and run back to the car.

Jack laughed at her for hours, called her the Snake Whisperer.

She pulled the blankets back over her head and wished the anger was enough, but the grief swallowed her whole. Sleepless, she leaked tears into the pillow until dawn, when she gave up and went downstairs.

By the time Skye woke up the next morning, Margot sat at the kitchen table with a cold cup of coffee in front of her. All the curtains in every room drawn. The air was gray and thick with shadow. Skye sat down beside her.

I'm sorry, Margot thought. *I'm sorry I can't protect you more.*

"How many?" Skye asked.

"Four."

From over their heads came a thump and Julia cussing through the floorboards.

"Uh oh," Skye said, and Margot smiled faintly. She was numb. All the way down to her bones. Julia came running down the stairs wearing an old Pirates T-shirt and a pair of underwear and nothing else.

"Why is it so dark in here?" Julia asked and reached for the curtains.

"Julia! Don't—"

But Margot was too late. Julia threw open the curtains and the guys out on the lawn lifted their cameras, the lights blinding. There were at least eight out there now. They were reproducing.

Julia snapped the curtains closed and whirled around to face them. "Is there going to be a picture of me in my underwear all over the internet tomorrow?"

"Probably not," Margot said.

"Well, shit," Julia said, and then snapped the curtains open again and lifted her shirt, flashing her boobs at the photographers outside.

"Julia!" Margot shrieked and then—amazingly—she was laughing. She could not stay numb with Julia. And Margot was grateful for it. "You're gonna regret that."

"I doubt it." Julia shut the curtains again and sat down next to Margot. Margot squeezed her sister's knee and Julia pressed a wet kiss to the side of her face. "You get any sleep?"

"Yep."

"Liar."

Margot rested her exhausted head on her sister's shoulder. Her sister probably knew she was up all night crying but she didn't say anything and for that she was grateful.

"Skye?" Julia asked. "What are you doing today?"

"We're trapped here, so . . . nothing?" Skye said.

"Well," Julia sighed. "You want to go to New Jersey?"

"Jersey? Why?" Margot asked.

"Because Rachel Horowitz has asked us to come visit her." Julia looked pointedly at Skye, who sat back in the banquette as if blown there.

"She answered the email?" Skye whispered. "She's alive!"

"Who is Rachel Horowitz?" Margot asked, looking between them. She currently had the memory of a goldfish.

"She wrote those Vanessa Purdy op-eds about Lady X and then vanished. She might actually *be* Lady X." Skye put her hand on Julia's arm. "Are you joking?"

"Not joking," Julia said. "She emailed back this morning."

"Read the letter," Skye insisted.

Julia opened the email on her phone and cleared her throat. " 'Dear Julia. What a pleasure to hear from you. I haven't thought of your mother in years, but since I got your email I can't seem to stop. If you're ever in New Jersey please let me know. I'd love to tell you a few stories. Sincerely, Rachel Horowitz.' "

"She knew Mom?" Margot asked.

"So it would seem. She knew Mom and she knew Lady X," Julia said. "What do you say, want to go to Jersey?"

CHAPTER 13

March 2024
New Jersey

Margot

Skye perked up like a toddler after a snack.

"Road trip!" she'd cried and went to pack what little she had with her. And like she understood what was at stake, she came back downstairs in a different disguise.

No eyeliner. Just a little mascara. Her black hair pulled back in a ponytail.

"Skye," Margot said, stunned to see this version of her baby looking back at her. "You look—"

"Like every other basic teenager in the world," she said.

"I was going to say nice, but whatever." Margot had her own disguise. She traded in her expensive leisurewear for jeans and one of Mom's old flannel shirts so soft the fabric was see-through in places. Velvet in others. Glasses, no makeup, and a Pirates cap from the front hall closet.

"We look normal," Skye said, and Margot wondered if that was what Skye wanted. A life outside of the fame and the spotlight and the money. Would that be easier for her?

Not that normal as the children of Jack Cooper was really possible, but did she have to lean in quite so much? Should she have fought harder to give them a taste of what she'd had growing up?

At the time she'd thought they'd exchanged normalcy for something better. Excitement. Bigger opportunities. A wider world. She remembered Skye's eighth birthday and the camera crew she'd had there, documenting the trip to the wildlife sanctuary. Skye was obsessed with animals at the time, and the sanctuary had reached out, excited about them coming as an opportunity to heighten awareness.

Skye had agreed, but had she really?

For Margot's eighth birthday they'd gone to the Shannopin Country Club pool. She'd been allowed to invite three friends. Mom and Dad had initiated a cannonball contest and Dad won, but split his trunks in the process. Mom laughed at him and he yanked her into the pool. They'd kissed in the deep end like teenagers.

Embarrassing their daughters nearly to death.

"You look like Mom," Julia said, snapping Margot back into the present and the cranberry carpet and flannel shirt. She smiled wanly at her sister. It wasn't true, but it was a lovely compliment.

The Jeep was in the garage, and in a parking lot down by Three Rivers Stadium a friend of Julia's was waiting with his car. They'd give him the Jeep and take his old Subaru the rest of the way.

"I feel like James Bond," Julia said, backing out of the driveway with Skye and Margot ducking in the back seat of the Jeep, a blanket tossed over them for good measure. "Do I really get in trouble if I accidentally hit one of these fuckers?" she asked, backing up at an alarming speed.

She rolled down the window and gave them all the finger.

Once they got out of Pittsburgh and it was obvious their switcharoo had worked, the miles passed quickly. Skye sat in front and took notes as she and Julia talked about Lady X.

Margot didn't listen, just stared out the window at the rolling farmland and wondered if Jack was right.

If after giving up school and her career, she'd been so desperate to be told she was good at something that she'd made her family a product.

Because it was the only thing she had.

"Margot," Julia said, snapping her attention to the front seat. Skye was asleep, her head against the window. Julia was looking at her in the rearview mirror.

"Hmmm?"

"He's an asshole who was trying to hurt you," her sister said, proving she could still read her mind.

"Okay," Margot said. "But what if he's right?"

New Jersey was actually the Jersey Shore. Not the part from that TV show. Long Beach Island, where the sand stretched for miles under a sky so blue it hurt. Mansions were set back behind a high dune. Half the houses were on stilts, repaired after Hurricane Sandy.

Julia had a friend at the paper who gave her the keys to her beach house for the week. Margot kept offering to send that friend money until Julia finally said, "Maybe you don't understand how friendship works?"

The gray, weathered house was a block from the beach and had a mountain of kids' sand toys by the door and tea towels that said *It's 5 O'clock Somewhere*. Skye loved it.

She claimed a room that was smaller than her closet at home with a single bed and a view right into the kitchen of the house next door. Luckily, it was the offseason and that house was empty.

"Let's go for a walk on the beach," she said, and what could Margot do but agree. Julia stayed home to do some work and the two of them twined scarves around their necks and put on hats and sunglasses and walked down to the beach, where they looked like everyone else.

A shaggy yellow lab mix beelined for Skye, who'd always had a thing with animals. A mutual love. They never got one for a million reasons, mostly, though, because Margot knew it would be her that would have to take care of it. And she'd been full up on taking care of things.

Her phone buzzed. She had it on silent, but someone was pushing through a notification. *Noelle Kim*.

Later, when she thought about it, she wouldn't be able to say why she picked up. Tenderized perhaps by seeing her daughter on the beach. Missing Noelle was certainly a part of it. In the *normal* time before this . . . surreal time, she and Noelle communicated almost hourly. Mostly it was Instagram DMs, but still.

But Jack's warning about their employees kept clanging like a bell in her head. Noelle was probably freaking out and fielding a lot of phone calls and messages from other people who were freaking out and Margot was a grown woman with a team. She couldn't put off her responsibilities indefinitely.

She didn't want Noelle to quit in the middle of this.

But mostly she wanted to know why Noelle gave Jack that statement. Why she talked to him at all. Their paths rarely crossed except in her kitchen or at the occasional function.

She called Noelle back.

"Oh my god," Noelle said, before the end of the first ring. "Are you okay?"

A barb caught in the back of Margot's throat, and she couldn't swallow it down. "I'm fine," she said around it. "You?"

Noelle laughed. "Not great, Margot. Not great."

"I'm sorry, Noelle. I just . . ."

"I know. I know." Noelle wasn't great at the soft things. She was hired for her organizational skills, clarity, and professionalism. Not for her EQ.

"Where are you?" she asked. "It sounds like a wind tunnel."

"The Jersey Shore. It's a long story."

She could hear a million questions in Noelle's silence.

But "How is Skye?" is what she asked. That barb sunk deeper and she blinked tears from her eyes.

"Good," Margot said, watching her daughter take a slobbery, sandy ball out of a dog's mouth without even cringing. "Being with my sister helps."

Noelle made a disapproving noise in her throat that delighted Margot. Noelle, like much of her Hollywood life, did not appreciate Julia's charm. "I'm glad," she said.

Margot took a deep breath and let it out. "I saw Jack."

"He found you," she said, like Jack was a parent who'd finally located their kid at a water park and everyone could breathe a sigh of relief. Margot went cold. She turned to face the water, sunlight reflecting and refracting over every ripple.

It was gorgeous. But all she could think was, there are so many sharks in that water. Riptides and jelly fish. Dozens of things that would hurt a person if given the chance.

"Why'd you give him that statement?"

The quiet on Noelle's end of the call buzzed and roared.

"Noelle," she said, having to laugh, "I know you did it. Authentic? That's your language."

"Someone had to do something," Noelle said, sounding defensive. "Someone has to *say* something. Margot—"

"Why?" Margot asked.

"*Why?!* I . . . I understand you're grieving, Margot, and you're in some kind of denial, or . . . whatever. But this is your life."

"You're right. It's my life, not my brand, and I don't appreciate you wading in like this."

"It's a little late to draw that distinction, don't you think?" Noelle asked, and Margot sucked in a breath—hurt, yes, but it was also exactly what she'd been thinking about herself.

I'm more than this business, she wanted to say. *I'm more than this marriage that's imploding.*

But she'd made a business that was all about her and her marriage. She couldn't blame Noelle for seeing only what they, together, as a team had created.

"Look, I know your sister probably thinks it's noble to stay silent. Like it's the high road. But it's only confusing," Noelle said.

To whom? she wanted to ask. Margot was still really fucking confused. How was she supposed to make it easier for everyone else before it got to be easy for her?

"Release the following statement," Margot said, staring at the water. "Margot Cooper asks for privacy for her kids in this difficult time."

"That . . . that's your statement?" Noelle clearly didn't agree with it.

"It's the statement I'm making right now."

"It won't even make a dent in the news cycle and will probably make things worse! Do you know what they are saying about Jack right now? About you?"

A woman in a red coat power walked between Margot and the water. She was undeterred by the incoming waves. By the sharks. By Margot and her collapsing life just a few feet from her.

Does that woman know what they're saying about me?

"At the moment, I don't really care," Margot said.

"What a luxury," Noelle said with shocking cattiness. "What incredible privilege. You have a voicemail on your office line from Skye's school. I've forwarded it."

She hung up.

Police in this city, like Officer Sherman Boyle, are worse than the rapists they are supposed to stop. Police like Officer Boyle use their power to bully and manipulate. Lady X is telling us something about him, demanding we listen. So, in the spirit of Lady X, I have delivered a petition with 5,000 signatures to the mayor's office demanding Officer Boyle's suspension and an investigation for harassment, extortion, and rape.

—VANESSA PURDY, *Village Voice,* May 28, 1977

CHAPTER 14

May 1977
New York City

Ginger

The hard slam of the apartment door woke Ginger like a gunshot. She sat up, panicked and disoriented, and it took her a second to realize where she was. Rachel's bed.

Rachel was curled up on the other side of the bed, facing the wall. Her old nightgown pulled taut around her shoulders. In the emotional aftermath of last night, none of them wanted to be alone, so Faye and Ginger both laid down with Rachel.

Faye left the bed at some point, but she'd stayed long enough to leave her smell on the pillow. Bergamot and butter.

Ginger had grabbed Rachel's dirty clothes from the bathroom while she took a bath last night. Ginger would go to her grave remembering the pale pink stain in Rachel's yellow panties.

"Throw them away," Rachel had said, her arms around her knees. Her hair a slick dark spill down her back.

We should have taken her to the hospital. Someone with more authority than Ginger and Faye should take care of her. A doctor? Her mother?

Ginger eased out of the bed and to the door. The pigeons were outside the window. More than just the one now.

What's a group of pigeons called? she wondered. *A family? A murder?*

She knocked on the glass and they didn't startle. They stared back.

In the living room, Faye had blue-cupped deli coffees, a grease-stained bag, and the morning papers.

"What's up?" Ginger asked, scratching her head. She felt hungover. Fuzzy.

"Nothing," Faye said. "All the papers and there is nothing. Nothing about Lady X." She handed Ginger the *Daily News*.

The headline screamed: *Son of Sam Taunts Cops with Clues.*

"That's good, isn't it?" Ginger asked. Not the Son of Sam thing, but that they weren't in the papers. Ginger didn't want what they did last night to be public. It was private. Them against an asshole. The press didn't need to get involved.

Rachel came out of the bedroom rubbing the sleep out of her eyes with a hand that despite her bath still had black spray paint on the fingertips. All three of them had black spray paint on their fingers. Like they were changing from the edges in.

"You got breakfast?" Rachel asked, and Faye tossed a sandwich over the back of the sofa, which Rachel deftly caught.

"How'd you sleep?" Ginger asked Rachel.

"Faye snores," she said, sliding down the wall to sit on the floor.

"Lies!"

"You do," Ginger confirmed. Faye threw a sandwich at Ginger and she peeled open the paper to let the steam out of the egg-and-cheese.

"Faye is mad that we're not in the papers," Ginger said.

"A little vandalism isn't going to get noticed in this city," Rachel said like she had lived in New York her whole life instead of just a few months.

"But it wasn't just vandalism, no? It was the word *rapist* over and over and over again. But no one cares. Only not enough police. Only Son of Sam." Faye lifted one of the papers she'd brought and handed it to Rachel.

"The world isn't going to change because we spray-painted one building," Ginger pointed out.

"Then we need to spray-paint more buildings," Rachel said, and Faye, her mouth full, pointed at Rachel like she'd proven her point.

Rachel pushed away the newspaper. The sunlight came through

the window in squares, and she sat in the middle of one, like she was being framed in buttery morning light. "I think it felt good to do something."

"I'm sorry about Officer Boyle," Ginger said.

"For what are you sorry?" Faye asked.

"That I made you go talk to him," Ginger said.

"It's hardly your fault he's an asshole," Rachel said with a wan smile.

She felt so painfully betrayed by him. He was a monster who hid behind a nice-guy mask, who was worse than the ones a woman instinctively knew to stay away from.

"How in the world is a woman supposed to get justice when guys like that are the cops?" Ginger asked. But her friends had no answers. Or not ones they could say out loud. There was no justice. Not for women. Not right now.

"You know why I got kicked out of my house?" Rachel asked. She was peeling the wrapper off her sandwich in tiny increments and giving the job all of her attention.

"Because you're gay," Faye answered.

"How did you know that?" Rachel gasped. Faye shrugged.

"Your mom kicked you out because you're gay?" Ginger asked.

Rachel nodded. "My brother runs with made guys and I get kicked out for kissing Lizzy Dror behind Fiore's."

"Your brother is in the Mob?" Ginger cried, thinking of that handsome guy with the good teeth. And then she thought of the friend in the tracksuit and all the gold chains.

"Kinda missing the point, Betty Boop," Rachel said with a laugh.

"Betty Boop," Faye whispered, and laughed.

"I'm sorry your parents kicked you out," Ginger said, knocking Rachel's bent knee with her own.

"Thank you," she said. "I'm sorry I lied about being gay when we came to visit the apartment."

"You didn't lie," Faye said. "You just didn't trust us."

Ginger nodded. "It's not really our business anyway." The neighborhood was full of people like Rachel, kicked out of their houses, looking for more accepting families in the men and women who hung out on Christopher Street.

"You know what my brother would do if he knew about the bookstore owner?" Rachel asked. She looked up and the light caught her eyes, turning them gold.

"He'd kill him," Faye said, and Rachel nodded.

"That is justice," Rachel said, jabbing the sunlight with her finger. Her sleeve rolling down her bone-white arm. "What we did is . . . a game."

"You think we should have killed that guy?" Ginger asked.

"I think killing him is not enough," Faye said, and Ginger could only blink at her in shock. How in the world were they going to keep this bloodthirsty animal on a leash?

"I don't want to kill anyone," Rachel said. "But it felt good to hurt him back."

"It was good being together," Faye said, surprising Ginger with the sweetness of that sentiment. Faye was a lone wolf if ever there was one. Ginger was honored to be considered part of her pack.

"Hear! Hear!" Rachel said, lifting her cup of coffee.

"Hear! Hear!" Faye and Ginger echoed, lifting their cups. Rachel and Faye didn't look at all like the women who'd applied to be her roommates. Shy and nice. Eager. Saying all the right things. Or in Faye's case, not saying anything at all.

The night had turned their smiles to snarls. Their eyes to flames.

Ginger could see shifting glimpses of the women who'd been hiding.

Of the women who'd been waiting.

The day was a new kind of day. So bright the city looked like a movie. Like when Dorothy got to Oz. Color so rich it was fake. The sun pooled on people's faces and got caught in their hair. People smiled at one another. Said hello to strangers. No one harassed Ginger on the street, and the subway didn't smell like urine.

The world was offering her its best face, and any day before today she would have believed in it with her whole heart. Ginger would have taken it as a sign of something good. She was doing the right thing. What she was meant to do.

But all that sunshine did was cast deeper and darker shadows.

And once you were aware of the shadows, that was all you saw.

At the studio Patty sat in the hallway putting on her character shoes. The air smelled like cigarettes and baby powder.

"Hey, you're doing the jazz class?" Ginger asked, sitting down next to her. She'd bought her character shoes at a second-hand store off Forty-second. They were too big and at the end of the day she'd have a blood blister the size of a quarter on her heel, but they were all she had.

"Yeah, but the teacher changed." Patty pointed to a piece of paper taped to the door. "It's Brady."

"No way," Ginger groaned, wishing she hadn't made the trek. It was hot out there and sweat was running down her spine and into her shorts. "Brady?"

"I was gonna go home, but I'm already here, so . . . I'll let him stare at my tits for an hour, I guess."

Ginger thought of the Piedmont bookstore and how that mother-fucker couldn't say anything about the graffiti without admitting to what he'd done. The power that assholes like Brady had was that the whole system bent their way with the weight of everyone's silence.

Brady came out of the fogged glass door of the men's room, wiping his nose and shaking back his hair like a knock-off Ryan O'Neal.

"Hey!" Ginger said, getting to her feet, which slid around in her too-big shoes.

"What are you doing?" Patty asked, trying to pull her back down.

Ginger shook her off and winked.

"Brady," Ginger said, approaching him outside studio B.

"Hey, Jennifer."

"It's Ginger," she said without a smile.

"Class is about to start," he said, coked up out of his head. His pupils were dilated to the size of nickels.

"Yeah, before we do that . . ." Ginger stepped closer. Behind them the door opened and let in a stream of students who were going to take his class. "I've been thinking about that spotlight of yours."

"This month is already set, but, honey, come on over to my place anytime and we can talk about getting you a spot in the next one."

"I think . . ." Ginger stepped closer again. Close enough that he was a little nervous with the crowd in the hallway, but also very interested in her cleavage. She thought about Faye telling her she was special and that she wanted to see her dance. And didn't Ginger deserve that? She'd put the time into a system that was rigged, and maybe she should get a little something for herself. "You're going to put Patty and me in the spotlight in two weeks and we're not coming to your place. Ever."

He glanced over Ginger's shoulder to where Patty stood, arms crossed. She was the only one who could hear Ginger, and she looked terrified and delighted. Like anyone when they got a front-row seat to top-shelf drama.

"Or," Ginger said, stopping Brady just as he opened his mouth, "I'm going to start saying the words *sexual harassment* real loud in this hallway. In fact, I might start screaming it. So loud your bosses hear it. So loud those scouts hear it. And everyone will know it's true because everyone already knows you're a dirtbag."

"Bullshit," he said, but his eyes flicked over her shoulder. People were starting to watch. Ginger could feel their attention on her shoulders.

"Try me," Ginger said, with all her teeth showing. "I'm begging you. Try me."

"Is there a problem here?" Antonio, another one of the teachers, an older man in a black turtleneck, came up beside them. He helped cast *Guys and Dolls* on Broadway last year and his classes were no longer open to newbies like Ginger. He was a demigod in these hallways. Even Brady looked starstruck.

"Brady and I were just talking about his spotlight this month," Ginger said.

"I've heard about your spotlights." Antonio looked at Brady like he was dog shit on his shoe. The insinuation was clear. Behind them Patty whistled through her teeth.

"Did you get cast?" Antonio asked Ginger.

"I did," Ginger said. "And my friend Patty." She stepped back and revealed Patty behind them.

Brady looked far from happy, but under Antonio's steely gaze he wasn't going to say shit. Ginger had taken some of that power away from him.

"They are," he said through thin lips.

"Glad to hear it." Antonio patted Brady on the shoulder and continued down the hall.

"You think you're real clever, don't you?" Brady said.

"I think I got what I want," Ginger said, cocking her hip. She knew how she looked. How men saw her. It was a game she could play all day. It was a weapon. Double-edged, but a weapon nonetheless. "Without having to suck your tiny dick."

There it was. That sizzle in the air. That advance warning system every woman knew. Brady wasn't going to hit her. But he wanted to.

"The spotlight is coming up in one week and you aren't good enough to be in it. You're gonna make a fool of yourself," he said before walking into the studio.

Ginger turned to Patty, who stared at her like she was a lit bomb. The way Ginger probably stared at Faye. "What did you do?" she asked.

"Made a wrong thing right," Ginger said.

Got us a little justice.

The Orbit Room looked magical in the watery sunshine coming in the front doors. The chandeliers had been cleaned and the crystals threw dozens of prisms across the rich red carpet and the gleaming gold fixtures.

Faye was already there, wearing her uniform that rubbed everyone's neck red. She was stringing coat check tags back onto hangers.

"How was Rachel?" Ginger asked.

"It is just another day, Ginger," Faye said, her pale blue eyes pitying.

"I don't think that's true," Ginger protested. How could it be true?

"She gets up, she gets dressed. She goes to work. Tries to do a good job. The world does not care that she was hurt."

Ginger cared. Faye too. If other people *knew*, they would care. But for some reason women kept those wounds to themselves. Applied their own first aid.

She thought of the way she'd delivered Faye to Shane's door for an interview and was so embarrassed. So full of shame. And so angry at the same time. Because she'd been delivered to that door too, and afterward felt like there was nothing she could say. No complaint she could make.

If everyone suffered through that, what made her think she was special?

Todd came running in through the side door, sweat streaming down his face like he'd run from the subway. He saw them and his eyes went wide with scandalized delight.

"Have you seen this?" Todd smacked the afternoon *Post* onto the half door. There on the front page was the Piedmont bookstore covered in tiny penises with the word *rapist* across the window. The headline: *Vigilante Village Vandalizer.*

Ginger could hear her blood in her ears. A roaring thump.

I am going to throw up.

"Front page." Faye's lips curled in a smile.

"Lady-freaking-X," Todd said, shaking his head. "Great name. I mean . . ." He kissed his fingertips.

"What . . . what does it say?" Ginger asked, handing the paper back to Todd, like she didn't care. But her hands were shaking and she was scared he'd see that and her bright red face and connect two impossible dots.

We thought we were so smart.

Ginger opened the half door and stepped into the coat check.

"Calm down," Faye whispered.

Faye loved this, Ginger could see it. Todd cleared his throat and read like anchor Peter Band on WABC. To Ginger he sounded like the teacher in *Charlie Brown* and she put a hand on the wall and told her knees to do their job.

"I think that bookstore owner knows exactly who did this," Todd said when he was done reading. "I think everyone knows."

"Who?" Ginger asked.

"His wife!" Todd said.

"No. Not the wife," Faye said, and Ginger wanted to tell her to shut her mouth.

Todd put down the paper and Faye scooped it up, folded it carefully, and walked to the corner of the coatroom to tuck it in her bag.

"Whatever. It was a woman he should not have fucked with." Todd rubbed his hands together. "I love it. I love seeing assholes get what's coming to them. Whoever Lady X is, I'm a fan." Todd blew a kiss over his shoulder as he walked down the red-carpeted hallway to the dark bar and Ginger collapsed against the wall, her hands on her knees.

"Calm down," Faye said. "There are millions of people in this city."

"Calm down?" Ginger cried. "Rachel was at that bookstore last night. Someone is going to ask her questions."

"You think she's the only one he's done this to?"

Ginger jerked back. She had not thought of that.

"My guess is plenty of women are mad enough to get a little revenge."

"That isn't comforting."

"I'm not here to be comforting," Faye nearly snarled.

Ginger thought of that flyer. The girl who looked so much like Faye and not at all like her either. *Dangerous,* that flyer said.

"Change into your uniform," Faye said. "You know how Shane feels about girls out of uniform."

VIGILANTE VILLAGE VANDALIZER
New York Post, May 9, 1977

Attacked! Dennis LeRoy, owner of the Piedmont bookstore, woke up to a phone call early Monday morning that his establishment, barely a year old and a labor of love for him and his wife, had been vandalized. The couple rushed to their building at West Fourth Street and Bank only to find a crime scene.

"Everything had been spray-painted," said LeRoy. "Every window. The door. The awning. And those awnings, do you have any idea how much they cost? A lot. They cost a lot. All of it ruined."

"The place was covered in little penises," said the employee who came to open the bookstore and then notified the LeRoys of the damages. "Like hundreds of spray-painted [redacted]. So many. I mean, someone was making a point."

"I didn't rape anyone," said LeRoy when asked about the accusations. "I'm a husband. A father."

When asked who might have done this, LeRoy had no answer.

"I don't know, man," he said. "Who knows why women do anything these days?"

CHAPTER 15

March 2024
Long Beach Island, New Jersey

Margot

Rachel Horowitz lived by the lighthouse at the north end of the island. Harvey Cedars. The fancy part.

"I thought New Jersey was supposed to be ugly," Skye said, glued to the window. Her face was red from their walk yesterday and the freckles were coming out. Margot hadn't seen those freckles in at least two summers. They reminded her of sandy sheets. The smell of sunscreen. Skye's little body curled up in a towel, ocean-cold and shivering.

The twins had texted this morning. Amelia was fine. Excited about an upcoming showcase for which she was making a suit. Her parents' imploding life seemed to not affect her at all. Which was par for the course. Amelia was always very good at looking after Amelia. She'd been twenty when she was two. Ellen was going to Spain for a week, to get away from it all. Alex emailed and asked if Margot had separate accounts or if everything was joint with Jack. So reasonable.

Julia had her briefcase with her, wedged in the back seat. Inside of it, Margot could see her yellow notepads and some of the newspapers from the attic. She'd made a joke about writing a book. But it didn't look like a joke.

"Julia, what are you planning on doing during this lunch?" Margot

asked, and even she heard the edge in her voice. Skye broke eye contact with that bright blue sky to look over her shoulder at her.

"What do you mean?" Julia asked, pretending to be oblivious.

"We're here because she invited us. Not to interrogate her."

"I'm not planning on interrogating her. I'm just going to ask a few
questions."

"Bullshit."

Julia's eyebrows hit her hairline. "You okay there, sis? You seem a
little wound up."

She *was* wound up. Last night she'd finally taken half a lorazepam
and dreamed that she was nursing the twins and looking for her lab in
Haines Hall. Every door she opened was the wrong one, and the twins
were fussy and wouldn't latch, and she was running late. She opened
the last door only to find her mom looking twenty years younger,
wearing a lab coat and nursing her own twins.

"You have to try harder, honey," she said, and Margot woke up in a
sick sweat and then couldn't get back to sleep.

"I just don't want to walk in there and reject her hospitality," she
said. Which was true but wasn't what was wrong with her.

"Well, that's good," Julia said. "I'm not planning on doing that."

Julia turned off Central Avenue onto Sixth Street. The road was a
dead end at a big white clapboard house on stilts with cedar shingles
and elegant black trim. Julia followed Rachel's instructions and parked
behind the pickup truck under the house. It looked from this side like
the house was built right into the beach.

Black-backed gulls circled over the roofline and then settled out of
sight.

Margot was out the door before the car was in park. Skye and Julia
tumbled out after her. Margot had to resist the urge to straighten their
hair and coats. Julia had gone business casual, which for her meant
leggings and a long blazer. An old black cashmere coat over it. Skye
wore sweatpants and Crocs.

At Margot's suggestion that she dress up a little, Skye had said,
"They're my good Crocs."

Margot had wanted to fight about it, just really get her teeth into the Crocs issue, but stopped herself. It was too bad there wasn't some kind of award for parents who didn't fight with their teenagers. The Battles Picked Award for Excellent Parenting. She'd have a bunch of those.

Jack didn't care what anyone was wearing. Once they went to a red carpet event with Alex in the Spider-Man costume he wore every day of third grade. Jack didn't even seem to notice, and she'd thought it was a sign of how he constantly met the kids where they were.

But maybe he just didn't care. Maybe he was actually that myopic.

"You gonna unclench your jaw?" Julia asked as they climbed the side staircase to the front of the house. "Maybe pull that stick out of your ass?"

"Shut up, Julia," she muttered under her breath.

"Do you want to wait in the car?" Julia asked, like Margot was the problem. She stopped, mouth agape. "I'm just saying you've got a giant thundercloud over your head."

"I'm fine." She turned the corner of the house to the beautiful, wide wraparound porch. There were comfy chairs with blankets thrown over the backs. A gas firepit. An outdoor kitchen. All facing the end-less rolling blue-green ocean.

At the side of the house was a red door with a rose window over it. A bucket full of shells beside it.

She took one of those yoga breaths that sometimes worked. It didn't this time. But she was trying.

That dream. Jack's visit. Max, the boy from Skye's school. Noelle. The endless grief. All of it a current in her chest, electrifying her body. She was working so hard just to act normal. One foot in front of the other. Smile.

Before Julia could ring the doorbell, the red door was pulled open and a woman with wild silvery-gray hair wearing a chambray shirt tucked into tan pants appeared.

"Julia?" the woman asked, her full mouth pulling into a wide smile. She wore silver bracelets and no shoes. A wide leather belt around her waist.

"Yes," Julia said. "Rachel?"

"Yes!" She threw up her arms, her face wreathed with genuine joy.

Margot let herself smile and did her best to shake the storm cloud Julia had been right about. "Oh my. Look at you. You don't look a bit like your mother, do you?" Rachel asked Julia, who hooted. Julia always loved a bold woman. Until they butted heads and it all went sideways.

"No. But my sister." Julia turned and held out a hand toward Margot.

Rachel put her hands to her mouth and her eyes filled with tears. Margot was strangely put off by all this emotion from a woman they not only didn't know but had never heard of.

"You're the spitting image of Ginger," Rachel said.

"I take that as a compliment."

"You should. Your mom was a smoke show. Come in! Come in!" She stepped to the side to let them all in. On the doorway was a mezuzah, and as Rachel walked past it she touched it and then kissed her fingers. A completely unconscious gesture.

"Hey, who are you?" Rachel asked as Skye walked past, in the rusty way of a teasing aunt.

"I'm Skye. Ginger's granddaughter."

"Granddaughter? Boop had a . . . My lord. Let me look at you." Rachel put her hands on Skye's shoulders and narrowed her eyes. "Yep. In the chin, there. Daring the whole world to take a swing. I can see her."

Skye, who hated being touched especially by strangers, only smiled.

"Ah! And the smile. Pure Ginger. Come in, come in. My wife has put together some food. I told her it wasn't necessary, but she doesn't listen to me."

A beautiful copper-skinned woman wearing a lilac linen tunic and darker purple leggings waved from beside a table crammed with food.

"I could eat," Skye said, which made both Rachel and her wife beam with joy.

"Nadia, this is Margot, Julia, and Skye," Rachel said, ushering them in.

"So nice to meet you." Nadia shook Margot's hand with both of hers. Then did the same with Julia and Skye. Her earnestness was sincere. "Rachel has been beside herself since your email."

"Beside myself?" Rachel said as if embarrassed. "I wouldn't say that."

"What would you say?" Nadia asked with the kind of teasing affection Margot knew inside out. Nadia pressed her hand to Rachel's neck and Margot had to look away, caught between envy and grief.

"Generally excited," Rachel said. "A normal amount." She winked at Skye. "Come sit. Or do you want a tour?" She turned to face the huge open concept living room that faced the Atlantic Ocean.

"That's the living room. We read there. Watch TV. Argue about what to have for dinner." She turned to face the opposite wall where the very modern kitchen seemed to be hiding in plain view. "That's our kitchen. It's camouflage. You can get a fridge that looks like cupboards, did you know that? About ten times a day I go looking for the fridge and find the pantry."

Margot, with her refined eye, looked at the kitchen and its marble waterfall countertop on the island. The Vouvray crystal light fixture. The custom cabinets in a lovely slate blue. It was a two-hundred-thousand-dollar kitchen. Easy.

It was a gorgeous house. A multimillion-dollar house.

Owned by a woman Mom had never mentioned.

"This is the dining area," she said, holding out her arms. The dining area was nestled in the middle of the house, between the kitchen and the living room. Classic modern concept, with a few pieces to give the appearance of rooms. Subtle changes in colors, from indigo to gray to orange to pink, mirroring a sunrise. Or a sunset. Rugs and accent pieces. Everything covered in books. Stacks of them.

It was very well done.

"Upstairs are bedrooms. My office. A toilet." Rachel turned, arms outstretched. "Good?"

Skye laughed. "Good." Even Julia smiled.

"We have tea or coffee. Some of that kombucha stuff or Diet Coke."

"We don't have Diet Coke," Nadia said.

"That's what you think," Rachel said with a grin, and Nadia gasped. "That's right. Secret Diet Coke, that's the kind of exciting life we live out here in the wilderness." Rachel put an arm around her wife's shoulders.

It was impossible not to be charmed. So charmed Margot felt tears gathering in her eyes. All this nameless, directionless emotion was landing on grief.

I used to have this.

Was it ever real?

"New Jersey is hardly wilderness," Julia said as she sat in one of the mid-century modern chairs. Margot would have picked something more informal to go with the beach house, but the teak chairs and matching table were excellent pieces. "This is a beautiful house."

"Thank you. I bought it when it was just a shack about twenty years ago. After Sandy knocked it down, we rebuilt it bigger and I don't know . . . maybe better?" She looked at Nadia, who laughed.

"The ceiling doesn't have any holes."

"I guess that's better," Rachel said.

"Margot?" Julia said. "Are you all right?" Margot realized her eyes were leaking. She wasn't crying. She was just . . . leaking. Like she was in bed with the covers over her head.

She could practically taste Skye's horror.

"Sorry," Margot said quickly. She even managed to smile before slipping into one of the chairs. "It's a beautiful house."

"First time it's made someone cry," Rachel said, generously trying to inject humor into the moment.

"It's okay," Nadia said to Margot, with earnest sympathy. "You've been through a lot."

There was a shallow puddle of silence. Rachel scowled and nudged Nadia's hip. Nadia winced. "I'm sorry," she said. "I didn't mean to bring up a sore subject."

"You've heard?" Margot asked, feeling exposed. "About . . . me?"

"It's . . ." Nadia and Rachel shared a look. "It's impossible to miss."

"We're staying off the internet," Margot supplied.

"Probably wise," Nadia agreed.

"Fuck that guy," Rachel said.

Nadia groaned and hung her head.

"Sorry, kid," Rachel said to Skye. "But fuck him."

Julia and Rachel shared identical razor-edged smiles, and Margot felt like everything was swelling and receding around her. The floor. The walls. Her head. Skye. It was like they were on the ocean and the waves were building.

"Can we not?" Margot asked, looking around the table but not seeing anything. "Please."

"Of course," Nadia said, and shot Rachel a quelling look.

"I'd offer you something stronger than Diet Coke," Rachel said as she sat down at the head of the table, "but we don't have it. I'm a recovering alcoholic."

"It's fine," Margot said with a smile. "Really. I'm fine. We're so excited to talk to you today."

"I'm pretty excited to talk to you too," Rachel said. Nadia sat down too, and soon everyone was around the table. "Ginger and I haven't talked since 1982."

"That's the year Mom and Dad got married," Julia said. Margot could see the whole timeline in her sister's head.

"I sent a blender." Rachel shrugged. Margot thought of that old Osterizer Mom refused to replace that sat in the corner of the kitchen. Tears threatened again.

"Do you know about the car accident?" Margot asked.

Rachel nodded. "I'm sorry. I would have sent a card, but I wasn't sure how much you knew about me." Rachel and Nadia exchanged a long, sad look.

"Were you lovers?" Margot asked. Was that why Mom never talked about New York City or this woman with bright, lovesick eyes?

Skye looked like she wanted to fold herself up into a black hole. Even Julia seemed shocked by her lack of tact.

"No," Rachel said with a laugh. "We were roommates in New York City."

"So she did live in New York City?" Julia asked with wonder, but all Margot felt was a growing anxiety. A mushroom cloud of unease.

"She did. A fifth-floor walk-up in the Village."

"Greenwich Village?" Julia said, like it was Oz.

"Yep. Above a pet store that sold crickets. We found those fuckers all over our apartment."

"Gross," Skye said.

"You're telling me," Rachel said.

"How long?" Julia pressed, the keeper of the timeline.

"She was there a year, maybe a little less. She moved to the city with a roommate who got pregnant and left for Pittsburgh."

"Bonnie Merkovich," Margot said. They used to take vacations to

Lake Erie with Bonnie and her kids. Bonnie and her mom were co-conspirators on the trumpet hiding. Bonnie's son may or may not have taken Julia's virginity.

And she never once talked about moving to New York with Mom.

Was it a secret?

Or a lie?

"Right. When Bonnie left, I answered an ad in the *Village Voice*. Something about being a people person."

"Mom was always ready for a party," Margot said. Ginger had been able to make a party out of nothing at all. The right song. A good hair day. The table pushed back so everyone had room to dance.

"She was," Rachel said. "I took one look at her and thought I had her pegged as some vapid party girl. But I've never had a friend like her before or since. She used to say she loved coming to the rescue, but I think it was just her way of being a mom to people when they needed one. And I think, more than a party, what she wanted was a family. Something reliable and loving to replace the one she came from."

Margot and Julia shared a dark look full of stories about a trailer at the edge of a steel town and the beautiful, controlling woman who died in it all alone.

"That tracks," Julia said quietly.

"We didn't know much about her mom," Margot said.

"I didn't either. She really only talked about her when she was blotto or a little high."

"High?" Julia asked. Julia who'd been grounded more times than a person could count for hiding joints in her Hello Kitty pencil case. "Mom?"

"Your mom was a lot of fun in 1977."

"She was fun all the time," Margot said, defensive for no good reason.

"Did she work at that club?" Skye asked, looking around at the adults in the room. "That Orbit Room?"

"She did," Rachel said with a smile. "She was a coat check girl and got promoted to the bar. But mostly she was training to be a dancer—"

"I told you!" Julia said to Margot.

Margot tried to smile, as if it was fun to learn that their mother was a total stranger, but it was breaking her heart. She shifted in her seat. Her jeans were too tight and making it hard to breathe. She could only get little sips of air.

"Was she any good?" Julia asked.

"I only saw her once at a showcase and you could tell she was mostly self-taught and a little raw, but when she was on the stage you couldn't look away from her. It was just too bad she left before all those dreams could come true."

Margot sat back, thinking about the nature of dreams and women getting older. Do they change, those dreams? Or do the women change? Or is that a story they tell themselves? Do women just give up one dream for something easier? Something out of reach for something closer? More reasonable?

Were women allowed to have two dreams?

In 1977? In 2024?

Sitting in this room with this woman she'd never met who had stories about a mother she didn't know—it felt like her mom couldn't. It felt like Ginger gave up one thing so she could settle for another.

A dancer in New York City so she could be a mom in Pittsburgh.

A biochemist at UCLA so she could be a brand in Hollywood.

Being a woman meant constant compromise.

That unease grew feverish and stomach-churning.

"She had a friend at the studio she went to, Patty? She became a dancer. A pretty big deal too. I went to see her a few times when she was on Broadway."

"We used to come into the city once a year," Julia said. "And we always went to see a Broadway show. I wonder if she was going to see Patty?"

"She was in *Miss Saigon*? I remember that."

"We saw *Miss Saigon* and *Les Mis* and *City of Angels*," Julia said.

"Then you went to see her," Rachel said. "I wonder if we were ever in the same theater." She smiled sadly. A wistful, longing kind of smile that didn't fit very well on her face. She was a woman who'd managed her regrets and didn't bring them out very often.

"I can't believe this," Margot said, pulling her collar away from her neck. Had her clothes shrunk? Why was everything so tight?

"I can," Julia said. "I can see Mom living that life."

"Why did she leave New York?" Margot asked. "Why didn't she tell us about you? Why are we only finding out about this now if it was all so fucking wonderful?"

Everyone at the table looked at Margot like she'd just farted. Like she was the one who was out of line, but this situation wasn't normal. They were acting like it was all this big lark that Mom kept secrets from them.

Big ones.

And you only kept secrets if they were bad. Shameful. Destructive.

"It was," Rachel said calmly, like she was tasked with talking down a jumper, "in the grand scheme of things, a really short time in her life. Eight months? I mean, it was a crazy year . . ."

"New York City in 1977?" Julia said, and whistled. And now Margot felt like an idiot for not knowing why that was such a big deal.

"Mom?" Skye whispered. "You okay?" She pointed to her own neck and Margot could feel the hives breaking out on her skin. She was itchy and hot. Miserable.

"Fine, honey," she said, putting her cool hands against her hot skin.

Nadia, watching all of this, poured juice in Margot's glass. Icy cold freshly squeezed orange juice. Margot took a sip and then downed it.

"The stories Ginger had from that year were probably not the stories you tell your kids." Rachel shrugged, her own cheeks pink.

"The Orbit Room?" Julia looked exactly like Mom in the kitchen after school asking for the good gossip from middle school. "It's as wild as we've been told?"

"Everything you've heard was true and then some," Rachel said. "It was sex, drugs, and disco every night, and your mom had a front-row seat. She went through Elton John's pockets one time."

"What?" Skye laughed, and Margot wanted to be happy to see her daughter laughing, but her skin was so itchy. "You're kidding."

"Nope. We could have sold the cocaine people gave her as a tip and bought a car."

"What did you do instead?" Julia asked.

"We did a lot of cocaine."

"Okay," Margot interjected. "I think that's . . . enough." Skye looked delighted.

"The place got closed down briefly and your mom and a guy she worked with stole all the champagne from behind the bar. We drank that champagne for a month."

"Mom. Our mom?" Julia said, like it was starting to wear on her how different this version of their mother was. Margot wanted to say, *Right? You're finally hearing this?*

"The Orbit Room got closed down because of Lady X, right?" Skye asked.

If Skye had picked up a plate and smashed it on the ground, she couldn't have changed the energy in the room more.

Nadia took a deep breath and held herself very still.

"Yes. Briefly," Rachel said, suddenly cagey. She didn't offer up any more information on Lady X.

"Speaking of Lady X," Julia said, reaching into her bag.

"Julia," Margot whispered. God. Her sister could not read a room to save her life. "Stop."

Julia ignored her and pulled out the newspaper clipping. The picture of the Lady X crime scene, their mom's face in the corner. *Is This Lady X?* in bold print across the top.

"Where'd you find this?" Rachel asked, quietly. The smile off her face. There was something very cold in her. Something dark and waiting.

And furious.

CHAPTER 16

March 2024
Long Beach Island, New Jersey

Margot

"I n my grandma's attic," Skye said into the heavy silence, "she has so many old articles about Lady X. We brought them. We can show you—"

Skye reached for Julia's bag, but Rachel stopped her.

"I don't need to see those again," Rachel said. "Once was enough. That spring—if it wasn't Son of Sam it was Lady X, and you'd think the way those *Post* assholes treated her she was just as bad as Berkowitz."

"Why is our mom in this picture?" Julia asked. "Why did they think she was Lady X?"

"After that picture was printed, she was the only lead the police had. So, I'll tell you what I told the cop that came to our apartment all the time, threatening to drag us down to the precinct. Ginger Daughtry was with me the day of that picture because I was writing about Lady X, and that photographer just happened to get her in the shot."

Julia looked deflated. She'd wanted to believe that Mom was more than just a mother and a wife. A bartender at a tiny country club outside of Pittsburgh. That version of their mother, the version Margot loved and held so dear, the version she'd modeled her life after—wasn't enough for Julia.

"How did you find me?" Rachel asked, and Nadia exhaled so hard her nostrils flared. "The email address you used was a relic. I was sure you found it in your mom's records."

"Vanessa Purdy gave us your name," Julia said.

"Jesus Christ," Rachel laughed, all razor wire and scorn. "Vanessa Purdy? Of course she rolled right over."

"She said you wrote her op-eds. That you were obsessed with Lady X," Julia said.

"Obsessed!" She hooted. "And she gave you my email? God, she really turned out to be just another politician. How disappointing."

"No," Julia said. "I found the email on an old newsletter."

"Well, that took some digging. You're the journalist, right?"

"How do you know that?" Julia asked.

"Your mom was very proud of you."

Julia's poker face was rocked right off and she was the woman sitting in that hospital waiting room beside her sister, praying her mother would make it through surgery.

"Your mom and I didn't talk much after she left New York, but I got a note from her when you graduated J-school," Rachel said. The chair creaked as she leaned back, like she was retreating from this conversation, and Julia leaned forward like she could change that. "She thought I'd like knowing her daughter was going to try to fight the good fight." The world swelled again, but this time it was Julia who had to blink her eyes. Clear her throat.

"You were a writer too," Julia said, her voice ragged around the edges. "Op-eds, some columns. A couple of big pieces for *New York Magazine*. You wrote about Lady X."

"Not that it did anyone any good. Least of all her."

"Why did you stop writing?"

"I didn't. I just wrote under a different name. Novels. Thrillers. A couple of movies. They paid for this house. You want to call me a sellout because I gave up journalism? Go right ahead. It won't hurt me." Margot watched a seagull land on the back porch, ruffle its feathers, look around like someone had pissed it off, and take to the skies again.

They are too much alike, she thought. *This can only end badly.*

"Why did you change your name?" Julia asked, a dog back to that bone.

"Because Rachel Horowitz was a drunk who burned every bridge that helped her get anywhere."

"But you wrote about her," Julia said. "You were trying to get the police to investigate the men she targeted. You were—"

"Stupid," Rachel said. "I was stupid. I thought I could make a difference and all I did was make angry men angrier."

Nadia reached over and pressed her hand to Rachel's, but she shook her off.

"You would think a little graffiti wouldn't even register in the city at that time. Every teenage boy walked around with a can of spray paint in his backpack. But because Lady X was a woman and she was screaming *rape* at the top of her lungs, they had to stop her. By the end of that summer, they wanted her blood. The press, the men she called out, the entire fucking police force, they wanted her dead. That picture and what they thought it meant drove your mom out of New York City."

"We didn't know any of this," Julia said.

"You stop and think there's a reason for that? Maybe your mom didn't want to drag herself through the mud again and now you're here getting ready to do it for her? Why don't you ask your sister how that feels?" Everyone gasped.

"Rachel," Nadia scolded.

"I'm sorry," Rachel said to Margot. "That was too far, even for me."

Julia had the good grace to look guilty. "I don't want to drag my mom's name through any mud. But the world has changed and Lady X is seen as a hero. Not a criminal."

"The world has changed, has it?" Rachel laughed and got to her feet. Nadia tried to hold on to her hand, but Rachel wasn't having it. "Violence against women has stopped, has it? Police believe victims now? Women don't have to walk down the street with their keys between their fingers? Young girls don't get married off to old perverts? A man's word doesn't count twice as much as a woman's?" Rachel grabbed a bowl that sat on the edge of the table and started throwing things in it. Samosas. Pakora of all types. A stick of meat. She tossed in some olives and chocolates. A half a wheel of brie covered in honey.

"So why did she keep it a secret?" Julia asked.

"People only keep secrets because they're ashamed," Margot said, unraveling like a badly knit mitten. "Because they're dangerous. Because they're hurtful."

"Or . . ." Rachel said, her angry face melting in the face of all the pain Margot was not able to hide. "Because they're protecting someone."

"Who was Mom protecting?" Julia asked. "You?"

Rachel smiled and leaned forward. The kind, teasing older woman was gone, replaced by a woman with no time for games. "Are you here to make accusations?"

"Were you Lady X?" Julia asked.

"I wish," Rachel said. "I wish I was Lady X, but I'll tell you something I've never told anyone. I'll say it once and never again. I'll give you one follow-up question and after that, the matter of Lady X is closed. For good."

Julia looked breathless with excitement, waiting for the decades-long secret to be revealed.

"Lady X was a woman named Faye Bouchard who worked at the Orbit Room with your mom."

"Are you kidding?"

"That's your follow-up question?"

"No!" Julia scrambled for her notebook and a pencil. "Did you know her?"

"Not at all."

"Where is she now?"

"That's a second question."

"Please," Julia said, and blinked wide eyes at her.

Rachel swore under her breath. "Dead. She was killed in July 1977. I think it's time for you to leave."

"No," Margot said, shooting to her feet. "No. Ignore my sister. Really, we just came to find out more about our mom. After the strokes and the accident, it's like she's there but she's not and, honestly, with everything that's happened, it would just . . . I just . . . I want my mom." Was she leaking again? A bright red hive? She didn't know; she was somehow in her body and floating above it. It felt like the fever she got after the twins were born. Mastitis.

Rachel looked at Margot for a long time, pursing and unpursing her lips like she was working on a problem that didn't have a solution.

"I'm so sorry," Rachel finally said. "For everything you're going through. And I'm sorry about your mom. It's not fair that she's going out this way. She was an excellent woman and a better friend. I only knew her for a little while. But that Ginger would say fuck your husband. Any guy who treats you and your kids like that isn't worth it. I don't care how good-looking or rich he is."

"What does that even mean?" Margot whispered. What were the action items on *fuck your husband*? What was the first step? The second? How did you know when it was done? How did you not tear yourself and your children to pieces in the process?

So many questions. Everywhere and all at once.

Not an answer in sight.

She put a hand to the table as the beautiful house and the angry stranger swam around her.

"A friend of mine once told me I was too nice," Rachel said, and not in a million years would Margot use that word to describe her. "And there are people in this world who live to kick the nice ones. You've been kicked. And he kicked you real good. So what are you going to do now?" Before Margot could say anything, Rachel turned to Julia. "I would have talked about your mom all day long. How she used to call me a sister and we slept in the same bed, telling each other secrets. Big secrets. Hard secrets. But I don't want to talk about Lady X. My desire for justice died with her. I'm an old woman, and your passion is boring to me. Here's some food." She handed Skye the bowl. "Safe drive."

"Rachel," Nadia sighed. "You don't have to be rude."

"She just ambushed me," Rachel said, pointing at Julia. "And I'm the rude one?"

Margot, Julia, and Skye found themselves ushered out the door.

"It's been a real pleasure, but don't be in touch," Rachel said, standing at the edge of the dining room where the day's shadows were crawling across the floor. "Except you," she said to Skye. "You I will talk to. I see my old friend in your smile."

"I'm sorry," Nadia said, following them out the door, onto the porch. The day had turned cold. Bitter. Clouds had rolled in and the ocean was slate gray and angry. White seagulls stormed the sky, pinwheeled, and vanished. "She's normally a very patient person, but Lady X is an extremely difficult subject for her. I think she feels responsible for Ginger . . . your mother . . . having to leave New York. And the police and press were honestly awful to your mom after that picture."

"Is that why she left?" Margot asked, and Nadia shrugged.

"How in the world was Rachel responsible?" Julia asked.

"She worked for Vanessa Purdy," she said with a shrug. "I'm sorry. For all of this." She pointed down at one of the samosas in the bowl Skye was still carrying. "Careful. That one is hot."

Back in the car they all sat in total silence, Skye staring down at the salad bowl of food, Margot staring daggers at her sister, and Julia staring out the window. Outside waves crashed against the sand, an endless roar.

"Well!" Margot cried when she couldn't take it anymore.

"Well what?" Julia asked, chewing on her lip.

"You're not going to apologize?"

"Why do I need to apologize?"

Margot made a strangling sound of incredulity. Even Skye looked like she was on Margot's side.

"You don't think you could have done that a tiny bit better?" Margot asked, holding her fingers a millimeter apart.

"All I did was ask one question."

"So of course it's not your fault. You're not going to take responsibility for what happened in there?"

"Margot!" Julia cried. "What are you talking about? I can't control her reaction."

"But you can control what you do and say once you see the reaction coming. Once you see what you're doing."

Julia looked at her. "Do you hear yourself?"

"Oh my god." Margot sat back, a headache pounding behind her eyes.

"You can't take responsibility for everything," Julia said. "It's exhausting, and look . . . it's fucking you up."

"There's a storm coming, and it's giving me a headache," Margot said, her eyes closed. The world was heavy on her head.

"Your husband did a dirtbag thing. A terrible thing. It's not your responsibility."

"I never said it was!" Margot cried. "And this isn't about me. She is the only person in the world we have to talk to about that part of Mom's life and you just slammed that door shut."

Julia humphed. "Yeah," she said. "That sucks."

Still not taking responsibility. How fucking Julia of her.

"But," Julia said, "you know what doesn't suck?"

"Samosa?" Skye asked with her mouth full. Margot sighed, always relieved to see her eating.

"Sure. But she told us who Lady X was." Julia started the car.

"Faye Bouchard," Skye said. "Who worked at the Orbit Room?"

"Let's go see what we can find out about her."

Back at their beach house, Skye rifled through the papers for the eight hundredth time and Julia tried to find anything she could on that Faye woman.

Margot took the food out of the bowl and assembled a dinner platter because they didn't have anything else to eat.

"Is there any aspirin?" she asked, her headache getting worse.

"Try the bathroom," Julia said without looking up from her yellow notebooks.

In the bathroom she tried very hard not to look in the mirror. The lighting did her no favors. She was sallow and wan and the dark circles under her eyes had their own dark circles. She found aspirin and took two, washing them down with water from the tap in her cupped hand.

There was a text from Noelle on her phone. A forwarded voicemail from the office. Margot had forgotten she was going to send that.

She pressed play and Dr. Ao from Skye's school sounded extremely dire. "Margot, I have attempted to reach you several times, and I understand that this is a difficult time for your family, but I feel we must come to a resolution on the harassment issue. I have scheduled a meeting with all parties to discuss the events between Max and Skye in the hopes we can come to an agreement on how to move forward. Please confirm if March 31 at 9:15 A.M. will work for you. Thank you."

She set her phone down on the edge of the bathroom sink. Braced her hands beside it, her wedding band and diamond clicking against the cream porcelain. March 31 was the day after tomorrow.

"Skye?"

"Yeah?"

"You need to tell me what happened with Max."

During the looting and rioting, 1,616 stores were damaged, 1,307 fires were responded to, and 3,776 people were arrested. Two people were murdered during the blackout. A drugstore owner shot a looter and an unidentified woman was found strangled in Washington Square Park. There were three accidental deaths due to fire, and one man fell off the top of an apartment building.

—NYC CRIME STATISTICS DURING JULY 13, 1977, BLACKOUT

CHAPTER 17

May and June 1977
New York City

Ginger

Her mother put Ginger in her first dance class when she was five. A parks and recreation ballet program. There were four other girls in that class and she knew within the first five minutes that she was better than all of them. And she knew in the first ten minutes that she loved dancing. Every class after that only reinforced what she knew to be true—she was going to be a dancer. She'd held on to that dream from Allentown to Pittsburgh to New York City. Through terrible teachers and amazing ones, awful classes and ones that inspired her beyond what she ever thought possible, and she never once doubted it. Not even her mother could shake her confidence.

Until Brady.

"I don't know," she told Faye and Rachel. The blood blisters had popped, and she was pressing a washcloth to one heel and soaking the other. "Maybe he's right. Maybe I'm just not good enough."

"He's not letting you be good enough," Rachel said. She was getting ready for a Vanessa Purdy meeting. After the bookstore, she'd asked if they could just host the meetings at the apartment and Ginger and Faye said yes. Tonight was the second one and Rachel was clearly nervous. She'd had some wine to calm her down, but all it seemed to do was amp her up even more. Ginger was beginning to wonder if she wasn't on something. Speed, maybe?

All the windows were thrown open, letting in a cool breeze and the shouts of teenagers in the park.

Rachel picked up Ginger's bloody socks and Keds and walked them down the hallway to toss them in her bedroom. "You said it yourself," she said, coming back into the room. "All he's given you is ... what are they called again?"

"Catch-steps," she muttered and slipped both feet into the bowl of hot water.

Since basically blackmailing her way into the spotlight she'd been relegated to the back row, with a tiny solo consisting mostly of steps so basic even a child could do them. Brady the asshole delighted in using terms she wasn't familiar with, showing her out for the bumpkin she was, embarrassing her in front of dancers who'd been in the studio for years.

Patty helped Ginger after class, but most of the others were laughing at her behind their hands. She was punching above her weight, as her mom used to say, and everyone knew it.

She wanted to claw his face, tell everyone she met what a dirtbag he was. She wanted to ruin him the way he was ruining her dream.

"You can't give up," Rachel said.

"Why not?" Faye asked. She'd made food for the meeting and set little toasts with something she called *creton* spread all over them. They didn't look good, but they were delicious. "Why can't she give up? She is young. If it's not the right dream, why can't she stop and dream something else."

"But . . ." Rachel looked from Faye back to Ginger. "What would you do?"

Get more hours at the Orbit Room. Have Faye teach her how to make bread. Take care of her friends, the way they took care of her. Maybe meet one of the nice guys she was sure existed somewhere in this city.

"My sister is not here," Faye said, staring out the window. That plastic trash bag was still in the elm across the street.

"You don't know that," Ginger said.

"I do. I know," Faye said. "That's the dream I have to give up so I can believe she is somewhere else. Happy. Safe."

It was reasonable but it didn't change how sad it was. Ginger reached over and squeezed Faye's hand and Faye squeezed back.

The front door buzzer went off, jerking them into action. Ginger grabbed her bowl of warm water and damp clothes and took them into her room, where she changed into something she thought might be appropriate for a feminist meeting. A tiered chambray skirt and a tank top because of the heat. She wore a belt low on her hips and big hoop earrings. In the hallway she ran into Faye, who'd gone the other way. She wore cut-offs and a tube top.

"So," a voice said from the living room, and Ginger and Faye stepped to the doorway. There were six women and four men in the living room. The breeze from the window wafted the smell of clove cigarettes and patchouli around the room. A woman stood near the spider plant, wearing bell-bottoms and a green crochet halter top. She had thick round glasses and hair cut into a long bob, frizzing up in the heat. She had an intensity around her that shimmered.

Rachel looked at her with adoration.

Vanessa Purdy.

"I think we have been given a gift," Vanessa said. "From out of the blue, we now have a cause, something we can rally behind. Something we can use to fundraise so we can get an office." The word *fundraise* rippled through the room like it was a secret code.

"Son of Sam?" one of the men said. "I have connections at the *Daily Mail.* I'm sure—"

"No." Vanessa shook her head. "Everyone is talking about Son of Sam; we can't get any juice out of him. I'm talking about Lady X."

Ginger clutched Faye's hands in the folds of her skirt. Across the room Rachel met their eyes with wide eyes of her own.

"What about her?" someone said. "She's just a vandal. There's a million of them in this city."

"No," Vanessa said, "she's more than that. She's clearly a victim of this violent patriarchy who has been ignored and pushed aside. And she is fighting back. How many women in this city can relate to that?"

Around the room women nodded.

"I want to find out everything we can about her," Vanessa said, and half the people in the room scribbled in notebooks like students at the front of the class.

"No one knows who she is," Rachel said.

"Exactly. Let's find out. Rachel, I'd like you to write an op-ed about how we need to listen to Lady X because she is trying to tell everyone how angry she is, how angry every woman in this city is, and if we don't listen now, things are going to get worse."

"You don't know that," Rachel said. "We might never hear from her again."

"Oh, Rachel," said Vanessa, like she was disappointed by her lack of imagination. "It's some spray paint and a name. Any of us can be Lady X."

The dance spotlight came up quick. Too quick, really. Rachel and Faye were there in the second row behind the casting directors and other bigwigs. Rachel had a little bouquet of daisies and Faye wore a beret and red lipstick that made her look so French that Ginger was immediately embarrassed about the dancing she was about to inflict on them.

Patty, whose talent was undeniable, had a gigantic solo that had all the casting directors enraptured. That, Ginger told herself, watching from the corner of the room, was at least some justice.

When it came time for her catch-step extravaganza, Ginger sold it with her whole soul. No one in the world had ever catch-stepped with as much panache as she did. Her part was small but she wasn't small, and Ginger figured that was a distinction she could live with.

The girls were waiting for her in the hallway next to a small table with a coffee percolator and cherry buns from Zaro's.

"You were wonderful, Boop!" Rachel said with a lot of conviction.

"Bravo," Faye said with slightly less conviction.

"It was a train wreck. You don't have to pretend." Ginger took the flowers from Rachel. "Thank you. These are nice."

Rachel put her arm around Ginger's shoulders and squeezed. Ginger felt a lot of pity in that squeeze.

Brady walked by, wearing his tight black T-shirt and tighter black jeans, belly pouching out over his waistband, sweat pearling his upper lip. He gave Ginger an ice-cold smile. "I hope you're satisfied." He smelled like English Leather and cigarettes and something, beneath all of that, that was sour. Rotten. Ginger looked at him and felt ignited.

A struck match, looking for something to light on fire.

"Let's go home," Rachel said, pulling them into action. "Ginger," she said with a laugh as they went down the long staircase to the street, "you were gonna claw his eyes out, right there."

Outside, Times Square was melting in the heat, drowning in its own filth. The porn theater marquees were lit up and the working girls were on the corners, bumming cigarettes off one another, their ass cheeks hanging out. Their johns and pimps circled them like flies. Like flies and jailers.

"I fucking hate this place," Ginger said as they walked in lockstep toward the subway. "Every other day I drag my ass up to this shithole, and for what?"

"Don't say that, Ginger," Rachel said, curling her arm through Ginger's. "You were good. You just obviously haven't been at it as long as some of those dancers."

"Every day some asshole—"

"Hey, honey." As if cued, a guy in a light blue sports coat and a combover stepped up to them. "Are you a package deal?"

"Fuck off," Ginger snarled at him.

"Jesus. If you're not a whore, how about you don't dress like one."

Ginger wore a black leotard and white shorts. Keds on her feet. There was no winning tonight.

Ginger burned in that subway car all the way to their stop at Fourth Street. She burned so bright and so hard that the addict asking people for money avoided them.

Officer Boyle stood at the edge of the fountain, his thumbs tucked into his gun belt like a hero in a shitty western. The girls he was talking to were barely paying attention, humoring him because he was a cop and had power over their lives.

What an idiot she'd been, Ginger thought. Trusting this man. Any man. She'd come to this city thinking she knew everything, thinking the rules that applied at home would apply here. But there were no rules. Faye was right, all that mattered was what she could steal and take for herself.

Once he saw Faye, Ginger, and Rachel, Boyle turned away from the working girls, and they took the opportunity to get away while they could. He stepped in front of the roommates, barring their way home.

Their choices were to stop or literally run away from him. Faye pulled like she might run, but Rachel held on to her. Her and Ginger both. "I'd like to ask you a few questions," he said, his intentions obvious in the corners of his tiny eyes.

"About what?" Ginger asked.

"About where you were the night of May eight."

"What happened on May eight?" Ginger asked.

"You"—he pointed at Rachel—"accused a man of rape. A family man, you said. Right? And then a family man's bookstore gets destroyed. The word *rapist* spray-painted all over the place." He stepped closer, trying to intimidate them. "Seems like quite a coincidence, don't it?"

"Not really," Ginger said. "Women get raped in this city all the time."

"Where were you that night?" Boyle asked.

"Talking to you in the park, if I remember correctly."

"After that? Come on, don't play coy with me."

"I wouldn't play anything with you, Officer Boyle," she spat.

"You know," he said, "you used to be a lot nicer before these two moved in." He waved his finger between Faye and Rachel like they were to blame for Ginger not smiling at him. Not stopping to say hello while he chatted up the working girls in the park. Not seeing what he really was.

"Isn't there a serial killer on the loose, Officer Boyle?" Rachel asked, linking arms with Ginger and Faye. "I imagine you have a lot more important things to do than talk to three girls coming home from work."

"I don't need you telling me how to do my job." Boyle stepped closer and reached for Rachel. "You can answer my questions here. Or we can do this down at the station."

"What?" Rachel cried, stepping back.

"You heard me."

He shoved Rachel. *Shoved* her. She tripped and would have fallen if Faye wasn't there to keep her on her feet.

"Hey!" Ginger cried, coming between Boyle and Rachel, who was going red with anger and surprise.

"She didn't have anything to do with Lady X," Faye said, pushing Rachel behind her. She and Ginger stood as a wall between Boyle and their friend. "We were together. She'd been hurt and we were taking care of her. If those are your questions, we've answered them."

"Shit, honey," Boyle said, a bully who was easily distracted. He focused on Faye. "You look really familiar. Do you work Forty-second Street?"

"No," she said. Boyle grabbed her by her arm and dragged her under the streetlight. He tilted her chin up so he could really get a good look at her. Ginger and Rachel shouted and tried to pull her away, but he swatted them back.

How is this happening? Ginger wondered.

"Swear to god I've seen you. What's your name again?" Faye jerked her head away and kept her mouth shut. "I never forget a face, honey. It's going to come to me sooner or later."

"We're leaving," Ginger said, pulling her friends forward. Enough was enough.

"That's right." He stepped back, his face flushed, and Ginger imagined he wanted to put them in their place so bad it was killing him to back down. "It's not safe in these streets for women. Not these days."

Faye stiffened and there was no question that was a threat. "I've got my eye on you three," he said, but the roommates walked past him, heads up, like they had nothing to hide.

The next night at the Orbit Room, Jasmine paced the hallway in front of the coat check.

"What's up, Jas?" Ginger asked, opening the half door and slipping inside. Faye followed and they put down their stuff, keeping their eye on their co-worker. "You're making me nervous."

"I had one rule, you know?" Jasmine turned, chewing a nail. She had a bruise under her eye that she'd tried to cover up, but in the heat of the club the makeup was evaporating and leaving the purple shiner. Ginger couldn't stop staring at it. Who in the world had the balls to fight with Jasmine? "I never got a friend a job here. They asked all the time but I said the Orbit Room wasn't hiring."

"Why?" Faye asked.

"Because of that shit Shane pulls in the interview. But I broke my damn rule and I brought a girlfriend to see about a job," Jas said.

The three of them looked up at that office door, and Ginger without a plan or conscious thought lifted the half door and started for the stairs. "What are you doing?" Jasmine asked, catching her arm.

"What I wish someone had done for me," Ginger said.

Before Ginger got across the hall, the door flew open and a furious woman with fingernails like talons came storming out. She wore a gold lamé bikini top and a pair of tight jeans. The kind of look on the kind of body that could get a job here no problem.

"This some kind of joke, Jas?" she shouted, drawing the attention of everyone in the foyer. "Ain't no job worth that. What the hell, girl? You can't warn a person?" She came racing down the stairs.

"Are you okay?" Ginger asked her.

"I'm fine." She threw back a curtain of long black hair that looked like it came right off Cher's head. "But that fool—" She jabbed one of her talons up at the office. Shane had the good sense not to show his face. "That fool better watch himself."

She stormed out of the club, Jasmine following her as far as the door, where they argued.

"Faye."

Faye shook her head, waving off the apology. "He didn't do anything. I bared my teeth and he pissed his pants, him."

Whether it was a lie or not didn't matter; Ginger was grateful for the forgiveness.

"Maybe we should bare our teeth more," Ginger said. The idea had a violent appeal.

Jasmine returned to the coatroom. "It's part of the job," she said.

"But it shouldn't be," Ginger said.

In the coat check Jasmine grabbed her compact and checked her makeup. When she saw how much of the bruise was visible she swore and glanced over at them, as if to see if they'd noticed too. Ginger looked away, making a show out of fixing her hat, but not Faye.

"What happened?" Faye asked.

"I ran into a door," Jasmine said, not even trying to make it sound believable. She shut her compact with a snap.

Faye shook her head and Jasmine laughed, the kind of laugh that wanted to be a sob. "Carl's had a bad season," Jasmine said. Faye reached for her like she might hug her and Ginger had to marvel at Faye's bravery, but Jasmine stepped sideways, out of reach.

"You don't deserve that," Faye said.

"Yeah, heaven help us if we start getting what we deserve, huh?" Jasmine said. "The men would be out of a goddamn job running the world."

Jasmine looked around the coatroom like she was just noticing it.

"There are no coats," she said.

"Heat wave," Ginger said. The coatroom was empty except for lost and found and staff stuff.

"Come on," Jasmine said, opening the door and waving Ginger and Faye out. "Come to the bar."

"But . . . Shane?"

"I can handle Shane," said Jasmine, who'd been promoted to shift manager at the beginning of May. "We're jammed in there anyway. We'll all swing out and make sure people aren't fucking in here."

It was an offer they couldn't refuse, to step onto the black glitter floor, under the disco moon. They walked down the red carpet like Dorothy with the Emerald City in view. A skip to their step, Shane and his bullshit forgotten.

"You're going to pick up empty glasses and bottles," Jasmine said over the funky beat of the Commodores' "Let's Get Started." "And bring them to the bar. Wipe down tables. That's it. You can keep the tips."

Faye and Ginger nodded and stepped into the inner sanctum of the Orbit Room. The music was so full, so everywhere. On the dance floor two men kissed and Divine and her giant white-blond wig danced with David Bowie.

Jasmine turned to face them, the bruise gone in the strobing lights. The sob forgotten. She was all smiles. "Makes all the bullshit worth it, right?" she said, and danced backward until she was absorbed by the party.

Faye and Ginger came out of the Fourth Street subway into air that was so still and so humid it did the impossible and made them want to go back into the subway where at least the trains created a breeze.

"When is this going to break?" Ginger asked, pulling her hair into a ponytail so it was off her neck.

"I like it," Faye said, sweat dripping down her chest. They crossed against the light, the intersection at Fourth and Washington Place quiet this time of night.

They stepped up onto the curb in front of Hongs and the quick yelp of police sirens made them jump. A squad car pulled up next to them and Officer Boyle got out.

"I need to see some identification," he said.

"Come on," Ginger said. "You know us."

"Identification, please. Two women alone at this time of night?" He shrugged. "Who knows what trouble you're getting up to."

"We're coming home from work," Ginger said, and fished out her old Pennsylvania driver's license to show him. He barely looked at it.

"What about you, blondie?" he asked Faye, a cocky smile on his face.

"I don't have my ID with me," she said quietly.

"No? Where'd you say you were from? Europe? You gotta have a passport for that, right? Where's your passport?"

"She doesn't take it to work," Ginger said, though as she thought about it, she'd never seen Faye with any ID.

He reached for his handcuffs and Faye stepped back, flattening herself against the brick wall behind her.

"You're going to have to come with me," he said.

"For not having ID?" Ginger cried.

"I'll take you too if you're not . . ."

The radio in his car crackled, the dispatcher calling for something that sounded far more dire than harassing two women coming home from work. Boyle hesitated.

"You better go," Ginger said. "Sounds like you have real work to do."

Boyle leaned in, pushing her up against the brick wall too. He smelled of sour sweat and fried food. She held her breath, her anger and bravado vanishing under the rush of fear. Being a cop didn't make him better, it made him worse.

Hongs's front door opened and Miguel the dishwasher stood there in a grease-stained apron. "Everything okay?" he asked, and still Boyle waited, breathing all over Ginger's cleavage.

"Everything's fine," Boyle finally said, and stepped back. He got back in his squad car and slithered down the street, sirens quiet.

Rachel's op-ed came out and all of New York City started weighing in on Lady X.

Host George Michael on TalkRadio 77 had a lot to say: "Don't we have enough with this Son of Sam madman? We gotta deal with this Lady X too? And what's the deal with these nicknames? Come on, cops. Help us out."

"Turn it off," said Faye. "I can't listen to him."

Ginger turned off the radio and the sound of the city came pouring in the open windows. It was another day without rain and the city was sweltering and bored.

Rachel burst through the doors with an armful of papers. "They're talking about Lady X in Jersey," she said, laying the paper down on the coffee table. "Queens and Brooklyn." She set down two more papers. "The *Times* picked up my op-ed."

"Vanessa's op-ed," Faye said from her spot on the couch. She hadn't gotten off it in hours. It was too hot to move. Ginger sat on the windowsill, catching the breeze limping in the window.

"Whatever." Rachel looked hungover this morning, and Ginger was pretty sure she put whiskey in her coffee. Ginger had been about to say something but Faye caught her eye and shook her head. "Apparently Vanessa's phone is ringing off the hook."

"That's good?" Faye asked, her eyes closed.

"It's good."

Some of the neighborhood kids had been working on a fire hydrant on MacDougal Street and there was a shout when they finally got it open and a geyser of water sprayed into the street. She knew it was her imagination, but Ginger could have sworn the air felt cooler.

She got to her feet. "Let's go," she said. "We can't stay cooped up in this apartment all day. We'll melt."

"What about Boyle?" Faye asked. He'd been hounding them all week. Faye especially.

"Fuck Boyle," Ginger said. "Honestly. We can't let him bully us into being shut-ins. Come on, the hydrant is open, let's go cool off."

Rachel stood. She wore a tube top and a terry-cloth skirt that looked like she might have worn it to play tennis in her former life. Faye protested but finally agreed.

"We should celebrate," Faye said as they all pushed their feet into the flip-flops they'd bought in the East Village at the beginning of May.

"Celebrate what?"

"You are making your boss famous," Faye said. Rachel looked as if she'd been slapped.

Outside the sun was so hot Ginger felt like an ant under a microscope. They were across the street and halfway to the hydrant before the squad car pulled up behind them. That blip of his siren, the quick flash of his lights, and Faye started to run. Ginger was so surprised she could only stand there, but Rachel turned to face the cop like she might slow him down if he decided to chase her.

Boyle got out of his car. Of course it was Boyle. Like he'd been waiting for them to leave the apartment. Just stalking them, waiting for the moment he could get his hands on Faye.

Boyle shoved right past Rachel, knocking her to the ground, and tackled Faye up against the brick building. She screamed as her face hit the wall.

"Shut the fuck up!" he shouted over her screams. He wrenched her arms behind her.

"Hey! What are you doing, man?" a man in tiny cut-offs and no shirt yelled. The street was full of people and half of them were slowing down and stopping to watch.

Ginger pulled Rachel to her feet and they rushed to help Faye. The door next to Faye and Boyle opened and a man in bell-bottoms and a Mets T-shirt walked out of Caffe Reggio. "What's going on here?" he asked Boyle like he'd just found a cat in his garbage.

"Mind your own fucking business," Boyle grunted as he pressed his weight against Faye's tiny body. She was gasping for air, her eyes wide and panicked.

Outraged tears burned in Ginger's eyes. She felt useless. If she grabbed Boyle she'd make it worse, and she could scream stop all she wanted but Boyle didn't give a shit.

"Stop, man!" a woman pushing a baby stroller yelled. "You're hurting her." The baby inside watched with wide eyes.

"She can't breathe!" Ginger cried.

Rachel tried to grab Boyle's elbow to pull him off but he swatted her away, driving his shoulder deeper into Faye's back.

A crowd gathered around them, people pushed outside and to the limits of their patience by the heat. Frustrated by a city plagued with crime and patrolled by cops who used the badge as a license to bully. Especially in this neighborhood. The drag queens were out, the gay guys who hustled on Christopher Street, most of whom remembered the Stonewall riots. The working girls and guys who sold dime bags of weed from the park who'd been tempted by the open hydrant. Single moms and neighborhood kids. The delivery guys in the white trucks. They were all gathering. They were all hot.

And they were all angry.

"She didn't do anything," Rachel shouted to the people watching. Stirring them up.

"Fuck, man," the crowd responded. "Don't you have better things to do than harass women?"

"Go catch this Son of Sam asshole and leave us alone," someone else yelled.

"Leave us alone" was echoed. And then echoed again. Until it became a chant.

Leave us alone!

Ginger shouted the words with her entire being.

Realizing he was causing a scene he had no justification for, Boyle stepped back and Faye darted sideways into Ginger's and Rachel's arms. Her face was scraped and bleeding. She was panting and shaking.

Boyle turned back toward them, pushing his hat up higher on his sweaty head. "This isn't over," he said, his red face slick with sweat.

He got back in his squad car and the crowd parted for him to pass, making a point of doing it slowly. Some of them smacked the roof of the car.

"He's not going to stop," Rachel said, her arm around Faye. The good girl who wouldn't say shit with a mouth full of it was gone and in her place was someone ready for a fight. Aching for one. "Not until he has proof of what we did or one of us is hurt."

The next day Boyle had all the working girls and drug dealers who'd seen him tackle Faye rounded up and taken to the station.

"That's because of us," Rachel said as they watched from the fire escape. Faye's face was a mess. Bruised and scabbed. She had to call in sick and got an earful from Shane. Ginger went alone at nine, relieved that Boyle wasn't waiting for her outside her apartment or in front of the subway. But he was waiting for her outside of the Orbit Room, sitting in his car across the street with the window open.

As she crossed the street, he caught her eye and waved. "Tell your boss the NYPD say hello," he called. She ignored him and hustled in. Jasmine was in the hallway outside the coat check, and when she saw her she shook her head. "You've got Shane in a tizzy," she said.

"I didn't do anything," Ginger said.

"Shane went out there to see what the trouble was and that cop told him he was just keeping an eye on you. He's paranoid enough. He's convinced someone on his staff has talked to the cops about the taxes."

"I don't know shit about his taxes," Ginger said.

"I know." Jasmine reached out and touched Ginger's arm. "But you can see how this looks. You should go home tonight. Let it blow over. Your next shift is tomorrow. Come back then, hopefully without the cop? Everything will be fine."

"This . . ." Ginger sighed. "This isn't fair."

"I know, honey," Jasmine said. "It's just the way things are."

Jasmine let her hang out in the empty coatroom until she could be sure that Boyle wasn't still waiting for her outside. Todd brought her a drink. They smoked a joint. Jasmine came in, took a hit off the joint, lifted her hair off her neck to try to cool off.

"Jas?" The swampy voice of her boyfriend cut through the music and the smile dropped from Jasmine's face before she could catch it.

"In here!" Jasmine yelled.

Todd got rid of the joint before Carl appeared in the open half door of the coatroom. He was tall and lanky with long arms and big hands at the ends of them. Ginger remembered Jasmine's black eye.

"There you are." That accent of his made it sound like he was smiling. But he wasn't. "What the fuck are you doing in here?"

"Excuse me." Todd lifted the gate to the coatroom and slipped out, Carl watching him go.

"You know I don't like you hanging out with other guys," Carl said, and Ginger laughed. Jasmine shot her a *shut the hell up* look, but it was too late.

"What's so funny?" Carl asked.

"Nothing," Ginger said, "just . . . Todd is gay."

"So?"

Ginger looked from Carl to Jasmine and back to Carl. Honestly, Jasmine might be one of the smartest women she knew, but what was she doing with this guy? "It just means nothing is going to happen. They're just friends."

"Come on, honey," Jasmine said, slipping out of the coat check and slipping her arm through his. "Let's go freshen up your drink, huh? See if Joe Namath is still here."

She led her boyfriend away and he cupped that big hand of his around her neck in a way that made Ginger's skin crawl.

When she got home, Faye and Rachel were sitting on the stoop in front of their apartment, looking up MacDougal to where it met the end of the park. Sweat gleamed on their skin under the streetlights. They were drinking cans of Tab that were dripping condensation onto the cement.

"You're home early," Rachel said, and Ginger explained what happened.

"Fucking Boyle."

"He's here," Faye said. "Well, there." She pointed up the street to where MacDougal met Waverly and Washington Square North.

"Has he been bothering you?" Ginger asked, surprised to see them outside if he was in the area.

"He eats at Hong's every Thursday night at ten P.M. Sometimes he'll have a few drinks," Rachel said.

"How do you know that?"

Rachel shrugged. "I talked to the girls in the park," she said. "And you think he's shit to us . . ." She shook her head. "At least we don't have to fuck him to stay out of jail."

"That's rape," Faye said, and Rachel nodded.

Ginger felt her lips curl with the rage that had been simmering for a week. Longer. Starting to boil over again. "He's gonna get me fired," she said.

"He wants to arrest me," Rachel said.

"He wants to hurt me," said Faye. It was so true, the motive under everything. He wanted to squish Faye under his heel just because he could.

Fuck him. Fuck that pathetic man. That bully.

"I've been following him," Rachel said. "What?" she asked when Faye and Ginger looked at her, astonished. "It's not hard. The guy is about as predictable as the moon. He's gonna be in that restaurant for an hour, if not longer. His car is parked in the alley."

That fucking car. Crawling behind them on the streets like a predator. Like a rabid dog they couldn't shake. That wouldn't leave them alone until they were bloody and beaten.

She wanted to destroy that car. Smash it to pieces. How much power did one man need? How much until he had enough?

How did men get away with it all the time?

Her body was exhausted. Her muscles tired. Her eyes burned.

But her brain was flooded. Her heartbeat too fast.

"Faye? You still have the spray paint?" Ginger asked.

There were a thousand reasons this was wrong. Police property and all. But Ginger didn't care. Faye got to her feet. Steely and full of rage that was always looking for cracks to get out.

Dangerous.

"*Oui.*"

They didn't change their clothes. It was too hot and the night was enough camouflage. They grabbed the bag from Faye's room and slunk back out into the shadows of MacDougal until they got to the alley.

And Officer Boyle's squad car.

Behind the car in the darkest shadows, Faye set down the bag and handed out the spray cans. Rachel took one, shook it, and wrote *rapist* in big letters across the hood.

The sound of the cans and the smell of aerosol paint filled the night. Two cats leapt away, leaving them with the rats. The carriage and row houses around them were dark. The lights from the bar where Boyle was eating illuminated the mouth of the alley.

Ginger slipped deeper inside of herself, until she practically disappeared. The way she did in that office with Shane at the club. She was instinct and a body full of violence.

Ginger drew the dicks and blacked out the taillight, but it wasn't enough. She dropped her nearly empty can in the bag and pulled out the crowbar. She liked how it felt in her hand. Like it could do damage. Like it was tougher than her. Harder than her. A weapon with no double edge.

She swung it back with her exhausted muscles, her teeth bared, her heart screaming, and smashed out the rear taillight.

The noise was shocking. A dog barked in one of the apartments around them. A light flicked on.

"Jesus, Ginger!" Rachel whisper-yelled. "What the hell?"

Ginger smashed out the other taillight and took two swings at the rear window. It cracked and splintered into spiderwebs. She climbed onto the trunk of the car and took out the cherries on top. She looked down at her friends and felt more alive than she'd ever felt. More alive than she could imagine feeling. She filled every inch of her skin.

Her friends looked up at her, eyes glowing. Teeth showing. They reflected a version of Ginger that she wanted to believe in. That she wished she was.

Powerful. Righteous. Magnificent.

They were glorious souls, those two. Finding Ginger when she needed them. And Ginger hoped, man, she *hoped*, she gave as much to them as they gave her.

I love them.

I would do anything for them.

Anything.

"Sign it," Faye said, holding out her can. Ginger jumped down and scrawled *Lady X* across the hood. In the cursive Mrs. Place taught her in third grade.

"*Et voilà*," Faye said. Without having to say a word to one another, they ran in opposite directions to toss the cans, the duffel bag, and the crowbar in different dumpsters.

One by one they found their way back home. Back to Rachel's bed, where they collapsed fully dressed, curled up like animals in her blankets, safer together and unwilling to be apart.

Hair smelling of aerosol.

Fingers black with the crime they'd committed. The vengeance they'd sowed.

The justice they'd delivered.

LADY X STRIKES AGAIN

Daily Mail, June 3, 1977

An NYPD squad car was found vandalized and destroyed near Washington Square Park in the early hours of Thursday morning. Officer Sherman Boyle, who was issued the squad car, claims he was in the neighborhood conducting a stakeout on a nearby apartment building.

"I stepped out to get a cup of coffee and a donut and I came back to a mess."

His squad car was covered in graffiti, the word *rapist* painted across the hood and doors of the car. According to witnesses, the car was covered in hundreds of little penises. The lights and rear window were all smashed out.

It was signed *Lady X.*

"It's nonsense," Officer Boyle says in his defense. "I've never hurt a person in my life. I'm a cop."

This is the second crime scene signed by Lady X. The first was a bookstore on West Fourth Street. According to sources there is nothing to link the crime scenes except the signatures and the nature of the accusations.

"I'm going to find out who this woman is. I'll find her if it's the last thing I do," says Officer Boyle.

Police are asking anyone with information to step forward and call the police hotline.

CHAPTER 18

March 2024
Santa Barbara, California

Margot

Julia came back to California with them. Whether or not it was necessary Margot couldn't be sure, but it was appreciated. She could feel, the moment she stepped off the jet onto the tarmac at Van Nuys, the claustrophobic sensation of phones lifted her way as she passed through the terminal.

"Breathe," Julia said, locking her arm through hers, her other arm securely around Skye's shoulders. All of them wearing dark glasses like they'd had a little work done in Costa Rica.

She remembered with sudden clarity coming home for Christmas for the first time after she moved out to Los Angeles. The way her sister slept in her bed that first night. And they'd breathed eggnog and Mom's garlic rolls all over each other. She'd slept so well that night, only to wake up and find her mom curled up on the other side of Julia.

The three of them in a single bed.

It hurt how much she wanted that moment back.

They stayed at El Encanto in Santa Barbara, a garden suite with two bedrooms. An outrageous expense considering she had a home only a few miles away, but she wasn't ready to go back to the house. Part of her was extremely content to pretend that house didn't even exist. Jack's infidelity had wiped that house off the face of the Earth.

Skye claimed one of the rooms as her own and vanished, having spent more than enough time with adults.

Margot and Julia watched her go. When the door clicked shut Margot collapsed on the pale linen couch.

"You okay?" Julia asked, sitting beside her so she could put her arm around Margot. The story about Max had spilled out of Skye on the way home to Los Angeles. She'd told them everything. Showed them the text messages and the pictures.

"Not even a little." She sighed. "When I think about what that kid did to her . . ."

"I know. I know," Julia said, and Margot looked up at the sun so she wouldn't cry. "But there is a plus side."

"He tricked her into thinking he liked her and then asked her to send him pictures of herself naked. What is the plus side?"

"Skye didn't send him half the pictures he asked for, and the ones she did send were pretty tame. And when he pushed for more, she reported him. That's some ballsy shit right there."

"But why didn't she tell me?" Margot whispered, and Julia sat back like she was stunned.

"You're kidding, right?"

"No, I'm not kidding. She told Jack but didn't tell me?"

"Because Jack was going to make it go away, before he got busted for doing the exact same disgusting thing."

Not totally the same, Margot wanted to argue, but she knew she was splitting hairs.

"Honestly," Julia said, "what a criminal lack of creativity. It's like they all follow the same scumbag playbook."

"I'm just so heartbroken for her. It seemed like she really liked him . . ."

"Oh my god, Margot, stop," Julia cried, and got up off the couch.

"Stop what?" Margot asked.

"Stop being so fucking sad. Sad for yourself, sad for Mom, sad for Skye, sad for fucking Rachel Horowitz." She laughed and then stepped forward, grabbing Margot's hands. "I love you, Margot. But when the fuck are you going to get angry?"

The meeting was at the Montecito New School at nine A.M. Julia insisted on driving them and then waiting in the parking lot, car running, in case they needed to make a quick getaway. She parked beneath the pinyons and sugar pines, where the shadows were blue-gray and buzzed with grasshoppers. The sunlight coming up over the ridge behind them was warm and sweet the way it always was in this part of California.

The breeze was cool and the first bell had rung so there weren't any kids standing around. Skye's friend Amber came up out of nowhere and tackle-hugged Skye. Amber was a solid foot taller than Skye and had been since kindergarten. Amber bent to whisper in Skye's ear and Margot felt that complicated grip of emotion she always felt when she saw Skye with her best friend.

Thank god, she thought.

And also . . . *I wish.*

Margot used to have friends like that. Kind of. But the kids. The business. Jack. They all pushed things like female friendship to the outskirts. To the occasional brunch. The quick catchup at yoga. She'd told herself that was the cost of having a busy family. A strong and healthy marriage.

But it was just another compromise she made without even being asked.

She glanced back over her shoulder at her sister, who gave her a goofy but sincere double thumbs-up.

Her sister was not easily pushed aside. And their relationship was one of those inflatable Bozo the clown dolls they had when they were kids. You could punch it all you liked, and it just kept coming back up with a grin on its face.

But she was so far away. There were no quick dates for coffee or hikes on the Peak. Wine after the kids went to bed.

Amber took off with a quick wave and a "see you, Margot" before the late bell rang. Skye watched her go with hearts and grief in her eyes.

"You've missed her," Margot said, stupidly.

"Yeah."

They crossed the yellow gravel of the parking area and the bark chip path that led past the outdoor classroom, the raised vegetable beds, and the butterfly garden. In the distance the sports field and swimming pool looked artificial and ever ready for whatever practices were scheduled for after school.

They paused at the back doors.

"You okay?" Margot asked Skye for maybe the millionth time. She was as tired of saying it as Skye had to be of hearing it, but she didn't know what else to say.

Skye shrugged. Pure teenager. Margot had no idea what that shrug meant.

Julia had painted Skye's nails a fresh glittery black and she wore her eyeliner like a weapon. She wore her school uniform even though she didn't have to. She'd said this morning that it would be weird to show up to school without it. But she'd modified it in subtle ways that didn't break dress code. One side of her shirt perfectly untucked. A line of safety pins on the blazer lapel. The tie pulled loose. One green sock and one blue sock pulled up to her knees. Combat boots.

She looked like she should be cast in a movie about angsty teenagers turning into angsty vampires.

Margot reached forward and squeezed Skye's hand. "I'm proud of you," she said, pleased her voice didn't shake. The secret Skye had been keeping was a doozy, and that she'd shouldered it mostly alone was—as Julia said—fucking heroic. "Like . . . so proud of you."

Margot dropped Skye's hand, thinking of her allergy to sincerity. But Skye immediately grabbed it back.

"Thanks, Mom. And thanks . . . for the road trip and . . . everything."

A thank-you from a teenager was so rare she had to resist the urge to look around to check if anyone else had seen it.

"My pleasure, honey," Margot said, feeling like she'd had no control over that road trip, but happy to take a little credit. "You ready?"

"I guess." She shrugged, such a complicated shrug. Such an unknowable language. Skye feigned indifference, but the two of them held hands walking to the principal's office. Margot pushed Dr. Ao's door open and greeted her assistant Daniel.

"Mrs. Cooper," Daniel said with a flat smile. The guy could not be starstruck. Jack walked in with a gift basket the size of a Mini Cooper one year and Daniel just asked him to set it on the counter and went back to typing. But when he turned to Skye, his face folded into basset hound authenticity. "Skye. I'm so glad to see you. We've missed you around here."

"Thanks, Daniel. Good to see you too."

"You all right? You need anything?" Daniel got up and squeezed Skye's shoulder. "I know this is hard."

"I'm good. Thanks."

Margot stared into the sunlight and blinked rapidly so no one would be embarrassed by her suddenly breaking into tears.

"Okay, follow me on back." They followed Daniel's turquoise V-neck sweater and khaki pants past the copy room to Dr. Ao's office. Daniel knocked and opened the door to reveal Dr. Ao sitting behind her desk the size of a lifeboat. In front of the desk sat a familiar floppy-haired kid and his two parents. A stern-faced father in a very nice trench coat and pinstripe suit giving every impression that he was missing an important meeting for this nonsense. And a red-eyed mother, who looked like she had no idea how she got here.

Margot was immediately exhausted. Like down to her bones exhausted.

She knew she was going to have to deal with their anger and grief—that their son, their baby, had grown into the kind of teenager who could send the texts he'd sent to Skye—on top of her own grief and anger. And that felt like a bridge too far.

How much, honestly, am I expected to hold? Aren't my hands already full?

"Mrs. Cooper." Dr. Ao stood up. She ran extreme marathons in deserts around the world and looked constantly sun- and wind-burned. Her age was unguessable. Her office was filled with accolades and honors, framed pictures of artwork made by students. Over her shoulder she had pictures of herself in different moon-like locations, wrapped in silver blankets, holding up medals. Dirt making raccoon eyes on her face.

Dr. Ao didn't have a family. This school and those marathons were her whole life.

For a moment, Margot was jealous. How simple. How clean. How . . . uncompromising. "Glad you could make it," Dr. Ao said like Margot was doing her a favor.

"Of course." Margot sat down between her daughter and the upset parents, hoping she could be some kind of buffer. "I'm sorry we have to wait for Jack."

"He's not coming," Skye said quietly beside her. "I asked him not to."

The pin that had been stuck in her side making it impossible to breathe or think past the dread of seeing him at this meeting was pulled free and she slumped in her chair. Thank God.

"Then let's get started." Dr. Ao cleared her throat and pressed her hands down on top of her desk. "As everyone is aware, the New School does not tolerate sexual harassment or bullying. Once Skye came to me with the texts from Max . . ."

"Alleged," the father said. "Allegedly from Max."

"They were from his number," Margot said. Skye had shown them to her on the plane. How innocuous they started.

Max: Hey, you got French notes I can borrow?
Max: Movie Saturday night? We can do a two man with Joe and Ashanti.
Max: What's up? I miss you.
Max: Pic?
Max: Awww . . . come on. Where's the skin?

"But you don't know that he sent them," his father shot back. "Max says it could have been a friend."

Skye scoffed and Margot leaned forward to get a look at Max. He was bright red and fascinated with his fingertips. "Really, kid? That's what you're going with?"

He blushed harder and the red-rimmed eyes on his mother leaked fresh tears. She was imagining teaching that boy how to hold a spoon and remembering his face the first time he saw a bird and how his hair smelled fresh from the bath.

"Don't talk to him," Angry Dad said to Margot.

"Max has said his friends took his phone from him." Dr. Ao stepped into the tension, hands spread wide on the mahogany desk.

The silence in the room was thick. "There were about twenty texts over the course of two weeks. Some of them came in the middle of the night. Some at school. And you're telling me a friend took his phone every time?" Margot asked.

She laughed because that was ridiculous. No one else laughed, and Dr. Ao went bright red.

"This is gaslighting," Margot said.

"No. This is reasonable doubt," Angry Dad said.

"Are you a lawyer or have you just watched too much television?" Margot snapped.

"Look, Max has got a scholarship, and a suspension from school puts that in jeopardy." He said this to Dr. Ao.

"Max asked my daughter, repeatedly, to send him pics of her in the bathroom. Touching herself. Your son has put my daughter in jeopardy."

"She sent a picture."

"Of herself in a swimsuit!" It had been maybe the most heartbreaking of all of it. Skye in a bikini Margot had never seen her wear, the bottom half of her face visible. She was biting her lip, trying undoubtedly to look older.

But she only looked young. And scared.

"That's worlds away from asking for a picture of my daughter in the third-floor bathroom," she snapped.

"Let's not get dramatic, honey," Angry Dad said.

"You did not just say that." Margot went white-hot and nearly blind. She lost the sensation in her hands.

Dr. Ao stood up, her hands out. "I know tempers are running high. But what would you have me do?" she asked Margot.

Margot jerked back. "Are you kidding me? I'd have you believe my daughter, who said she'd been harassed for months by Max."

"You don't have proof of that," the asshole said.

"We have a pretty damning text thread from Max."

"You don't have proof it was him."

Rage like Margot had never felt—not even on her own behalf—filled her up like helium in a balloon. Her eyes pounded. Her fingertips were numb.

She looked at Dr. Ao. "You're agreeing with this?"

"I'm just saying we can't suspend him if there's no proof."

"My daughter's word isn't enough proof?" Margot asked, her voice whisper thin. "The time-stamped texts from his phone aren't enough proof?"

Dr. Ao looked at Skye and back at Margot and then over to the father, who sat there, smug and righteous, because he was a man saying something. A man bending the world to his will despite the evidence.

"I have to be fair to both students."

"And I think in light of some of the trouble your husband is in," Angry Dad said, "you might not want the words *sexual harassment* said in the same breath as your daughter's name."

Margot was on her feet. Her hands in fists at her sides.

If she had a can of spray paint, what would she write?

Fuck you.

"Mom?" Skye reached up and tugged on the sleeve of the camel-colored coat Margot wore over that cheap acrylic sweater. "Let's just go."

Margot looked down at her daughter's face. The baby girl she'd been still in her cheeks. Her wide eyes. But she was building up her walls. Margot could see it and she hated it. She was just a kid; she shouldn't be protecting herself.

That was Margot's job.

She'd read those texts from Max. And she'd read the way Skye had tried to handle it. And Max over there just kept coming for her.

"Mom?" Skye said, like she was suddenly nervous. "What are you doing?"

Margot patted her daughter's hand. Too little too late, but someone was going to show this girl that she was worth fighting for. Worth burning down the world for.

"What a mistake you're making," Margot said, laughing because she had nothing to lose. Not one thing. She'd lost so much already and she'd fight to the death to show this girl that they had each other. "Not just because Skye will be leaving this school along with her father's massive checkbook. How big is your checkbook?" she asked Smug Dad but then waved her hand. "Doesn't matter. Oh, and I won't be the fundraising chair anymore. So, good luck with that silent auction."

"Margot," Dr. Ao said, looking like a person strangled by her own lack of convictions. Margot had no pity. "You don't need to do anything so drastic."

"We just wanted to talk. You're being unreasonable," Smug Dad said, shifting in his chair. Taking a swing even as he was going down.

Margot sucked in a deep breath and caught fire. "The real problem, and you wouldn't know this, Dr. Ao, and you certainly wouldn't . . . whatever your name is," Margot said to the father who wasn't looking so smug anymore. Who in fact was looking nervous. "But my sister is a journalist. What kind of journalist is she, Skye?"

"Investigative."

Dr. Ao went pale and began to fidget around her desk, lining things up on the blotter.

"That's right. An investigative journalist. And I thought, post MeToo, that we were in the business of believing women. I'm sad that's not the case at this school. But you know who does believe Skye? Her aunt. And she will make sure that none of this happens to another girl under your leadership, Dr. Ao. I'd polish up that résumé and"— she looked at Smug Dad and Devastated Mother—"I'd get a lawyer. Skye? You want to go?"

Skye was already at the door, smiling just a little.

"Margot?" Dr. Ao said when they got to the door. She looked so small behind that desk, completely compromised. "I'm sure there's a way—"

"Yeah, there was. But you blew it."

The kid had the good grace to look uncomfortable. And, frankly, guilty.

"Max?" Margot said. His mother beside him got to her feet, turned to face them. "You're just a kid, but you're running out of time. You let this stand and you're just as bad as him." Max looked at his father, panicked and more than a little scared. If the guy could be such a flaming asshole in the principal's office, it was a safe bet he was a million times worse in his own home.

"I'm so sorry," the mother said, surprising Margot. "Skye, for what it's worth, I believe you."

Skye startled so hard, her hand knocked into Margot's and Margot grabbed it.

Too little too late, Mom. Get out of that situation and try to take your son with you.

"Thank you," Skye said, and Margot got them out of there. They practically ran down the hallway like the office was about to blow up behind them.

"Should I get my stuff?" Skye said, skidding to a halt.

"Later," Margot said.

Skye did not need to be convinced. They hit the door, ran across the parking lot surrounded by eucalyptus and pine trees to the dark sedan where Julia was waiting for them. She jumped when they opened the doors and after one look at Margot's face peeled out of the parking lot.

"Seems like it went well in there," Julia said.

"Max says his friends took the phone, and they don't believe Skye. He is coming back to school."

"Oh my god," Julia breathed. "Let me at them."

"They are all yours. Particularly the father."

Julia took East Valley Road North. "Am I taking you home?" Julia asked. "Like home, home?"

Margot turned to look at Skye in the back seat. She watched the eucalyptus bushes and pine trees as they flew past in a blur.

Her dad used to tell a story about a strike at a foundry in the seventies and all the bosses with soft hands and pressed shirts had to stay in the mill for days, making sure the fire was always going and the foundry never went cold.

She was never going cold.

"I'm so proud of you," Margot said to her daughter, who had the guts to do the right thing and walk into the office full of people who would doubt her word.

If Skye could walk into that office, Margot could walk into her home.

"Thanks, Mom," Skye said, a brief smile appearing on her lips.

"Yeah," Margot said, crossing her hands in her lap. "Take us home."

"Is Dad there?" Skye asked.

She didn't know. Margot had put her head in the sand and hoped for the best when her life was falling apart in a real way. No more denial. No more rationalization.

"I'll find out," Margot said, and texted her husband.

Margot: Are you at the house?

Jack: Margot! How did it go at school?

Margot: Are you at the house?

Jack: Yes.

Margot: Skye and I will be there shortly.

Jack: What happened at school?

Margot: We'll talk when we get there.

She put down the phone. "He'll be there," Margot said. "But if you don't want to see him, you don't have to."

At a stop sign at Hot Springs Road, Julia looked up and met Skye's eyes in the rearview mirror. "Let's get boba and go to the beach?"

Skye nodded and Margot reached out to grab her sister's hand, gratitude only making the fire burn hotter.

Once after a bike accident, Margot spent a week walking around her life like it was someone else's. Nothing looked familiar. The Whole Foods, her office space. The house. The school. Everything in such sharp, clear contrast. Details she'd never noticed in bright relief.

Lorna, her therapist, said it was the lingering effects of a panic attack. Fight or flight.

It would go away, she said.

Now she was looking at her house with the same clarity. Her muddy boots at the door, next to the heels she'd worn to lunch with Jack two weeks ago. Her denim coat. The keys to her car in the clay dish Alex made.

Her house. But not.

Her things. But not.

The remains of the meeting that had ended so quickly, still on the table. The cinnamon rolls hard as rocks on the counter.

Was that just four days ago? Five?

Her favorite mug had a smudge of her lipstick on the edge.

She put it in the sink with the rest of the mugs from that ill-fated meeting. Had she done that? Cleared the mugs? Had Noelle? It didn't seem like something she would do. Jack, maybe. He was very good at doing part of a job. Clearing the table but not doing the dishes.

That kind of thinking used to feel unfair.

Not so much today.

"Margot?"

Jack came into the kitchen wearing the Browns T-shirt the twins got him for Christmas. They got him the T-shirt and tickets to the home opener so they could all go together. It had been the hit of that Christmas.

"Where's Skye?" he asked, looking around like she was hiding.

"She didn't want to come."

"She didn't want to see me?"

"Something like that."

Anger welled up, clenched his jaw, narrowed his eyes, but he tamped it back down.

"How did it go at school?" He stepped farther into the kitchen. His socked feet on the hardwood floors she'd picked out during the renovation, and she couldn't even stand that. Couldn't even stand to be on the same floor as him. She walked around the long harvest table to the living room with all its bright windows. The dark leather couches and family pictures.

"Bad?" he asked, following her.

"Stop!" she said, holding up her hand like a crossing guard. "Just stay there."

"In the kitchen?" he asked through the open doorway. In the fall she bundled herbs from her garden, tied in string and hung in that doorway to dry. During Christmas she hung lights and garlands.

"Yeah," she said, and unbuttoned her coat. It was an old one from Pittsburgh. Fake cashmere. A relic from some high school trip to New York City with Mom. A second-hand store on Canal Street.

"School?" he nudged, like he was getting irritated.

"She's not going back."

"What?" He had the balls to sound furious.

"They didn't take her word for it. They were going to let Max back into school."

"You're kidding," he said.

"I am not." Margot blew out a long breath. It was hard to breathe in here. She tilted her head back to the dark exposed beams and the creamy white ceiling. She pulled the neck of her shirt away from her body.

Was this menopause? Perimenopause? Fuck, she was so hot.

"That's all you're going to tell me?" Jack asked, again, so irritated with her.

"That kid did the same thing you did."

"Not quite the same thing," he said in sad defense of himself. "I wasn't harassing an innocent fifteen-year-old."

Oh, the same hair she'd split. How disgusting.

She turned to face the fireplace. Prairie stone imported from someplace. A prairie, obviously. It had seemed so crucial at the time. That authenticity. Now it was ridiculous.

Jack made the mantel in his *I'll be like Harrison Ford* phase. It was fine. Lopsided, but she would never tell him that. On the mantel was a picture of their wedding on the beach and a picture of each of the kids and the bat from that baseball movie that won him the Oscar.

It was signed by the cast and crew.

He loved that bat.

"Okay," Jack said in his *If you're not going to be reasonable, I guess I'll be reasonable* voice. She hated that voice. Every woman probably hated that voice out of their partner's mouth. "We should talk about next steps."

Oh. Fascinating. What did he think they should do next?

"I've had Andre reach out to some of the networks. Oprah. Katie Couric—"

"Oh my god, are you talking about the statement again?"

Then, "I want a divorce." The words sprang out of her chest. Forged in fire.

"We can . . ." He looked ill. Like seriously ill. And for a second she thought, poor guy. She really did. That poor guy getting his heart broken. "We can talk about that. After our statement."

"I'm not giving a fucking state—"

The floor between the kitchen and the hallway that led to the bedrooms had a squeaky plank right in the middle of the doorway. Everyone in the house knew how to avoid it.

When it squeaked, she shut her mouth.

"Margot . . ." Noelle stepped out of the kitchen from the doorway that led to the garage. Maybe it was the adrenaline making her life seem like a bad movie, but it took Margot a second to realize that Noelle was real. And she was really there. "You both need to make a statement that will allow you to have careers after this. Cancel culture—"

"What the hell are you doing here?" Margot asked her assistant. Her trusted assistant who was practically a part of the family. Who had keys to her house. Who was here. Right now. Without a coat.

Barefoot. Not just no shoes, but . . . barefoot.

"I called her here," Jack said in his imperious voice. All authority. Don't question me. A man saying something and bending the world to his will. "To help me convince you to see reason."

In a heartbeat she saw what an idiot she was. What a pure lamb to slaughter. A laughingstock in her own house. Suddenly, that bat, that prized possession that held a position of such honor in their family as to have its own fucking lighting, was in her hands.

She curled her fingers around the wood. She remembered him saying something about how the bat had been made by the grandson of some guy who did something with Babe Ruth. He told her like it should matter when it didn't. Not at all.

"Margot?" Jack said, his hands up. "What are you doing?"

"How long?" she asked, pointing with the bat from Jack to Noelle.

"What are you talking about?" Jack said. Now he was using his belligerent voice. Margot ignored him. The truth was all over Noelle's face. The tears standing out in her eyes.

"I'm sorry," she whispered.

"Jesus," Jack swore.

She choked up on the bat the way her dad taught her and just started swinging. She cleared the mantelpiece, sending all those pictures in pieces to the floor, where they shattered spectacularly. The table in the corner with more of Jack's memorabilia mixed in with the twins' grad photos. Skye, young and chubby-cheeked, playing the piano at a recital. She cleared it in one swing. The stained-glass piece hanging in the window that he got her for her birthday a million years ago. She smashed the grate in front of the fireplace. Tried to take down the mantel, but the impact sent electric pain up her arms.

"Calm the fuck down," Jack said, coming at her like he might wrap his arms around her, but she dodged him, taking the two steps from the living room to the kitchen. Her dream kitchen. Every decision hers, in service to her family. To this ideal. This fucking story she believed.

She took a bat to all of it. The cinnamon buns. The coffee cups she loved so much.

She didn't realize she was screaming until her voice caught on a sob and she choked. She threw her hand up to cover her face and her fingers were covered in little flecks of blood. All that ceramic. She wiped her face with the sleeve of her old coat and it came away covered in snot and tears and blood.

The bat fell from her hands and her ears throbbed in the silence.

"Margot?"

"Julia," she sobbed and turned to the doorway. Glass crunching under her feet.

"Holy shit," Julia said with a wide, manic smile on her face. "Got mad, did you?"

"Julia," Jack the idiot said. "Try and talk some sense—"

"Hey, fucker." Julia wrapped her arm around Margot's shoulders and led her back toward the garage. "If it was me, I'd take that bat to your face. So count your blessings."

"Skye?" Margot whispered.

"In the car. We've had some developments on Lady X," Julia said. "Skye is turning into quite the investigative journalist."

"Get me out of here," Margot said, unable to look back at the mess that had been made of her life.

So she didn't see Noelle, carefully putting her phone back in her pocket.

CHAPTER 19

June 1977
New York City

Ginger

The picture of the cop car was on the front page of the *Village Voice*.

"It's gorgeous," Rachel said, spreading the front page of the *Post* out on the coffee table. The black-and-white picture was so sharp the flared feathered edges of the spray paint on the word *rapist* was visible. All Ginger's little dicks.

Lady X Looking for Trouble was the headline.

What felt so urgent and necessary last night just felt risky this morning. Foolish. They were making it too easy for Boyle to connect the dots right back to them.

It's done, Ginger thought. *Can't take it back now.*

There was a phone call for Rachel and she took it in the kitchen, every word on her end an excited *yes* and *of course.*

She hung up and said with triumph, "Vanessa is holding a press conference at the park. Today."

"About what?" Ginger asked, and Rachel looked at her like she was an idiot.

"About Lady X. You heard her at the meeting, Lady X is someone women can rally around. And going after a cop? This is going to get attention."

"You can't tell her it's us," Faye said.

"Why not?" Rachel asked.

"Because we don't know if we can trust her?" Faye said, and Ginger had to agree.

"I trust her," Rachel said, shoving her notebook and pen into her bag like that should be enough for them.

After Rachel left Faye sighed and said, "She is half in love with Vanessa Purdy. And that will be a problem."

Faye and Ginger went to the press conference and stood at the back of the crowd, which was surprisingly big.

She heard people arguing that it was just more graffiti in a city filled with it. But there were also women carrying signs that said *Stop Corrupt Police*. A few journalists gathered near the fountain, taking pictures and asking Vanessa questions.

Rachel stood beside Vanessa, getting people to sign the petition on her clipboard.

And there were a lot of cops. More than a protest this size deserved. Lady X had kicked over a hornet's nest last night.

"This is happening so fast," Ginger said. It wasn't even noon.

"It is not happening fast enough," Faye said. She wiped the sweat off her neck with the back of her hand.

Rachel handed Vanessa a bullhorn and she got up on the lip of the fountain and lifted her arms over her head. Camera flashes went off and the crowd settled down.

"What are the cops hiding?" Vanessa asked through her bullhorn, and a ripple went through the crowd. Flashbulbs went off. "How many rapists are they protecting? And what are they going to do about this Officer Sherman Boyle that Lady X has so clearly accused of rape?"

By the time the afternoon papers hit, Lady X was on the front page of all of them.

Police Officer in Lady X Attack Suspended?
Angry Officer Says: No Man Is Safe

That night the Orbit Room doors opened at nine and the guests streamed in, wearing outfits so spectacular they bordered on outrageous. Feathers and sequins and everyone with their nipples out. Eyeliner on the men. Neckties on the women. Everybody covered in glitter.

Ginger and Faye had officially been moved into the bar, where the energy was manic. The city felt like it was pulling apart at the seams. Rome burning kind of vibes. And this crowd was going to dance while it burned.

In the VIP section, the men were grabby. Like they had to reassert something. Establish the ground rules. Ginger walked around with her arms bent at her waist, blocking the "accidental" brushes against her breasts. She twitched sideways to stop the guys who would grab her ass. Some got it anyway.

"Lighten up, sweetheart. You'd be a lot prettier if you smiled," more than one said, and she rolled her eyes behind their back.

The women at the club laughed louder. Danced freer.

Ginger and Faye were on their break, sitting on the throne in the back of the coat check, when Rachel came in around midnight, through the side door. Dante was used to her at this point. She wore her best flares and a men's dress shirt tied in a knot at her waist.

"Hey!" she said, kissing both Ginger and Faye on the cheeks. "Good night?"

"Weird," Ginger said.

"*Sauvage*," Faye elaborated.

"Have you seen the papers?" Rachel asked, eyes bright. She smelled of wine and weed.

"Shane talked about it at our staff meeting," Faye said.

"Well, he's the kind of guy who should be worried," Rachel said, glancing back at that staircase and the office door on the second floor. "Maybe . . ."

"No," Ginger said. "We're done. Aren't we?"

"I don't know." Rachel stretched her arms out wide. Her hips starting to shake to the beat of Cameo's "Funk Funk." "I feel like we're doing the good lord's work in this godforsaken city."

"Hallelujah," Faye said. Ginger scowled at both of them, but they only clutched each other and laughed.

Rachel stepped back as a group of women approached. All of them tall and thin and blond, with the kind of beauty that verged on alien. Models. Each of them wearing a tiny baby-doll T-shirt with the name *Lady X* written across it.

"Your shirts . . ." Ginger said, but couldn't finish the thought.

"Andy made them," one of the women said, holding out the bottom of her light blue shirt. "Aren't they amazing?"

"They are," Rachel said. "They really are."

Faye, Ginger, and Rachel watched the models vanish into the strobe-lit darkness of the bar, confetti raining down on them, like they were disappearing into another world.

"Andy?" Faye asked.

"Warhol," Ginger said. "Andy fucking Warhol."

"I've heard of him," Faye said, again like that was a seal of approval.

Todd met Ginger and Faye at the edge of the VIP section, where a group of women had taken over the best banquette, usually reserved for Shane's special guests.

"Boss is in a mood," Todd said. "Those models with the T-shirts?"

"He saw them?" Faye asked. Confetti clung to Todd's chest and the side of his neck, stuck in sweat like flies in amber. Faye peeled it off him one piece at a time.

"Not a fan. And now he's got a little group of assholes in the back of the VIP section talking about how they need to hunt this Lady X down."

Both Faye and Ginger craned their necks to the booth in the back corner. It was shadowy, but she could make out Shane and Jas's boyfriend Carl.

"Hunt?" Faye said.

"Who is the short guy with them?"

"The dentist? He's like a known dirtbag. Every gay guy in the Village has turned him down, so he knocks his male patients out and fucks with them."

"How can it be so well-known and no one does anything about it?"

"Because his victims are gay and passed the fuck out, so who is going to believe them?" Todd said, and Ginger was on the receiving end of a scathing look.

"Sounds like a job for Lady X," Faye said, blowing smoke rings.

"Fuck yeah it is," Todd said.

The "*Ahhhh* freak out" of "Le Freak" started and Todd rolled his eyes. The three of them picked up the whistles around their necks. Every time this song came on, staff in the bar were supposed to blow these whistles, stop what they were doing, and dance. Ginger thought it was fun. She put down her tray and bumped Faye's hips with her own, making her laugh.

Todd wore the expression of a man who was tired of a good time. A man who could use twelve hours of sleep, some green vegetables, and a glass of water.

"Todd!" Shane said as he walked out of the shadowy section of the VIP area. He snapped his fingers and pointed toward the dance floor.

Todd waded into the crowd, blowing that whistle like his life depended on it. A woman dressed all in silver stopped him. She grabbed his ass with both hands and he tipped his head back, blowing that whistle up at the moon.

It looked like the worst good time that ever was.

"Is there a problem, ladies?" Shane asked, like he was just waiting to fire someone.

"No problem," Ginger said, smiling.

"Then get to fucking work."

Faye watched the burning end of her cigarette like she was considering the benefits of pressing it to the walls and watching it all burn.

"No," Ginger said.

"No what?" she asked.

"We're not doing anything to this place. We need the paychecks."

"What about that dentist?"

"No!"

"Why not?"

"Because we're not vigilantes for hire."

"We could be."

She stepped past Ginger and picked up her tray, the whistle and dance forgotten. "You know, I will die remembering you on top of that car..."

"Faye." Ginger looked around, scared someone would hear her.

"*Magnifique*," she said. "You should be like that more often."

CHAPTER 20

June 1977
New York City

Ginger

Rachel opened the front door of their building and they stepped into an echoing wall of noise. Someone on one of the floors was fighting in the main hallway, everything ricocheting off the walls. A door slammed and footsteps hammered down the concrete steps.

Ginger, Faye, and Rachel stopped on the landing for the second floor as Officer Boyle and another officer turned the corner. The hallway lighting made him look green.

"I've been looking for you girls," Boyle said, revealing the scared bully all that apple-cheeked friendliness had been hiding.

"Here we are," Rachel said, the stone-cold woman all that polite friendliness had been hiding. "What are you doing in uniform? I thought you were suspended."

"Yeah, you'd like that wouldn't you? Hate to disappoint but I'm still an officer of the law. Now, let's go on up to your apartment," he said. "We have some questions for you."

Ginger could feel her face getting hot. A muscle in her eyelid twitching.

"Go then," Faye said, pointing them back up the stairs. Her face was totally normal.

"No, no, honey," he sneered. "After you."

Ginger smiled her wide coat check girl smile and let Faye and Rachel go first so that it was her ass Boyle and his partner were staring at. Ginger gave it some extra sway just as a general fuck you as they climbed the rest of the stairs to their apartment.

Faye opened the door and said very quietly, "Everything is fine."

Nothing felt fine. Where were the clothes Ginger wore the other night? Was there paint on her shoes? There had to be paint on her shoes, the soles? From when she climbed onto the car?

Rachel met Ginger's eyes, lifted her eyebrows. *Calm the fuck down.*

Boyle shut the door behind him and Ginger's armpits went hot and prickly.

Ginger thought of those clothes in their rooms; hers were right there on the floor. She thought of the soap on their bathroom sink stained black from the spray paint on their hands.

Thank God they threw away the paint cans. The crowbar.

Oily sweat oozed down Ginger's spine.

"Tea?" Faye said into the charged silence.

"I'd love some," Boyle's partner said, only to get glared at by Boyle. "Never mind."

His partner started looking around the apartment. He kicked over Ginger's boots, revealing the soles. She could see the black paint at the edge, but he just crouched and set them back to rights. He looked at the little table, their keys. A pack of cigarettes. Some gum. He recoiled from a box of Tampax.

"How about we cut to the chase," Boyle said. "I know it was you three who destroyed my patrol car."

"Oh," Ginger said, sitting down on the couch and putting up her aching feet. "I hadn't heard. What happened?"

Boyle swept his hand across the table under the phone, sending everything crashing to the floor. The three girls jumped but managed not to scream. The silence was painful and all Ginger could do was breathe through it, her heart pounding in the back of her throat.

"If you had any proof we'd be in jail," Rachel said, so calmly Ginger wanted to applaud her.

"You bitches think you are so smart," Boyle said, walking around the apartment. He picked up the coffee mug Rachel had left by the window and hurled it against the ground. He took a painting off a wall and smashed it over his knee. As if they'd taken an oath, the three of them did not react. They held hands on the couch and didn't even look at him.

He stood in front of them on the other side of the coffee table, his chest heaving.

He's going to hit us, Ginger thought. *And there's no one here to stop him.*

But he only picked up one of Rachel's half-full Chianti bottles and drained it on the rug and then smashed that on the ground. He heaved the whole coffee table against the fireplace. They couldn't help but flinch, glass splintering everywhere.

On the mantel were the stacks of newspapers Rachel had been keeping.

He tore them to pieces and threw them in their faces. A scrap clung to Ginger's sweaty chest. Rachel pulled a piece out of her hair.

"You have any idea the kind of trouble I'm in?" he asked.

"Probably the kind of trouble you deserve." Rachel, instead of shrinking at the unspoken threat, seemed to get bigger. She took up more space on her own terms. And if she was afraid, she didn't give him the satisfaction of showing it. Ginger didn't know if this was who she was after the rape? Or because of the booze?

"They're talking about taking my badge!" he shouted, spittle raining down on his uniform. Ginger squeezed Rachel's and Faye's hands, urging them to be quiet. "Where were you Thursday night?" he asked.

"You saw me go to work," Ginger said, lifting her eyes to meet his.

"You saw me in the park," Rachel reminded him.

"But I didn't see you," he said, leaning down into Faye's face. "I never forget a face, and yours I've seen before. You know what I think? I think you've been printed and when they get done dusting my cruiser, we're going to find your prints all over it."

Faye gave him nothing. A blank stare.

Boyle smiled and Ginger wondered how she ever thought it was friendly. It was a shark's smile. All teeth.

"My partner and I are going to look around your place."

They broke the dishes in the kitchen. All the makeup in the bathroom. Boyle came out of Ginger's room with a pair of pink silk panties. "You don't mind, do you?" he asked, tucking the underwear into his pocket.

Cold chills and hot rage filled her.

Pig, she thought.

Boyle took his time leaving the apartment, looking over everything like he was appraising its price. "I've got my eye on you," he said.

"How fun for us," Ginger said, and Doyle's partner grabbed his elbow, pulling him out the door.

Boyle shut the door behind him, and the three of them collapsed. Faye against the couch, Rachel right down to the floor. Ginger braced her hands on her knees and tried not to pass out.

"That was . . ." Ginger couldn't even finish it. The sentence. The thought.

"Close," Rachel said. "That was close."

"We can't do that anymore," Ginger said. "No more."

"Or?" Rachel said. "We just need to be smarter about it."

"No! No." Rachel grinned at Ginger. Eyes alight. "I'm serious, Rachel. He knows . . ."

"He doesn't know shit," Rachel said. "Faye, tell her."

"Oh, he knows. But he can't prove it." Faye waved her hand. "And . . . we will take a break. Till things calm down."

"And then what?" Ginger cried. "This isn't like . . . a thing we're going to do forever?"

"No. Only until men stop being assholes," Faye said, and Rachel thought that was just hilarious.

The next day there was a crowd in front of the Orbit Room and Ginger and Faye couldn't get through to the doors. There was a woman up front yelling through a megaphone, but from so far back it was too distorted to understand.

"Todd!" Ginger yelled, seeing his head over the crowd. He fought like a salmon upstream to get back to where Ginger and Faye were standing. He brought Jasmine with him.

"Is it Son of Sam?" Ginger asked, because it was a big crowd with a weird energy.

"No! It's Lady X!"

Ginger stepped back, her head light. Faye's arm in hers was a vice.

"She must have written *rapist* on the front of the building like seven hundred times. *Lady X* right across the glass doors. He's got a crew painting over it right now, but it's too late. There was a television crew here. Dozens of reporters," Jasmine said, like it was the beginning of the end and she was sad to see it go.

"Who is on the megaphone?" Ginger asked, but she already knew the answer.

"Vanessa Purdy."

"Is Rachel here?"

"I haven't seen her," Todd said.

Dante the security guard came out and moved people along and all the staff went down the side alley, where it was drippy and wet no matter what the season was, and it felt like you were meat about to be packed.

"Faye?" Ginger said, watching the pale skin of her neck, the bones of her spine as she looked down so she didn't step in a puddle.

"*It was not me,*" she said, and looked over her shoulder at Ginger. "I swear."

"Was it Rachel?" Ginger asked.

Faye didn't have an answer.

That night the cops came right through the front door past coat check and into the bar. Immediately, a flood of people went running past, little bags of coke and joints tossed out of pockets like it was seed-planting season. Shane came out, red and sweating. He led the cops up to his office.

Standing in the hallway, watching, was Jasmine's friend, with the hair like Cher and the fingernails like claws. Her smile sent chills down Ginger's spine.

"What do we do?" Ginger asked Faye, but when she turned Faye wasn't there.

"Faye!" Ginger yelled as she fought the crowd to get to the bar.

Todd came running out, bottles of champagne in his arms.

"Take these!" he cried. "I'll get more."

The music screeched to a halt and the cops cleared everyone out, shutting the club down. Not even the cleaners could stay.

"Where's Faye?" Ginger asked, but Todd hadn't seen her.

Todd came back to the apartment with Ginger, each of them carrying four bottles of champagne. The good stuff. From the VIP section. Rachel was home. She'd found a Smith Corona Electra typewriter outside a brownstone in the West Village, swore it contained the revolutionary spirit of Patti Smith, and when she wasn't drinking, she was writing. Sometimes she did both at once.

Todd filled her in on what had happened at the club.

"Shut down?" Rachel repeated.

"For the time being. You can thank Lady X and your boss." Todd's eyes went round. "Do you think Vanessa knows who Lady X is?"

"No," Rachel said. "I don't."

"Do you think Vanessa Purdy is Lady X?"

"No," Rachel said. "I don't."

"Too bad," Todd said, going into the kitchen to put some of the bottles in the fridge. "Lady X is the real fucking deal. She's gonna change shit."

"Have you seen Faye?" Ginger asked once Todd was out of the room.

Rachel shook her head.

"You think . . . ?" Rachel said but didn't finish the sentence. She didn't need to.

"She said she didn't."

"Do you believe her?"

"I don't know."

LADY X BRINGS THE ORBIT
ROOM DOWN TO EARTH
Daily Mail, June 6, 1977

The Orbit Room, the exclusive nightclub of the rich and famous, was shut down yesterday after the building was the site of another Lady X crime scene. Owner Shane Romero arrived at his club only to find the word *rapist* graffitied over seven hundred times.

"When are the police going to do something about this woman?" says Romero.

Police have no suspects at this time.

When asked why the police shut the club down, a representative of the police department said they cannot talk about ongoing investigations.

Vanessa Purdy, a political activist and feminist, says police need to investigate the allegations against the Orbit Room and Shane Romero as well as Officer Sherman Boyle and bookstore owner Dennis LeRoy, who Lady X also accused of rape.

"I'm a citizen," Romero says. "I pay my taxes, and if this Lady X says different, she's a liar. I'm the victim here."

CHAPTER 21

March 2024
Montecito, California

Margot

There was glass in Margot's hair. And she was shaking.

"Mom?"

"I'm fine." Margot put her hand over Skye's.

"You're bleeding!" Skye cried, picking up Margot's wrist. There were rivulets of blood running down the back of her hand from her fingers.

"Blood?" Julia asked in the front seat of the car, like she was their driver. "Margot? Do we need to go to the hospital?"

"No." Margot opened her purse and fished out a Kleenex. "I'm fine, it's just—"

"Did Dad . . . ?" Skye trailed off.

"No, honey. No. God. No." Margot pulled Skye against her side and kissed the top of her head over and over again like she did when she picked Skye up from kindergarten, having missed her for five hours straight. "I . . . did this myself. I broke a bunch of glasses."

"Your mom took a baseball bat to everything," Julia said. "It was magnificent."

"*The* baseball bat?" Skye asked.

"Yeah. *The* baseball bat." Margot remembered when he put that bat on the mantel and all the things he took off to make room. Pictures of the kids. Mom and Dad posing next to that Willie Stargell statue in

Pittsburgh. Julia and Margot at Halloween when they were kids, dressed up as cats.

Margot put those pictures in her office on the second floor.

"That bat changed our lives," he'd said, and Margot agreed. She put those pictures away happily. Made room for his success, happily. Quietly and completely over the years, she made his success the center of their whole lives.

And then he changed it again. To this new dumpster fire. And it felt like Margot had no choice. She was a passenger, and he was calling the shots. He could do what he wanted, and they had to work around it.

"It's badass, Mom," Skye said, and Margot leaned back, looking at Skye's face. And, to her surprise and delight, Skye let her. "It was badass in the principal's office too." Margot couldn't remember the last time her teenage daughter allowed Margot to look her in the eye, and Skye looked right back. A smile on her face.

Funny. All she had to do was destroy their home and threaten Skye's school.

All she had to do was be honest about her life and get mad.

She used the Kleenex to wipe the sweat off her forehead and some of the mascara she imagined smudged under her eyes. She'd really worked hard destroying shit.

"Well, it sure was messy."

Being a badass was messy. Breaking the rules. Ignoring expectations. Setting things straight with a bat. With a can of spray paint.

"You're like Lady X," Skye said, and Margot laughed, exhausted.

"I wouldn't go that far." Margot leaned her head against the headrest and looked out the window. Julia took the 101 on-ramp heading south to Oxnard.

"Where are we going?" Margot asked. She wasn't sure she cared, as long as it wasn't here. As long as it wasn't her life.

"To New York."

"What?" Margot cried, sitting up, no longer exhausted.

"You want to stick around here?" Julia asked, meeting Margot's eyes in the rearview mirror. "Go for broke with that bat? Talk to Jack some more?"

"No . . . I . . ." Margot pressed a hand to her head. "But Skye's got school."

"You just blew that school to pieces, Margot," Julia said.

Margot looked down at her daughter again, who was nearly unrecognizable in the clarity of the sunlight through the windows. That fragile disdain that covered all that teenage insecurity, it was like she'd taken a bat to it, revealing the bright-eyed, curious, and engaged girl underneath. For that girl . . . God, she'd do anything.

"You want this?" Margot asked.

Skye nodded.

"We can take the time to figure out where to send me to school." Skye said all the right words, and Margot was jelly in the back seat of that car.

"We can go back to Pittsburgh after," Julia said, and Margot made a breathy sound that was very nearly a sob.

"I'll go back to Pittsburgh with you," Skye said, and Margot had to laugh. That was too far. "They have schools there."

"Not where Jack Cooper's daughter goes. Not after what he's done. Honey, I just don't think . . ."

"Show her the email," Julia said, and tossed her phone into the back seat.

"What email?" Margot asked, while Skye pulled something up on Julia's phone.

"It's from Nadia. Rachel's partner," Skye reminded her.

Margot reached up in her hair for her glasses, but they weren't there. Skye took the phone back and read the email out loud.

"*Julia, I am so sorry about what happened today. That time in Rachel's life was a tumultuous one, and she rarely talks about it. She has, over the years, told me things that I had truly hoped she'd share with you. One of those things is the friendship she had with your mom. Your mother helped Rachel through an incredibly difficult time in her life. The way she talks about your mother is with love. The Lady X drama ended in bloodshed that cost your mother and Rachel their friendship and so much more.*' "

"Bloodshed?" Margot asked, freaking out, right on cue. "What is she talking about?"

"Keep reading, Skye," Julia said.

" '*Rachel was so excited to meet you*,'" Skye continued. " '*Had been talking about you since the moment you reached out. She feels so bad about how today ended and she knows I'm sending this email.*'"

"Well, that's sweet," Margot said.

"Keep reading," Julia said.

" '*There is someone else you should talk to*,'" Skye continued, the thrill in her voice indicating that she was getting to the good part. " '*He knew your mother at that time, and he also knew Lady X, and he is the one who should be answering your questions. If you'd like to reach out after you talk to him, I would love to hear from you. Best of luck, Nadia.*'"

"This is the number?" Margot asked, pointing at the number at the bottom of the screen. "Did you call it?"

"Yeah."

"I guess we're going to New York."

They stayed in a boutique hotel on a cobblestone side street just outside of Greenwich Village. They got a suite and room service because Skye was smiling again after years of her not smiling and Margot didn't want it to stop.

Currently, the food was set up on the dining room table in the suite, and Julia and Skye had every article they'd pulled from the attic spread out alongside it. The suite smelled like French onion soup and musty attic. Margot would leave a bigger tip for the housekeeping staff.

"Rachel Horowitz said that Faye Bouchard died on the last night of the July blackout in 1977. But there are no death certificates for Faye Bouchard," Julia said, looking up from her laptop. "There were a lot of heart attacks and fires that night. A man fell off a roof not far from here. There was one confirmed murder. A Mob thing in Brooklyn. And there was a Jane Doe found strangled near Washington Square Park."

"You think Faye Bouchard was Jane Doe at the park?" Skye gasped.

Margot could say *I told you so* but refrained.

"Right now, she's a blank space. I don't have a death certificate. I don't have a marriage or birth certificate. All we know is she worked at the Orbit Room around the same time as Mom."

"What do you think?" Skye asked Julia.

"I think Lady X was killed," Julia said with finality. "And there's a really good chance she's the Jane Doe at the park." Skye moaned low in her throat, exhibiting grief for a person she didn't even know about a few days ago. "So, it's obviously not Mom or Rachel. Maybe she went too far. Fucked with the wrong person. Or someone found out who she was." She lifted up one of the newspapers with a headline that said: *Lady X Must Be Stopped*. "They were hunting for her."

So dramatic, Margot thought. She stepped over to the table with all their notes and old newspapers with their inflammatory headlines.

Police Officer Suspended After Lady X Points Finger.

Beneath the headline was a picture of a cherub-faced police officer in his dress uniform, smiling into a camera. And another picture of a vandalized cop car.

Officer Sherman Boyle has been suspended by the NYPD after accusations of rape by vigilante Lady X.

"We take accusations of police misconduct very seriously, and the officer in question has been suspended until we can get to the bottom of this," said Police Commissioner Micheal Codd. "The Knapp Commission was created to handle this sort of thing. We're on top of it."

"There's already a police shortage," said Vincent D'Mateo, 35, a cab driver from Queens, "and we got this Son of Sam on the loose, what are we doing getting *rid* of cops?"

She picked up another newspaper with the headline *Baseball Hero's Hand Ruined*.

There was a small picture of the baseball player's hand, swollen and Frankenstein-ed with black surgical stitches. It was shocking. Scary even, the evidence of such violence.

"I can't believe anyone thought Mom would do this to someone," Margot said. Mom caught spiders under a glass and put them outside. "This Faye woman did it?"

"That's what Rachel says."

"I wonder what he did to Faye," she murmured.

Her phone buzzed with a call from Jack and she turned it off. A few minutes later Skye's phone rattled against the table.

"You need to talk to Dad," Skye said, glancing down at her phone.

"Says who?" Margot asked.

"Dad." Skye looked up. Another thing so much like Julia. That worried knot right above her eyes.

Margot walked away from the table to the long, low couches against the wall. The upholstery was weird and eclectic. Bright floral hot pink and kelly green. They'd have to remodel every few years, because this eccentric old lady vibe they had wouldn't be popular forever. Or maybe it was timeless. Margot didn't know anymore.

"Margot," Julia said, following her across the room and holding out her phone. "You need to call your lawyer. And then you need to talk to Jack."

Lawyer? She didn't have a lawyer. She had Jack's lawyer, who treated her business like a cute little side hustle. Like she was running a lemonade stand. Getting a new lawyer had been on her list for ages, but there just never seemed to be the time.

"Margot?" Julia said, and Margot faced her sister. Whatever it was. It was bad. It was . . . very bad. Because Julia didn't look mad.

She looked scared.

She took Julia's phone and read the text from Jack.

Tell my wife to call me or I'm going public with this and I'll get custody of Skye and I will rebuild my career on top of her ruined reputation.

And attached was a video of Margot, her old coat from Canal Street whirling around her as she screamed like a woman unhinged and took a bat to her own home.

I could kill you for this!

She screamed that, a few times. Plain as day.

Twice, she watched it. The first time she told herself it wasn't that bad. The second time, she let herself feel exactly how bad it was. And all she could think was *custody of Skye*. In a few years she'd be old enough to make her own decisions but not yet and maybe never if that video was released. Jack would get the sharkiest shark that ever sharked and she would be painted as unstable and she might not even get visitation rights.

He wouldn't do that, she tried to tell herself.

But she never thought he'd do any of this.

And here we are.

Somehow he had all the power again. And this betrayal was worse than the first. It was cold-blooded and premeditated. Fucking around with beautiful girls on the internet was just gross.

This was evil.

And never in her life would she have said that Jack was evil.

"Don't promise him anything," Julia said, her voice lowered so Skye couldn't hear. Julia had herded her into one of the bedrooms, the view of lower Manhattan like a scene in one of Jack's movies. *This is Jack's world*, she thought, *and I'm just living in it.*

"I've never been so scared," she whispered. She would die if she lost custody of Skye.

"You want me to stay in the room while you talk to him?" Julia asked, and Margot nodded. "Put it on speaker."

"You can't . . ." *blow anything up* was what she was going to say. But wasn't it all blown up? Wasn't it all ruined anyway? What could Julia do, really?

"I'll be silent," Julia promised. "I'm just a witness. I can record it."

Was that necessary? It seemed ludicrous, but she nodded.

She pressed Jack's number, put it on speaker, and put the phone on the bed, and the two of them, like they used to, put their knees on the floor and rested their elbows on the mattress.

"Margot," Jack said, and her breath hitched. "I'm sorry to have to do this. But—"

"What do you want?" she asked, her voice as calm as she could make it, and it still sounded like she was calling 911.

"Margot. Can we please just talk?"

"You're blackmailing me, Jack," she said. "So clearly not."

"You're not responding to me, Margot. I don't want to do this, but my hands are tied."

Julia made a growling scoff sound in her throat and buried her face in her pillow.

"I'm here," Margot said. "Talk."

"I have agreed to a sit-down interview with the *Today* show. I want you by my side," he said.

"Why?" Margot asked. "After this bullshit you must understand there's no future for us."

"I know," he said. And that fucker had the audacity to sound sad. He pulled the pin on the grenade, and he sounded sad? "And I feel awful—"

"Why. Do. You. Want. Me. There?"

"Right now there is speculation all over social media that I was on Epstein's island—"

"Were you?" Margot shrieked, and Julia pulled her head out of the pillow.

"No. No. I swear."

"Your word doesn't mean shit."

"I was not on Epstein's island. I was not a part of a pedophile ring."

"Then just say that."

"It's not just me. There are rumors circulating about you too. About our family."

Margot rolled her eyes, but Julia winced like it might be true.

"The twins have agreed to be on the segment. But Alex is waiting to talk to you and Skye isn't answering my calls."

"You talked to the twins?" Ellen agreeing to this made sense; she'd do anything for her father. But Amelia?

"They want this shit put to bed too," Jack said. Margot could hear him huffing and puffing and she wanted to ask him what he was doing. Last week she would have asked him and he would have made a joke about trying to tie his shoes and they'd laugh about how they both woke up with sore wrists just from sleeping; the memory was a jagged knife right in her gut.

"No Skye," Margot said. "She's not on camera."

"Okay."

"I'll talk to the twins and tell them they don't have to do this."

"Margot. Please—"

"Jack. Don't be this guy. Don't be the guy that makes a mess and needs his whole family to fix it. If you and I going on camera and holding hands and I don't know . . . crying doesn't work, then it doesn't work."

"You'll cry?" God. He sounded so pathetically hopeful.

Julia started to laugh and put her head back down in the pillow.

Margot imagined, in all honesty, it would be very difficult not to cry.

"When is this interview?"

"Friday."

That was four days away.

"Where do we film? And do not say our home."

"New York," he said. "That's . . . that's where you are, right?"

The credit card bills. The jet. Of course he would know. Maybe Margot should be grateful he wasn't demanding his way into the suite.

"Fine. Four days. Send me the details."

"Margot, thank you. Seriously."

"I'm not doing it for you," Margot said. "I'm doing it for Skye. You file for custody and I'm taking all this to a lawyer."

"She wouldn't want to come with me anyway," he said, having the gall to sound like he had regrets.

"You shouldn't have filmed me, Jack," Margot said.

"I didn't, Margot. I just used it."

Julia looked up, eyebrows furrowed, and it dawned on them at the same time. "Noelle."

"I'm sorry—"

Margot hung up on him before he could say one more word.

Julia, like she knew the betrayal of her assistant and friend was the most crushing of all, put her hand over Margot's and squeezed. Hard. Like Margot was hanging over a cliff and Julia was trying to pull her back to solid ground.

CHAPTER 22

June 1977
New York City

Ginger

"I didn't do it," Faye said the morning after the police raided the club. Faye put down the paper, the headline yelling at them from the coffee table. *Lady X Brings Orbit Room Back to Earth*. She was pink in the sunshine, but the bags under her eyes were dark.

"You just vanished!" Ginger cried. "I turned around and you were gone."

"I went to the bathroom. When I came out . . ." Another one of her infuriating shrugs. She sipped her tea and winced when it was too hot. "I left."

"You didn't come home," Ginger said. It felt like they were on the show *Baretta*, interrogating Faye. They just needed a dark room and some handcuffs.

"I did," she said. "Just later than you. Todd was passing out on the couch."

"Where were you?" Ginger asked.

"We must spend every day, every minute together?" Faye asked. "I got a hot dog."

"You're the one so eager to keep Lady X going," Ginger said.

"Not where I work," Faye said. "I need that job. Why aren't we asking Rachel?"

Rachel held up her hands. "Why me?"

"Because you wrote that article. Because it all got bigger when Vanessa Purdy got involved," Faye said. "Because I think you'd do anything to impress her."

"I didn't have anything to do with the Orbit Room. But, you should know, Vanessa has asked me to write another op-ed."

"Come on, Rachel! You can't tell her no?" Ginger asked.

"I don't want to tell her no. I believe in this. I believe in what we've started. But I didn't do the Orbit Room. I swear," Rachel said, pointing at the newspaper. "I think it was someone else. Someone else with a bone to pick with Shane."

"Like who?" Ginger asked.

"Any one of the millions of people he doesn't let into the club?" Rachel ticked off. "Any one of his suppliers he doesn't pay. Any one of the women he's asked to suck his dick to get a job. Shane is an asshole. I bet hundreds of people would love to see him go down."

"This is true." Faye took Rachel's feet into her lap so they could both stretch out their legs. Dust motes floated in the air around them like they were blessed by pixies. "I believe you," she said to Rachel.

"And I believe you," Rachel said to Faye.

Ginger didn't believe either one of them.

The Orbit Room reopened after being shut down for a week. Shane said the raid had been about fire codes, which didn't seem *impossible,* so everyone believed it. But when the second Vanessa Purdy's op-ed came out, it sent Shane into a meltdown.

One by one, Shane called all the female employees up to his office "for a chat." He sat behind his desk, the watery light from a rainy day making him look skeletal and paranoid. A third-rate crime boss.

Behind him was Dante and a new security guy Shane had hired, who had a gun tucked into the hip of his jeans. Ginger would have laughed if she wasn't so scared.

Ginger didn't sit in the chair where she had sat during her interview, choosing instead to stand and ignore it.

"What's going on?" she asked, looking from Shane to the security guy and back to Shane. An icy cold finger of fear touched the back of her neck.

"That's what I'm trying to find out," Shane said, wiping his nose. "What do you know about this Lady X bitch?"

Ginger swallowed a terrified laugh. "Nothing. I mean . . . only what everyone else knows."

"That girl that comes in here, your friend . . ." Shane waved his hand around.

"Rachel?"

"Whatever the fuck her name is, she works for Purdy, doesn't she?"

"How do you know that?"

"Because I know everything that happens in my club!" he shouted, which was obviously not true, but Ginger wasn't going to say anything.

"Yes, Rachel works for Purdy."

"Is she Lady X?"

"No."

"But she knows who is?"

"No, she doesn't."

Shane waited her out and she remembered the feel of him in front of her in that chair she was ignoring. His dick in her hand. The feel of his belly against her knuckles. She swallowed down revulsion and a scream.

"She can't come to the club anymore. She's banned. And you better be careful or you'll be fired."

Faye was waiting for Ginger downstairs, biting the edge of her thumb like she used to when she first moved in. "*Ça va?*" she asked, and Ginger had to laugh.

"Not *ça va*, Faye. Not *ça va* at all."

The next morning Rachel pounded on their bedroom doors. "Up and at 'em, girls!" she cried.

"What's wrong?" Ginger asked, stepping out of her dark room into the sunlit living room. She got cut at three A.M. and it was too damn early for this.

"Get dressed," Rachel said. In the kitchen she poured coffee into a thermos.

"For what?" Ginger asked. She wore a Steelers shirt that Bonnie had left behind and nothing else.

"It's too early," Faye said as she stepped into the sunshine. "Why are we awake?"

"Because there is a march on city hall," Rachel said.

"Another anti-nuclear thing?" Ginger asked.

Faye groaned and turned back around for the bedroom. "No," Rachel said. "No! It's a women's rights march on city hall. Vanessa is calling it the Lady X march."

"No," Ginger and Faye both gasped.

"Yes," Rachel said, ducking back into the kitchen with her eyes wide and smiling. "Come on. Don't you want to see what we've made?"

"Rachel." Ginger grabbed her roommate's arm as she walked by with a paper bag full of sandwiches. "Listen to me. Shane called every female employee into his office to ask what we knew about Lady X. He asked about you. He knows you work for Vanessa Purdy."

"Lots of people work for Vanessa Purdy."

"He's banned you from the club," Ginger added, and for a moment Rachel looked hurt. Stunned.

"How . . . how does he even know my name?"

"Someone must have told him. Look, we are too close to this. People are connecting dots."

"Fuck that guy," Rachel said, shrugging off Ginger's hand. "And fuck that club."

"Rachel—"

"We're doing the right thing. Vanessa is doing the right thing. This march is the right thing. All those assholes are mad because we're right and they're wrong," she said, defiant. "And you know that."

Ginger did know that. She did. She'd stood on that cop car and felt in her bones the rightness of what they were doing.

Rachel put the sandwiches and the thermos in a bag and slung it over her shoulder. "This is happening. You can come or not."

"I'm coming," Faye said, and went back to her room to change.

"You're kidding!" Ginger cried.

"I want to see what we made," Faye called from her closet.

Ginger rolled her eyes but went into her own bedroom to change. Rachel clapped. "This is going to be fun!"

They took the subway down to Chambers Street and Broadway and when they climbed the steps to the street it was mayhem. Already more women in one place than Ginger had ever seen. Hundreds of women. Some carried signs that said WE ARE ALL LADY X.

"Holy shit," she breathed. She didn't feel pride. Or if she did it was buried under fear. This was . . . too much. Too much attention. The air was oppressive and the Hudson smelled swampy in the heat.

"Right on," Rachel cried. "I have to meet up with the team. You want to come—"

"No," Faye said, putting her sweaty, sticky arm through Ginger's. "We will watch."

Rachel ran off to find the people she worked with, and Ginger and Faye moved along Chambers Street with the rivers of women gathering at city hall.

A chant started up from somewhere in the back, and soon the women around them had joined in.

"One, two, three, four, we won't take it anymore! Five, six, seven, eight, no more violence, no more rape!"

"This can't be real," Ginger kept saying.

"Women are mad," Faye said with her shrug that said *What can be done?*

Women were linked arm in arm with their anger. Walking in step. Hugging one another before joining the chant. The march. Some were crying. The communal nature of it all, seeing in one another's faces the same pain. The same rage.

It was miraculous.

Cops were there, but they mostly looked on like angry spectators. Elbowing one another in the ribs as women walked past. Some catcalling.

A dark-haired woman in front of them turned and spat something at a cop, who stepped forward, glad to have a reason to get rough with the protesters, but the woman's friends pulled her back in line.

They smiled at the cop, their most pacifying smiles. Lowered their heads like servants. They apologized for her, over and over, to mollify him. Walking faster until he would look stupid chasing them down.

It was so wrong. So out of place here.

They walked arm in arm down the gravel avenues of City Hall Park to get as close to the stairs in front of the columned entrance to the building as they could. The crowd was deep around them, shoulder to shoulder.

There was the crackle of a megaphone. Vanessa Purdy, tall and broad with dark, serious glasses, stood at the top of the steps and welcomed everyone to the new world.

"A world where we don't have to bear sexual violence or harassment. You know what I really like about this Lady X?" she asked, and women shouted a bunch of things back at her. "Yeah," she laughed. "Her giant brass balls."

A group of men lingering in the shadows of trees at the edge of the park started to heckle the women around Ginger and Faye. Most women ignored it. A few of them sneered, made bold by the safety of the numbers surrounding them, gave the men the finger, and turned back to Vanessa on the steps.

But the dark-haired woman . . . she was not letting it go.

"Fuck you!" she shouted at them.

"You wish, you hairy dyke," some asshole shouted back. He cupped his dick through his jeans and made kissing sounds. As far as catcalls in this city went, it was pretty tame. But apparently for her, it was too much. It was unignorable. The very last straw.

Her friends tried to hold her back, but she shook them off and stepped toward the catcaller and his two friends, who looked delighted that their extremely basic effort at goading a woman into action had worked. They were apes one step above throwing their shit.

"Cherie!" one of the woman's friends shouted, trying to pull her back toward what felt like the safety of the crowd. Now, others had turned, and they were shouting things at the stupid men standing next to the small cast-iron fence. Suddenly Cherie had a force of women with her, fingers jabbing the air, their faces contorted with anger.

"The cops won't let anything happen," an older woman next to them said. Ten feet away two uniformed police officers watched the growing drama and twirled their billy clubs as if bored.

But Ginger and Faye knew better. They knew what was coming before it happened. One of the men hauled off and slapped Cherie, hard across the face, knocking her to the ground. His friend kicked her in the ribs and the other one spit on her before the cops could be bothered to even blow their whistles.

The men ran off and a few women chased them, but in the end the cops stepped in front of the women, arms out like they were corralling animals, and the men went free.

Cherie was helped to her feet, bloodied and clutching her stomach, spit clinging to her cheek.

Ginger stepped forward to help, but Faye stopped her.

"The last thing we need is to be arrested," Faye said, and Ginger couldn't argue with that. The two of them walked away, calmly and casually.

Until they saw Boyle standing beneath a tree, watching them. He wore civilian clothes, a crumpled pair of khaki pants and a T-shirt with sweat stains under the arms. He drank from a bottle slipped inside a paper bag. She wasn't close enough to smell him, but she knew he reeked of body odor and booze.

And anger.

He lifted the paper bag, a toast with nothing but malice behind it. Faye grabbed her hand and they ran for the subway and home.

WOMEN'S MARCH TURNS VIOLENT
New York Times, June 22, 1977

One woman was sent to the hospital and five were arrested after an altercation at Vanessa Purdy's Lady X march on city hall. Witnesses claim a group of men were harassing the peaceful protesters, but according to police reports a woman attacked a bystander and he defended himself. Police cleared the area and arrested protesters who became violent.

"The only thing violent about this protest," says Vanessa Purdy, "were the men who instigated the fight. This was a peaceful protest. And these actions by the male spectators and the police only proves why we need justice."

"A woman swung at me," said one of the bystanders who was caught up in the fight. "What was I supposed to do? They want equal rights, don't they?"

CHAPTER 23

June 1977
New York City

Ginger

That evening before opening, the main bar was dark and cold. And she felt watched in every room.

Todd filled the wells with ice. Made sure they had lots of champagne. Lots of cream. Peppermint schnapps. Crème de cacao. Shane had them trying a new drink.

"Midori?" Ginger said, looking at the bottle. The liquor was a kind of fluorescent green.

"Comp it," Shane said. "Comp lots of it. And if anyone so much as mentions Lady X, they get the boot."

"You're kidding," Todd said. "After what happened at that march today? Everyone is going to be talking about Lady X."

"I don't give a shit, Todd," Shane snarled and stormed off, leaving them with a case of Midori.

"He invested," Todd whispered. "It's all the rage over at Studio 54. We will just make sours. Squeeze more lemons."

"Jasmine is late," Ginger said as they squeezed lemons until their hands hurt.

"That's never a good sign with her."

"Is she late a lot?" Out in the coatroom they never knew what was happening in the main bar. It was ground central for gossip, but terrible for truth.

"It's the fucking boyfriend," Todd said.

"Right," Ginger said, remembering Jasmine's black eye and the way he held her neck.

Two hours later the club was filling up when Jasmine ducked under the flap and put herself behind Ginger, who was pulling dirty glasses from the bar.

"Jasmine?" Ginger said, trying to get out of her way, but she was glued to Ginger like a sequin. "What's . . ."

Carl came up to the bar with his nostrils flaring, looking like a bull at a fence line. He was tall and rangy with blond hair he wore in a mullet and a handlebar mustache, the ends damp, like he kept sucking them into his mouth.

"Jas!" he shouted, with a good old boy accent. She'd guess he grew up somewhere hot and swampy. "Come on now."

"It's fine," Jasmine said from over my shoulder. "We can talk about it later."

"We're going to talk about it now—"

"You need a drink, handsome?" Ginger asked, leaning forward, making sure he got a good shot of her cleavage. Ginger found her cleavage could derail just about any man.

And sure enough, Carl fell for it, distracted by the way the dress pushed her breasts up to her neck. "Let me get you something special." Ginger poured him one of the Midori sours and slid it over the bar to him.

"Thanks, darlin'," he said. "Jas? This ain't over, honey."

He walked away, his head brushing the bottoms of helium balloons that bounced off the dance floor.

"You got a lot of nerve flirting with my boyfriend right in front of me," Jasmine said, but even Ginger could tell being tough was an act.

"Just trying to get him off your scent," Ginger said. It was dark in the bar and the strobe lights didn't make anything clearer. Looking at her face, Ginger couldn't tell if she'd been hurt, if she was scared, or what. "You okay?"

"Carl had a bad game is all," Jasmine said, tugging the edges of her short skirt and then straightening the stupid silver collar.

"Bad game?" she asked.

Jasmine blinked at her. "He's a pitcher for the Mets?"

Ginger had no idea; she couldn't give a fuck about the Mets.

"He takes his bad games out on you, does he?"

Jasmine shot Ginger a dark *mind your own business* look and walked off to her station on the far side of the bar. She would have been regal if it weren't for the antenna bobbing on her head.

It was busy, but Ginger had one eye on Jasmine all night. Jasmine didn't come out from behind that bar unless she was with her or one of the other waitresses. She didn't take a break unless it was to go with Ginger to the bathroom.

But around midnight Sylvester Stallone came in with Joe Namath and about thirty other people and the crowd went nuts. Doors closed at three and most folks cleared out, but some stayed to party with Shane, including Sylvester and Joe. Faye got cut and Ginger just assumed Jasmine left at the same time.

At five A.M. Todd and Ginger turned in their cash registers to Shane and went to the coat check to change and head home. The lights were off, and it was just Todd with her so she didn't even bother going back in the far corner with the lost-and-found coats and the tiny bit of privacy they gave a girl. She pulled off that itchy dress and those awful bloomers and pulled on her loose peasant dress.

"Todd, I'm gonna get a cab. You—"

"Ginger?" a tiny voice said from that dark corner.

Ginger jumped, startled.

"Faye?"

"No. It's . . ." A pale hand reached out from the coats. "Jasmine."

Todd and Ginger shared one quick look—the whites of Todd's eyes fully visible around his dark irises—then slowly pushed the coats back to reveal Jasmine. Collar torn. Hair down around her face. Hand cradled to her chest.

And a black eye that covered half her face.

Ginger took her home. Todd came too, helping Jasmine in and out of the cab, his arm around her waist. Ginger got the door to the apartment open and turned on the light.

"Girls?" Ginger called, and Faye's door opened, her pale head sticking out into the hallway.

"Hello, darling," Todd said. "Bit of an emergency here."

Faye shut her door and reappeared in that rainbow-sleeve T-shirt of Rachel's and a pair of blue underpants. She padded into the living room and saw Jasmine on the couch.

"Oh. *Chérie.*"

"It's not as bad as it looks," Jasmine said, trying to wave her hand, but her wrist made her wince. "Honestly."

Faye looked at Ginger with a dozen questions, but she didn't have any answers.

"You want a drink, honey?" Ginger asked Jasmine, who nodded gratefully. "How about a change of clothes?" Another grateful nod. Faye went to get the wine and the mugs the girls usually drank it out of, and Ginger grabbed some clothes from her room.

"Where's Rachel?" Ginger whispered to Faye in the kitchen. "Is she back from the march?"

Ginger had sudden visions of Rachel in jail or worse.

"She was here when I got home," Faye said. "She's working on something. Nothing but clickety-clack."

Rachel spent a lot of nights in that room with a bottle of wine, working on op-eds.

Ginger gave Jasmine a pair of soft sweatpants and a T-shirt. "Do you need help?"

"I can do it," she said, but she could not pull the dress off her shoulders or over her head, which was the only way to get out of it. Before Ginger could step in, Todd was there.

"Trust me," he said with a soft smile and a wink. "No matter what Carl thinks, I am unmoved by your breasts."

Jasmine smiled gratefully and Todd undid the collar and pulled the dress as carefully as he could down her body. Revealing other bruises. Older bruises along her ribs.

"What the fuck happened?"

It was Rachel coming out of her bedroom, hair a mess and smelling like a bar. If the energy in the room wasn't so soft and careful, Ginger would have rolled her eyes at her.

"Todd and I found her like this in the coatroom," Ginger said.

Jas turned down the wine and Faye made her tea instead.

"Hey, Jas," Rachel said, coming to sit beside her on the couch. "Looks like you took a punch from Rocky himself."

Jasmine smiled but didn't laugh. "It was Carl. I tried to give him time to cool off, but . . ."

She looked down at her hand, tried to move her wrist, but hissed in pain.

"Can I take your hat off?" Ginger asked her.

"Please," Jas said, and Ginger pulled the last remaining bobby pin that kept that hat cockeyed on her head and another bobby pin that let her black hair fall down around her shoulders.

"I hate those damn things," she muttered.

Ginger made a soft sound of agreement.

"He did this at the club?" Faye asked. She sat down on the floor, pulling the T-shirt over her knees.

Jasmine nodded. "He had a terrible game today and I try to give him lots of room, you know? But he was just spoiling for a fight."

"It was a fight, huh?" Rachel said. "How many licks did you get in?"

Jasmine took a sip of tea and sloshed some of it on her bare leg but didn't even flinch.

"He's been out of control all season," Jasmine said. "They'll never make the playoffs, so I thought I'd stick it out and then leave him when it was over."

"Why wait?"

"In the hopes that he doesn't kill me when I pack my bags?"

She said it like a joke, but no one laughed. "He knows where I work. He knows where my mom lives. I mean . . . I can't get away from him. The best I can hope for is to leave when he doesn't care as much."

"As exit strategies go, it's not bad," Rachel said. "How long have you wanted to get away?"

"Months. I mean . . . the day after I moved in, but . . ." She finished that thought with a sad shrug. Unlike Faye's shrugs, this one was easily translated.

What can I do?

"We'll move you out," Rachel said. "And you can stay here."

"What?" Jasmine said. "I can't . . ."

"One of you is sleeping in a closet. You don't have the room," Todd pointed out. "You can come stay with me. That asshole will never dream you're living with two queers on the Upper East Side."

"I can't," Jasmine said.

"Why not?" Faye asked with her direct bluntness.

"Work?" Jas asked, like she was reaching for straws.

"You won't be working for a while with that wrist anyway," Todd said.

"He's pretty sure he's gonna get traded or dropped at the end of the year, and he's old so this is the end for him, and he knows it." That was why he was taking everything out on Jas. Mom had a guy like this once. Ginger knew—this wasn't going to get better, it was only going to get worse.

"All the more reason to get out now," Rachel said.

Jas was losing her reluctance. "He's got a team meeting tomorrow. Practice at Shea . . . He'll be gone all morning."

"Then we go in the morning," Rachel said.

"So this is like a proper caper," Todd said, kicking his legs over the side of the couch to sit between Faye and Jasmine. "Count me in."

"Your boyfriend won't care?" Jasmine asked.

"Oh, he'll blow a gasket, but I have his number," Todd said with a wink. He grabbed a mug of wine and downed it. "And it's not forever, right, hon? You just need a safe place to get on your feet."

"I can't believe you're doing this for me," Jasmine said.

"This?" Rachel said, catching Ginger's eye and then Faye's. "This is nothing."

Ginger woke up a few hours later and Faye had already made coffee while Todd and Jasmine were on the couch looking like they hadn't slept at all.

"What's wrong?" Ginger asked into the heavy energy of the room.

"I think Jasmine needs to go to the hospital," Todd said. "This wrist."

Jas held it out and her wrist was bruised and swollen twice its normal size. "Oh shit."

"I think that fucker broke it," Jasmine said, dark circles under her eyes.

"I have aspirin," Ginger said, stepping to the kitchen, but Faye was already there, shaking three pills into Jasmine's hand.

"I think the caper is off for the day," Todd said.

Faye shook her head. "We'll go. Give us your key, you."

Rachel came out of the room wearing her *Little House on the Prairie* nightgown. "Don't you have a doorman?" she asked, stretching. "If we leave with all your stuff, he'll call the cops."

"Not Dominick," Jasmine said. "He's cool."

"Yeah, there's cool," Ginger said, "and then there's cool with robbery."

"No. He's . . . helped me before. When Carl lost his temper. He's been trying to get me to go stay with his sister in the Bronx."

"So," Rachel said. "If we tell him you gave us your key and we're moving you out before Carl comes home?"

"He'll hold the elevator for you."

"Far out," Rachel said. "Sounds like we've got a plan."

The apartment was a few blocks east of Central Park, on a quiet street with a couple of full-sized trees and some old ladies walking their poodles. There was less trash up here and the air smelled different.

"Money," Faye said, her lip curled.

They found the building, and as they approached the door a man in a uniform who looked like he might have played football in college until he hurt his knee, which was how Jasmine described him, opened the door for the three of them.

"Hello, ladies," he said with a smile. He was immediately likeable. "How can I help you?"

"We're friends of Jasmine's," Rachel said, and the man's eyebrows lowered in sudden suspicion.

"Everything okay with her?" he asked.

"Well, not so much. She's at the hospital. We're here to move her out."

"That motherfucker Carl?"

"He put her there. He doesn't know we're here."

"Well, you timed it right, ladies. He drove his big old Cadillac out of the garage about an hour and a half ago. You got a key?"

The truth was, Ginger had her suspicions. And maybe she was jaded about nice guys after that bullshit with Boyle. Ginger didn't think that if the rubber hit the road, Dominick would really help them. If Carl showed up, Ginger would bet money Dominick would offer them up without a second thought.

"Three-oh-two," he said. "Second door on the right. The back door takes you to a stairway to the garage if you get in a pinch."

Ginger, Faye, and Rachel stepped into the elevator, and he waved as the doors slowly closed.

"Seems nice," Rachel said. Faye and Ginger both made scoffing noises in their throats. "Yeah." Rachel shrugged. "You're probably right."

The hallway had a dark blue carpet that looked expensive and freshly painted white walls. There was even art.

"Classy," Ginger said, looking at a picture of two girls standing on a beach, another girl flying a kite in the distance.

"*Allez*," Faye said, all business as she pushed open the door to the apartment. Rachel and Ginger followed, closing and locking the door behind them. The hush of the apartment was so loud.

"Jeez," Rachel said, looking around. "Get a load of this place. What a trip."

The living room was carpeted in wall-to-wall white shag. A low red couch and a matching chair. Silver mirrored wallpaper on one wall that reflected a distorted view of the room and everything in it, including the three of them.

"It's like a fun house mirror," Ginger said, lifting her arms. She looked like a fat, round bird. She crouched and looked like a tall, thin bird.

There was a hookah in the corner and a teak liquor cabinet. A hi-fi and the biggest television set Ginger had ever seen. On top of the television was a red lacquered statue that looked, disturbingly, like a giant erect dick.

"He's kidding with that, isn't he?" Rachel asked.

"You think Carl is compensating for something?" Ginger said, and Rachel laughed. Even Faye cracked a smile.

"Come on," Rachel said. "We're wasting time."

Ginger followed her down the hallway past the kitchen that looked like it was never used. A second bedroom that Jasmine said Carl used as his office. Ginger peeked her head in and saw a wall full of trophies and plaques. Medals hung up on hooks around the room.

"Holy shit," Ginger said, looking at one of them. "This was from his Little League team in Florida."

"So?" Rachel called out.

"Who hangs up their Little League shit?"

"Little League men," Faye answered. "Come help me."

There was a huge desk in the room with a stack of framed pictures and a hammer on the corner. There was a jumping rope and a bunch of dumbbells by the window.

"Ginger!" Rachel cried.

"Coming!" Ginger joined them in the bedroom, where a king-size bed dominated. Rachel was clearing out the bedside table and Faye was in the closet.

"You think she wants these?" Rachel asked, using one finger to pull out a pair of handcuffs. "Or this?" She pulled out a long, black blindfold. They all looked at those handcuffs and blindfold like they were evidence of a crime scene.

"Maybe she ties him up," Ginger offered.

"Little League men don't like to be tied up," Faye said like she had some authority on the subject.

Rachel put the toys away and pulled out a small picture album Jasmine had asked her to grab. Some lotion. A tiny jewelry box. Faye plopped a soft-side Samsonite suitcase on the bed and started to dump Jasmine's clothes into it. She emptied out the dresser drawers.

"I'll get her stuff out of the bathroom," Ginger said.

"What did she ask for in the living room?" Rachel asked.

"Some of the records," Ginger reminded her. "She said everything good was hers. Everything garbage was his."

"All right," Rachel laughed, and they filed out of the bedroom. Ginger went to the bathroom and Rachel walked past her to the living room. The bathroom was full of tiny white-and-black tiles. The toilet, sink, and bathtub were black.

A vase full of feathers sat on top of the toilet. Ginger opened the medicine cabinet and grabbed Jasmine's birth control and a prescription for an antibiotic she was taking. Her inhaler.

Ginger was putting them in the bag she'd brought when she heard a door open.

And a man whistling.

"Jas?" he called, and Ginger felt every bit of blood drain from her face. Panicked, she jerked backward and hit the vase of feathers on top of the toilet. It rattled against the wall before she could catch it.

"Baby!" he drawled. "I know I was out of line, but you made me so mad and you know how I am when I'm—"

He stood in the doorway of the bathroom, looking big and blond and mean. Whatever apology he was pretending to give vanished, and his eyes went cold. "What the fuck are you doing here?"

CHAPTER 24

June 1977
New York City

Ginger

Did he recognize Ginger? Out of her uniform and without makeup? Wearing normal clothes? *God, please don't let him recognize me.*

He looked at the bag in Ginger's hand, then back at Ginger. "Where's Jas?"

"I'm just . . ."

"Where the fuck is Jas?" He took one lunging step into the bathroom and grabbed Ginger's hand, wrenching it back until it felt like her wrist was going to pop. Ginger screamed and pushed at him, but he kept coming, pushing her back toward the bathtub. She put her good hand out against the wall and knocked down a shampoo bottle. She had no idea what he was saying, but spittle was flying from his mouth like he'd never meant anything more. Ginger was sure he was about to kill her.

Then there was a thick gong sound, and his eyes went wide and his mouth stopped moving and he slumped in slow motion to the floor. Behind him, holding the big red penis, was Rachel.

"Shit," Ginger said.

"Are you okay?" Rachel asked.

Faye ran into the bathroom. "Come on. Before he wakes up, let's tie him up."

"Let's just leave!" Ginger cried, but Rachel and Faye already had their hands under his armpits and were pulling him from the bathroom toward the living room.

"Jesus, for a string bean he weighs a bunch."

"Ego is heavy," Faye grunted.

"There's nothing to tie him to in here," Rachel said, looking at the long, upholstered couch and the matching beanbag chair. They switched direction and pulled him back down the hallway toward the bedroom.

"Here!" Ginger said, still holding her arm against her body as she pushed open the door to the office. Behind the desk was a ladder-back chair. She grabbed it, putting it beside the desk.

Together the three of them heaved him up onto the chair. Faye grabbed the jump rope from the corner and Rachel ran back for the handcuffs and blindfold.

"It's too late for that," Ginger said as Rachel put the blindfold on him. "He already saw me."

"But he didn't recognize you."

"I don't know for sure." She didn't look anything like she did at the club, but she wasn't willing to bet on it.

"Well, let's make sure he doesn't see any more of you. And keep your mouth shut if he wakes up." She pulled his arms behind the chair and put the cuffs on him, all while Faye tied him to the chair with a series of intricate knots.

She looked up and caught them staring. "I had a goat. He was an escape artist."

"Get the rest of her stuff and let's get out of here," Rachel said.

Ginger went back to the bathroom and picked up the bag she'd dropped. She just started throwing things into it. Toothpaste and hairspray. Perfume.

Rachel finished in the bedroom, and they met in the hallway.

"You get everything?" Ginger asked in a whisper.

"I think so. I found a roll of twenties in his dresser. Grabbed that too."

"Nice."

"Jasmine!" Carl roared. They ran into the office, where Carl was struggling to get himself out of the chair. Faye was at the blank wall, a big black marker in her hand.

Lady X was scrawled across the wall.

"Jasmine, I know you're in here. Untie me and we can chalk this up to a misunderstanding, right?"

The three of them looked at one another, wild-eyed and frantic. Well, Ginger was frantic. Faye looked like this was going exactly as she'd planned. The depth of this betrayal wouldn't fully register for weeks; right now, it was just panic heaped on panic.

"Jasmine, I'm serious. You're pissing me off, darlin'. You don't want me to be pissed off, right?" He tried to stand; he rocked on the chair. None of those knots would hold forever.

Rachel started to back out of the room, her finger to her lips. *Let's just go*, she mouthed. But Faye was watching Carl.

Faye wasn't listening. Faye didn't seem to be in the room.

Or in her body.

"You stupid bitch," Carl snarled, his face savage. "You stupid fucking bitch. I mean, not only are you stupid. You're dumb." Behind his back he twisted and suddenly his hands were free. He lifted them, wiggling his fingers. "Remember, you begged me to get the kind of handcuffs you could get out of without a key." He reached for the blindfold, and Ginger dove for his arm, grabbing it and using all her weight to hold it down.

Go, she mouthed. *Run*. He'd already seen Ginger, but if they left now he'd never know Rachel and Faye were there. Carl struggled, but Ginger was fueled with the adrenaline of survival.

He started punching Ginger with his other hand. Grabbed a fistful of her hair and tried to pull her off him. Ginger felt strands getting ripped from her scalp, but she kept her scream behind clenched teeth.

Faye, cold and distant, locked someplace in her own past and their combined frantic present, reached forward and grabbed the hammer at the end of the desk and smashed it down close to his hand.

The violence was startling. Everyone went still.

"Let go," Faye said, in a voice Ginger had never heard before. Carl's fingers slowly released Ginger's hair. Ginger's breath sobbed but she didn't let up on his arm. His fingers were spread wide as he tried to use the desk to push himself back against Ginger, knocking her off balance.

"Stop," Faye said.

"What are you going to do? Huh? What do you think you can do to me, bitch? You're fucking worthless. You're nothing. You can't even—"

Faye lifted the hammer high above her head, like some Viking priestess in the middle of a blood sacrifice. She brought it down on his hand. For a second everything was quiet. And then Carl screamed, a blood-curdling, animal scream. Ginger reeled back, sick. His hand was broken. All the way broken. A dozen different parts held together by skin.

"Jesus," Rachel said, and then she pulled Faye into motion. Ginger ran around the frantic and sobbing man tied to a chair and the three of them grabbed the bags and got out of there.

They sprinted down the hallway, jabbed the elevator button twenty times until it opened in slow motion. The elevator doors closed behind them while "The Girl from Ipanema" played in the background.

"Faye!" she cried. "What the fuck?"

Faye was shaking as she shrugged. "*Il est un animal!*"

"He saw me," Ginger said, and pushed Faye. "He saw me. And you wrote *Lady X* and . . . you broke his hand. Faye!" She didn't even seem to care. Ginger shoved her again. Again, until she was in the corner. Ginger was levitating she was so angry. This wasn't vandalism. It was assault and battery. It was jail time.

It's the end of my life.

"Hey, stop," Rachel said, getting between them. "I don't think he recognized you. Honestly."

"The doorman saw us!" Ginger cried.

"Jas said he's cool," Faye whispered.

"Yeah, how cool is he going to be when the cops show up and it's us or his job."

"I'm sorry," Faye said. Her eyes were her eyes again. She was in her body and in the moment. She touched Ginger's hand. Grabbed her shoulder. Wrapped her arms around Ginger's neck. A torrent of French came out of her, so fast Ginger couldn't keep up. Ginger pushed her away, unable to accept her apology. All she saw was how that woman at the march had been attacked, dragged down to the ground by a bunch of men who would have killed her, just for supporting Lady X.

The elevator doors opened with a *bing*. Dominick got one look at them and the smile fell from his face.

"He came back."

"You can do whatever you want," Rachel said. "Tell the cops, don't tell the cops, but he deserved what he got."

"I never saw you," Dominick said, like he was giving a vow. "There haven't been any visitors to three-oh-two."

There was no way Ginger was going to trust this guy, who had probably been nice to Jasmine just so he could get in her pants.

"Come on," Ginger said, and pulled her roommates into action. They ran out of the building, picking up speed as they raced to the subway station.

They held their breath and dodged the garbage and made the 6 Train south, just as the graffitied doors were closing.

"You've . . . you've got to leave. Today," Faye said.

"And go where?" Ginger cried.

"Pittsburgh," Rachel said. "You can stay with your friend, right?"

"Bonnie?" Ginger nodded. She was short-circuiting. All she could do was look at Faye and feel a rage so pure it was like being high. She didn't know herself. Had no idea what she would do.

Faye had just ruined her life. Sent her backward. She was closer to that fucking trailer than she was to making it in New York City. And she was furious.

"Go to the train station right now." Rachel pulled out the roll of twenties she'd swiped from Carl's dresser. "Don't go back to the apartment. Don't do anything but get on the next train out of this city."

"I can't believe . . ." Faye put her hands to her eyes and then her lips. "I didn't plan it. I don't even remember thinking. Yes? I just . . . the hammer was in my hand, and he was saying such . . ." She closed her eyes and tears raced down her cheeks.

"It's okay," Rachel said.

"No, it's not," Ginger snapped. "The way the press went nuts over a bookstore, a dance club, and a vandalized cop car? They were going to lose their marbles over a New York Mets pitcher with a broken hand. No matter how much he deserved it.

I'm going to throw up.

"He's going to accuse Jasmine," Faye said.

"She's been at the hospital," Rachel reminded her. "With Todd. Probably getting that wrist set. Lots of witnesses."

Ginger looked down at her own wrist. It was red and swollen but she could move it all right. That fucker had a patented move. He walked right up to a line but didn't cross it.

"What will we say?" Faye asked.

"Oh," Ginger snapped. "You're worried about your alibi?"

"Keep your train ticket," Rachel said. "And call when you get to Pittsburgh. Call everyone in the city you know."

"It's going to be okay," Faye said again. And her efforts to make it seem like no big deal enraged Ginger. She was swollen and floating with anger. She wanted to *squeeze* Faye as hard as she could.

"It won't," she said. Faye went pale and shrank even smaller in the subway seat. "You know it. I may . . . I may never be back." She might get arrested. Attacked like the woman at the march. Whatever her life was before this moment, it was going to be totally different after this.

And it was Faye's fault.

Suddenly every question she never asked this girl seemed like a mistake. Ginger knew that day Faye walked into the apartment that she was hiding something, and Ginger had thought—like the fool her mother believed her to be—that Faye was cool. Mysterious.

She was just trouble.

"What were you thinking when you lifted that hammer?" Ginger asked. "Who did you really want to hurt? What aren't you telling us, Faye!"

Faye swallowed but stayed silent.

"If you cost me everything, don't I have a right to know?"

"I will leave," Faye said, not answering the question. "I can move. You are right, it's not fair what I have done. You are paying for my price."

"Why did your sister run away?" Ginger said, and Faye's eyes went wide, panicked. She was a cornered rabbit. "Why are you so scared of the cops? What are you hiding?"

The subway slowed and finally stopped. And Faye gave her nothing. Not an answer. Not another apology. Whatever she was hiding was more important than Ginger.

"Fuck you, Faye," she said, and got to her feet. "How long do I have to stay gone?"

"A week. You'll be back by next weekend at the latest."

A week. Ginger could do that.

She swayed as the bodies around her stood and headed for the doors about to open.

"We'll be fine. All of us," Rachel promised. The doors *bing*ed and the world rushed past.

"Boop," Rachel said. "You have to go."

"*Oui*," Faye said. "Be careful."

Ginger slipped between the closing doors and transferred twice until she was in the belly of Penn Station. And within twenty minutes she was heading north to Boston, where she would go west to Pittsburgh.

WANTED LADY X: DEAD OR ALIVE

Daily Mail, June 24, 1977

Lady X's latest victim and Mets pitcher Carl Fitz, who last year pitched a no-hitter against the Phillies and this year had a respectable 4.0 ERA, has had three surgeries on his hand and his future in baseball looks bleak.

"I have no feeling in my pointer finger," he said. "Doctors say I'll never be able to move my thumb again. This woman took my career away from me. I'll never be able to throw a baseball again."

Fitz is offering a $5,000 reward for any information on Lady X that ends in her being found and arrested.

"I don't care if the police find her or if I do, I just want her punished for what she did to me. So, yeah, five grand to anyone who can bring me the identity of Lady X."

CHAPTER 25

April 2024
New York City

Margot

"Stop watching the video," Julia said, sitting down next to Margot on the beautiful but exceedingly uncomfortable couch in their suite. Julia put her feet up on the marble coffee table, nudging aside the gold horse head fruit basket filled with apples that were probably replaced every day.

"I'm not," Margot lied. She couldn't stop.

Noelle filmed this, she thought. This private, awful, unhinged moment. That Noelle never should have been a part of. And she *filmed* it.

Margot was furious with her husband. But she was terrified of what she felt about Noelle.

"I could kill you for this!" she shrieked on the screen. She'd never seen her face like that. Hateful. Murderous.

"I hate it." Margot pressed play again. Julia watched from her spot against Margot's shoulder.

"I love it," Julia said as, on the screen, Margot's bat got tangled in the tapestry that had been made by a local artist she'd featured in the magazine.

The tapestry had been a gift.

Jack said it looked like a big pink vagina hanging on the wall.

Video Margot got the bat free and pointed it at Jack.

A text appeared at the top of the screen.

Talking points for the interview.

It was from Noelle.

"Is she for real?" Julia asked, grabbing the phone away from Margot. "She's giving you talking points? How about point one, fuck, and point two, off."

Margot had cut all of Noelle's access to her businesses. Noelle had willingly turned in her laptop and phone at the office. All the passwords had been changed. She'd even had the office locks changed.

And then, free of one member of her team, she'd let go of the rest of them. With plenty of severance. She'd closed her social media accounts. Paused the Substack. The brand was in suspended animation. Floating in space. "Why haven't you blocked her number?" Julia asked, reading the text.

Margot shrugged. How did she explain the different flavors of her rage. What she felt for Jack right now was difficult. It was pain and anger, sure. But it was also guilt and resentment. It was confusion. So much confusion.

But this . . . what she felt about Noelle? It was pure. White-hot. Sharp as a blade. Delicious. Murderous was better than being hurt. She was so tired of hurt.

"'Don't talk about the kids except to say they are loved and getting support,'" Julia read the rest of the text. "'Don't talk about your business other than saying that your team is exceptional. Don't talk about the future except to say that you are working together for your family.'"

Julia looked at Margot and then back down at the screen. "It's a good list."

"She always was good at her job," was all Margot could really say. Good enough that she knew there would be value in filming her meltdown.

"Why in the world is she trying to help you?"

"She's not. She's trying to help Jack. She's giving me a script and telling me to stick with it."

Julia nodded, eyes wide. "Bitch."

"In this case," Margot sighed, "yes."

The door to Skye's room in the suite opened and she came out wearing a pair of leggings and an old UCLA sweatshirt of Margot's. She'd been wondering where that thing went.

"Ready?" Skye asked.

Margot wanted to put her feet up on the couch, order three martinis from room service, and try to get drunk enough that she could sleep for a few hours.

"Come on," Julia said, her hand out. "You can't stay here and get blotto." Her sister was still reading Margot's mind. It was annoying.

She got to her feet and the three of them glanced in the mirror at the door. Margot put on sunglasses and a Pittsburgh Pirates ball cap. Looking at herself, she felt like a disguise was hardly needed. She was gaunt and gray-faced. Her eyes red-rimmed and swollen. Her entire body shriveled one terrible degree. She looked older. Plainer. Sadder.

She was never a beauty. But she'd always had a certain look. Jack always said that she was a classic. A throwback. *They don't make women like you anymore.*

She used to think it was a compliment, now she wasn't even sure what it meant.

Beside her in the mirror, Skye added some Carmex and Julia stuck out her tongue at the two of them.

The good news was New York really didn't care about her. The world moved too fast here, and they'd already seen it all. Her life and her drama were far too small to be interesting.

Which was comforting.

"It's nice. Let's walk," Julia said, linking her arm through Margot's, forcing her into a pace that was somewhere between a run and a sprint. But soon her heart was pounding and her cheeks were flushed and Margot wrapped an arm around Skye's shoulders and all three of them did a little skip like it was the yellow brick road and not the cobblestones of Crosby Street.

"Looking good, ladies," a guy selling hot dogs cried.

The coffee shop was airy and bright with soaring ceilings and a lot of plants. The floor was indigo-and-gray patterned tile. There were a dozen little round tables surrounded by stools. Every one of them was full, some with three people crowded around them. Every person casting sideways scornful glances at the four luxurious booths along the wall with velvet seating and plugs for computers. Each booth had one person in it. A twenty-year-old assistant type, just sitting there. No computer. No coffee even.

Sitting in the booth in the middle, a luxurious round affair with a chandelier above it, was an elegant black man with a full head of silver hair. Laugh lines around bright black eyes. A stern mouth that did not look like the kind that smiled enough to give him those laugh lines.

Everything about him looked serious and slightly imposing.

"Is that him?" Margot asked.

"I have no idea," Julia said.

Skye, who had managed all the communications, lifted her hand to the man and smiled warmly at him, like they were old friends. "Todd?" she asked, walking away from Margot and Julia, who still stood arm in arm like reluctant hens.

"Skye," he said, coming to his feet. He wore a navy three-piece suit and a gorgeous Versace tie from the latest collection. Pink and orange phoenixes rising from light blue ashes. A matching orange pocket square tucked with an artful flourish in his breast pocket.

They shook hands like bankers and Margot blinked back tears.

"This is my mom Margot and my aunt Julia," Skye said.

"Pleasure," Todd said, sizing them up. "Would you like something to drink?"

"Coffee is fine," Margot said. "We can—" She turned toward the counter, where other people were lined up to get their caffeine. But Todd lifted his hand to the barista and held up two fingers. He looked at Skye and then back at the barista and said, "Last week's special."

Julia, beside her, was not impressed. Julia had a real *eat the rich* mentality that she barely kept in check around Jack and Margot. "We can order our own coffee," she said.

"I'm sure you can. And you can wait in line, or . . ." Like he'd timed it the barista came with a small tray. Two coffees, a pitcher of cream, and a charming little hammered tin sugar bowl. Beside the coffee was a hot chocolate with a brûléed marshmallow on top. The barista set that down in front of Skye.

The crowd of people at the counter just looked on in annoyed silence. The same annoyed silence the people crammed around the small tables had. Like this was something they were used to. They didn't like it. But they didn't have a choice.

"You own this place?" Margot asked.

"No," Todd said, offering no other information. "Please, sit."

The three of them took off their coats and slipped into the booth. In front of him Todd had a coffee cup, a phone, and a small stack of envelopes.

The envelopes looked like they had been around the block a time or two. The edges were curled and soft. The front of the envelopes, where the writing would be, were face down.

And she got the sense that was by design. Everything about this man was by design. They would not know anything he didn't want them to know.

"Thank you for meeting with us," Julia said.

"Well, Rachel didn't give me much of a choice, did she?" he asked. "What can I help you with today?"

"I understand you knew our mom," Margot said. She took off her glasses but left on the cap. She was sitting between Todd and Julia; if someone wanted to recognize her, they were going to have to work hard.

Todd nodded, carefully lining up the edge of the envelopes in a straight line with the edge of his phone.

"I knew Ginger," he said with a smile that didn't match his polished indifference. Real emotion slipped out between this man's buttons. And it was pure. Lovely. "I adored Ginger. We worked together for about six months at the Orbit Room. We had some wild times." He winked at Skye.

"She's never told us about living in New York," Margot said, the question implicit. *Why?*

Todd looked at her for a long moment, as if doing some very complicated mental math.

"It did not end well for her in this city," he said.

"What does that mean?" Julia asked.

"You've seen the newspaper picture?" he asked. "Your mom in front of a crime scene?" They all nodded. "Well, despite the Son of Sam fever, there were still plenty of men who wanted to see Lady X pay for what she'd done, and your mom was a fine enough scapegoat for them."

"That's why she left?" Margot asked, suddenly outraged for her mother. That she'd had to let go of a dream that up until a few days ago Margot had never even heard of.

"It wasn't because of our dad?" Julia asked.

"No. She did not leave because of your father, and as far as I know yes, she left because of Lady X."

"Did you know Faye Bouchard?" Skye asked.

Todd looked at Skye with wide eyes and she only looked right back at him, steady as she goes. Three weeks ago, Margot would have been slightly embarrassed by her boldness, thinking it walked right over the line into impolite, but the lines had been redrawn over the last few days. Her boldness made Margot sit up straighter.

Todd turned to face her in the booth, giving her his full attention. Probably hoping to intimidate her. "She worked with your mother and me at the club. Coat check."

"Did you like her?"

"She was very . . . cool," Todd said.

"Cool like cold or cool like interesting?" Skye asked.

"Both."

"Was she really friends with my grandmother?" Skye asked.

Todd pulled the cuff of his shirt sleeve past the wrist of his suit. A stalling tactic and not a very smooth one. "In a sense."

"What does that mean?"

"It means Faye lied about a lot of things. And how real can your friendship be if it's built on lies?"

"Did you know Faye was Lady X?" Skye asked.

Todd lifted his hand and pressed his pinky finger into the tear duct of his left eye. "Is that what Rachel told you?" he asked, like he was just exhausted by the whole mess.

"Yes," Skye said.

"Well, that was stupid." Todd dropped his hand and opened his eyes. "Do any of you smoke?" he asked.

"Not for years," Julia said.

"A vape pen?" he asked Skye.

"No," Skye said, looking sideways at Margot.

"Hmm," Todd sighed, and Margot, who was not in a position to trust anyone anymore, wondered if he wasn't flustered. Because it felt like he was flustered. "That is a shame. I wonder if . . ."

"Did you know Faye was Lady X?" Margot repeated with a fervor that had Skye and Julia turning to look at her.

"I did not," he said. "But I am not surprised."

"So? Who the hell was she?" Margot asked. "Our mom had nothing to do with Lady X and she ended up paying the price for this bullshit. Harassed and chased away from this city, her friends, her dreams."

Everyone turned to stare at her. They loved the bright glowing mythology of Lady X, but Margot only saw the cost.

"It wasn't bullshit," Todd said carefully. "It was important. And Faye was a . . . friend."

"What kind of friend betrays another like that? What kind of person sets up their friend to take the fall? She sounds like an asshole to me."

Margot could feel Julia looking at her. It was a strange and delightful twist. Julia seemed worried that Margot was going to blow up some social dynamic. Make a scene.

Todd's eyebrows, as much as they could move, were arched in a way that might have been surprise. "She wasn't an asshole. She was tired of being a victim and tired of being silenced. She was . . . angry." Todd gave Margot an up-and-down side-eye. Like she should understand.

She wanted to laugh. *You think this is angry? You should see this video on my phone.*

I could kill you for this!

"How did she die?" Skye asked.

"Faye was killed. The night of the blackout," Todd said, regurgitating what Rachel had said.

"But a body was never found," Julia said, unable to ignore her journalistic impulses.

"No body that was identified as Faye."

"You're talking about the strangled Jane Doe in Washington Square Park?" Skye asked.

"You've done quite a bit of research," Todd said.

"Why didn't you find out if that was her? I thought you were friends," Skye asked. Margot couldn't even imagine what Skye would do if something happened to her friend Amber. There would be no way she'd stop looking. It would become the defining moment of her life.

But they just moved on. Rachel to her beach house, this man to his Versace tie life. Mom buried Faye with Lady X and never said a word. Was it because she was the one being hounded by the police and the press? Because she was the one whose life was derailed?

Or had something else happened? Had her mom been keeping a bigger secret?

Once she thought it, she couldn't shake the idea. Did Mom have something to do with Faye disappearing?

"We didn't know. It wasn't like today. There was no database. No photographs on the internet. There weren't enough cops on the streets or medical examiners. Women went missing in the city all the time."

"But she had family, didn't she? Someone would have looked for her, wouldn't they?"

"I don't have an answer for that," Todd said. "If anyone did look for her, we never knew about it."

"Who would have killed her?" Skye asked. Yes. Indeed.

Who killed Lady X?

"The baseball player?" Julia asked. "The one whose hand she broke? I mean . . . she ended his career."

"His career was already ending," Todd said, droll and unimpressed. "Nobody gave two shits about him until he claimed he'd been one of Lady X's victims. After that, his success was exaggerated by the press to stir up more ire toward Lady X."

"Who else would be mad enough?" Margot asked. Someone across the restaurant had their phone out and was pretending to take a selfie but it was pointed her way. "Whose life did Lady X really ruin? Who was falsely accused of her crimes and chased away from the dreams she'd had and the friends she'd made? Who spent her whole life keeping this a secret from her family? And why would she do that if she wasn't hiding something?"

"Holy shit, Margot," Julia laughed. "Are you listening to yourself?"

"You think Ginger killed Faye?" Todd murmured.

"In the right moment, at the right time, anyone is capable of anything," Margot said.

Todd laughed. Uproariously.

"Just for the record," Julia said, reaching across the table to put her hand on Skye's, "your mom does not really believe your grandmother killed her friend." Julia looked at Margot, eyebrows raised. "No matter how angry she is with Noelle."

"Who is this Noelle and what did she do to you?" Todd asked.

"Nothing," Julia said.

"Betrayed me," Margot answered. She wanted so badly to just lean forward and give the people staring at her the finger. Just look right down the barrel of those cameras and give everyone watching the finger. But Noelle had taken that away from her with the looming threat of that video going live. She was back in a straitjacket of celebrity and the fear of everything being taken away from her if she did something wrong. Only the stakes were custody of Skye. And she wouldn't risk that for anything.

"Worse betrayal than your husband?" Todd asked.

"You've been reading the news," Margot said.

"It's hard to avoid. Much like my question."

She smiled, despite herself. He was quick. And charming. Smart. A little mean, which if you were on the inside had its appeal. She could see her quick and charming mother being friends with this guy.

"Of course it's not worse than my husband's," Margot said. "But that doesn't mean it's not awful."

Todd hummed.

Mom could be volatile. Passionate. She remembered Mom and Dad fighting all the time when Julia was in high school and giving them trouble. Mom had thrown a plate at Dad's head. A coffee cup. And more than once she'd thrown his coat and the keys to his truck on the lawn and told him to find some other place to sleep.

If she'd had a bat in her hand at the wrong time . . . who was to say?

"Personally"—Todd pressed a well-manicured hand to his chest—"I always thought the disgraced cop had the most motive."

"Why didn't you stay in touch with my mom?" Margot asked.

"That's the way she wanted it. She met your father and seemed very keen on putting us, and that year, behind her," Todd said.

"Maybe," Margot said. "Or maybe she was so scared of what was happening with this Lady X bullshit, maybe she was so mad at this Faye woman for getting her in trouble, that she just washed her hands of the whole thing. Put the lot of you in her rearview mirror and never looked back."

"Maybe," he said, but he didn't sound convinced.

"Or *maybe* after her life was ruined, she got so pissed at this Faye woman . . ."

"She killed her?" Julia asked. "Listen to yourself."

Todd looked like he was biting his tongue, and Margot wouldn't have him pegged as that type. The restrained type. He seemed like the kind of man who said what he wanted, cutting and clever, and damn the consequences.

But whatever he'd been expecting with this meeting was not what he was getting, and she took a little delight in that.

"People do terrible things all the time," Margot said. "Loving a person doesn't change their capacity to do terrible, awful things. Just because we think Mom wasn't capable of something like killing a person doesn't mean she didn't."

"My lord," Todd said. "Your mother did not kill Faye."

Margot wasn't sure she believed that. She wasn't sure she wanted to. It was better to think of Mom as a killer than a victim. If the woman who had trouble getting out of her chair, who'd lost half her memory and her beloved husband, if that woman, who'd been the victim of a life-altering accident, if she had a secret life—she didn't want it to be one where she was the victim of a photograph taken in the wrong place at the wrong time. Or the victim of a friendship that used and forgot her.

She'd rather her have some control. Some power.

It was insane, she knew that. But ever since they opened that box in the attic everything had been tipping toward insane.

She was just, finally, rolling with it.

"You don't believe me?" Todd asked. The three of them looked at him like they didn't know who to trust, but it sure wasn't him.

He started to laugh, pressing his fingertips to immaculate dark eyebrows. "Okay. I see how this is. I see . . ." He swirled his finger around the table. "How you are. Sure, Ginger took the blame and had plenty of reason to be furious with Faye. But she was like a sister to Faye. To Rachel. They were roommates for that summer, best friends. Your mom got Faye the job at the Orbit Room. And there was nothing they wouldn't do for each other."

"That's . . . this . . ." Julia looked at Skye and back at Todd. "Is new information." She scrambled in her messenger bag for one of her yellow notebooks.

"Honest to god, your mom would have a fit if she knew I was telling you this."

Julia and Skye fell for this like stones. Margot could see it on their faces, their dumbstruck delight. Margot was too angry to be dumbstruck, by anything.

"Don't pretend like you knew our mother," Margot said to this stranger. This slick stranger she wasn't sure if she liked.

"Honey," he said, leaning forward. "I'm going to forgive you because the stress you're under is criminal. And I don't want to break your heart, but the woman I knew was as fierce as they came and she couldn't bake a cake to save her life. But the rules of this agreement were set in stone, and I won't be the one who breaks them no matter what the hell Rachel says." He picked up his phone and tucked the envelopes in the inside pocket of his coat. "Excuse me, Skye," he said, and then stood, tugging and smoothing his elegant suit back into place. He really was a handsome man. Too thick for his age, like someone who'd found human growth hormone with a little testosterone. Jack had done that too, in the desperate year when the first leg of his career was coming to an end. The irritability and constant raging hard-on had made him impossible. It had been like living with a horny badger and she'd been too old for that shit. Margot wondered if he'd been cheating then.

It seemed depressingly likely.

If Todd said goodbye she didn't hear him, lost in thought about Jack's penis and how after all these years, she would never see it again. Maybe she wouldn't see another penis again for the rest of her life.

Oddly, she wasn't mad about it. Not right now.

The twentysomething assistant types left their booths, following behind Todd like he was the pied piper.

"Holy shit, who is that guy?" Julia asked. The people on stools stood and cracked sore backs before flooding into the more comfortable seating Todd had clearly kicked them out of.

Todd stopped at the small table of people who'd been pointing their phones Margot's way. He said a few words and they all went silent. As he stood there, they all opened their phones and showed him something and then appeared to delete it. Todd nodded at them one by one as each of them did the same thing.

"Oh," Margot said, not changing her opinion, but modifying it perhaps.

"What are we supposed to believe?" Skye asked.

"Well, we're not believing Mom strangled someone in a park and left her there," Julia said.

"I don't know," Margot said. And she didn't. That was the truth.

"Stop it. All we know is this guy isn't telling us the whole story, and Mom had more to do with Lady X than we thought."

They gathered up their coats.

"Do we have to pay?" Skye asked, turning toward the barista just as the front door opened and Todd walked back in like a storm cloud, muttering to himself, his tie pulled slightly askew.

"You don't deserve this," he said, coming to a stop at the table. "I want that to be crystal clear. You don't deserve this."

"What?" Skye asked.

"My help." He reached inside his jacket and Margot expected him to pull out the envelopes, with their soft frayed edges and the coffee stains. But instead it was a card.

A business card.

He smacked it down on the table hard enough that Skye jumped. "I already regret this," he said to Margot. "But you need this, and your mother was a force of fucking nature. Come by Friday at noon."

"I can't," Margot said.

"I'm sorry?" Todd asked in the way of a man who was not used to being told no.

"Friday morning I have to sit on national television and hold my husband's hand while he tells everyone he's deeply sorry for breaking the vows of our marriage with girls young enough to be his daughter."

"Shit," he said, with wide eyes. "That fucking sucks."

"It does, thanks."

"No wonder you've got murder on your mind."

Margot laughed, an awkward loud bark. "Indeed."

He sucked his teeth and looked over at that wall of plants. He heaved a gigantic sigh like he'd come to the worst possible conclusion but what could he do?

"Come tomorrow. Ten A.M." He turned and left again. Without stopping anyone this time. Without paying the bill. He was there, and then he wasn't, and the room felt different.

"Do I love him or hate him?" Julia asked.

"Love," Skye said. Margot was inclined to agree, but she wasn't going to commit to anything yet.

"He's a lawyer," Julia said, looking at the card and passing it off to Margot.

Todd Ackerman Esq. and Associates
   21 Prospect Street West

"He thinks you need a lawyer," Skye said. "He's probably a pretty good one."

It was a nice offer. One she would take. "He does seem like a shark, doesn't he?"

Margot walked up to the cashier to pay for the coffees they didn't drink.

"It's on his tab," the barista said. "Don't worry about it."

Margot stuffed a twenty in the tip jar and joined her sister and her daughter out on the street. It was April in New York City; the sun was bright but the wind was wet. "What should we do now?" she asked. "Pizza and back to the hotel?"

Skye looked eager and so she let her daughter look up the best pizza in Manhattan and they walked a few blocks to John's on Bleecker and then hopped in a cab to go to another place. Margot and Julia sat in the back of a double-parked cab with greasy bags in their laps while Skye ran in to get more pizza.

"You know what I can't stop thinking about?" Margot asked her sister.

"That our mother killed Lady X?" The way Julia said it made her laugh.

"What if she did?" Margot said, because it could be as true as anything. "But no."

"It's what I'm thinking about, so thanks for that."

"Well, you won't like this either."

"Margot," Julia sighed and rolled her head against the greasy cab headrest.

"Mom got chased out of New York, right? Everyone we've talked to has said that. She took the blame for Lady X and had to leave town."

"Yes," Julia said with a nod. "Everyone agrees with that."

"Did Mom meet Dad and they fell in love or was he her escape route?"

"What are you talking about?"

"Did Mom love Dad the way we believed she did? Or was it just one more lie we've been told?"

"You think Mom and Dad didn't really love each other? Jesus, Margot, that's really cynical."

Margot shrugged. The chemistry of her brain had been changed and it just seemed so unlikely that the fairy tale their parents sold them was real.

They both turned and looked out the car window at Skye buying more pizza. She waved at the guy working the cash register and the guys in the back all waved back at her before she came out the door smiling.

"The only thing I know is real," Margot said, "is how mad I am. And how much I love that girl. And you. That's it. That's all I know."

Julia put her hand over Margot's and squeezed, the paper bag crinkling. "Solid start, honey. Solid start."

CHAPTER 26

June 1977
Ben Avon, Pennsylvania

Ginger

"You never cooked like this when we were roommates," Bonnie said, her face swollen and puffy from the hormones. She and Ginger sat at the Formica kitchen table tucked into the corner of her kitchen. The air was heavy with cigarette smoke and the smell of Sanka.

"I didn't know how," Ginger said. "Eat."

Bonnie ate every bit of the crusty bread and the herby soup with garlic croutons Ginger had made. When it got too hot in the house they went for a walk, or a waddle as Bonnie called it, around the block. Bonnie wore John's slippers because her feet were so swollen.

In the afternoon, Ginger painted the nursery while John was at work and Bonnie sat in the hallway because the paint fumes made her dizzy.

"So, how is dance class going?" she asked. She had her foot braced on the opposite wall of the hallway and was trying to paint her toenails but was having a hard time reaching over her belly.

"I quit." Ginger hadn't yet said it out loud. With the drama around Lady X and Boyle, dancing had just slipped off her plate. She hadn't even missed it. How wild was that? The thing she'd loved more than anything else and it was gone and she didn't care.

She remembered Faye once telling Rachel that she hadn't met very many interesting people and Ginger thought maybe she'd picked dance because it had been the most interesting thing at the time. And it had kept her busy until something better came along. And maybe things would've been different if she'd come to the city with better training or could afford it once she got there. But she knew in her heart time wasn't on her side, and she didn't have what it took to make it in New York City.

It was a gift to let it go with no hard feelings.

"What?" Bonnie's blond curls bobbed as she spun to face Ginger. "You quit dance?"

Ginger told her about the spotlight.

"I always knew he was a cheap Fosse knock-off," Bonnie said.

Standing there in the tiny nursery with the window that looked out on Bonnie's mother-in-law's house next door, Ginger almost told her why she was really there. Why her wrist was swollen and bruised. How she got the split lip.

Faye, who'd thrown her under the bus.

How something that had started as revenge had grown . . . so out of control.

The next morning before everyone woke up she borrowed John and Bonnie's car and drove into the city to the Hilton hotel, which got newspapers from all over the world. It had been three days and she just wanted to see if the New York City press was still covering Carl Fitz and Lady X.

To her shock, the East Coast papers were dominated by Son of Sam.

Son of Sam Strikes Again

Two people, a man and a woman, were shot outside a club in Bayside, Queens. They both survived.

Ginger drove home and immediately called the apartment.

"We're fine," Rachel said. "I mean, the city has gone absolutely nuts, but we're okay. Son of Sam has taken the heat off Carl. The press won't be interested in him again probably ever."

Ginger let out a huge sigh of relief. "So I can come home?"

"Not yet. Faye said he was at the Orbit Room last night talking about Lady X. He upped the reward money and is telling everyone he wants Lady X dead or alive."

He was pretending to be a knock-off Clint Eastwood. It was pathetic. And chilling.

"How is Jas?" Ginger asked.

"Fine. The hospital was an excellent alibi."

"What about you guys? Did you figure out an alibi?" Ginger asked, twisting her finger in the cord.

"We didn't need it. I'm telling you, all anyone cares about is Son of Sam. Except for Boyle."

"Is he harassing you?"

"He got suspended. They've taken his badge. The force is making an example out of him, like they can prove they're cleaning house if they get rid of one scumbag."

"What about Faye?" Ginger asked.

"Boyle follows her everywhere." She heard the clink of a bottle hitting the edge of a glass. "Truthfully, Ginger, I'm worried about her. The night of the shooting she went to Queens and I think she's gone back every night."

"Queens? Why?"

"She says she wants to get a look at Son of Sam."

Bonnie bit into the cake Ginger had made. Her first attempt. The cake was from a box, but the frosting was something she'd seen Faye make. Tons of butter, tons of powdered sugar, a little vanilla, a little milk. Didn't seem so hard. She'd put in a drop of blue food coloring on account of Bonnie hoping the baby was a boy.

"Honestly!" Bonnie cried. She put another forkful in her mouth and closed her eyes. Ginger smiled, happy to be earning her keep. Happy to be making someone happy. Happy that it could all be simple. Without the competition, she and Bonnie had settled into something sweeter. Kinder.

"Bonnie!" The front door opened, letting in the smell of early summer and motor oil. John. Ginger and John had come to a kind of peaceable understanding brokered mostly by Bonnie telling him he could go sleep at his mother's next door if he was gonna fuss anymore about Ginger being there. "I brought Pete. Like ya asked."

Ginger scowled at Bonnie, who only shrugged, pretending to be innocent. "Cut them some cake," she whispered.

Ginger shoved the pan over to her. "Do it yourself," she said, and got busy at the sink.

"Heya," John said, and bent to kiss Bonnie's flushed, round cheeks. Walking in behind him was a garage-door-sized man. So tall he had to duck his head. Wide too.

Not Ginger's type. So Bonnie could stuff it. She liked her guys like artists. Not like linebackers.

"Peter," John said. "This is Bonnie my wife and her best friend Ginger."

"Charmed," Bonnie said, holding out her hand. Ginger smiled despite herself. Bonnie was wearing a housedress and hadn't seen her feet in weeks, but she greeted him like the queen.

"Hi," Ginger said, lifting her hand from the dishwater. Peter set a six-pack of Rolling Rock on the counter and shrugged out of his denim jacket. He wore a Steelers T-shirt that . . . wasn't a bad look on that broad chest of his.

"Hey," he said, coming closer while John and Bonnie talked about their days at the table. "You need some help?"

Oh brother, Ginger thought. "No. I'm good. Have a beer and take a load off."

"If I help you, you can have a beer with me and also take a load off." He had a moustache that lifted in the corners when he grinned.

"Listen," Ginger said. "I'm just visiting. You can save your charm."

"Oh, good," he said. "I'm always running low. So, how about we cut this short. I'll wash, you dry because you know where things go, and we can sit down and play some cards. Stop all this jawing. I hate it."

Ginger smiled despite herself.

"Fine," she relented, peeling off her yellow gloves and handing them to him, never expecting him to take them, much less wear them. But he put on the gloves like he just didn't care about looking ridiculous.

"How do you know Bonnie?" he asked, digging into the water. Behind them, John took a beer and Bonnie went to find cards.

"We were in a few beauty pageants together."

"No fooling?"

"No fooling," Ginger said. It seemed like a million years ago now. "We moved to New York together."

"You like it? New York?"

"I do," Ginger said honestly. "I really do."

"Even with this Son of Sam asshole?"

She wanted to say New York was full of assholes, and the ones women had to worry about most were bosses and dance teachers and bookstore owners. They were cops and baseball players. Husbands and boyfriends. There were men in that city—every city—who did as bad or worse than Son of Sam every day. All the time.

"Even with that asshole," she said.

"I was there for one week before deployment. I ate at Katz's Deli every day. By the time I got to Vietnam I was half pastrami. Half pickle."

He handed Ginger the bowl she used to make the frosting and she dried it with the flour cloth towel. "You were in Vietnam?"

He nodded. "Marine Corps."

"Drafted?"

He nodded again. "My birthday is September 14, 1952."

Ginger didn't know what to say to the guys who came back, looking haunted and hunted. Truthfully, she tried to avoid them, so she didn't have to say anything. Suddenly in front of this guy with his twinkly eyes, that felt cowardly.

"I'm sorry," she said. "And . . . thank you for your service."

Surprisingly, he laughed. "That about covers it, doesn't it? I'll take your gratitude, but you can keep the pity. I'm going to school on the GI bill, and I met some real good men I'm happy to call friends."

"Is John one of them?" Ginger asked, looking over her shoulder as Bonnie separated the deck and John finished his first beer.

"I went to high school with John," he said in a low whisper. "He was that kid who couldn't stop running his mouth, and I just tried to keep him from getting the stuffing kicked out of him."

"Noble work," Ginger said with a laugh.

"Speaking of, John said you were a real good dancer. Is that what you're doing in New York?"

He said it without a leer, which was . . . refreshing. Lots of guys heard *dancer* and thought she was stripping.

"I thought you hated jawing?"

"You bring it out of me, Ginger. What can I say?"

"You guys gonna play cards, or what?" John yelled. Peter pulled the plug on the sink and took off the yellow gloves, winking at Ginger as he did it, and she got flustered. A funny little striptease from a man the size of a house. A joke from a guy who could laugh at himself.

Peter Evans really was a surprise in every way.

On the first of July, the phone in the kitchen rang and Bonnie answered it, her hand braced on her lower back. "Yeah," she said into the phone. "Sure. Just a sec . . ."

She stretched the phone out to Ginger where she sat at the kitchen table reading an old *Cosmo*. "It's for you. Some foreigner."

Ginger turned her back on Bonnie and pressed the phone to her ear. "Faye?"

"*Bonjour*," Faye said. "I am sorry to call like this. Rachel gave me your number."

"It's all right. Is everything okay?"

Faye made a soft noise. Part despair and gratitude, part relief and surrender. Ginger waited for that spike of anger. But the last week had softened its edges and it was just a nudge. Annoyance really. Letting go of it was such a relief. She was not meant for anger. Or grudges. It took too much work, and she missed her friends.

"Rachel got fired," Faye said.

"What! No! Why?"

"She says it's because Boyle told Vanessa that Rachel was Lady X, but I think it has more to do with the drinking. She is never sober, her. I am worried."

Ginger heard the snick of a lighter and Faye's quick inhale. Ginger could see her on the couch, the phone cord stretched across the floor and over her shoulder, and in an instant Ginger missed the apartment and Faye and Rachel so much it hurt.

At once it was decided. She would go back. Her friends needed her.

"Rachel said you are trying to find Son of Sam."

Faye laughed like it was the best joke. "So many terrible things in this city and everyone only cares about him. Son of Sam."

"It's not safe, Faye."

"No place is safe. Don't we know that?"

The next morning, Ginger got ready to leave and Bonnie did plenty of protesting, invoking Son of Sam over and over again. In the end, Bonnie gave Ginger a long hug on the porch. John would drive her into the city to the bus station.

"Hon," Bonnie whispered. "I'm not a fool. No woman shows up without her purse, no clothes, and bruises all over her face and isn't running from something. I'm not going to make you tell me your secrets. But if you need help, real help, I'm here."

A bright red Mustang pulled up in front of the house and Peter got out.

"Bonnie," Ginger sighed, knowing she'd told him Ginger was leaving.

"Honey, that is a special man. What kind of friend would I be if I didn't try and set you up," she said with a grin.

Ginger hugged her one more time and walked down the pathway through the overlong grass of Bonnie and John's front yard.

"What are you doing?" Ginger asked. She didn't have any clothes with her when she arrived, but Bonnie had loaned her some of her pre-pregnancy stuff and was letting Ginger leave with a few things. Bonnie also gave Ginger twenty bucks for the train ticket.

"John said you were leaving. Thought you might like a ride."

"I have money for the train."

"Save your money. Let me give you a lift."

Ginger narrowed her eyes at him, because honestly, what was this guy's angle. "I'm not sleeping with you."

He gave her a long, unreadable look and then asked, in a quiet voice, "Is that what you think I'm after?"

"Most guys are," Ginger said, crossing her arms over her chest.

"Well, I'm not most guys. I just want to get you into the city safely and get myself a pastrami sandwich. That's all."

Peter had her at pastrami. Ginger agreed, and he popped open the door for her. Peter waited for Ginger to sit inside, her paper grocery bag full of Bonnie's cast-offs on her lap, before shutting the door. He got behind the steering wheel but didn't immediately start the car.

"Second thoughts?" Ginger said.

"No. I'm just thinking. I know there are guys like that . . . like you mentioned, who would do something nice for a gal expecting something in return. And maybe those guys wouldn't ask for permission to take that something. And . . . you, looking the way you do"—his eyes cast sideways at her for just a second—"and being as smart as you are. And fun. I guess you've probably run into more than your fair share of those guys."

"I've met a few," Ginger said, thinking of Boyle and Carl and Brady and Shane at the club.

"I'm sorry," he said. Startled, she looked at him. Their eyes met and she felt something new, something green and bright, poke its way out of her cynicism and disappointment.

This was a man a girl could count on. A man a girl could build something with.

And wasn't that a kick in the pants?

He started the car. "You want to make a list of those guys and maybe I can pay them a little visit? Give them a lesson in manners."

"I already took care of that, Peter."

Peter laughed out the window as they drove down the hill to the river and highway 65, which would take them east, back into the city.

CHAPTER 27

April 2024
New York City

Margot

Margot actually slept, and when she woke up the next morning she just... didn't give a shit. Not a single shit. And, she could admit, it was alarming. She did not need her daughter's wide-eyed panicked stares or her sister asking if she was feeling all right every ten minutes. She knew her hair was a disaster, and she wasn't wearing makeup. And the clothes she had on were the same as yesterday. The jeans had a grease stain on them from the pizza.

"Mom, you're freaking me out," Skye said.

"Women all over the world are not wearing makeup or doing their hair and they don't freak people out."

"They're not you," Skye said.

At some point in the night, she'd realized something. All those years of yoga and Pilates. Expensive facial treatments and Botox. The tasteful boob job she got after Skye when her breasts were just empty envelopes on her chest. Calorie counting and all the rest of the ridiculous tortures she put herself through: It was all fear.

Fear that she would be scorned. By the people who worked with Jack. By the press. By the barista at the coffee shop.

Or worse, that she would become invisible. Forgotten. A middle-aged woman the whole world looked right through.

In the clarity of three A.M., she realized it had happened anyway. She was scorned, pitied, forgotten, and invisible. All at the same time.

And it had nothing to do with how she looked. Or anything she could control.

Not giving a shit was freeing.

It was, in fact, one of the most freeing things that had ever happened to her.

Skye, Julia, and Margot stood in the lobby waiting for their car to pull around. They had debated wearing hats and sunglasses again but had ultimately decided not to because none of those assholes who'd been taking videos yesterday at the coffee shop had posted them. Thanks to Todd.

Margot wore her jeans from yesterday because they were her favorites, the UCLA sweatshirt that she'd stolen back from Skye, and her favorite bright red lipstick. The one her team said was too much for her skin tone, which probably meant it was too much for her age.

"I think you look great," Julia said. Skye shot her a rich side-eye and Julia nudged her in the side. "Like yourself. Like the old you."

Margot had no idea if she looked like the old her, because she wasn't entirely sure who the old her was.

They took the Brooklyn Bridge over the river, Skye watching the stone towers as they passed. Brooklyn didn't look like Manhattan. It didn't smell like Manhattan. It had a whole different vibe. They passed a school. A park. Basketball courts. Girls in school uniforms were hanging out on a corner, flirting with a bunch of guys.

"It looks like a neighborhood," Skye said, watching everything go by with teenage wonder all over her face.

At home, Skye got dropped at school and picked up and then taken to friends' houses only to be picked up again a few hours later. Margot knew that sometimes she and Amber went to Freebirds in Isla Vista and pretended they were UCSB students, just so they could feel a part of something.

They drove around a park to a tree-lined corner and the Uber stopped in front of a beautiful stone building with arched windows on the first floor and a second-floor balcony from the center window that faced the park.

"Wow," Skye breathed as they all got out of the car.

Skye and Julia stood on the sidewalk, the park behind them, staring up at the house. Margot didn't have time to be intimidated by a house. Or wowed by architecture.

She went up the front stairs to the beautiful big wooden door set back with a tiled vestibule.

There was one big lion-faced knocker in the middle of the door and a Ring doorbell.

Margot pushed the doorbell and waited for a voice to ask her who she was, but instead the door was thrown open and a thin woman with short silvery white hair stood there in a pair of leggings and a flannel shirt.

"Holy shit," the woman said with a tiny bit of an accent. "You look just like her."

Margot felt a little dizzy. Her heart was beating hard. She was scared she might throw up.

"Hi. I'm Margot."

"Of course," she said. "I'm Faye."

Margot could not stop laughing.

Skye looked like she was going to die from embarrassment, and Julia was furious.

"Get it together," Julia hissed at Margot as Faye—or Lady X, who was supposed to be dead—gave them a tour of her stunning Gilded Age home. There was wood and marble everywhere. There were fireplaces and chandeliers in every room. Velvet fainting couches.

It was *ridiculous.*

"I'm sorry," Julia said as Faye glanced over her shoulder at Margot, who was doing her best to smother the laughter behind her lips, but it was impossible. "She's had a terrible week and might be having a small mental breakdown."

"She is allowed," Faye said, and led them from elegant room to elegant room until they got to the back of the house, where there was nothing but windows and views of trees.

The kitchen was small and old-fashioned, and Todd was there in his three-piece suit, making espresso.

"You want?" he asked all of them as if he'd known them forever.

"Please," Julia said, because she never turned down coffee.

Honestly. Coffee? Now? "You want something stronger?" he asked Margot, with an imperial arch of his eyebrow.

"I'm fine," she lied.

"I told you your mother didn't kill her," Todd said like this was all a lark.

"You told us she was dead."

"Rachel told you she was dead," he clarified. "I was just following her lead."

Faye sat down on the banquette, with the budding trees behind her. The sky a feathery gray. She patted one of the pillows and two tiny dogs appeared out of nowhere and leapt onto the cushion, turned three times, growled at each other, and settled down.

Faye stroked their ears with her fingers.

"Why . . . would your mother kill me?" Faye asked.

"Because she took the blame for everything you did."

"*Moi?*" Faye put a hand to her chest.

"Don't be a bitch," Todd said with tender affection. He leaned against the wall over Faye's shoulder, sipping his own espresso.

Faye shot something back at him in French so fast Margot's two years of high school French could not keep up.

"I am not dead. Your mother did not kill me. And Lady X started as the three of us and grew . . . grew to be so many people in the city," Faye said. "A proper movement."

"Three?" Julia asked.

"Myself, your mother, and Rachel."

"Rachel said—"

"Whatever she said," Faye said, lifting a hand before Julia could get worked up, "it was to protect your mother and perhaps me. It is a habit she cannot seem to break."

"Start at the beginning, darling," Todd said. "I'm afraid you're breaking their brains."

Faye stroked the soft ears on one of the dogs and whispered something quiet to the other. "The beginning is not my story to tell. It's

Rachel's. But we vandalized the bookstore, and the cop car, and we broke into the baseball player's apartment."

"But what about the Orbit Room?" Skye asked.

"Not us," Faye said. "I don't know who it was. By that time, Lady X had taken on a life of its own. And truthfully, your mother didn't hurt the baseball player. That was me, and she did shoulder the blame. For a long time. But that cop car ... that was all Ginger." Faye whistled and one of the dogs looked up like she understood the language. "Your mother stood on top of the car. Possessed with fury. And she looked at Rachel and me like she would kill the next person who hurt us."

The dogs whimpered as if feeling some of Faye's tension. Outside the wind blew and bent the trees toward the window, where they clicked and scraped against the glass.

"And then she did," Faye said.

"What?" Margot gasped and then laughed, certain she must not have heard Faye right.

"You came here for the truth, correct?" Faye asked. Julia, Faye, and Skye all nodded with varying degrees of eagerness.

Faye nodded at Todd, who opened his briefcase and pulled out three file folders. He set down one in front of Skye, Julia, and Margot. Julia opened hers first.

"An NDA?" Julia laughed. "You're kidding."

Faye's face said she was not kidding.

"I'm not signing this," she said, while Margot was already signing hers with a flourish.

"I hate to burst your bubble, Julia. But you won't be writing a book," Todd said.

"You know, Todd, I'm getting a little tired of your three-piece-suit attitude," Julia said.

He smiled and Faye laughed. "You won't be writing a book because you don't want to implicate your mother in murder, do you?" Faye's words hung in the air for a second.

"You're lying," Julia said, her eyes narrowed.

"Sign the agreement and I will tell you everything you want to know."

"Sign it," Margot said. "Just sign it, Julia. You know you have no choice."

Julia scowled but signed it, and Skye did too.

Todd collected the folders and put them back in the briefcase.

Faye leaned forward, silver bracelets clacking against the old wooden table. Her bright blue eyes sparkling with delight, like she'd been waiting a long time to tell this story. "Here is your truth. That year. That wild, incomprehensible year with those two beautiful souls who saved my life—ended in murder."

CHAPTER 28

July 1977
New York City

Ginger

Peter parked illegally and insisted on walking Ginger up to the apartment, carrying her paper bag luggage that didn't weigh more than five pounds. Across the street in the park she could have sworn she saw Boyle, but when she looked again he was gone.

She was so jumpy she was seeing Boyle everywhere.

Ginger barely had the apartment door open before Faye was up over the back of the couch and wrapping her arms around Ginger's neck, apologizing in French over and over again.

Rachel came out of her bedroom, and when she saw Ginger she threw her arms around her neck too. "You're back," she cried, and Ginger was falling to the wall and sliding down to the ground as the three of them laughed and cried like it had been years and a war since they'd seen one another.

"Hello there, handsome." Todd, who Ginger hadn't seen by the window, gave Peter a flirty wave. Peter, filling the doorway, laughed.

"I see she's in good hands," Peter said. "Ginger?" Ginger glanced his way over Faye's head as he set her paper bag down on the floor. "My number is in there if you ever need a ride. Or help with the dishes."

"Thank you, Peter." Ginger tried to push her roommates off so she could get up and give him a proper goodbye.

"No," he said with that twinkling smile. "Don't get up. I'll see myself out. Call. Anytime."

Faye reared back to look him in the eye, upside down.

"Oh, *bonjour?*" she said.

"*Bonjour,*" he said with a pretty good accent. Good enough that Faye's eyebrows went up. And then he was gone.

Ginger sat up against the wall and her three friends bombarded her with questions. "Stop. Stop. He's just a nice guy."

"Hmmm," Faye said, plenty dubious.

"Come on, come on, what have I missed?" Ginger asked, leaning forward to jostle Faye's knees. It was so good to see her again, and she regretted every terrible thought she'd had about Faye, even if some of them were deserved.

"Well, there have been no more copycat Lady X's," Rachel said.

"Todd knows?" Ginger loved Todd, but they were trusting him with this kind of secret? The week in Pittsburgh had made her feel so far away from this.

"Honey." Todd scowled. "I figured it out. You went to get Jas's stuff and then suddenly her boyfriend has a broken hand and *Lady X* is scrawled on his wall? I'm pretty but I'm not dumb. And," he said, flopping down on the couch, "I'm proud of you. All of you. I knew I liked that Lady X bitch, I just didn't know how much."

Ginger got up off the floor and crawled over the back of the couch to sit beside him. Papers from the last few days were all over the coffee table, Son of Sam on every front page, but there were a few articles about Carl's broken hand and Lady X buried in the local news section.

"The good news"—Rachel squeezed in between Todd and Ginger. Faye joined her and they were all crowded on that couch, mashed together—"is that Dominick has been rock-solid. He's been interviewed at least a dozen times saying no one had gone up into that apartment all day. And the security guy in the garage said Carl's car was the only one that left and came back." Rachel dug through the papers until she pulled out the one she was looking for. She opened to the op-ed page and handed it to Ginger. "Someone, not me, wrote this . . ."

"'Did relief pitcher fake his own injury to prevent embarrassment?'" She put the paper down. "Wow. That's incredible."

"Well, don't get too excited. Carl has hired a lawyer and that little cabal at the club has only grown. There are a lot of men in the city who are hunting Lady X."

Hunting. That sounded . . . awful.

"That's not all," Faye said, and she pinched Todd.

"Ouch," he said. "Honestly, woman, stop pinching the messenger. Some of the guys at the club are talking about Lady X-ing the dentist."

"What?" She looked from face to face. "What does that even mean?"

"You're a phenomenon," he said. "You are a movement."

"We're a verb, apparently." Rachel smelled vaguely of whiskey and her face was flushed.

Ginger reached up and touched Rachel's cheek. "Are you okay?" she asked. "Faye told me you were fired."

"Fine," Rachel obviously lied. "There are lots of papers to write for. Lots of women to make famous. I'll land on my feet."

"The drinking?" Ginger asked. The room was quiet and still, everyone looking at Rachel.

"Under control," Rachel said, another lie. This is what happened when women couldn't just box up what had been done to them and put it away. The trauma had to get out somehow. "And right now, not important." She turned back to Todd. "You have to stop those men who want to Lady X the dentist."

"I've been trying," he said. "But people are furious. People are tired of watching the assholes win. They want to get even."

"Well, they can figure out their own way," Ginger said. "Lady X is retired."

Faye and Todd had told Shane that Ginger had a stomach bug, and he didn't ask any questions about why she'd missed a week of work.

"Looks like you put on some pounds," was all he said. The prince. Her first night back she was behind the bar filling up the coolers with ice while Todd sliced limes. The collar and little capped sleeves of her space-girl dress cut into her skin. She hadn't gained any weight, but the uniform was still all wrong. The places it rubbed and scratched and pulled were multiplying.

Carl walked up, his arm in a cast and sling. Ginger's heart stopped in her chest. If she'd had any advance warning she would have ducked and hidden behind the bar. But the asshole was coming right toward her.

Todd stepped closer to her.

"Rum and Coke," Carl ordered, and she got busy making it, shorting him on the rum because fuck him. "Hey," he said. "I'm talking to you." Ginger looked up to meet his swamp rat gaze. "You know I got robbed a week ago." He lifted his hand. "They broke my hand."

"Sorry to hear that."

"I could swear it was you."

"Me?"

"Yeah. You got them big tits and red hair and the woman in my apartment had big tits and red hair."

"That's crazy," Ginger said, shrill and loud and guilty. "I was out of town visiting my friends in Pittsburgh. I'm real sorry about your hand. How is Jasmine?"

Jasmine with her broken wrist staying at Todd's.

"Don't get me started on that bitch." He grabbed the glass, some of the Coke sloshing out the side.

Carl walked off to that VIP section where Shane had gathered his group of assholes.

"You know," Ginger said to Todd, "if you went around the city and asked men what they thought of Lady X, the ones who are angry, who feel called out or victimized, the ones who call her a bitch or say she needs to be punished—they're guilty. All of them."

"Yep," he said. "It can start to feel like there aren't any good ones left."

"There are," Ginger said, thinking of Peter.

An hour later the cops came.

Carl met them at the door and ushered them to Ginger like a maître d'.

"Miss?" one of them said, shouting over the music. He had a thick black moustache and plaid tie that looked like it had never been tied right. Half the dance floor noticed what was going on and turned to stare. "I'm Detective Bui with the NYPD. You need to come with us." He gestured back at the other cop, who was still talking to Carl, who was foaming at the mouth with delight.

"Why?" Todd asked.

"We just have a few questions for the lady."

"Am I being arrested?" Ginger asked.

"Nope. Just some questions," the man shouted over the music.

"Jesus Christ, Ginger," Shane said, coming up to the bar. "You're causing a fucking scene. Get going and don't come back."

"You're firing me?" she cried.

"Of course I'm fucking firing you!"

There was a solar eclipse when Ginger was a kid. Fourth grade, maybe. And they had this great teacher, who loved science. And the day of that eclipse he took everyone outside when all the other teachers had their students in class, windows drawn, so everyone's eyeballs wouldn't get burned out. Which was what Brian Lang said would happen if they looked at the eclipse. But Ginger's teacher took two paper plates and poked a hole in one of them and the class watched the eclipse on the other paper plate.

That was Ginger's life right now.

Crisis coming through a pinhole, and she was staring at a paper plate, wondering if it was real and terrified to look because her eyes would burn out.

"Can I . . . change my clothes?" she asked Detective Bui. It was one thing to be questioned by the cops; it was another thing to be taken in wearing a silver space dress and a pair of bloomers.

"Sure," he said, and Ginger went into the coat check, where Faye met her.

"I'll tell them the truth," she whispered. "It was me."

"No, you won't." Ginger gave her a smile she did not mean. She shouldn't have come back from Pittsburgh. She should have stayed and played that tie-breaker hand of euchre and made more cake and fucked Peter. "I'm not being arrested. I'm just answering questions."

Ginger changed quickly, kissed her cheek. "I love you," she said. "Tell Rachel I love her too."

And she walked with Detective Bui into the hallway and then out into the night.

Ginger watched the Orbit Room vanish in the back window. Carl and Shane out front, looking like they'd won. And there standing in the shadows was Boyle, not a figment of her imagination. Not a paranoid vision. Boyle. He lifted his hand and waved.

In the end, Bui put Ginger in a tiny room that smelled like urine and BO. They gave her a cup of coffee that was so strong it immediately went sour in her stomach. And then they made her wait. And wait.

Finally, Detective Bui with his loose plaid tie came in looking like there were a million things he'd rather be doing.

"We just have a few questions for you." He sat down across the tiny table from her. She almost asked if she could go to the bathroom, but Ginger wanted this over just as much as he seemed to.

He asked where she was on the day of the break-in and she told him about going to Pittsburgh. "Do you have your train tickets?" he asked.

"Probably. At home. But you can call my friend Bonnie. I stayed with her."

He asked her about her friendship with Bonnie and she told him Bonnie was pregnant and Ginger painted her nursery. Made her a cake. She felt tears well up.

"You okay?" he asked.

"Fine. This is just . . . scary."

"Do you have any idea why Carl would say it was you that broke into his apartment?"

"I'm friends with his girlfriend. Ex-girlfriend."

"Jasmine Herrerta. The girl he sent to the hospital."

Ginger nodded.

Detective Bui blew a long breath out of his nose, and Ginger realized why he seemed so put out. It had nothing to do with Ginger. He wasn't interested in solving this case. Sitting in front of her was one of the good cops.

"Here's the thing," he said. "We've found a set of prints on a statue that was used to knock Carl out. If I fingerprint you and prove that it wasn't you, this could be over. Right now." His tired eyes brightened for a second. "And we could both go home."

Ginger's fingerprints weren't going to be on that statue.

"Sure," Ginger said. "I have nothing to hide." She wiggled her fingers at him and he smiled.

CHAPTER 29

July 1977
New York City

Ginger

Two hours later Ginger raced into the apartment, down the hall, and into the bathroom, where she pulled down her pants and barely made it to the toilet before peeing.

"Ginger?" Rachel cried, and both she and Faye crowded into the bathroom door. "Are you okay?"

"Fine," Ginger said, eyes closed with bliss as she peed like she'd never peed before. "Starving."

"I'll make something," Faye said, and vanished from the doorway.

"What did they want?" Rachel asked.

"Fingerprints." Ginger showed her the black tips of her fingers.

"You gave them to him?" she asked, horrified.

"They lifted your prints off the statue. Not mine. I just exonerated myself."

"That's what they told you! They could have other prints from the bathroom. Or the doorknobs? Ginger!"

Well, shit. She'd felt so smart.

"I don't think he was tricking me," Ginger said.

"Yeah, because we've had such great experience with cops."

There was a knock at the door, the kind of sharp hammer that only Mrs. Reznick or Officer Boyle used. Or maybe Detective Bui. Shit.

"Shit," Rachel said, and shut the door so Ginger could finish up in private.

Ginger heard the door open and the murmur of voices, one of them a man's.

This is it, she thought, unable to meet her own eyes in the mirror. She went into the living room to pay the piper.

Expecting Bui, she was surprised to see Boyle in a pair of jeans and a coffee-stained gray T-shirt.

"How did you get in here?" Ginger asked.

"I heard you were released," Boyle said, ignoring her. He looked pissed at the way things had shaken out.

"I didn't do anything wrong," Ginger said with a shrug.

He scoffed.

"There's a word for this, you know," Rachel said, her arms across her chest. "What you're doing showing up here."

"My job?"

"You're suspended," Rachel said. "And this is harassment."

"*Harassment*. It's like every woman in the goddamn city learned the same word at the same time."

"What do you want?" Faye asked, sitting on the couch.

Boyle's beady little eyes lit up at the sight of her. "You," he said. "I wanted to talk to you."

Despite the heat, cold prickles of alarm spread over her neck and back. Rachel and Ginger stepped closer to the couch, but Faye just looked bored.

"Well, here I am." She lifted her hands.

"Remember how I thought I recognized you?" he said, like they were old friends. "Months ago, the first time we met."

"No," Faye said.

"Well, the other day I was in the Port Authority and there it was . . ."

He paused, waiting for her to respond, but she didn't give him the satisfaction.

If she wasn't freaking out, Ginger would applaud.

From his back pocket he pulled a folded-up piece of paper and took his time unfolding it, revealing the edge of a grainy picture . . . a goat, a girl with long, dark hair. The gap between her two front teeth.

Ginger braced her fingers on the back of the couch.

"A while ago it was on every light post in Times Square and all the bus terminals and Grand Central." He laughed, trying to straighten the creases. "It took me a while, you know, because I think you cut your hair and"—he lifted his hand and wiggled his fingers around his head—"dyed it or whatever you gals do. But that's you." He pushed the paper in her face and Rachel stepped forward.

A guard dog with a pen behind her ear.

"Watch it," Boyle said, lifting the paper away from Rachel's reaching hands, waiting a second, and then handing it to her. A childish game from a childish man. "Tell me that's not your roommate. With . . . a different name. A different look. The goat is a nice touch." He turned and faced Faye. "Someone is looking for you. Someone went to a lot of trouble papering the city with a picture of you. Someone thinks you"—his eyes walked all over Faye, who seemed unbothered but for the frantic pounding of her heartbeat in her throat—"killed a man."

"It's not me," Faye said, without looking at the paper.

"It's not her." Rachel shoved the flyer back at Doyle. "She's from Austria. That girl's from Canada. And except for the teeth, she doesn't look anything like her."

Boyle pushed her hand back at her, paper and all. "Keep it," he said. "Take another look. Put it on your fridge. You'll start to see I'm right. You'll start to see she's been lying to you." He smiled at all of them. The apple cheeks. That good-guy veneer. His own lie.

And then he was gone.

Something about the apartment was shattered, like the furniture had been rearranged and the walls were closing in.

Ginger and Rachel both turned to Faye, who sat there and spread the flyer flat against a cushion, using the back of her hand, over the picture of the girl.

She was still, not like the deer in the forest behind the trailer but like the hunters who were after them.

"I am not from Austria."

"We know," Rachel whispered. She looked up at Ginger, who nodded. Those mornings by the percolator that seemed like a lifetime ago. "We always knew."

Faye made a grateful gust of a laugh that ended on a sob. She put her hand over her mouth. Rachel reached for her, but Faye turned her face away, stopping Rachel in her tracks.

"Is that you?" Ginger asked her, pointing at the flyer.

"You better sit down. I have something to tell you."

Faye was from a small town. Northern Quebec. There was a pulp mill and a church and that was it. One church. One religion. Church every day.

"Every day I prayed for forgiveness for sins I didn't understand. Felt shame for things I'd never done. Was punished . . . we were all punished," Faye said. "Every girl. Every daughter. Every mother. Every wife." In the course of telling her story, Faye had adopted a strange tic, like she was tucking her hair behind her ear, but there was no hair to tuck. Some lingering muscle memory from her life before.

Every few years a girl made it out. Got to the highway and hitch-hiked or convinced some trucker to take her across the ice.

"We'd never hear from her again and were told she died. Froze to death in a cornfield, or murdered by non-believers who used her body before her throat was slit. But then . . . my sister made it out." A faint smile. Ginger squeezed her hands. They sat on the couch, the three of them, touching, holding hands. Braving the truth. "She ran away in the middle of the night without a word. We were told she was dead, like always. But then two months later . . ." Faye got up and padded down the hallway to her room. She came back with the postcard. "I got this."

I'm safe. Come find me. xoxo

"They had a meeting to discuss me getting this postcard and de-cided that, to keep me from leaving, they would marry me to the hus-band my sister ran away from. And he would redeem himself to the elders by keeping me under control."

Rachel closed her eyes. Ginger felt tears build in hers but blinked them back.

"I was fifteen. He was forty."

Ginger didn't even know what to say. All she could think was *fifteen*. At fifteen she was stuffing her bra and dancing to Tammy Wynette at her first pageant.

The next year was a different story. But at fifteen, Ginger was still a little girl.

And Faye was married? Cooking some man's food. Having to sleep with him.

"How long did you stay?" Rachel asked.

"Three years," Faye said. "It was . . . bad."

"Of course it was bad," Rachel said, but even Ginger knew they had no idea how bad it was.

And Faye wasn't going to elaborate.

"I had a bike because I made sandwiches and sold them outside the mill during the week. So, one night while Henri was sleeping, I rode for hours to the next town, where there was a bus station. I rented a locker and put a change of clothes there. Scissors and a box of hair dye. Paid for it with money I had kept aside from the sandwiches. I thought this was how my sister had done it too. I knew I needed money, so I took a little bit each day. But he found the money and . . ." She shook her head. "If another wife left him, everyone would turn their backs to him. It would be better for him, easier for him, under-standable . . . if he killed me instead."

"Oh my god," Rachel breathed.

"But he stopped, obviously. He stopped," Ginger said. She knew her hunger for the happy ending, for the breath of relief, made her a sucker.

"I stopped him," Faye spat. "I grabbed the poker from the fire and I hit him over the head until he fell down and then . . ." In her silence, Ginger thought of Faye in Carl's apartment. The look on her face as he called her names and she lifted that hammer. "I hit him again and again until there was nothing left of his face. Nothing left . . ."

Ginger pulled her into her arms, holding her while she shook. She killed him. Faye killed her husband. When she said she made it so he couldn't hurt her again, it wasn't because she left. It was because he was dead. Ginger squeezed her until the shaking stopped.

"Breathe," Rachel said, and Faye sucked in a deep breath like she'd been holding it for ages. Since she'd picked up that poker. Since she ran away in the night, bruised and beaten and bloodthirsty.

"I walked away," Faye said. "Middle of the night with just the clothes on my back and all the money I could steal from my husband's dresser. I took the bus to Montreal and then the train to Toronto, where I thought I would be safe, but the flyers showed up at Union Station and on the subway." She lifted the flyer Boyle had left. "So, I left again on the bus to New York City."

Ginger thought of that bruise on her hip, green and yellow with that rotten purple middle. It had been old when she saw it and it had still been so shocking.

"And your sister?"

"It's been years," Faye said. "I think she probably moved on. I hope . . . I hope she moved on."

All of them thought of those posters on the lamp posts in Times Square and on Forty-second street.

So many missing girls. So many families left wondering. Hoping their sisters and daughters and friends had boarded a bus or a train and left the city. Hoping they'd moved on.

"Who is looking for you?" Rachel asked, picking up the flyer.

"I can only guess it's the elders. They wouldn't go to the police," Faye said. "They don't want me arrested; they want me back. There aren't enough women."

Faye touched the picture. The goat. "I saw the flyers too. Ripped down the ones I could. But I haven't seen anything new in months."

"I saw one in Times Square months ago," Ginger said. "I tore it down. Threw it away."

"You knew it was me?" Faye said.

Ginger shrugged one of Faye's shrugs that meant yes and no. Of course and never.

Rachel tilted the flyer to the light. "I'm sorry but I'm not calling you Ginette."

"She is dead, her."

"What's the phone number for?" Ginger asked, pointing at the number at the bottom of the flyer. Right under "suspected of murder."

"Our church," she said.

"Why aren't you more scared?" Ginger asked, and Faye looked at her with the oldest eyes in the world and the answer was obvious.

"The worst has already happened," Ginger said. But she was wrong. There was worse. There was having to go back to that after the taste of living for the last few months. Worse would be having all of this ripped away. Worse would be jail.

Worse would be Boyle.

"Boyle is going to call this number and tell them where you are," Ginger said.

"I am not scared."

She reached out her hands and Ginger and Rachel grabbed them.

Rachel was determined to believe in her. To fight with her if it came to that. But Ginger had spent the night in the police station. Ink still stained her fingers black. Fear in the back of her head that she'd believed, once again, the wrong man and he would use that belief against her.

"Maybe you should go stay with Todd. Just until this dies down," Ginger said.

Faye shrugged and Rachel's laugh was bloodthirsty. Full of razor wire and the blunt, deadly end of a hammer. Rachel looked proud. Righteous. She too had seen the worst and was still standing. She wasn't scared either.

Which made Ginger the only one.

And I am terrified.

A few blistering days later, the three of them walked home from the Pioneer grocery store, telling themselves they were going to stick to their diets and eat the sprouts and grapefruit they'd just bought, even though they all knew they'd be getting egg rolls at Hongs that night.

"Holy shit," Rachel said, coming to a stop in front of the old Piedmont bookstore. It was boarded up and closed. A For Sale sign in the soaped-up window. The torn awning flapping in the stifling-hot breeze off the Hudson.

Rachel looked it up and down and then cleared her throat and spat on the ground.

"*Zol er krenken un gedenken*," she said.

"What?" Faye asked.

"Let him suffer and remember," Rachel answered.

"Amen."

Next door the hardware store had a kiddie pool in the window. "Hey," Ginger said, pulling some sweaty crumpled bills out of the pocket of her cut-offs. "How much money do you have?"

Together they had enough for the plastic pool and a hose, and Faye and Rachel carried the groceries while Ginger put the hose over her shoulder and that baby pool on her back like a turtle and followed them back home.

They hooked the hose up to their sink and ran it out the window and onto the roof, where she filled up their new best friend.

"It's ready!" Ginger yelled, and yanked on the hose. Someone turned it off downstairs. A few minutes later, Faye came up the ladder, pale and nervous in a tank top and shorts.

"That railing," she said. "It's not safe! Someone could fall."

Ginger helped her around the worst of the tar until she got to the pool. Faye sank into the cold water with a shiver and then a sigh of ecstasy. Rachel followed carrying a grocery bag of ice-cold beer and a pack of cigarettes rolled up in her sleeve.

The sun hit her curls and a pair of sunglasses of Ginger's she'd co-opted as her own.

"Faye is scared of heights," Rachel said. "Never thought she was scared of anything."

"I'm not," Faye said, resting her head against the edge of the pool. She lifted a hand, eyes closed, and Ginger put a cold beer in it. "I am aware of heights. I am not scared of anything."

"Hey," Rachel said, and handed Ginger something. "I grabbed this at the hardware store. Made me think of you."

It was a Betty Boop doll, covered in colored gems. Red for her dress. Black for her hair.

"Boo boopy doop," Ginger said, doing the dance. Making her friends laugh. Ginger set her on the chair some other neighbor had brought up to the roof and she watched the girls drink beer and get sunburns.

July 13, the phone woke her up out of a hard sleep. "Jesus," she muttered, flinging herself out of bed and down the hallway to grab the phone receiver off the wall.

"What?" she said.

"Took you long enough." It was Todd. Ginger looked at the windows where the sky was turning pink. Sunrise. "Listen, I want to warn you. They went after the dentist last night."

"They?" Ginger rubbed her eyes and winced; her face was so sunburnt it hurt to touch. "What dentist?"

"Ginger," he snapped. "Wake up. Get it together. The dentist. The one from the club. Some of the men he's fucked with went to his office last night and vandalized it."

His words seeped in. "No, Todd."

"They put *Lady X* all over it."

Ginger woke up Faye and Rachel and they decided to go to the dentist's office and see it for themselves. Faye called Todd and got the address and he agreed to meet them. By the time they took the subway up to Lenox Hill, it was daylight and the press had already been alerted.

There was a throng of people in front of the brownstone.

"Whoa," Rachel said. The outside of the building looked a lot like the outside of the bookstore. There weren't any of Ginger's tiny penises, but the word *rapist* was written over and over again. Big and small. Cursive and print. Three stories of it. They must have had ladders? Or climbed down somehow from the roof?

And there, across the gold plaque by the door, was *Lady X.*

"This is insane," Ginger muttered, stepping closer. The rage coming off this vandalism was palpable. Even hours later. In the bright light of day. The men who did this? They were enraged.

"I had no part of this," Todd said when he came up the sidewalk to meet them. His partner was with him, an older lawyer who walked a floppy-eared dog.

"*Tabernak,*" Faye spat.

"He didn't," the lawyer said. John, maybe? Todd rarely spoke of him. This relationship of theirs was not love in any way Ginger understood it, but they'd been together a long time.

And maybe what Ginger knew of love was all wrong.

"But you know who did," Ginger spat.

Todd nodded slowly. "I tried," he said. "To talk them out of it. But the more I argued the more it seemed like I was on the side of the rapist. And I am not."

Rachel patted him on the shoulder. "It's all right."

"You gotta stop saying that," Ginger snapped.

"The cat is out of the bag," Rachel said with a shrug. "Lady X is out of our hands."

"That's not true," Ginger said. One of them had been fingerprinted.

"If something comes of this," John said, "I will represent you. Pro bono." The dog sniffed the small bit of grass around a tree behind a black wrought-iron fence, jumped inside, and peed on that grass.

"I guess that's something," Ginger said.

The front door opened and a small, balding man with round glasses and wearing a robe stepped out and was blinded by the flash of cameras on the sidewalk outside the building. The man flinched and held up his hand to shield his eyes. The crowd started shouting questions and he was baffled at first and it was almost funny watching him realize what they were talking about. He turned and faced the accusations spray-painted across his building and it was unmistakable. The sudden fear. A man caught red-handed.

Ginger hoped the photographers caught that.

"Ginger," Faye cried, and Ginger turned and was blinded by the flash of cameras. She ducked to get out of the shot and walked back to where Faye and Rachel, Todd and John were standing.

Ginger picked up her last check from the Orbit Room. No one was there to say goodbye to her except for Dante, who leered at her tits one last time. Working there had been the best part of her life and the worst at the same time. She wasn't smart enough to put it into words, to hold both things in her mind at once. It was a magical place and she'd been glad to be a part of that, but she was Dorothy in Oz and she'd seen behind the curtain.

It was Todd's night off and he came over to the apartment to cheer her up with Faye and Rachel, who was trying hard not to drink.

"What are you going to do?" Todd asked.

"Whatever I want," she said.

"What do you want?" Rachel asked.

That she didn't have an answer for. But the apartment was filthy and she decided it was time to mop the floors and do the dishes. Rachel was guilt-tripped into helping, keeping her hands busy so she didn't drink. But Faye and Todd laid on the couch, listening to the guys playing music in the park across the street.

The buzzer rang and Ginger stepped from the kitchen to the living room, sudsy water dripping from her yellow gloves. Todd and Faye sat up. Rachel poked her head out from the bathroom. She had this dread that it was Boyle. That it was always Boyle. Or worse, some elder from Faye's church coming to drag her home.

The buzzer rang again.

"You want me to get it?" Todd asked.

She shook her head no, took off the gloves, and ran downstairs to look through the peephole. It wasn't Boyle or a stranger from Quebec. It was Detective Bui.

She opened the door. "What are you doing here?" she asked.

He held out a newspaper. "You seen this?" he asked.

Front page, *The Mail*, was a picture of the dentist's office this morning. There in the corner, turning to face Faye when she yelled her name, half her face a blur, the other half razor sharp and undeniably Ginger.

"Why were you there?" he asked. "Miles away from your apartment, before it was reported."

"A friend called."

Bui nodded, his dark eyes piercing. "You understand how this looks," he said.

Not good, Ginger thought, and gave him back his newspaper. Ginger channeled as much of her roommates as she could. Brave and bold and chin up. Because if she was going down, she was going down swinging.

"How does it look?" she asked with a saucy grin. "Honestly, Detective, aren't you supposed to be finding the person who is murdering people in their cars instead of going after—"

"I'm too busy for this shit," he snapped, his hand scrunching up the paper and shoving it in the pocket of his coat. It was a million degrees outside and he wore a sports coat and a tie. He must be boiling.

"But there are three men who are convinced you are Lady X. Three men who are making my life difficult, so you're going to have to come down to the station with me."

"Haven't we done this dance before, Detective?"

"We can do this the easy way or I can get my handcuffs out and we can cause a scene."

Right. There was only so far bravado could take you.

"No need for cuffs," Ginger said.

"I'll call John," Todd said, standing on the first-floor landing. "Don't say shit until he gets there."

Detective Bui walked Ginger in the front door of the Sixth Precinct station off West Tenth Street and John was already there. He wore an elegant suit and carried a briefcase the size of a small suitcase, and Ginger had never been so glad to see someone in her life.

"I'm Ms. Daughtry's legal representation," he said, stepping around the drunk in a trench coat who was waiting to be put in the drunk tank.

"Great," Detective Bui said. "Just what we need."

"She had nothing to do with this crime. As I'm sure she's stated."

"She's stated plenty," he said. "Let's go talk where it's quiet."

"Are you arresting her? Pressing charges?"

Detective Bui sighed. "No."

"Then we really don't need a quiet place to talk, do we? You've already brought her in once and, as I understand it, gotten fingerprints." He looked at Ginger like she was his dog jumping over wrought-iron fences so she could pee on grass. "Did you find any prints on the dentist's office that matched hers?"

"No," Detective Bui said.

"Then I think we're done here."

"The men who think it's her are serious. And they're not letting it go," Detective Bui said. "If she doesn't answer my questions now, I'll only be back."

"Then come back," John said. "Until then, get better evidence."

Detective Bui opened the front door for them, and John led her right back out into the free world. Hot and ripe with garbage.

She turned and caught the door before it closed and Detective Bui before he went back inside. "You should talk to Shane at the Orbit Room about the second set of books in his office. They're in the ceiling of his private bathroom. Or . . . that's what I've heard."

"I'm sorry, what now?" Detective Bui asked, his eyes wide.

She shrugged. "Thought you might find that interesting," she said, and Detective Bui grinned at her and shook his head, letting the door finally close.

"Wow," Ginger said. She thought that kind of thing only happened on TV.

"Indeed," John said, pulling the cuffs of his shirt past his coat sleeves. "You are . . . full of surprises."

"Thank you."

"You're welcome." He smiled at Ginger with a wealth of haughty kindness, of reserved affection, and she saw what Todd saw in him. Solid-gold loyalty. "Call me. Anytime. Any friend of Todd's is a friend of mine."

"I wish there was something I could do to repay you." Ginger imagined his hourly billing was in the hundreds.

"You can, actually. Try to talk sense into Todd and convince him to go back to law school."

Ginger didn't even know Todd had been in law school. "I'll try," she said.

And then, proving he was magic, he lifted a hand and a black sedan came purring up to the curb, its bumper gleaming in the moonlight. It was nine P.M. and he insisted on giving her a ride back to her apartment. The sedan made its way through cross-town traffic from the East Village to Greenwich like a hot knife through butter. *Rich,* Ginger thought. *This is what being rich will get you.*

"Good luck, Ginger," he said when they were stopped in front of her building.

Ginger wasn't sure what she needed luck for, but she thanked him and hopped out. The sedan eased back into traffic and disappeared into the night. She stood at the door and rang the buzzer, waiting for one of her roommates to come and let her in.

"Hey!" Rachel said, opening the door. "How did it—"

A man wrapped his arms around Ginger and shoved her and Rachel back in the doorway. He kicked the door shut behind him but didn't let go. He smelled of stale booze and BO.

"Jesus Christ! They let you go again?" he spat, squeezing her so hard she couldn't breathe.

Boyle.

Rachel tried to push him off, but he shoved her back against the step. She got up and came at him again and he backhanded her.

"You fucking bitches aren't getting away with this. I know it was you. I know it."

Boyle wrapped his fingers around her throat. Shook her. Whatever had happened to Boyle since being suspended had eroded him. He was running on animal instinct and out for blood. Her blood.

Fear, real fear, more fear than she'd ever felt before, flooded her system.

"You think you're winning?" he said, and she shoved against him. Clawed at his hand. Rachel tried too. "You don't get to win," he said in her ear, and pushed her into the wall. Every breath was shallow and not enough. Her heart pounded against her rib cage. Her vision was going dark. Cloudy. She kicked at him with her stupid Keds, but he only squeezed her neck harder.

He was going to kill her. Right here in this dirty foyer.

She braced her hands on his arms and, finding her moment, brought her knee up into his crotch as hard as she could. His eyes bulged and his face went red and the second his grip on her throat loosened she shoved him away and she and Rachel sprinted up the stairs, throwing the deadlock closed behind them.

Faye came out of the kitchen.

"What's wrong?"

"It's Boyle," she said, and put her hand to her neck. Would he have killed her? Was she being dramatic? What did her body feel was real?

"He was going to kill you, Ginger," Rachel said. "He wants to kill all of us."

And then the lights went out.

CHAPTER 30

July 1977
New York City

Ginger

"What the hell?" Rachel whispered, and watched through the big windows as the whole city went black. Restaurants, buildings, and streetlights. There was a sudden honking of horns and shouting. There was the screech and crash of metal as cars collided in the chaos.

"A blackout?" Rachel asked. "Now?"

A heavy fist pounded on the door and the three of them gathered in the living room's unbroken darkness. There was barely any moonlight, even, through the windows.

It felt thick. Isolating.

Terrifying.

"Open up!" Boyle yelled. "I just want to talk."

Rachel pulled the phone receiver off the wall. "I'm not even getting a dial tone," she said. "Wait. No ... it's gone again."

There was another heavy pounding on the door. "Open up. I've got some information for Ginette."

Faye stared at the door like she wanted to go through it. It was the same look as when she brought that hammer down on Carl's hand. A woman who'd had enough. Who would not be a victim again.

"Faye," Ginger said, "he's lying. You open that door and he won't stop until he's hurt all of us."

"Maybe I'll hurt him." She ducked into the kitchen and came out with her long knife, its edge gleaming in the thin light coming in the window. "Maybe he will know what it's like."

"We have to get out of here," Rachel said. They'd closed the windows to clean them, and she threw them open again.

"Why?" Ginger asked. "He won't . . ." *be able to break the door* was what she was going to say just as he pounded on the door so hard something splintered. "Oh shit," she said.

"Hey! What are you doing up there?"

From the hallway they heard Mrs. Reznick's voice, shouting up at him from the floor below, and the pounding of his feet as he left. She screamed after him. Curses, Ginger was sure of it.

Faye sagged against the wall, the knife clattering to the floor. She put her hands over her face, and Rachel and Ginger rushed to put their arms around her.

"It's okay," Ginger said, when it wasn't.

There was a quiet knock. Soft.

"Girls," came Mrs. Reznick's voice, and they all made laughing sighs of relief. Rachel pulled open the door and Mrs. Reznick, looking like an eighteenth-century ghost carrying a candle, stood in the doorway. "Do you know what happened to the lights?" she asked, stepping into the apartment, looking out the window at the dark city that was getting darker as it got closer to ten P.M.

"Blackout," Rachel said. "We should—"

There was the heavy clang of someone running up the fire escape, and before they could pull themselves together he was there. At the window. At the window they'd just opened like an invitation. He wore a blue shirt with heavy sweat stains beneath the arms and dark pants.

Mrs. Reznick screamed.

"You fucking bitches," he said, and began to climb in through the window. "You are going to get what you deserve if I have to do it myself."

Faye lifted the knife and charged him. She was a berserker. Screaming into a night full of screams. Ginger couldn't be sure if Faye meant to actually stab him or just scare him enough to get him out of the apartment.

But Boyle was big, and she was small, and there was a reason they'd had to resort to anonymous vigilantism. Faye didn't get close to him with that knife before he batted her aside like she was nothing.

The violence of it, to the rest of them standing there, was shocking. So shocking they gasped. He knocked her so hard she fell against the windowsill and crumpled to the floor, the knife skidding across the hardwood. She tried to get to her knees, but she was like a deer who'd taken a bullet and didn't know yet that she was dying.

"You stupid, worthless cunt," he spat. "I'm going to send you back to where you came from." He reached for her, like he was going to take her limp body and throw it over his shoulder.

Faye fought enough that he couldn't get a grip on her, and Ginger charged across the room, ducked under the window, and put both hands against his stained shirt.

Ginger got the impression of cherubic cheeks and a sinister smile. Eyes that were empty.

She shoved him. And the only reason it worked was because she caught him by surprise. Then Rachel was right behind her, shoving him again. He staggered back. He reached for Ginger, got her wrist, and half yanked her out the window, but Rachel grabbed Ginger's waist and didn't let her go. Rachel braced her feet against the wall and Ginger felt like she was being torn in half.

Mrs. Reznick was there, trying to help.

Faye got up, punch-drunk and concussed, and did the only thing she could. She bit him. Hard enough there was blood. Hard enough she'd spend the rest of her life remembering how flesh could give under teeth.

Hard enough he let go and, with one last shove from Ginger, arms windmilling, he fell over the railing of the fifth-floor fire escape.

There was a fat, fleshy thud on the cement below and then . . . silence.

The three of them looked at one another, shocked and trembling.

"I told you," Faye said. "Someone could fall."

COP FOUND DEAD DURING BLACKOUT

New York Times, July 15, 1977

Suspended police officer Sherman Boyle was found dead outside a Washington Park apartment building. According to police on the scene, Boyle had fallen off the fire escape or roof of the apartment and died instantly. According to the coroner's report, he was under the influence of multiple substances and his blood alcohol content was double the legal limit. Police have ruled his death an accident.

Boyle was suspended by the NYPD earlier this summer for his involvement with Lady X. Vanessa Purdy, community organizer who is planning a run for city council next year, gathered over 10,000 signatures demanding his suspension.

CHAPTER 31

April 2024
Brooklyn

Margot

"Murder," Julia said. Outside, the trees clicked against the windows. Bony, reaching fingers tipped with green buds, brand-new leaves. "You're saying the three of you murdered a man."

"A cop?" Margot said.

"He was suspended. And it was involuntary manslaughter," Todd said. "And self-defense."

"Was there a trial?" Julia asked him.

"There was no trial," Faye said. "We were never arrested."

Todd handed Faye a small folder and Faye opened it, revealing the envelopes that he had at the coffee shop and a blue flyer.

Featuring a girl with a gap in her front teeth, hugging a goat.

Missing, it said.

Murder, it said.

Margot looked up and Faye smiled, revealing the same gap-toothed smile.

"What did you do?" Skye asked. Margot had to wonder why Skye was handling this so calmly. Margot felt like Alice in Wonderland and all the cats were conspiring against her. "That night? After you pushed him?"

"Brushed your teeth," Julia said, and Faye thought that was hilarious. Even Todd cracked a smile.

"Mrs. Reznick saved the day. Again," Faye said. "Because of the blackout, the streets were crowded with people. Bars were serving all night long. She sent the three of us down to the street so people could see us. She told us to drink at a bar and stay all night. Be loud. Be memorable. So we did. We went to Minetta Tavern and stayed until the sun came up. Your mother kissed a bartender. Rachel played poker and lost a lot of money. I started a fight. Mrs. Reznick finally got through to the police. By the time we got home the next morning, drunk and sweating, Boyle was gone."

Julia sat back, mouth agape. Margot felt similarly gobsmacked.

"We waited for the police to come and question us. But they never came. The blackout had turned the city upside down. So I packed my bags and left. Hitchhiked down to Florida, but after years of cursing winter I found I could not live without it, so I moved back."

"To New York?"

"It was five years later, and the world seemed to accept that he'd been drunk and fell off the roof."

"The bite on his hand?" Margot asked.

Faye shrugged. "He'd burned enough bridges with the NYPD that they were happy to have the story of his death buried quickly. No one protested for him. No one demanded an investigation. He was buried on Long Island without a police funeral send-off."

"He got what he deserved," Julia said, and Faye nodded.

"What about the Jane Doe in the park?" Skye asked.

"We think she was one of the girls who worked the park, that Boyle harassed all the time," Faye said.

"Did Boyle kill her?" Julia asked.

"It seems likely," Todd said.

"Did you ever find your sister?" Margot asked. Faye shook her head no, and it was obvious after all these years that it still hurt. That not knowing woke her up on cold nights and she felt the loss of her sister like a missing limb.

Julia and Margot shared a long look. If she lost her sister, Margot didn't know what she would do.

"What about Rachel?" Skye asked.

"Rachel stayed in the apartment and drank herself to rock-bottom before she cleaned herself up and ended up doing very well for herself."

"What about our mother?" Margot asked. There were still gaps in this story they'd never been told. Between the woman who shoved a man off a fire escape and the mother they knew.

"The second night of the blackout, she called your father, and he came and got her."

"He drove into the blackout?" Julia asked like it was proof of their father's love. The epic climax of a fairy tale.

"Got there at three A.M.," Faye said. "She packed up the newspaper articles that I had been keeping so they were out of the apartment, grabbed the stupid Betty Boop doll Rachel gave her, got into his Mustang, and was gone."

"But she came back, right? You guys saw each other again." Skye looked at each of them. But the answer was clear on Faye's face.

They did not see each other again.

"Why?" Skye whispered.

"At first, we were scared. You can imagine. Boyle had been a cop and your mother was already under a lot of scrutiny for Lady X, and it just felt . . . safer not to see each other. And then I was in Florida and Rachel was in rehab and then getting herself together. And your mother was . . . happy. And it seemed like maybe we were just bad memories for one another. We'd write a few letters, but then, once in a while, someone would be interested in Lady X and start asking all the questions again, and we all seemed to agree it was best to just be silent. But then you came along," Faye shook her head, a fond smile on her face. "Rachel cracked like a nut."

"Rachel sent you to me," Todd said. "Like she was asking permission to finally tell the truth."

"She kicked us out of her house," Julia said.

Todd and Faye nodded like they expected nothing less.

"You were friends. Best friends," Skye said, a teenager who knew that word with an intimacy that every adult in the room had forgotten about. When friendship was a thing that you needed to tell you who you were. And who you wanted to be.

"We were. I loved them like sisters. I miss them like I miss my sister."

"Margot?" Julia asked, squeezing her hand. "Why are you making that face?"

Margot pulled her hand away. Did she really have to say this? Did she have to shit in the smiling faces of these people who wanted to believe the lie?

I guess I do.

"Mom was happy? Really? Or did she just know which sucker to call to get a ride away from a murder scene?" Had she, like Ginger, picked the path of least resistance? The safest route. After making so many decisions and fighting so hard, had she just thrown her hands up and gone along for the ride?

"Whoa," Julia said, sitting back in her chair like Margot had blown her there. "You don't believe that."

"What else are we supposed to believe?" This was what she never wanted to find out. This was the truth she'd been avoiding. Fine. Whatever. Her marriage was a lie; she was going to figure out how to deal with that. Years of therapy. Horses. A new career as a doula. Whatever. But this? That her foundation was bullshit. That her memories were fool's gold. That the person who had made her had made her out of a lie.

It was the last straw. Or the first falling domino. It was something. Everything. It was a devastation so complete she wasn't sure how she was going to get out of this chair. She'd been hovering at the edge of the abyss for days, only through sheer will keeping herself from crawling into her bed and pulling the blankets over her head and never coming out. And with this reveal given to them by a woman with such effortless cool, her will was gonzo. Bye-bye. Her hands were ragged, bloody stumps where she'd been holding on so hard for so long.

Maybe she'd just crawl on this floor here. And let the world go on without her.

Faye pushed the envelopes across the table toward her. "Read this one first," she said, lifting one from the middle of the pack like she had them memorized.

Margot didn't even have the will to open it. She raised her hands as if to show her sister the bloody stumps and let them drop again on the curved teak arms of the seven-thousand-dollar chairs they were sitting in.

Julia lifted the envelope and opened it, pulling out a piece of painfully familiar stationery. Stationery that after Dad's funeral and Mom's hospitalization Margot had taken back to California with her. She put the small box in her own desk and looked at it every day and remembered how Mom wrote angry letters to teachers and principals, grocery store managers. And she also wrote dozens of thank-you cards to other teachers, other principals. The manager of the pool. The waitress at their favorite diner.

She included a little handwritten note at Christmas with all their utility bill payments.

In the 1990s, this stationery was scattered like parade confetti all across western Pennsylvania.

And now it was here.

Pale blue-lined paper with *From the desk of Ginger Evans* across the top.

Julia cleared her throat before reading out loud:

Faye, I heard you were back in New York and I'm glad to hear it. I hated thinking of you in Florida. You are the least Florida person I know. I kept having this dream of an alligator trying to eat you and you crawling out of its mouth with a cigarette and a teacup of wine. I'm married, but you probably know that. Todd is doing a good job of letting me know what all of you are doing. Rachel is back in rehab. I'm scared that I might have sent her back there with a letter I wrote her. I think I am too much a part of her life that she is trying to forget? But I want to tell you I am okay. I am safe and I am loved. Remember when we were scared there weren't any good guys left? I got one. Maybe the last one. I don't know how I deserve this man, or how in the insanity of that summer he found me, but he's mine and I'm not letting go. I won't tell him about that summer. I've taken all the papers I packed up and put them in a box in the attic. I won't look at it again. But I like that it's there. It's like having a piece of you in my house. I make your meat pie and your bread and I think of you. And I look at my daughter (Julia is her name) and I hope she's as strong as you. As fierce. As wild. I love you. I'll never forget you. I hope you are as happy as I am. Ginger.

Julia put the letter down, folding it carefully and handing it back to Faye.

Everyone was silent. Tears were sending mascara down Skye's face like war paint for a dramatic teenage battle.

"Well," Margot whispered.

"Yes," Faye answered.

"I guess . . ." Margot didn't know what to say and she looked at Julia for help, but Julia had tears in her eyes too. Julia shrugged as if to imply there was nothing to say.

Mom had been Lady X. Mom had loved their father. Mom had killed a man. Mom had sisters.

"It's a lot," Margot said, which for some reason was hilarious. It was an understatement with no hope of wrapping its arms around everything they'd learned.

And they all started laughing. They laughed until the tears were knocked loose, until Margot and Julia were clutching each other's hands. Until Skye had cried off all her mascara and was snorting with laughter. Faye laughed until she had to turn her face to the window and one of her dogs leaned up to lick the salt from her cheeks.

"We wrote one another," Faye said, pushing the letters forward. "Not a lot. But we stayed in touch."

Margot fell on the letters like a starving woman.

Dear Faye, I've had another girl. She has my hair and my eyes. I look at my girls and I think of you and me and Rachel. I miss you . . .

Dear Faye, you know, the more I think about it, dancing was just a way to be adored. And being adored is all I ever wanted. To come to the rescue and be loved . . .

Dear Faye, did you read that article in the Times about Lady X? Vanessa Purdy sure is riding Lady X all the way to the Senate! Rachel must be furious!

Dear Faye, I don't think I can meet you and Rachel at the shore next month. That podcast mentioned my name and I'm scared to get pulled back into Lady X. I know you think I'm ridiculous, but I have too much to lose . . .

Margot put the letters down and wiped her eyes.

"How is your mother?" Faye asked, the edges of her voice cracking.

"Do you know about the accident?" Julia asked.

Faye nodded.

"She lives in a lovely assisted living facility, and she has good days and bad days," Julia said. "The good days are a miracle. It's my mom the way she's always been."

"The life of the party," Faye whispered, and Julia nodded, the same sad smile on their faces. "The bad days?"

"They're bad," Julia said, an understatement that left room for interpretation.

"I have wanted to see her." Faye lifted a hand. "I know, it's selfish. But I have thought of her, every day. Every day all these years, and I know Rachel has done the same."

"You've stayed in touch with Rachel?" Margot asked, thinking of that lunch and how Rachel stuck to the story they'd agreed on with one major difference. That must have been hard. Or maybe Rachel just came equipped with outrage.

"Off and on," she said. "Once she was sober, she reached out. I go to her book launches. Todd is her lawyer."

The three of them turned to the handsome man in the three-piece suit.

"You went back to law school?" Margot asked.

"I did," Todd said. "The girls were very convincing, and I figured if I was going to stay friends with them, one of us should be a lawyer."

"What happened to your partner John?" Julia asked.

"He died," Todd said quietly. "AIDS in 1987."

"I'm sorry," Julia said.

"Don't be too sorry," Faye said. "He gave us all his money."

Todd laughed, an outraged bark, and shook his head at Faye. Faye reached out and patted his hand.

Dark humor was their love language.

"You never married?" Margot asked. "Never had a family?"

"One marriage was enough. I have friends who I see. And once or twice a man I liked enough to try and have children. But it never happened. I have all the family I need." She squeezed Todd's hand and went back to petting her dogs.

It was a declaration of platonic love. Of found family. A friendship with ties that bind.

"Now," Todd said, smoothing his pale pink tie, "let's discuss Friday."

"Friday?" Margot asked, looking blankly around the room. "My Friday?"

Todd's polished veneer bent to allow a smile. "Yes, your Friday. You are filming a segment for the *Today* show?" he asked, and Margot nodded. Her phone on the table seemed to glow green with that video's menace. "What is your plan?"

"I haven't made one."

"You should tell him to fuck off. To fuck off and continue to fuck off until he has fucked off to the ends of the earth," Faye said, and then realized that Skye was sitting there. "Sorry," she sighed. "That's awful of me."

Skye seemed to shrink in her chair. The feral woman morphing again into the scared and embarrassed teenager.

I should have protected her more.

Margot should have had conversations when Skye wasn't around. But after years of being in her room, distanced by eye rolls and half-grunted answers, Skye had been delightfully by her side through all of this. Margot had enjoyed it. Relished it, really. Asking her to leave or treating her like a child had felt wrong.

But that was probably a mistake.

Skye was going to need some serious therapy.

"Well, I wasn't going to do the segment," Margot said. "I didn't want to make a statement. And then . . ." She lifted the phone and pulled up the video. She handed it to Todd, who sat beside Faye to watch it.

She saw the video in their reactions. Faye's bloodthirsty delight. Her glitter-eyed agreement with Margot's violence. A woman who helped push a man over a balcony after nearly taking a mouthful of flesh. Todd's elegant silver eyebrow crept millimeter by millimeter toward his hairline. The video came to an end and he watched it again.

"He's forcing you to sit by his side?" Todd asked. "To hold his hand and nod as he weeps or he'll . . . what?"

"Sue for custody of Skye."

Todd turned to Skye. "How old are you?"

"Sixteen."

"You have an old soul, kiddo," he said, and Skye seemed to grow three inches. "But you do not need to be scared of this." He tapped a few things on her screen and then put the phone down, pushing it across the table back to Margot.

"I threaten to kill him," Margot said, in case it wasn't clear.

"And yet, he lives." Todd shrugged. "There are angry parents demanding he be put on the registered sex offender list for sending unsolicited dick pics to minors. Something, during a custody case, I would be sure to bring up."

"Oh my god," Margot breathed.

"What an idiot," Julia said.

"Honey." Margot reached out for Skye's hand. "I'm sorry. I'm sorry this is happening. We won't talk about it in front of you."

"You think that will make it go away?" Skye asked. "You think whispering about it where I can't hear you will change any of this?"

Margot didn't know what to say. Skye leaned forward.

"Mom, do you think sitting on that segment and holding his hand and agreeing with everything he says will help anything?" She said that last part like Margot was an idiot.

"Maybe," Margot said.

"Well, maybe it shouldn't go away," Skye said.

"It's your father, honey. I don't want this to be worse for you."

"It couldn't be any worse!" She leaned over the table, looking Margot directly in the eyes like she was beaming information right into her head. "Mom. The worst has already happened."

Faye gasped and then laughed.

"Well said, *chérie*," she said.

"What can I do?" Margot asked, the mother's prayer bursting out of her, echoing through the centuries. "What can I do to make it better?"

"Nothing," Skye said, like Margot just wasn't getting it. "Nothing. It's his mess. Don't clean it up for him."

"I'm happy to be your representation," Todd said, and Faye nodded.

"You're a divorce lawyer?" Margot asked.

"No," he said, with a smile like she was so cute for asking. "I'm *your* lawyer. I put my number in your phone. Text me the details and I'll meet you at the studio on Friday." He checked his watch and stood. "I have to take a few calls. Why don't you order food and tell them about the time someone left their baby with us in the coatroom at the Orbit Room. I'll be back soon."

They stayed for a late lunch of sushi and fried brussels sprouts. Pastrami sandwiches and ramen soup. All ordered from different restaurants. All Faye's favorites, like she was trying to show them the best she had to offer.

And Margot knew they were stand-ins for Ginger. But they were happy to do it. Happy to hear the stories. Happy to receive the gratitude Faye had been storing up for years.

"Your mother," she said when the day was over and she was walking them to the door. A black sedan they had not ordered waiting for them at the curb. "Sometimes I think what would have happened to me if she hadn't let me stay in her closet." Faye stopped and grabbed Margot's and Julia's hands. "Your mother saved my life more than once. I am here only because of her."

Margot sucked in a breath and squeezed Faye's hands. "You are welcome here anytime," Faye said. "My home is yours."

"This is your home?" Skye asked.

Faye nodded. "I am the associates in Ackerman and Associates."

The dogs circled her feet, looking for attention, and she picked one up, tucking it under her chin. The other got bored and wandered off to one of the couches in the palatial sitting room, where the windows were open to let in air that smelled spring green. "I'm glad you pushed to be here," Faye said. "We were so scared of what we'd done, we never saw how this moment could be joyful. But I am joyful you found me."

"I'd like to speak to you some more," Julia said.

"Oh, you I know have questions." Faye smiled at Julia and reached out to touch Skye's shoulders. "And you, I imagine. The two of you would like to discuss that NDA."

"The story is so epic," Skye said, looking at Julia and back at Faye. "Like, it needs to be told. Lady X is iconic."

"Lady X was angry and hurt and scared," Faye said.

"All of us are," Margot whispered. "But she *did* something about it."

Margot looked into Faye's pale blue eyes and imagined her mother doing the same nearly fifty years ago. She felt for a heartbeat, as if her mother was standing right next to her. She could smell her perfume and feel the weight of her arm around her waist.

And then the heartbeat was over and the pain of missing her mother was as fresh as it had ever been.

"Come back. We will discuss," Faye said.

That night Margot lay in bed staring at the ceiling and listening to her sister not quite snore. Julia had fallen asleep the way they had when they were kids, between one excited run-on sentence and the next. Margot was too tired to sleep. Her brain was fighting her every step of the way.

There was a quiet knock on the door and Margot sat up.

"Skye?" she whispered, though nothing would wake up Julia.

"Mom?" Skye crept into the room wearing her pajamas. An old pair of sleep shorts and a Lilo and Stitch T-shirt that hung down to her knees. "Did I wake you up?"

"No. I can't sleep."

"Me neither."

"What are you thinking about?" Margot asked, and scootched to the middle of the king-size bed, giving her daughter an invitation she hadn't taken her up on in years. But to her surprise Skye crept forward and crawled into Margot's bed, curling up on her side to face her.

"I'm thinking about Gran," Skye said.

"Me too," Margot lied. *I'm thinking about you.*

Margot pushed a tiny silky piece of black hair out of Skye's eyelashes. Her face was moon-shaped and bright. The most beautiful thing in the universe.

"Do you think she was scared?"

"Pushing that guy off the fire escape?" Margot whispered. "Yeah."

"No. I mean when they went to the bookstore. The first time they stood up for themselves. The first time they broke the rules."

"I don't know," Margot said truthfully. "Would you be?"

"So scared. Like . . ." Her eyes lifted to the ceiling and then back down again.

"You did it though, you went to the principal about Max. You stood up for yourself."

"It doesn't seem like the same thing."

"I think it is."

"I'm glad they had one another," Skye said. "You know. Like Gran did it for Rachel. And for Faye. I'd break the rules for Amber."

Margot laughed a little, making the mattress shake.

"It's hard to do it for yourself," Margot said.

Skye nodded. "Whatever you do on Friday, Mom, you're doing it for yourself. But you're doing it for me too."

Margot sucked in a breath.

"For Alex and the twins. Everyone Dad hurt."

"Skye," she breathed. *I'm not brave enough to do what you're asking.* "I'm no Lady X, honey. I'm sorry. But . . . I'm not."

Skye sighed and smiled, and then to Margot's astonishment and tear-prickling delight, Skye kissed her forehead and got out of bed.

"Goodnight, Mom," she whispered, and closed the door behind her. Leaving Margot alone with the ceiling, her softly snoring sister, and a decision to make.

CHAPTER 32

April 2024
Today Show Studios

Margot

Jack looked tired. Artfully so. Not so tired he was unappealing, but tired in a heroic kind of way. The way of a husband sitting beside his wife's hospital bed. Or driving to pick up his runaway daughter from a phone booth the next state over.

He had the best makeup team money could buy, after all.

Margot had declined Todd's not-so-subtle insistence that he get her an appointment with his Botox clinic. But she accepted the facial and the color touchup and blowout that Faye provided at her home.

"I don't think she leaves the house," Julia had whispered as she enjoyed a scalp massage from one of the army of technicians Faye had brought in for the impromptu spa day. Skye had even deigned to have her hair cut. And to Margot's amazement, the stylist, who appeared to be absolutely poreless, convinced her to lighten the dark hair she insisted on keeping the color of a black hole. Now there were lowlights and caramel highlights and Skye smiled with confidence at her own transformation.

They'd selected Margot's wardrobe, using phrases like "Does this look like she still has a working vagina?" and "Does this make her look like she wants to put stones in her pockets and wade into a fast-moving river?"

They settled on middle-aged but not dead. Background but not wallflower. Grieving but respectful of the real victims of her husband's crimes.

Funny how a beige sweater set with a pink band around the neck and wrists, gold hoop earrings, and cream linen pants seemed to thread that particular needle.

At the studio, Todd wore his full lawyer regalia. Black three-piece suit with a bloodred tie and pocket square with subtle purple details. So impressive that Jack looked at him with worry in the corners of his eyes. It was delightful.

"Do not talk unless you are asked a direct question. If you don't want to answer that, say 'I am not prepared to answer that.' Okay?" Todd crouched so she had to look him in the eye.

"Okay," she said, giving him a feeble smile.

"Take your time. Don't be afraid of silence."

"Okay."

"Or?"

"Or what?"

"You could burn it all down," he said with a wink. "Make this whole show a little more interesting."

Todd walked away, joining Julia on the other side of the camera. They'd be offstage but in her sight lines. She and Jack would be sitting on a set that looked like a very wealthy person's living room. Like it could be their living room. There was a brown love seat, where she'd be forced to sit beside him. Her hand on his knee perhaps. His arm over her shoulders. There was a table with Kleenex and two mugs of water.

"Skye didn't come," Jack said, approaching her makeup chair.

"A little much for her, don't you think?" Margot asked. Her rage was banked someplace low. Squashed by adrenaline.

"Yeah," he said. "Margot. I'm so sorry. For all of this. I'm . . ." He shook his head. Not acting. Not lying. A sorry soul laid bare.

And she felt nothing.

"Let's get this over with," she said, getting to her feet.

"You look nice," he said.

"I look like a prop," Margot snapped, and walked across the sound set to the fake living room. The sound crew came in with their little microphones.

"I need to . . ." a tech said, gesturing to Margot's sweater. The tech was a woman. Young. Dark hair pulled back in a cap. She didn't meet Margot's eyes.

"Of course." Margot lifted her chin so the tech could clip on the tiny microphone and then hide the wires down her sweater.

"It's calibrated for soft voices," she said, still not meeting Margot's eyes.

"So don't yell?" Margot asked, and the girl smirked.

Was she smirking at me? Or with me?

A lovely brunette wearing glasses and a color-block jacket by Sacai that somehow said she was both stern and fun, stepped up to their fake living room set.

"I'm Aubrey." She shook both of their hands. "I know you're old pros at this, but we just want to be sure you both have a chance to say what you need to say. What you want the public to hear."

She said *both* but she was looking at Jack.

"Thank you, Aubrey," Jack said with the old Jack Cooper charm.

"Any questions for me?" she asked, her eyebrows raised. "No? Wonderful. A reminder. This is live, so there are no options for editing or redo. Swearing will be bleeped out, but that's it."

There were a few more light checks. Sound checks. A quick dusting of powder for all of them. An extra dusting of blush for Margot.

"You look a little washed out, honey," the makeup tech said, and Margot could have throat punched him.

The lights blazed and she blinked a few times, getting used to it. Aubrey sat up so dramatically and perfectly straight, Margot gave up trying and cheerfully slouched against the edge of the love seat.

"Quiet," the director yelled. "Rolling. Sound." There was a complicated series of hand gestures and then the camera man pointed, it seemed, right at her, and a small red light on the camera illuminated.

Like an unblinking eye.

Aubrey, who was using a voice that made her sound like a sad fifth-grade teacher who had to take away recess for her class but wasn't happy about it, went through her intro, detailing the depth and breadth of Jack's betrayal.

"Twenty-seven women," Aubrey said, "have come forward."

"Twenty-seven?" Margot cried and, unable to help it, laughed. Just once. "Sorry." She lifted her hands. She could feel Jack's sudden tension beside her.

Behind the cameraman, Julia's eyes were wide with delight. Noelle was there, looking guilty. Looking sorry and small. That seemed good. Right. She'd bounce back though. A lesson learned, hopefully. A bruise on her psyche that might wake her up, flinching in the middle of the night for the rest of her life.

Beside her, Jack started talking and she realized she'd missed the first question.

Jack put his hand on hers, wrapping his long, thick fingers around hers. His thumb on her knuckle. She looked at that thumb like it was a giant cockroach.

This whole time she'd spent wondering what her mother would do. And she pretended like the answer was difficult because of the strangeness of the situation. The celebrity and the attention. But she knew.

Even before she knew that her mother had pushed a man off a five-story building. Before Margot knew that she'd gotten a dirty cop suspended. And a club shut down for cooking the books. Before Margot knew that her mother risked everything over and over again to teach men like Jack a lesson.

She knew all along.

"My mom would be horrified," she said. Out loud. Aubrey's face fell open. Just wide open. Eyes and mouth. Then she pulled it back together. "Your mom?" she asked, like it was a planned follow-up to a question she never asked.

"I mean"—Margot started to laugh—"horrified." She turned to Jack. "What you've done to our family. Your kids. Your *kids,* Jack." The laughter dried up like it never was. Rage made her skin prickle. "Your fucking kids."

Jack's face went red. Rage and embarrassment not even his professional makeup job could hide.

"Margot," Aubrey said, reaching out a hand like she had a shot at getting control of this interview.

"My mom would be so mad at me for sitting here and trying to help you clean up the mess you made," she said, right into his beloved blue eyes. The man she'd been with for twenty-five years. Skye had his eyes. Alex too.

She shook off his hand and he let go, his hands resting on his thighs. He was terrified, she could see, and he was also resigned. He'd tried to make it go away but, deep down, under all that bullshit, was the man he'd been.

And he couldn't pretend he didn't deserve this.

Instead of feeling sympathy, like she might have days ago, she felt only disgust.

She shifted so no part of her body touched any part of his and faced the camera.

"We will be getting a divorce, Aubrey. I don't want his money. Or the fame. God, I don't want that flesh-eating disease anymore. I want to spend the next two years helping my daughter through high school. My twins through college. I want to watch my son put someone in space. I'm sorry to the women my husband victimized. The women he harassed and put in uncomfortable or scary situations. I'm so sorry. But you . . ." She turned to Jack, who was red-faced. So angry and humiliated she wondered if maybe he'd have a heart attack. That would solve a problem or two. "Can fuck yourself," she finished, then wrestled with the microphone.

Too long.

Her exit was being ruined by the microphone, so she stood up, tiny little cord trailing. The sound of her panicked, huffy breath amplified through the sound stage.

The tech who wouldn't meet her eyes rushed forward, smiling. Bright eyes. A flame where there hadn't been one before. She unclipped the microphone, freed Margot from it, and turned it off before whispering, "Nice job."

The makeup tech who said she was washed out high-fived her as she made her way to where her sister was doing an elaborate victory dance that looked like karate.

"Way to burn it to the ground," she cried, wrapping her arms around Margot's neck. "So fucking proud of you, sis. You know who else would be?"

"Mom."

"That's right. Mom."

She was proud of herself. *Herself.* Not the team she'd built. Not her kids. Not the brand. Or the house. Not her goddamn marriage. Herself.

She hadn't felt this way since college.

It was unfamiliar, heady.

A small army of suited men were descending on them. The consequences of her actions wore pinstriped Hugo Boss.

Todd, like Superman, stepped between them and Margot and Julia.

"I'm Mrs. Cooper's legal representation. You can contact me with any of your concerns." He handed out his cards like Chinese throwing stars, then turned and ushered them toward an exit sign and a black SUV that was magically waiting for them.

They crawled in and peeled away.

Julia handed Margot her purse, her phone inside dinging like a thing possessed.

Alex: Nice job mom. Proud of you.

                    Amelia: Mom! That was unhinged.

Ellen: How could you do that to dad? On national tv?

                    Skye: Thank you, Mom.

"Faye is popping champagne," Todd said, his thumbs a blur over his phone. "His lawyers have already called. This will get messy." He said it like a man with an appetite for mess.

Julia put her hand over hers, and Margot, numb and giddy, squeezed it. Held on for dear life. *Thank you, sister. Thank you for getting me here. Thank you for reminding me of who I am and what I want. I love you.*

"You know what that was?" Julia asked, her voice thick and rough with emotion.

"What?"

"Some real Lady X shit."

It was.

It really was.

In recent years, thanks to podcasts and Reddit posts and the internet's successful shrinking of the world, the mythology of Lady X has spread around the globe. An Olympic skier in Switzerland who had been denying serious allegations of sexual misconduct with a teammate had *Lady X* scrawled across his locker in the Olympic Village. Photos from other athletes posted online. A politician in New Zealand had a harassment scandal in his past resurface thanks to *Lady X* written across the hood of his car. And the day of Donald Trump's second inauguration, women posted pictures of their hands, the words *I am Lady X* written across their palms. Not bad for an urban myth. In the end, Lady X was just a woman. Any woman. Every woman. Maybe there were a dozen of her. And maybe, hopefully, there will be a dozen more. Because her work isn't done.

—Skye Cooper, college application essay to NYU

Margot

I t was a good day, they'd been assured. And the old women were going in. Quietly. One at a time. If Mom didn't recognize them, they wouldn't push it. Margot begged them to meet Mom where she was at.

"What the fuck does that even mean?" Rachel asked, staring out the cracked window of Julia's Jeep on the way to the facility in Sewickley.

"Don't push her, don't . . . hound her. Don't make her scared," Margot said from the back seat where she was wedged with Faye.

"We're not monsters," Rachel said, and Julia and Margot shared guilty looks in the rearview mirror, haunted by that day they'd scared Mom so badly she needed to be sedated.

"Tell me, Julia, why this Jeep?" Faye shouted over the wind whistling through the gaps in the soft top.

"It's a classic," Julia said, which did not appease Faye at all. Faye in her old age had embraced being a snob with the kind of zeal that was nearly inspiring.

The last year had been busy. Margot moved to Brooklyn, into her own Gilded Age mansion, with a solarium, a second-floor ballroom, and a dumbwaiter. It was beautifully outrageous, and it was just across the park from Faye. They had dinner once a week and went for walks along the promenade. Margot was working on a garden, and Faye came over to sit in the sun, her dogs in her lap, and critique her efforts.

Skye moved to New York with Margot, finished school at Basis, and was headed to NYU in the fall. Ellen moved in a few months ago while she figured out "what was next on her journey." So far that seemed to be hot yoga and dating a drummer. Alex came home for Christmas and Margot visited him in the spring. They went for long walks along the beach where he lived and watched birds nesting in the dunes and she wiped bittersweet tears from her eyes.

Amelia went to her father's for Christmas. And as hard as she tried, Margot could not seem to repair what had been damaged after the interview.

Margot went to a lot of therapy about it.

Julia still lived in the house in Pittsburgh. The cranberry carpet was still there and so were the boxes in the attic, but she'd turned their parents' bedroom into an office and recording studio and she was working on a long-form investigative podcast on the Jane Does found strangled under the bridges in Pittsburgh four summers ago.

She'd finally accepted some financial support from Margot, who, thanks to Todd, had come out of the divorce with more than a little extra money. Julia had hired a producer, an engineer, and a research assistant and was going to be able to launch the podcast at the end of this year.

All of this Margot could have predicted, but what came out of the blue was Julia connecting Margot with friends and colleagues who were investigating stories about women who'd been hurt. Trafficked. Or had broken the glass ceiling in their field. Had won gold medals. Defied the odds. Escaped horrific circumstances. Were changing their communities. Changing the world.

If there was a woman out there telling women's stories and she needed money to build a platform—Margot was quickly becoming a fairy godmother.

And an executive producer.

Julia pulled into the parking area beside the care facility and turned off the engine. The four of them sat there, staring at the brick building.

This was the first time the old friends were meeting since the night after they sent Officer Boyle over the fire escape.

"Are we going?" Rachel asked, and as if to answer, Faye popped open the back door and jumped out of the Jeep.

"If she gets agitated, we leave," Margot said.

"We heard you the first million times you said that," Julia said. "She'll be fine."

"You don't know that," Margot said. She and Skye had made it a mission since they moved to the East Coast to see Mom more often, and it seemed to help. Mom usually recognized Skye and knew that she was finishing high school and had already been accepted to NYU. She got confused and thought Skye was going into science, but only because Margot had done that.

"If she gets agitated," Rachel said, and squeezed Margot's hand, "we will leave."

Once they were buzzed in Faye and Rachel were treated like visiting royalty.

Rachel had greased the wheels with signed books for the staff who were into that kind of thing. And Faye had lunch catered for them. All the good stuff from Bar Marco. The mood was really good. Excited.

Everyone who worked here was invested in seeing Mom happy. The head nurse Anthony led them down the hallway to Mom's door.

Margot felt tears behind her eyes. A thorny ball in her throat.

She wanted this to work, so badly. She wanted this to be a beautiful homecoming. A moment for three old friends who'd sacrificed so much.

Let them have this, please let them have this.

"I'll go first," Rachel whispered.

"Why?" Faye asked.

"Because I look like I could be a nurse and you still look like a coat check girl at the Orbit Room," Rachel shot back, gesturing at Faye's entirely normal jeans and T-shirt. Rachel, on the other hand, was wearing hemp pants and a shirt that said "Fuck the Patriarchy."

The nurses didn't wear that kind of thing.

Margot loved these two together. It was like her and her sister but harder. Sharper. They never pulled their punches. Since Margot moved to Brooklyn, Rachel and Nadia were frequent visitors. And Rachel had invited everyone to her beach house over the summer for a beautiful week.

"You're so mean to each other," Skye had said one night at the beach house when it felt like Faye and Rachel had gone too far.

"Mean?" Rachel cried. "We're not mean. Are we, Faye?" she asked, like she didn't just call Faye a bitch.

"You are beautiful," Faye said, resting her head on her old friend's shoulder. They sat together, right next to each other. A room full of seating and they had their legs in each other's laps. Like cats. Like the way Skye and Amber sat when Amber came to visit in New York.

Like teenagers who never grew up.

Suddenly the cracked door to Mom's apartment opened wide and Ginger stood there. Her hair piled up on her head. She wore a black sweater with a V-neck that most grandmothers couldn't get away with. "What is everyone out here whispering about?" she asked.

Behind Margot, Rachel made a low sound of pain and Faye murmured something soft in French.

"Hi, Mom," Julia said, her own voice breaking.

"Julia!" Ginger said. "Margot! I didn't know you were coming today!"

"Surprise!" Margot came in and wrapped Mom in a hug, absorbing her Shalimar and coffee smell.

"Where's Skye?" Ginger asked.

She was at home, furious she hadn't been allowed to come along. The essay she'd written about Lady X had gotten her into NYU and now she and Julia were in fact working on a book. A book that could not be published until all three members of Lady X were dead and could not be implicated in the crimes they'd committed. But Skye was diligently conducting interviews, and Faye and Rachel were indulging her like beloved aunts.

Faye, just to piss Skye off, promised to live forever.

"She had school," Margot lied. "I'm here with my friends." She turned sideways to reveal Faye and Rachel, who held on to each other with a white-knuckled grip.

Ginger's face went very still, her eyes moving from Rachel to Faye and back again. The moment stretched and Margot watched her mother's eyes fill with tears and she nearly pulled the plug on this whole idea.

But Mom took a deep, shaking breath and pressed her fingers to her lips. "Are you . . . real?"

"Hey, Boop," Rachel whispered, and Ginger's breath left her body on a sob.

Faye stepped forward, Rachel right behind her, and they took Ginger's hands, wrapped their arms around her waist, kept her standing when she would have sagged. "*Chérie*," Faye said in a quiet voice, dense with love.

"Long time no see," Rachel said.

"Is it safe?" Ginger cupped Faye's face in her soft, wrinkled hands, dotted with age spots. Faye closed her eyes, like she was receiving a blessing. "Boyle?"

"No one figured out what we did."

"Carl?"

"In the end, no one gave a shit," Rachel said, and Mom reached forward to put her hand on Rachel's face too. Rachel turned her cheek so she could press a hard kiss to Mom's palm and then covered Mom's hand with her own, keeping it on her skin.

"Todd?"

"A lawyer. A very good one," Rachel said.

"He's my roommate. Not as good as you two though," Faye said.

"No," Ginger laughed, and it came out as a sob. "No one could be better roommates than you two."

The three of them sat down on the small love seat, all together.

Heads together, laughter filling the room, they didn't seem like vigilantes. Or shit disturbers. Or problem-makers, all the things they'd been called over the years.

They just seemed like women. Friends, for whom the worst had already happened. And they'd helped one another through it. To the other side.

Margot reached out and grabbed her sister's hand. She'd made it too. But without a doubt she knew she wouldn't have. Not without Julia.

Not without Faye and Rachel. Skye.

Lady X.

Without Lady X, none of them would have survived.

ACKNOWLEDGMENTS

Every time I sit down to write the acknowledgments for a book, I'm reminded that publishing is a team sport. I've been in this business for a long, long time, and I've never had a publishing experience like this one, and it is all thanks to this top-tier team. I appreciate SO MUCH the people who saw what I did in *Lady X* and helped her get here—into your hands.

To the author friends who brainstormed and took my calls and pushed and pushed me to try a little bit harder and reach beyond my comfort zone—Annika Martin, Zoe York, Brighton Walsh, Selena Blake, Adriana Anders, Skye Warren, Simone St. James, and Stephanie Doyle. I'm so lucky to have you all in my corner.

Pam Hopkins, who ushered me through so much of my career with friendship, professionalism, and grace.

Sophie Cudd and the entire team at The Book Group—I actually don't even know what to say. When you make a list of dream agents and agencies and then actually have the privilege of working with them? Thank you seems so lame. But thank you. Sophie, your plans for this book outpaced my wildest dreams.

The most surreal and delightful part of this experience is working with Shauna Summers again. All these years later and it's still such a privilege. (And so much fun!) The entire team at Ballantine has been incredible. Mae Martinez, who came in clutch with big ideas that made *Lady X* a riskier, more powerful book. Melissa Churchill, given the thankless task of cleaning up my internal timeline. Jessie Bright, who made this brilliant stop-you-in-your-tracks cover. Taylor Noel and Melissa Folds, who shouted about *Lady X* from the rooftops and got her out in the world in such a creative way.

Bhavna Chauhan and everyone at Penguin Random House Canada, you make me feel like a hometown hero, and it's been such a pleasure working with you.

To the women in my life who inspire me every day—I owe you so much. Hopefully you found yourselves in this book. Steve Osgoode, my lucky charm at the beginning of this process. Don't argue.

From the readers who have followed me from Harlequin to this point and to those who have just found me—THANK YOU.

Mom and Dad, your pride and love have sustained me. The rent checks helped too. Thank you for believing in this dream (and keeping it to yourself when you didn't!).

Mick and Lucy, I'm so proud of the people you are and the way you look at the world. You are inspirations.

Adam. There just aren't enough words. Thank you.